"DARION!" Elienne's cry raised a gust of wind. Glassware tumbled. Then the air before her split, cloven by sorcery. Within the rent appeared a tall figure clad in wet riding leather and gray wool cloak. Soulfocus light blazed down on sodden white hair and the familiar lined face of Taroith.

"My Lady!" Taroith's summons cut urgently through the soft sigh of the flames. "Come to me, quickly."

But a thin, red bar of light shot between them, barring Elienne from the Sorcerer. Golden and surly in his spoiled black doublet, Faisix lifted his voice in challenge. "If you wish the Lady's company, Master Taroith, you must win it from me."

Taroith said, "You are foolish to contest me."

"Spoken like a true and loyal Master of the League," Faisix sneered. With the grace of a panther, he stepped across the tangled wreckage of his study. "If you want the woman, *fight for her.*"

"Strike first, then," Taroith said softly. "And remember whose choice initiated this conflict...."

Janny Wurts

Sorcerer's Legacy

BANTAM BOOKS
NEW YORK · TORONTO · LONDON · SYDNEY · AUCKLAND

SORCERER'S LEGACY

A Bantam Spectra Book / published by arrangement with the author
Bantam edition / April 1989

ISBN 0-553-27846-0

Published simultaneously in the United States and Canada

Bantam Books are published by Bantam Books, a division of
Bantam Doubleday Dell Publishing Group, Inc. Its trademark,
consisting of the words "Bantam Books" and the portrayal of a
rooster, is Registered in U.S. Patent and Trademark Office and
in other countries. Marca Registrada. Bantam Books, 666 Fifth
Avenue, New York, New York 10103.

PRINTED IN THE UNITED STATES OF AMERICA

O   0 9 8 7 6 5 4 3 2 1

For E. K. Payne,

whose early enthusiasm first led me
to put stories into words,

    and

For D. P. Mannix IV,

who has been friend, advisor, and example

Chapter 1

Timesplicer

"So you are the Duke of Trathmere's widow," said the ugly, smooth-skinned man who called himself Prime Inquisitor to the Khadrach Emperor.

A sudden rush of grief forced Elienne to look down. Scarcely an hour had passed since the Khadrach army had claimed her home and her husband's life, and the words had a lonely, unreal sound. The heavy, blood-crusted boots of halberdiers still seemed nightmarishly out of place against the glass mosaic floor of Trathmere Keep's great hall.

"Answer me, bitch!" said the Inquisitor.

Elienne bridled at his tone, forgetting her torn, soot-stained gown and swollen face. She raised her head and glowered at the rat-faced Inquisitor.

"You dare," she spoke quietly, "*you* dare call me that? Khadrach *mervine*! May Hell's own Demons defecate on your tongue. It seems fit for little else."

The Inquisitor blinked, hot eyes framed in a reddening face. His jeweled collar of office glittered like blue flame in the torchlight as he sat back, slowly. Anger always made him careful.

"So." He licked thin lips. "The *Lady* can curse like a mercenary."

Elienne glared.

The Inquisitor laced his veined hands on the table before him. "Woman," he said, "you're a Duke's widow, less, even, than the little worm that hatches a fly. You have no worth. Unless, of course, you carry the Duke of Trathmere's unborn heir?"

Without pausing for her answer, the Inquisitor flicked a glance over Elienne's thin body.

"I see not," he observed.

Elienne again shut her eyes. The night before, Cinndel had come to her bed for the first time in weeks, perhaps knowing it was fated to be his last. There was a small chance . . . but Elienne crushed the memory at once. Children were not conceived by husbands worn and hardened like flint before the tides of a hopeless war. And scarcely a week past, Elienne had had evidence she was not with child.

She opened her eyes as the Inquisitor went on.

"As mother of Trathmere's heir, you would have some stature in the eyes of the Emperor. As Trathmere's widow, you are an obstacle in his path. By Khadrach Law, only women of blood descent may inherit. The Duchy of Trathmere, therefore, becomes a prize of war, and yourself, my sharp-mannered *Lady* . . ." The Inquisitor paused, smiling venomously. "You become chattel of the estate, less, even, than the hens in the byre, for at least they and their eggs may be eaten."

Elienne felt her neck warm beneath the thick, dark knot of hair that had fallen loose across her shoulders. Despite the fear that nestled like a toad in her stomach, she drew a long, steady breath. "Tell me, Inquisitor"—her tone became acid—"do all Khadrachi carry their manhood in their bellies?"

The Inquisitor shot half out of his chair before he could curb his temper. He rearranged himself like a snake coiling to strike, and rage splintered abruptly into laughter.

"That was a foolish challenge, Little One." He turned to the halberdiers. "Have her brought to my chambers at sundown. She will learn quickly how a Khadrach officer likes his bed warmed. Until then, lock her away. I find her manner offensive."

"Touch me, and you'll learn regret!" said Elienne. The Inquisitor ignored her. He nodded to the halberdiers.

A gauntleted hand prodded Elienne's back. Rather than allow herself to be driven like an animal, Elienne gathered the tattered ruin of her skirt and walked from the hall. Though she did her best to ignore the clanking presence of her escort, pretended indifference did nothing to loosen the terror that circled her thoughts like a garrote. She had acted rashly. Cinndel was dead. What had she thought to gain by further resistance?

"I love you for your horrid, saucy little tongue," Cinndel had once said to her. The memory brought tears despite her attempt at control. She stumbled blindly. The misstep earned her an ungentle shove from a halberd haft. Elienne blinked quickly to clear her eyes, and found herself guided around a corner and down another corridor. Lancet windows cast patterns of light and shadow like a game board, herself the pawn haplessly manipulated across its wide squares. Elienne shivered. Already the sun slanted toward late afternoon. Night would be upon her all too swiftly.

The halberdiers stopped at last before a portal bound with ancient, rusted iron. Lurid orange stains streaked the oak panels between, caused, Elienne knew, by condensation from Trathmere castle's dungeons. In her memory, the door had never been opened. But the shock and revulsion she felt only inspired amused laughter and grins from her guards.

"Got cold feet, little Lady?" said one. "Inquisitor'll warm 'em, sure's fire."

The door opened with a torturous groan, spilling a wash of damp air. A man was sent for a torch. Elienne waited in silence and struggled to contain her apprehension. The cresset's guttering, smoky light revealed a littered stair that plunged down into darkness. Elienne forced an outward show of courage. Cinndel had disliked women who were silly and afraid. The chilly touch of a halberd against her shoulder pressed her forward.

Gritty stone met Elienne's slippered foot, and cobwebs trailed like ghost fingers through her hair as she descended. Daylight faded behind, replaced by the fitful flicker of torchlight. The stair ended in a corridor so low the soldiers had to stoop. Confined, the reek of tallow and sweat became stifling. The curses and clangs as helms scraped against slime-caked stone made Elienne want to stop her ears.

The soldiers thrust her into the first available cell. A thin slice of light fell through the barred slot in the door while the soldiers wrestled slide bolts jammed with rust. Elienne heard an annoyed order accompanied by the jingle of steel mail as her escort unslung weapons and pounded the bolts home.

"Bide well, little Lady." Rough voices and torchlight receded, leaving Elienne in darkness. Minutes later, she heard the moaning complaint of the upper door being drawn closed. The echoes died slowly into thick silence broken erratically by the sullen drip of water. Elienne reached out to orient herself. Her hand met stonework soft with slime, and something wet squirmed away from her touch.

Elienne flinched back. The curse she uttered would have embarrassed a stablehand, but the effect was ruined by the shuddering sob that followed. Cinndel had frowned upon tears, but he was dead. The spirit he had admired in her had earned no less than the shame of the Inquisitor's bed. Succumbing to the despair that had driven her since Trathmere's fall, Elienne allowed herself to cry. Better here, she felt, than before Khadrach eyes.

She quieted after a time. The tears dried on her cheeks, and the water drop's monotonous song became predictable and familiar to her ears. It reminded her of the water clock her uncle had tried to rig with chimes. The mechanical portion had never worked properly, and it was forever striking the hour out of sequence. Elienne pushed the memory aside and leaned wearily back against the door. The Khadrach had burned both her uncle and his silly clock. The Emperor's armies had marred almost everything that had ever given her pleasure, and uttering another stinging curse, Elienne lapsed into silence.

Time passed, but Elienne had no way to mark the hours. The waiting was long—perhaps the Inquisitor had forgotten her? More likely the dark, damp solitude stretched minutes to hours below, while above the sun had not yet set. Then, abruptly, she realized she was no longer alone. The darkness remained impenetrable as before, the water drop an erratic solo against stillness; yet, for no apparent reason, Elienne sensed a presence with her that had not been in the cell before. It evaded definition.

Uneasy, but not yet afraid, Elienne pushed herself away

from the door. She reached out, but groping fingers met nothing. There *was* nothing there, she thought, stung by self-reproach. No tangible cue sparked her imagination, only nerves. Still the feeling persisted. Something, or *someone,* had invaded her solitude.

Half in annoyance, Elienne reached out again. This time her fingers encountered the sharp, cold prickle of an Enchanter's craft.

Elienne gasped and drew back. The Enchanters were surely dead, all of them; Guild Tower had been mercilessly leveled by Khadrach. Any survivors would have learned better than to practice loremagic within the Emperor's lands. And what could an Enchanter offer but illusions anyway, Elienne thought. Anger at her helplessness followed.

"Show yourself, meddler," she said sharply. Her troubles were great enough without a stranger intruding on them. "Show yourself! I am sick to death of guessing you out."

A faint light sparked into existence before her. With a thin snap, it flared into startling brilliance. Darkness shattered, knifed into sudden shadows. Elienne shielded aching eyes with her hands, half-blinded, and found herself face to face with a Sorcerer.

He was dressed richly in the heavy blues of twilight, his cloak lined with red. His features were mapped with the usage of centuries. The light, brilliant and dense as a winter star, hung poised over the palm of his hand. Without asking, Elienne realized he hailed from no Guild in Trathmere, or in any other land listed in the archivists' records. This was no dabbler in images.

"Who are you?" she demanded.

The Sorcerer dimmed his light and, with a flick of his finger, set it adrift. His mouth reflected forced patience, and light eyes regarded her with the dispassionate intensity of a snake. "I am called Ielond."

"Searcher," translated Elienne, wondering even as she spoke. The name derived from no language she knew. Meaning could have come only from Ielond's own touch upon her mind. Overwhelmingly awakened to the fact she confronted a wielder of intense and dangerous power, Elienne was unable to curb the question that rose like a challenge to meet him.

"What do you seek in Trathmere's dungeons, Gifted? Khadrach have no love for your kind."

"I seek a bride for the Prince of Pendaire."

Elienne's temper flared, heated by memory of Cinndel, whom she loved without thought for another. "Myself, Gifted? Am I the one you came for?"

Staring upward, Elienne read her answer in the Sorcerer's impassive silence. "Devil and Demons take that idea! Keep your Prince, Gifted. Better I take my chances with that *mervine* of an Inquisitor. Himself I am free to hate."

"Keep still." Above Ielond's shoulder, the light flared like a small sun. "You will wed my Prince only if you prove worthy—and your manner with strangers shows regrettable lack of courtesy."

"Then search elsewhere, I beg you." Elienne fought to contain sudden tears, overcome by the sensation that there was nothing understandable left in the world.

Quiet for a long moment, Ielond stood with his head bent, perhaps listening to the lonely splash of the water. Elienne glared at him through swimming eyes and noticed his face had softened a little.

"*Will* you leave, Gifted? I have little desire to be any man's companion."

Ielond spoke at last with measured, forceful phrases. "I will go, Lady Elienne, if that is what you wish. But before you speak, hear me. Your choice will also affect the life of the child you carry within you."

Elienne stepped back, clumsily, into the door. Her hands moved instinctively to her middle. "Last night," she whispered, and felt chilled. Could it be true, after all, that Cinndel . . .

Ielond finished the thought with icy abruptness. "Fathered a child upon you, yes. Before you allow yourself hope, hear what alternatives await you. The Inquisitor will take you to his bed, come nightfall. He will be startled by your beauty, for he did not notice it this afternoon beneath the dirt. If you manage to control your tongue in his presence, he will take you on as consort. Cinndel's son will be claimed as his own blood without hope of proof to the contrary."

Elienne gasped, suddenly pale beneath soot-streaked skin. "Never. Not while I live."

"That is but one alternative," Ielond continued remorselessly. "There is another. You will slight the Inquisitor with your customary lack of tact. He, in a subsequent fit of temper, will break your neck. Mistress, it will take you eight months to die, and your child will miscarry."

Elienne pressed against her prison door, wrung speechless with horror.

"Or you can come with me," Ielond said, "and perhaps be saved. I cannot promise such choice will be without peril, but the Prince is a just man, and your son would become heir to Pendaire's throne."

Elienne dragged air into her lungs to curse, but her throat locked against words. Suddenly she wished Ielond had not told her of the child, for that knowledge made her yet more vulnerable than before. She was also afraid. No Guild Sorcerer ever known could appear at will behind locked doors. What sort of man was the Prince of Pendaire, who sent an adept powerful as Ielond to search for his bride?

"You must choose, and quickly." Ielond gestured impatiently. The stamp of booted feet could be heard descending the dungeon stair, and stone walls threw back unpleasant echoes of male laughter. The guardsmen had spent a busy interval celebrating their victory with drink. Gripped by sudden revulsion, Elienne made her decision.

"I will go." She hoped the Inquisitor's wrath would kill him when he learned of her escape.

She had no chance to reflect further. Ielond seized her wrist in a crushing grip. The light exploded above him with a splitting crackle, enveloping them both in a starry skein of sparks. A great rush of wind followed. Elienne's hair whipped her face, and through stinging eyes she saw her cell dissolve into spark-shot darkness, replaced impossibly by an expanse of ocean viewed from tremendous height. Stars shone cobalt and white against the indigo depths of the sky.

Fear prickled like an insect down Elienne's spine. Ielond's

hand on her arm was her only contact with the sorcery that held her suspended over the void. Her predicament was no trick of illusion designed to awe the ignorant; the distant splash of whitecaps and the salt smell in her nostrils was distressingly real.

Such power over natural law lay beyond comprehension. Elienne shut the sight away behind closed eyes. Abruptly oppressed by the unnamed host of implications her simple consent might demand, she had a perverse desire to pull free. The Prince of Pendaire was none of her concern.

Without warning, the night was split by an icy blast of air. Ielond's cloak streamed like a flag. Elienne was hurled forcefully into his shoulder; the sorcerer shouted instructions, but the words were unintelligible to ears dazed by a screaming rush of sounds. The wind struck again. The gale flung Elienne like a kite. Ielond's iron fingers burned her wrist. He shouted again, urgently, but Elienne could not understand him. Wind filled her mouth and lungs thick as water. Speech was impossible.

The demon wind eddied. Elienne twisted like a toy. Wrist, hand, and elbow flamed in sudden agony. Ielond's grip loosened. The wind screeched and tore, then gusted with the shriek of a titan and broke the Sorcerer's grip.

The sky upended. Elienne's stomach twisted with the plunge as she plummeted through a tumbling panorama of sky and seafoam cold-lit by starlight. She lost sight of Ielond. A dark, damp streamer of cloud swallowed her effort to find him.

Panic-stricken, Elienne stifled an urge to scream. Instead she flung out both hands and groped.

Her fingers grazed cloth. "Ielond!"

Hands fumbled, then gripped her. Strong arms caught her shoulders, bundling her roughly against a hard, male chest. Muffled in cloth that smelled faintly of spices, Elienne struggled to free her face, without success.

The Sorcerer's grip only tightened. Pressed so close she thought she would suffocate, Elienne fell limp. To her, dizzied by stormwind and darkness, it seemed as though Ielond would bear her through the Eye of Eternity before the howling fury that buffeted her would abate.

Yet abate it did, finally, with such a wrench the very earth might have stopped turning. Elienne's feet struck solid ground. Ielond transferred his grip to her shoulders, anger cold and still upon his face.

"Listen with care," he said. "I have enemies who are powerful and ruthless. They seek your life, for they would rather my Prince remained childless and unwed. So long as you stay within my sphere of influence, you have my protection. But should you, even in thought, wish yourself elsewhere, you imperil us both."

Elienne covered her face, blocking the Sorcerer from sight. She was shaking. Her skin prickled with apprehension, and her thoughts still echoed with the horror of her fall.

"You made your decision." Devoid of compromise, Ielond's voice trapped her wandering attention. "Stand by your word, Elienne of Trathmere. Your life depends upon your commitment. Look upon the extent of it."

Ielond's hold shifted. Elienne felt herself twisted about.

"Look well, my Lady," commanded the Sorcerer.

Elienne lowered her hands and gasped. Bathed in azure twilight, a desolate expanse of icefields spread before her, uninterrupted by habitation or settlement. The blocky spine of a mountain range cut the horizon into hard-edged angles. Elienne gazed upon that eerie, empty landscape and wondered why she felt no sensation of cold.

Ielond spun her gently back to face him. The light Elienne had noticed earlier in the cell drifted above his shoulder like a captive star. He said, "You are protected by my sphere of influence. Three paces from my person, your flesh would freeze to powder in seconds. Take warning."

Elienne gave no indication she had heard. Trembling and arrogant, she stood still as Ielond fingered the torn ruin of her dress. Her emotionless gaze followed as the Sorcerer summoned his light and balanced it on the tip of his finger. Neither did she blink as that finger extended toward her and the hot, prickling energy of enchantment burned across her face. She simply held still and endured.

The Sorcerer's touch roved across her person. Where it passed, it transformed. Tangled, sooty hair became combed and shining. Torn clothes and abraded skin knit without trace of flaw, and spun wool acquired the watery, smooth sheen of butter-colored silk.

Ielond paused to admire his handiwork. "That should serve well enough."

Elienne examined the gown that clothed her. The hand she raised to touch was weighted unfamiliarly with gems at wrist and finger. They were heavy and cold; real.

"The traditional gold of Pendaire's brides becomes you well," Ielond observed, and this time his words drew reaction.

Elienne stiffened. Anger bloomed across her pale cheeks. "Would you marry me to a stranger on the day of my husband's death?" Hysteria edged her voice, and her eyes sparkled with sudden tears. "Well, would you, Gifted?"

Ielond declined answer. "You are overwrought," but his intended kindness was lost upon Elienne. She stepped back as he reached for her.

"Overwrought!" said Elienne. "Your heart is cold as Eternity, Gifted. Let Pendaire's Prince seek his own bride, if indeed he has the manhood."

Ielond caught Elienne as she turned, pulling her to him. She expected his immediate anger. She received instead a view of raised brows and a startled, rueful smile.

"I see I did not err in my choice. You must forgive my haste. If we survive the consequence of what you just wrought, I promise you won't regret."

"Consequence?" Elienne shrugged coldly, but Ielond did not release her.

"Just that," said Ielond, and at that moment the whirlwind caught them. Ice-edged and furious, Elienne recognized the same force that had torn her from Ielond's grasp earlier. Chilled through her thin silk, she braced herself with a rising sense of apprehension. When the Sorcerer's arms encircled her from behind and gathered her into a bear hug, she did not struggle.

The wind rushed and eddied, carving the ice crystals underfoot into whirling patterns until the air became saturated, opaquely white. Ielond's cloak snapped back on itself with whipcrack reports. Yet he stood as a rock does when battered by storm and surf, Elienne held secure in his embrace.

The wind passed as swiftly as it had sprung up. Ielond and Elienne stood in silent sheets of settling snow, neither one moving. At last Elienne drew a hesitant breath and spoke. "*I* caused that?"

Ielond nodded. "You stand within my sphere of influence, under my protection. When you resist me, even in thought, you match your polarity to that of my enemies, augmenting their strength. You provide them opening, since you are within my defenses, and through your dissent I am made vulnerable. This is why I urge you to guard your thoughts."

Elienne stared. "Then I could have destroyed you?"

"You might yet," said Ielond flatly. "I consider it worth the risk."

The snowfall had thinned, relinquishing its hold on sky and landscape. Yet instead of relaxing, Ielond's grip on Elienne tightened.

"We have been overtaken." His tone went suddenly cold. "Whatever your sentiments, Mistress, you would be wise to hold them neutral until I am through."

Elienne followed the Sorcerer's eyes. Thinly veiled by the last drifting flakes, a rider stood before them, cowled in black. Decorative borders of gold threadwork adorned his neck and hood, framing features incisively lean. His hands were gloved with mail, also of gold. His mount was equine in shape, but its flesh glinted like brass newly polished. Scaled like a snake, it emanated viciousness from armored crest to spiked tail, and its master seemed possessed by the black stillness of Eternity.

"Faisix." Ielond's voice startled Elienne.

The rider moved. Pale lips turned upward into a thin smile. "Ielond. Is my projection that good?"

"Adequate," said Ielond. Elienne could feel the beat of the Sorcerer's heart through her back, and his arms tightened like a vise around her waist.

Faisix laughed, the sound like a whisper against the cold

expanse of the icefields. "By that, I assume you realize I am here in flesh."

Ielond declined answer. The laughter ceased.

"The woman is unwilling," Faisix said abruptly. "Twice she has expressed her desire to be released from your care. I answer her call."

"I refuse your claim," Ielond responded. "Return whence you came."

The thin smile repeated itself. "I have brought news from Pendaire. Would you dismiss me before you have heard? Or are you no longer interested in your royal ward?"

"There is little you could tell that I do not already know."

Faisix crossed his arms and leaned on his mount's neck. "Indeed? Not even the fact that, in Pendaire, Summer's Eve is already past? Your Prince failed to meet his deadline, my friend. His seed is sterile. The Council has named him unfit for the crown and the continuance of a royal line. By its decree, the execution ceremony will occur on the morrow."

"Why!" Elienne burst out. "Do you murder a man in Pendaire because he cannot father a child?"

Faisix transferred yellow eyes from Ielond, and, feeling his gaze upon her, Elienne was suddenly cold.

"It is custom only for Kings, Mistress." The words were gently stated but somehow inspired no confidence. "Princes have supporters. If the crown must pass into other hands, peace must be kept. There cannot be excuse left for uprising. It is an ancient law, seldom invoked, perhaps because few Princes are born with such an unfortunate affliction."

"You have the justice of a toad," said Elienne hotly, "and your councilmen have the minds of fishes. Certainly Ielond will stop this execution you speak of."

Faisix shook his head slowly, a final smile thinning his lips. "Certainly Ielond would if he could. But my second piece of news proves otherwise. The Sorcerer known to us all as Ielond died Summer's Eve in Pendaire."

"Liar!" cried Elienne. The man at her back was warm, alive, and solidly real.

"Ask him," Faisix invited. "He will tell you so."

Elienne turned and searched the face of the Sorcerer who

held her. His expression was all seams and twilit shadows, impossible to fathom.

She said, "Is it true?"

"Yes," said Ielond. "Faisix has named my true death. He has also unwittingly brought me word of success."

"Can dead men succeed?" gibed Faisix. "Then your Prince will succeed with you, Ielond."

He returned his gaze to Elienne. "You called me, Mistress, and I have come. Shall you forsake that corpse's company? Come to me. It was your desire."

Faisix extended his hand. "Come," he repeated. The word seemed to release a torrent within Elienne's mind. All the confusion she had experienced since Cinndel's death welled up at once, pressuring her to step forward, away from Ielond's prisoning grasp.

"Be wary," said the Sorcerer in her ear. "His promises will not be what they seem."

Elienne gave no sign she had heard. Her face remained drawn with indecision. The small jewels that adorned her throat trembled like pale green waterdrops.

"Ielond cannot hold you." Faisix's voice was honey and ice. "If he crosses your will but once in my presence, Mistress, I can destroy him for you."

Elienne's face drained entirely of color. "I thought you said he was dead." Her voice shook, uncertain.

Faisix ignored the challenge. "Come to me, my Lady," he urged, and raised one slim hand from his mount's neck and lifted the cowl from his head. A haze of golden light bloomed under his fingers. Lean features softened and flowed as the illumination touched them, transformed the face to a gray-eyed, chestnut-headed man pleasantly proportioned.

Elienne flinched as though struck by a physical blow. She gasped aloud. "Cinndel!" Her small frame quivered with tension like a harpstring plucked by an unskilled hand.

"Come to me, beloved," the mounted man said softly. "Come."

"My Lord is dead." Elienne's inflection was lifelessly flat. The torn, bloodied corpse she had dragged from the weapons of the Khadrach had been real enough to shatter even this skilled fantasy. Her husband's death had been final as Eternity itself. The image on the horse mocked her with false promise. Drawing a great shuddering breath, Elienne broke.

"Mindbender!" she shouted. "Defiler! Release my husband's likeness. You aren't fit to wash the clothes he wore. I'll not have you dishonor his memory with sorceries."

Cinndel's features unraveled, exposing the face of Faisix. Anger clothed its delicate, narrow bone structure, and the golden eyes held murder.

"Woman, still your viperish tongue," he said, whetting his consonants with menace.

But Elienne had passed beyond caution, and the pain within her could no longer be restrained. "Beside you, the abominations of the *mervine* are the picture of innocence. Your presence itself is an atrocity. I would sooner welcome the foulest demon of Hell than suffer the sight of you."

Elienne twisted in Ielond's grasp, violently presenting her back to the subject of her insults. She buried her face in the Sorcerer's cloak, and he, gathering her weeping body close, faced his adversary over her heaving shoulders.

"It would seem your offer has been refused," he said quietly. "Go from this place."

Faisix gathered the reins in his mailed fist. For a prolonged moment he sat and glared, the image of fury. At last he pointed to Elienne. "She," he said coldly, "will regret her words through the Eye of Eternity before I am through," and like powder blown before wind, both he and his mount dissolved, leaving the ice plain empty in the deepening shadow of night.

Ielond placed his hands on Elienne and gently pried her away from his chest.

With his eyes caught on her tear-streaked face, he said, "What in the Name of the Most Holy is a *mervine?*"

Elienne stared back, blank with shock. Then her thin face transformed and a broken laugh escaped her throat. "It's a relative of the weasel." She caught her breath. "And more properly phrased as a creature of Hell. The dominant offspring of each litter consumes its siblings at maturity. If the surviving kitten is male, it will also couple with its own mother before leaving the nest. Have you no *mervine* in Pendaire?"

"We have Faisix and a very corrupt Grand Council," said Ielond. "That is share enough of the Devil's handiwork."

Elienne closed her eyes and shuddered. "What are we going to do about them?" Her voice still sounded strained, but there was a fresh spot of color in her cheeks, and the set to her lips proved she had spirit still in reserve.

"Ma'Diere's Saints!" The light about Ielond's shoulder lit his sudden smile. "We're going to change history, my Lady, and send Faisix to his Damnation. But it cannot be done from here."

"Then Faisix was wrong. You'll not be dead on Summer's Eve," said Elienne quickly.

The Sorcerer's smile faded at once. "Summer's Eve in Pendaire is the locus of my true death." His tone was suddenly clean of inflection. "Every action has its consequence, Mistress. That is one I cannot change if my Prince is to survive to claim his heirship."

Elienne shook her head vehemently. "But if you died in Pendaire, how can you be alive in this place? Your words are like riddles, impossible to understand."

Ielond placed an arm around Elienne's shoulders. "Walk with me, and I'll explain."

Chapter 2

Icebridge by Sorcery

Ielond took a long stride forward. Imprisoned by his physical hold, Elienne had little choice but to follow. The Sorcerer had promised her understanding of facts that appeared to conflict without compromise. Worn thin by the weariness that dragged at her body and mind, Elienne resolved that such explanation had better satisfy her beyond all doubt. Life and Death by Ma'Diere's Law were profound and final opposites. If in Pendaire the law of mortality was so fluid as to be reversible, she knew she could never endure such a place. Why seal herself in marriage to a stranger if Cinndel could be restored to life by a Sorcerer's touch?

Ielond interrupted Elienne's thought. "I must begin with the Prince. His fate brought us both to this place. When he was still a child, his royal parents died in a fire, and, following custom, the Grand Council of Pendaire appointed a Regent and a Guardian. The offices are separately held by law, lest a single man be tempted by his power as Regent to lessen his responsibility as Guardian.

"Faisix took the Regency of Pendaire. I was given charge of Prince Darion and his elder sister, Avelaine."

Ielond paused. The coarse crunch of ice crystals crushed by his boot soles accentuated his silence until Elienne gave way to curiosity.

"The Prince has a sister?" she said. "Then will the girl not inherit in his stead, since the Council has ruled him unfit for the succession?"

"Avelaine is dead." Ielond spoke abruptly, his voice suddenly roughened with grief which had slipped restraint. "An accident with a horse took her life at the age of fifteen."

Bitterness touched the Sorcerer's face. "The Grand Justice himself ruled her death a mishap. Yet, Eternity witness, treachery claimed her. Avelaine could ride the black Damnation itself, had it come shaped as a horse."

"You had no proof," said Elienne in sudden sympathy.

"None." Ielond fell silent again, and this time she did not interrupt. The wind sighed over the ice, chasing loose crystals ahead like sand. The scratchy whisper of their passage set Elienne's teeth on edge. When at last Ielond resumed, the sound of his voice made her start.

"The loss of Avelaine alerted me to the possibility Prince Darion might likewise be threatened. He was then twelve years old. Every protective ward in the spectrum of White Sorcery did I cast about his person. Ofttimes the boy complained the lights of my enchantments kept him from sleep. Yet I dared not dilute the potency of my work.

"For five years the wards remained untampered. Then, the day of his seventeenth birthday, Darion returned home stripped of all protection."

Ielond stopped in his tracks. His pale eyes seemed to stare through Elienne, and though darkness obscured his face, his words were forced as steel forged over a flame of anguish.

"The Prince's clothes were streaked with blood. He said he had gone hunting with his cousin Jieles, and that they had made a fine kill. But he could remember nothing of the beast he chased, and his knife was clean in its sheath. His very aura rang with the reverberation of Black magic. When light was brought by my apprentice, my worst fear was confirmed. The bloodstains formed recognizable symbols, evil ones, and I knew if I probed their origin, I would find them to be the heartblood of a maid."

Ielond's hand tightened painfully on Elienne's shoulder, yet she did not shrink from his touch. "Then Black Sorcery made your Prince sterile?"

"Just so," said Ielond. "There was only one in all of Pendaire with both power and motive for such an act. Faisix of Torkal. It was he who possessed the horse that killed Avelaine. And now, if he has his way, the Grand Council of Pendaire will murder the Prince lawfully without his needing to soil his hands a second time. Jieles will assume the crown in Darion's stead, and as ready a pawn for Faisix's hand was never conceived in human form."

"Could you not lift the curse, Gifted?" asked Elienne.

Ielond's hand fell from her shoulder, and he resumed walking. "I could. But to do so I would have to transgress Ma'Diere's Law. Only through Black Sorcery may the Prince's affliction be reversed. The counterspell would require the death of another virgin."

"You would be twice Damned," said Elienne softly, and expected silence to follow her comment. But Ielond's response was explosively swift.

"I'd suffer Damnation gladly, Mistress, if I could spare Darion! But my Prince forbade me permission to work the darklore. He would not have me take a maiden's life to save his own, Eternity take his courage."

Impulsively Elienne reached for the Sorcerer's hand. His grasp was light, almost hesitant. Plainly, he held himself responsible for the fates of both of his wards. Elienne suddenly understood his lack of sympathy for her own grief at the loss of a husband, motivated as he was by the anguish generated by such inner guilt.

"Then you think Cinndel's child can be passed for Darion's own," said Elienne at last, hoping to draw Ielond from his brooding.

The Sorcerer's hand tightened on hers. "Yes. But it's hardly so simply arranged. First, since I am Darion's Guardian, it is my charge to present the Council Major with a candidate for betrothal. They, in turn, will establish the fact she is not pregnant, and virgin, by sorcery. Following their endorsement, by written law the Prince has until the end of his twenty-fifth year to get her with child. Royal marriages by tradition follow conception."

Elienne stopped cold. Her fingers went lifeless in Ielond's hand. "I can't help your Prince. I wouldn't pass a blind midwife's examination for virginity. And you told me I carry Cinndel's child."

Ielond was at once clinically brisk. "Virginity can be re-created with a simple healer's spell. As for your pregnancy,

I have spent years at a stretch studying the process of conception. I have learned things about the body of a woman only Ma'Diere would remember from Her Creation. Mistress, it will be another two days before any Sorcerer in Pendaire could detect Cinndel's child, and that is all the time you will have to establish paternity."

Elienne found herself trembling in the grip of fresh anger. The idea of false virginity was abhorrent, and thought of strangers, Sorcerers, scrutinizing her body made her flesh crawl. Was there no end to the indignities she might have to perform over Cinndel's grave?

Ielond grasped her shoulder and lightly shook it. "Have a care, Mistress. Another outburst from you will bring Faisix back. I doubt we could stand against him a second time."

Elienne opened her mouth to utter a heated protest, but Ielond cut her off with rebuke.

"Should my Prince die for your dignity, Mistress?"

Elienne's temper dissolved into tears. She had no spirit left for resistance. Ielond drew her close in his arms, and emotional exhaustion overtook her at last, like a wave dashed ragged against rock. Stroking her smooth hair with his fingers, Ielond said in her ear, "Lady, I have been seeking you through Time and Space, for thousands of years. Know that I cherish you as I would a daughter, and strive for understanding. My actions are those of a father whose only son is threatened, for I love Darion as a son."

Elienne's head spun. How could any man, Sorcerer or otherwise, live for thousands of years? Her mind was too numb to grapple with impossible concepts.

"I'm tired," she said simply.

"Rest, then." Ielond traced a symbol over her forehead with his thumb. Sleep rose in a dark tide, drowning the well of Elienne's thoughts. She sagged against the Sorcerer's shoulder and, hoisting her like a child, he took her up into his arms and began to walk.

Elienne dreamed. She knew a place of moonlight and rocks. The sky was starless, black as Eternity, and against its featureless, velvet expanse a crescent moon gleamed like

Ma'Diere's Scythe, the one She carries in Her Left Hand to gather in the Dead.

Elienne stood alone in that dream place and silently waited. Her body gradually assumed the fixed patience of the stone under her feet, and her mind became balanced on the needle-fine instant that comprises the present. All thought was fenced by an implacable cage of discipline and, moment to moment, she was able to contemplate only what was.

The moon traced a low arc above the horizon, dragging dawn after its lower limb. The sun rose, hot and white as the Seed of Life Ma'Diere holds in Her Right Hand, and still Elienne waited.

Her body seemed to melt and flow, conjoining with the barren gray rock. Muscles, sinews, and joints became as rigid as statuary, enduring as the stone itself. Unburdened of its transient, mobile casing of flesh, Elienne felt her mind free itself and expand. She beheld the plain where she stood as part of a round, spinning planet. The sun swelled into sphericality, and Elienne's perception broadened further, until it embraced the stars in their multitudes and encompassed the Pivot of the Universe.

Elienne felt herself merge and become one with the vast ebb and flow, Ma'Diere's Right and Left sides that balance Life with Death. Still she waited, until her concentrated thought honed itself into a weapon and finally shattered the taut pinpoint of the present. Consciousness broke through. Time became visible, a shining white ribbon that streamed before her across the void, until perception became dimmed by incomprehensible distance.

The stonelike rigidity released Elienne's flesh. Compelled by impatience, she stepped onto the path of Time and began to follow its track. Her mind restlessly overtook the plodding of her feet and roved ahead, gathering speed until space, stars, and universal reality whirled past as a featureless blur. Time spun onward, sweeping Elienne's awareness with it like thread cast haplessly from a spool. Aware its nether end passed straight through the Eye of Eternity, beyond which lay the heart of Ma'Diere's mystery where no mortal may enter,

Elienne tried to brake, to slow the rush of thought. But the effort only served to reunite her sluggish flesh with her mind.

Flung beyond control, Elienne glanced back, frantically searching for sanctuary. But instead of a haven, she found a wide, light sky peppered black with shapes. Hell's Demons were extended in full pursuit. Beneath the straining pinions of their wings, claws and fangs gleamed like steel polished in anticipation of blood and killing.

Elienne yelled in stark fear and stumbled. Faisix and his snake-scaled horse led the Hell's Horde, and the creature's forked red tongue tasted her presence. It quickened pace.

Elienne screamed again. Terror froze her thoughts. She forced herself to run. Time unreeled futureward under her, but its course was no longer straight.

Cut, spliced, and rewoven repeatedly, the Timepath's clean line had been altered to the point where the eye could scarcely follow its spiraling tangle of convolutions.

Elienne had no chance to wonder whose hand had meddled with the thread of natural progression. Her pursuers drove her forward without mercy. She fled over the first splice in the Time-track, her only thoughts of escape.

The universe splashed into fragments. Darkness reigned between one step and the next. Reality re-formed as Elienne's foot came down, but its shape was unrecognizable, utterly changed. Hardly had her senses encountered an impression when a second junction came upon her. Another void opened underfoot, replaced by yet another sequence of existence. But the alien reality of that Time-borne place held no comfort to human perception, and it was shortly spliced away in favor of still another.

Elienne glanced behind, saw Faisix and the Horde had fallen back. More junctions passed beneath her step. Time-track interwove with Time-track in blinding progression, until each successive reality fell into the next like a toppling row of dominoes whose faces defied counting. Then, without warning, Time's line straightened out.

Elienne knew a world, a land with customs separate from any she had ever known, and in that place a woman. Almost it could have been herself, so fresh in the stranger's mind was grief for a lost husband and ruined home. Elienne felt herself sift through the woman's existence, body, mind, and emotions, striving to match character and circumstance with a pattern she found embedded like a signpost along the path she traveled. The woman failed to fit, and Time bucked underfoot, spliced into change with unarguable purpose.

A second woman waited on the other side, and beyond her, women by the thousands in tireless succession. Each had suffered the recent loss of home and lover, and each carried a newly conceived child. Elienne entered the lives of all of them, mercilessly driven by the meddler who had carved Time to fit his purpose and left his pattern at every turn.

"Release me!" she wanted to scream, yet she knew such outcry would be futile. Faisix and the Hell's Horde were still behind, and she could stop only when a woman was found whose character and circumstance meshed with her predecessor's requirements.

She traversed mind after mind. Her nerves became frayed by others' pain until humanity itself wearied her, and the lives she experienced became numerous and petty as the movements of insects. Yet pursuit denied her a second's rest.

Elienne felt her feet become heavy; every mortal instinct balked at the distance she had wandered from her proper Time. She glanced often over her shoulder, each time horrified to discover that Faisix and his Hell's Horde had gained.

Dulled like water-polished stone by fatigue, she dragged herself over another seam in the Time-track. The woman on the other side had met despair with mulish defiance. Elienne invaded her consciousness with flat distaste, stunned by a startling discovery; the master pattern that had so long gone unsatisfied at last had found its match. A closer look at the woman who had met the Timesplicer's qualifications shocked her anew. She faced her own self.

Elienne felt herself hurled headlong into a scene similar to one she had lived only hours earlier in the darkness of Trathmere's dungeons, but in her dream she was present also as observer. Dirty, tear-streaked, and possessed by grief and wild anger, her former self stood braced against the prison's barred door. At her feet knelt a Sorcerer magnificently clad in blue. He had cut through the stuff of Time with what she now saw revealed to be a focused projection of his living soul. It shone like a winter star, hard, brilliant, and blue-white. He took the severed strand of Time into his hands, and in growing horror the dreaming Elienne became aware he intended to make a loop; join it back into itself at an earlier point in its own past.

"No!" she cried, momentarily set adrift by revelation; the path just followed had been a Sorcerer's condensed perception of five thousand years' search for a Prince's bride. "You must not!" Newly wise to the laws of Time, she was aware crossing a Time-track back into itself would cause death to its wielder.

The Sorcerer, recognizable as Ielond, glanced up, his face pale with weariness. Yet beneath lay a will too strong for mortal interference.

"I must," he said simply. "By the time I had unraveled the mysteries of Time and learned to alter its sequence, Darion had already stood before the Grand Council and been condemned. If he is to be saved, the past must be changed."

Elienne shook her head, blinded by swelling tears. Her throat squeezed shut, trapping her protest unspoken, and the soul brilliance that drifted over Ielond's hands distorted into starred slivers as her eyelids spilled their salty burden down her cheeks.

Ielond rose from the cell floor. The lining of his cloak echoed the red of Cinndel's wounds as he stood before her, immovable as chiseled stone. "Elienne, you mustn't weep," he said gently. "It is the Prince's life or mine. I make the choice with peace in my heart."

The words were spoken aloud, and their sound woke Elienne from sleep. Disgruntled and shaken, it was a moment before she realized that she had passed the night in Ielond's arms. Over his shoulder, an orange sun topped the mountains at the edge of the icefield's bleak expanse.

Elienne felt rested. Yet the dream's impact remained irrevocably inscribed into waking memory. All she had been forced to witness through the night was sharp as direct experience, and the tears on her face were real. Elienne stared up at the sliver of light that drifted always in Ielond's pres-

ence. No Guild Sorcerer from her own land could have
disciplined self-will to a focus so precise that soul became
manifest, a visible pinpoint of force.

Conscious of the Sorcerer's gaze upon her, Elienne spoke,
embarrassed to find her voice shaky with the effect of her
tears. "I understand, I think. You splice Time. That is what
gives you power over Destiny."

Ielond shifted his grip and gently lowered Elienne to the
ground. "I can influence all destiny but my own," he said
carefully. "It makes little difference. I have built my lifework
around Darion's future. If he dies, my efforts have been
wasted. Since I will not be alive to see them through to
completion, I rely on the resources of the woman I send to
Pendaire as his bride. Lady, if you fail, there can be no other
after you. Are you prepared to devote your life to a man who
is a stranger?"

Elienne stared at her feet, reminded by the unfamiliar
jeweled slippers which covered them that Ielond's words
carried the weight of finality. A long minute passed before she
answered.

"I go only to preserve a life that is dear to you, for you
saved my life, and the life of Cinndel's child." She met the
Sorcerer's intent gaze. "I'll give you my best effort, and my
son for the royal heir. But I cannot promise I will love your
Prince. Husband he may be, but only in name. My heart is
not available for bargain."

"So be it," said Ielond. "I can ask no more."

The Sorcerer's attitude turned brisk. He unpinned the
neck of his cloak and drew forth a heavy gold chain. A filigree
pendant dangled from its end, set with a glassy, transparent
gem that shone like dew on silver in the dawn light.

Ielond cupped the ornament in his hand. "This is a
mirrowstone. It will react to any living substance that comes
into contact with its surface. This one has been set over a
strand of Prince Darion's hair. You will see his current location reflected within, provided no other influence is touching
the stone."

He extended the gem to Elienne. "Take care when you

look. Handle it only by its setting, otherwise you will see nothing but yourself."

Elienne accepted the jewel gingerly, the gold a hard, warm weight against her palm. With an eerie sense of foreboding, she gazed within. The mirrowstone's reflection jolted her like a physical blow.

Elienne gasped, "Ma'Diere's mercy!" It took an extreme effort of will not to fling the object away into the snow. Framed by the ornate grace of the setting, she saw a slim, chestnut-haired man; he wore black, unrelieved by device or embroidery. Manacles adorned his wrists. Whatever emotion lay beneath the pale mask of his face was shuttered behind forced control. Hazel and wide-set, the eyes were haunted. And beyond the stiff line of his shoulder stood a hooded executioner with an ax.

"Do something!" cried Elienne. "They'll kill him."

"That is for you to determine." Ielond was remorselessly curt. "Now listen, because time is precious. That stone has been interfaced by enchantment. In the locus of Pendaire, it will also act as a means of communication; you have only to touch the stone and speak, and Darion will hear you. Do you understand?"

Elienne nodded, not trusting herself to speak.

With steady hands the Sorcerer pulled the chain from Elienne's fingers and slipped it around her neck. He then summoned his light and carefully joined the end links until no seam remained. When his work was complete, the mirrowstone could be removed only with a file.

"I am going to splice us into my personal study in Pendaire." Ielond ran his hand over the chain one last time before letting it fall. "The time will be Summer's Eve. You will find on my desk a sealed writ presenting you to the Grand Council as candidate for the Prince's betrothed. My tower is situated in the west wing of the palace. You should have little trouble getting the writ from there to the chamber where the Grand Council will convene by noon the following day."

Ielond placed his hand on the small of Elienne's back and gently pressed her forward. "I will further alter your own

Timepath to converge with Pendaire but an hour past the moment your son was conceived. This will give you a full three days for the Council to affirm your candidacy. You must bed the Prince at all costs before the close of the week."

Elienne's expression went wooden. The Sorcerer appeared not to notice. He strode at her side and drew breath to resume his list of instructions.

Elienne interrupted. "And you will die," she said bitterly, and followed with a curse.

Ielond loosed an explosive sigh. "Mistress, it's inevitable. My life has already passed through Summer's Eve on Pendaire. My reemergence there will create an impossible differential between past and present. The same reality cannot exist twice in a single location."

The Sorcerer's brisk manner plainly indicated he wished no more said on the subject. Elienne walked on in mutinous silence as, slowly, the sun's rising disc stained the horizon yellow-gold. Disturbed more than she cared to admit that Ielond would not survive the transfer to Pendaire, she realized he had won more than cooperation during her short time in his presence. Elienne worried. Denied the stability of his presence, her wayward, outspoken manner would make it difficult to mind her promises concerning Darion. Cinndel had been entertained by her quick tongue; another man might learn to hate it.

Ielond stopped so abruptly Elienne almost bumped into him. Shaken from thought, she looked up and saw they had reached what appeared to be the uttermost edge of the world. The icefield ended almost underfoot. As though chopped by a giant's cleaver, the plain dropped off sheer into a glassy, crystalline precipice. The base lay thousands of feet down beneath an ocean of dawn-tinted sky.

Ielond gave Elienne no time to recover her breath. "This is the point of our departure, Mistress. Time-wielding requires much space. Since we will be leaving a wide change ripple behind us, it is important the site be uninhabited."

Elienne said nothing. She knew if she framed her thoughts into words, the useless, angry emotions damned within her mind would prevail. Ielond took a braced stance. He extended his right arm with his light cupped beneath his palm and uttered four words.

Wind sprang up. It swept in from behind, a demon's howl of cold that clutched Elienne's skirts wildly against her ankles and whipped her hair like a horse's mane. The gale mounted, ice crystals driven like a scourge before its fury. Yet Ielond effortlessly bridled the forces of his summoning and funneled the result through the pinpoint focus held balanced between finger and thumb.

The wind keened through the vortex. Faintly over the rush of noise, Elienne heard Ielond speak again. The pull of those three words tugged her soul, made her yearn to escape the confines of flesh and merge with the nexus of power that converged beneath the Sorcerer's hand.

Ielond raised his voice a third time, and two more words built like a pyramid upon those which had preceded. Elienne experienced a physical wrench, compelled to grasp Ielond's wrist to maintain her footing.

The light waxed brighter and blazed. Through burning eyes, Elienne saw the ice begin to alter. Fine crystals blew loose and streamed, separate as table salt, over the abyss. Tossed into empty air, the particles spread like a cloud and visibly swelled; from specks, they expanded rapidly to the size of rocks, then touched and intermeshed to form a solid, crystalline bridge whose hard facets shattered sunlight into colors. The sight was one of indescribable beauty. Yet even as Elienne paused to admire, Ielond capped the pyramid of his incantation with one final word. The light shot like a meteor from his hand, trailing a tail of fire over the gleaming arch of ice.

"Come." Ielond took Elienne firmly by the arm and drew her onto the narrow span of the icebridge. The path was precarious, barely wide enough for the two of them to pass single file. Elienne felt as though the breadth of the sky had expanded, engulfing them like specks poised on a thread above the Eye of Eternity. The icefield fell behind. Ahead, the slender walkway led upward and disappeared through the blazing heart of Ielond's light.

"You may confide in my apprentice, Kennaird." The

Sorcerer's words fell as a whisper in that wide space. "He will attend to the details after my death. Taroith, also, is trustworthy. He heads the Sorcerers' League and also holds a seat in the Grand Council. Heed his advice, and look to him for guidance."

Ielond towed Elienne onward, oblivious to her growing alarm. The orange sun hung off to the right as though suspended, and awash in torrid light, the icefield glimmered behind like the Plains of Hell. Following Ielond's footsteps, Elienne saw the steady brilliance of his focus begin to shine through the solidarity of his person. At the next step, his cloak glittered like frost-shot glass and sparkled into transparency. Elienne felt the cold tingle of enchantment pierce her inner-most flesh. She wanted to stop, but the Sorcerer pulled her relentlessly forward.

"We have entered the threshold of the Timesplice." Ielond's voice seemed diffracted, and both hands and feet disappeared after his cloak. "Ma'Diere's fortune go with you, Lady Elienne. You are Darion's last hope in life. Abandon him, and his death is certain."

The Sorcerer moved directly through the dazzle of light that burned, hot as a star, at the end of the icebridge. The solidity of his body unraveled into a blaze of blue-white sparks and vanished. Elienne felt herself gripped and hurled after him into oblivion. The light snapped out with the speed of a lightning flash, and sky and icebridge fell away into darkness.

Elienne could neither hear nor see. Her throat would not answer her desire to scream, and her very soul was plunged into cold darkness, fathomless as Eternity.

Chapter 3

The Council Major

Elienne wakened rudely to the stinging, bitter taste of a strange liquid; fumes scoured her nostrils and made them burn. She choked, supported by strange hands. Through watering eyes she caught the blurred impression of an anxious face lit by a candle. All else was darkness.

"My Lady?" said a voice. "Can you hear me?"

Elienne nodded, unable to speak. Whatever she had been made to swallow bound her throat in knots. The cold lip of a flask brushed against her mouth. Fearing a second draught would be forced upon her, Elienne turned her head violently to one side.

"No more," she managed to croak, and coughed wrackingly so that her objection could not be ignored. Rewarded, after an interval, by the thin clink of glassware being set aside, Elienne blinked away the tears that dammed her eyes.

She lay on a thick-piled carpet magnificently patterned with birds of paradise. Her shoulder was propped against the knobby, carved foot of a dragon whose middle region supported the seat of a chair; and, in the trembling light of a hand-held candle, a sandy-haired man bent over her, thin face drawn with concern.

"Ma'Diere be praised," he said in a rush. His blue eyes protruded slightly, lending a faintly surprised expression, but his mouth was kindly and generously proportioned. "I was afraid we had lost you too."

Elienne struggled to sit. "Ielond," she said, and stopped. Her eyes had begun to adjust to the dim room. Over the young man's shoulder she saw a figure in blue velvet robes sprawled awkwardly across the top of a paper-littered desk. Horror and loss wrenched a gasp from her lips. "No!"

"He is beyond help." The young man swallowed. "Dead."

Elienne bit her lip and restrained an obscenity. She was less successful with the urge to weep that followed.

The man gave Elienne's hand a self-conscious squeeze. "I know how you feel." His own voice betrayed grief. "Master Ielond has instructed me since my fourteenth year. I loved him better than my own father."

"Then you must be Kennaird." Elienne blotted her face on a silken sleeve. "I was told to trust you."

She disengaged her hand from Kennaird's clasp and began to rise, but, overcome with dizziness, she made it only as far as the cushions of the dragon chair. "Hell's Damnation, what's the matter with me!" The room began to swirl in sickening circles.

Kennaird confessed with embarrassed haste, "It's the elixir I gave you. It will only bring you sleep."

Elienne struggled to stand. "Where is Darion? I wish to speak with him."

"You must not. Not before the Grand Council has sanctioned him as your betrothed." Kennaird's words sounded as though they were funneled across a wide distance.

"Eternity take the Grand Council!" Elienne struggled for control. Her tongue seemed swollen and thick. "I have to see Darion."

But Kennaird remained stolidly unsympathetic. "Ielond guessed as much. It was his final will that I keep you safely in this tower until tomorrow. A little sleep will do you no harm, and it might improve your temper."

"Damn you," Elienne responded, shaping her consonants with extreme effort. Her tongue had grown as sluggish as her eyelids. "Damn yooouuu...."

Her eyes closed. For a long moment Kennaird stood and regarded the small, almost delicately proportioned woman intended as Prince Darion's bride. Ielond had said he would seek a lady of spirit. The apprentice blasphemed with uncharacteristic fervor. "Ma'Diere's everlasting mercy! He's sent us a veritable harridan."

* * *

Elienne woke to warm sunlight. She stirred languidly. Her clothes had been removed, and whoever had done it had also left her in a marvelously soft bed. She felt rested and pleasant, but for the pestilent itch that had developed in the area of her crotch.

Elienne shot upright, sending pillows and bedclothes in a cascade to the floor. More than sleep had invaded her body during the night. She'd have bet every jewel Ielond had given her that Kennaird had also blessed her with a convincing reconstruction of her maidenhead. The thought raised blistering anger.

The apprentice sorcerer chose that moment to poke his head through the door. "Good day, my Lady."

"You," Elienne accused scathingly, "have the manners and the morals of a billy goat." She made no move to cover herself.

Kennaird gaped. The tops of his ears turned scarlet, and he retreated hastily, slamming the door as he went. Through the thick, carven panels, his voice sounded strangled. "Missy, what was done was for Darion's sake."

"He damned well better be worth it." Elienne flung the coverlet aside in anger. "I'll not suffer every churl and his brother sticking his hands beneath my skirts without granting the courtesy of asking first."

"Missy, please."

"You're not forgiven," raged Elienne. "Let me be."

The door opened. Kennaird stood braced as though expecting a blow. But Elienne merely slipped out of bed and stood, wrapped in the chaste folds of a sheet like a barefoot queen.

"My Lady," the apprentice said coldly, "kindly dress at once. It is already half-past eleven, and you must appear before the Council within the hour. Ielond recommends you to them as a Prince's bride. Act like one, whether it pleases you or not, or another will pay with his life."

"Goat," said Elienne.

Kennaird departed. But he paused on the far side of the door to loose a snort of laughter into his sleeve. Over his work the past night, he had envied Prince Darion the mate Ielond had delivered, but no more. That missy the Prince could have all to himself, and his Grace would be lucky if his hair wasn't gray before the turn of the season.

Kennaird sat at Ielond's desk sorting through papers when Elienne merged from the bedroom. Alerted by the sound of the door latch, he looked up and studied her with light curiosity. Ielond had fashioned dress and jewelry with the finesse of a master. Golden silk and tourmalines complemented Elienne to the point where it was impossible to imagine her dicey temperament, far less her waspish tongue.

"I am glad you're not one to fuss overlong with dressing," said Kennaird. "Ielond's death has put an already delicate situation squarely on top of a nest of chaos. The Council will be in knots arguing over Darion's succession, because but seven days remain before his twenty-sixth birthday and he has not fathered even a bastard child. You are the first and only candidate for the Prince's Consort whom Ielond has entered, and suspicion is already high because he waited so very late. Your case must be presented at the earliest possible moment."

Elienne offered no response. Instead she gazed about the study with unconcealed interest. Absent were the flasks, braziers, and phials that would have cluttered the dwelling of a Guild Sorcerer from her own land. Though Ielond's walls were tiered floor to ceiling with the usual rows of dusty leather books, she found no implement of a Loremaster's practice anywhere in the room.

"Ielond's sorceries were crafted entirely of mind and will," said Kennaird. "His art was discipline; his power, self-awareness. He had no need of gimmicks."

Elienne stared. "Was it he who taught you to read thoughts?"

Kennaird shook his head. "I was guessing. My training has not progressed so far." He tapped a sheaf of papers with a finger. "But Ielond left much information on you and the place you came from. He had established knowledge of your existence before he broke the barrier of Time and left Pendaire. He had only to locate you and return."

"Why are you telling me this?"

"I wished you to know just how much faith Ielond placed in you." Kennaird rose hastily from his chair, heated for argument.

Elienne interrupted. "I think I already know." Her annoyance showed. "Ielond gave his life, and I my word, for the sake of Prince Darion's succession. I realize I am a sorry substitute for your Master's living presence, but that was his choice. Honor his memory by respecting it." Elienne paused to rein in another stampede of tears. She was through crying over what could not be changed. "Don't take your Master's death out on me," she finished shakily. "And quit trying to shepherd my conscience."

Kennaird looked down at the papers beneath his hands as though they held an answer for his uncertainty. The brown jerkin he had worn the night before had been replaced with a heavy black robe bordered at the cuffs with a triple band of blue. The deep colors contrasted harshly with his light hair and complexion, and morning light only accentuated the fatigue that ringed his eyes. For a moment, Elienne regretted her outburst. Ielond had not left his apprentice an easy legacy. But before she could offer apology, Kennaird rose and collected a document crusted with seals.

"My Lady, the time has come to present you before the Grand Council of Pendaire." With evident annoyance, he scooped the remaining papers into an untidy pile. Then he flung wide the study door and motioned the Lady of Ielond's choosing over the threshold.

Elienne waited on the balcony that overlooked the head of a spiral staircase while Kennaird set a ward to guard the doorway. His focus resolved after an interval of profound concentration. Compared with Ielond's brilliant manifestation, the apprentice's effort shone dimly, no more than a faint bluish gleam over his spread palm.

Yet Elienne watched without criticism as he traced a pattern over the oaken panels above the knob. None of the Guild's followers could have done as much with so little. Completed, the ward sparkled to invisibility.

Blotting sweat from his brow, Kennaird nodded toward

the stairs. "I hope you are as sturdy as you are stubborn. It's a long way down."

The words were no understatement. By the time they reached the bottom, Elienne was grateful she had led an unfashionably active life for the wife of a Duke. She wondered briefly whether she would be as free to indulge in hawking and riding as wife of a King.

Kennaird led her through an arched portal at ground level. The view beyond stopped Elienne in her tracks.

The tower opened into an immense garden completely enclosed within a courtyard. Blue, orange, and yellow flowers bloomed in a magnificent array, framing fountains, lawns, and hedgerows with breath-stopping artistry. Above, washed in golden summer sunlight, and brilliant with pennants, rose the spires and battlements of the royal palace.

"How beautiful," exclaimed Elienne softly, but that moment she caught sight of a flaw amid the garden's perfection. A dirty, dark-haired child sat huddled beneath an evergreen beside the path. She glared at the two of them, a scowl printed on her smudged oval face.

"Hello," said Elienne.

When Kennaird turned and saw whom she had addressed, he stopped at once and bent imposingly over the bush and the child it sheltered. "What are you doing here? Does your governess know where you are?"

"No!" The girl shrank into her thicket of needles, hands clenched tightly around scuffed knees.

Elienne grasped Kennaird's elbow. "Must you be so harsh with her?"

The girl seemed no older than twelve. Elienne stooped and offered her hand, but the child backed violently away. Branches whipped, dealing Elienne a stinging rebuff, and the girl escaped at a run across the emerald expanse of lawn on the far side.

"You insolent brat!" Kennaird yelled after her. "I'll have you punished."

Elienne frowned. "Let the poor child be. She was obviously frightened to death of you."

Kennaird presented her with a startled glance. "That was

Minksa," he said angrily. "She's Jieles's bastard and, incidentally, one of your enemies. You've a lot to learn about this court and its ways before you question my judgment, Missy. Remember that."

Kennaird strode off before Elienne had time to reply. She was obliged to hurry as the apprentice hustled her without sympathy through an exquisitely carved entry and down a maze of hallways. The decor within reflected the same restrained artistry as the garden. Though Elienne longed to linger and stare, Kennaird's hasty step prevented her.

He slowed at last before a wide doorway with broad double panels and a round stag device chased in gold. The knob was set with gems.

Kennaird addressed the liveried steward who guarded the entrance against intrusion with urgency. "I bring with me Ielond's candidate for the Prince's Consort." He waved the sealed document. "This writ was the Master's last in life. Let me and the maid pass. She is the one chosen to share his Royal Grace's destiny."

The steward raised eyebrows in surprise. "You bring a missy endorsed by the Prince's Guardian? Enter, with my blessing. They're fighting in there like the two halves of Eternity over His Grace's future, and—"

"I know. Excuse me." Kennaird pushed past the steward and opened the door, motioning Elienne after him.

Neither the garden nor the exceptional elegance of the palace halls prepared her for the sight of the Grand Council Chamber of Pendaire. The room was oval-shaped. Loftily domed, a triple row of galleries filled with seated councilmen tiered its entire circumference. The floor was tiled with a mosaic depicting Ma'Diere's seasons, fall and winter beneath her shining Scythe, and spring and summer lit with the warmth of the Seed of Life. A dais centered this array, upon which sat an exquisitely dressed collection of notables.

"Which is the Prince?" whispered Elienne in Kennaird's ear.

"Hush." The apprentice was sweating. Something had made him nervous, and, searching that vast chamber for the reason, Elienne began to take note of the proceedings.

An emaciated old man stood on the dais. Heavily ornamented red and black robes draped his stooped back, and though his poor health was evident from a distance, his tremulous voice carried clearly the breadth of the room.

"... since his Guardian's death, his Grace has done nothing but drink himself senseless," the elderly man said with succinct clarity. "Were he a Prince worthy to rule, he would not indulg 'iimself to the point of shameless exhibition. It is my opinion this Council wastes time seeking a formal Consort. What can his Grace achieve in seven days that he hasn't already tried with every scullery drudge and loose wench he could find to fill his nights? My Lords, your Excellency, I say Prince Darion is unfit for succession. The sooner that sad fact is faced, the better for the well-being of this realm."

Elienne wondered how anyone could listen to such a hidebound outburst; but like the first warning of stormwind on a still afternoon, murmurs of assent swept the packed galleries. Elienne's temper roused, stripping away the last vestige of restraint. Caution abandoned, she slipped past Kennaird and walked boldly onto the floor.

"Fools!" she said scornfully. "Would you listen to that lame old rooster? Fathering children is a pastime for the young." She shot a withering glance at the elder, whose jaw quivered with outrage in a face gone red to the top of his bald skull. "Or had you forgotten that, in the advanced state of your senility?"

Hard hands gripped Elienne's arm, and a flurry of black velvet rippled against her skirts. "Will you shut up?" hissed Kennaird in her ear. The council chamber had fallen silent, and every eye in the room was upon them. At that moment, Elienne noticed who sat in the great chair at the top of the dais.

She had not looked closely at the man when she first entered, but now his golden gaze drew all of her attention. Fear knotted her stomach. Though unfamiliarly framed by a court setting and a collar of burgundy brocade, the fine, light hair, high cheekbones, and sculpture-perfect features were indelibly etched in Elienne's memory.

"Have you business here, woman?" Faisix said softly. "If

so, it had better be exceedingly important. Your abusive contributions are not welcome." His eyes passed lightly over her gown of yellow silk. "And the clothing you wear is a royal affront. How dare you, without this Council's approval, dress yourself as Prince's Consort?"

Kennaird objected loudly. "She has Ielond's endorsement." He flourished the writ in his hand, and confusion erupted across the council chamber.

"Silence!" The uproar reluctantly subsided as Faisix nodded pointedly at the document. "Bring that here."

Kennaird bowed neatly from the waist. "Your pardon, Excellency. I was instructed to give this only into Master Taroith's hands."

Faisix seemed unperturbed. "Very well. Taroith?"

A tall, white-haired gentleman rose from a seat on the dais. Robes of silver-gray covered a spare body, and the eyes, brown and kindly, were set in a face molded by wisdom and compassion. From the first glance, Elienne knew she confronted Ielond's equal, a Sorcerer she could both trust and like.

"Kennaird," Taroith said immediately. His step, as he descended the dais, was that of a man half his years. "I see you wear mourning for Ielond. You have my sympathy. He was the finest Master Pendaire has ever known."

Taroith gave Elienne a smile of reassurance and with honest curiosity accepted the writ. "Welcome, my Lady." He looked down and briefly inspected the seals on the document. "Pendaire could benefit under a Queen such as you. I wish you the best of fortune with the Prince."

The Sorcerer broke the seals with swift efficiency in a certain prescribed order. Though bent with age, his fingers moved like lightning. As the last wafer of wax parted, a bright blue glyph blazed into view alongside the light of his focus.

Taroith smiled and addressed the Council. "That is Ielond's own ward. It could have been set only by his living hand. Therefore, what it sealed lies beyond our right to question here."

The chamber became still as death. Taroith quickly scanned the written lines and at last raised his eyes from the parchment.

"Your Excellency," he said to Faisix. "My Lords." He

directed a respectful glance toward the galleries, momentarily preoccupied; then, with a confident gesture, reached out and grasped Elienne's hand. "The writ of Ielond, Guardian of the Royal ward, Darion of Pendaire, recommends to us this maiden, Elienne, as candidate for Consort. Ma'Diere bless her presence. She has solved a difficult problem."

A tumultuous wave of talk rose, drowning Taroith's last words. Beckoning to Elienne, the Sorcerer nodded toward the dais.

"Go with him," said Kennaird. "And good luck, Missy."

Elienne moved forward, aware the uproar in the council chamber centered on her. Taroith led her up the steps to the dais. The insulted elder stood at the top, shakily glaring at their approach. Elienne ignored him. He was a known enemy. Surrounding her, as yet undeclared, were others. Elienne studied the faces of the notables on the dais before their first startled expressions could be replaced by less revealing ones.

Taroith placed Ielond's writ is Faisix's hands and drew Elienne forward. "His Excellency Faisix of Torkal, who serves Pendaire as Regent until the Prince's rights of succession have been confirmed."

Elienne curtsied, since courtesy demanded it. Strangely, no trace of recognition appeared on Faisix's features. He would not recall the meeting on the icefield until a fortnight hence, Elienne realized. Ielond had spliced her back in time; for Faisix, the encounter had not yet taken place.

Faisix's light, chill gaze broke through her thoughts, rapt with the curiosity of a predator whose hunger is temporarily quiescent. At last his glance returned to the writ.

"Ielond's choice," he mused. "Your Prince has been made to wait a long time for you, Missy."

Abruptly the Regent rose and addressed Taroith. "Circumstances are hardly normal. The Prince's grace period is nearly over. I will urge the Grand Council to adjourn at once, that the ten Select may meet separately over this matter." Faisix turned and spoke anxiously to a portly individual who stood nearby. Though confusion still prevailed on the main floor and in the galleries, his words brought gradual order to those on the dais.

Taroith gave Elienne's hand a light squeeze. "Formalities, only. Don't let them upset you. Ielond's word will stand. It cannot be otherwise. There may be inconveniences added to satisfy a few malcontents, but nothing overly serious. Ielond without a doubt had compelling reasons for selecting this hour for your presentation. Anyone who knew him as I did will trust his judgment, and the rest must acknowledge his legal writ."

Elienne stared at the richly patterned carpet under her feet and wondered how much Taroith knew of Faisix and the Prince's curse. Obviously the Sorcerer endorsed her cause. But if the unsettled emotions she had noticed among the council members had accurately gauged their reaction to her presence, she would need more than support. She required nothing less than an ally who was guarded against treachery, and of those present Ielond had placed trust in only one.

"Gifted," said Elienne to Taroith, turning so Faisix would not overhear. "Gifted, one present wishes the Prince to fail his succession. He has powerful followers."

Not a flicker of expression altered Taroith's countenance, but he drew Elienne away from the crowd of notables promptly. "Missy, if Ielond told you who the Prince's enemies were, you had best name them to me now."

They reached the stairs and started down. Taroith's focus lit features that were calm but receptive; and, drawing a deep breath, Elienne plunged ahead. "Don't ask me to explain," she said in a low voice. "I know this much first hand, without Ielond to warn me. Your Regent wants Prince Darion dead, Gifted, and my own life to him is but a grass stalk before the Scythe of Ma'Diere."

Taroith directed a swift glance over his shoulder. Faisix lingered yet on the dais, though the Select of the Grand Council had begun to heed his summons and gather into a group. Looking back to Elienne, Taroith said, "Whatever you do, don't mention him directly by name. He is Sorcerer enough to follow what concerns him, and no ward of secrecy is possible in this place."

As they reached the level of the mosaic, Taroith ushered Elienne across its echoing expanse toward a small side door.

"Your accusation is a grave one, Missy."

Elienne dodged around a message boy who had stopped in her path to stare. "Gifted, Ielond left me but two names I could trust in all Pendaire. Yours was one of them. He said I was to look to you for guidance."

Taroith regarded Elienne long and steadily as he walked. "Ielond gave his life to bring you here, didn't he?"

Elienne nodded, avoiding speech. The Guardian's death was too recent for her to contemplate without emotional interference.

"Well then." The Sorcerer reached the door, pushed it open, and briskly drew Elienne after. "We mustn't fail him in his final wish. You have my protection, Lady. We will soon see who would rather Darion fails his inheritance."

"Jieles, also," Elienne added.

Taroith made a noise in his throat. "That one I already know to be grasping and selfish."

With a wave of his hand, the Sorcerer set his focus about the task of igniting the wall sconces. Thin new flames lit a white-walled room trimmed with gilt molding, and furnished with a long table and chairs. The last wick had barely caught fire when the door opened wide to admit the Grand Council's Select. They were all past middle age, and as brilliantly dressed as a flock of rare birds.

Pendaire must be a rich kingdom, Elienne concluded, or else its peasantry was excessively oppressed. The last of the Select filed in, the elder Elienne had insulted entered among them, supported on Faisix's arm.

"We can also assume that old Garend there is no friend," murmured Taroith in Elienne's ear. "You touched his pride with your slight to his manhood, I'm afraid. He is one who holds a vicious grudge."

Confronted close hand by Garend's crumpled cheeks and pinched, miserly features, Elienne found it difficult to regret her hasty words. The man reminded her of sour milk. Never one to bury dislike under innocuous courtesies, Elienne accepted the chair Taroith offered without comment. The Select of Pendaire's Grand Council would no doubt provoke response from her soon enough; she had simply to wait and to watch.

Faisix opened by having Ielond's writ read aloud by a scribe. The document was lengthy, detailed, and formally phrased, yet the Select listened without interruption until it was complete. The silence held as the scribe returned the writ to Faisix and departed, leaving the liveried door steward the only other nonofficial in the room beside Elienne.

"It appears Ielond has left us an eminently qualified candidate," said Faisix to the assembly. "All that remains to satisfy the procedure of the law is this Council's signature of endorsement."

A subtle and clever opening: Faisix had used simplicity as a gambit in a trap to be sprung by the Prince's own supporters, Elienne realized immediately. Her suspicion was swiftly confirmed.

"There are but seven days left for Prince Darion to conceive an heir," said one of the Select. "Ielond's timing has given him poor odds of fulfilling the terms of the Law. I move that he be allowed a twelve-month extension, lest he be condemned without fair chance."

The debate was opened. Faisix sat back in his chair, ambiguously silent, as another voice contested. History held record of six royal executions. Not one of Darion's predecessors had been granted additional time.

The original defendant was quick to point out that those six unfortunates had been paired with a legal Consort for years. But Garend struck down that argument with a specific.

"What difference, my Lords?" he said in his rasping tenor. "King Mistraèl II had no legal Consort at all. He was granted his rights of succession on the evidence of four illegitimate children. This Prince of ours has lain with enough women to demonstrate the potency of his favors. He has sired no bastards. The Grand Jury would have no choice but to rule out his case."

Murmurs of assent underlined Garend's statement, but argument prevailed. Words grew heated, and delicately, without Faisix's prompting, the Select swung their questioning from Darion to Ielond's own motives for revealing an unknown candidate at the bitter end of the Prince's trial period. Garend's contributions figured heavily. His was the first attack to be targeted at Elienne, and even through dignified phrases his malice was apparent.

The accusations prompted Taroith, who had remained silent, to speak out at last. "Garend," he said with firm finality. "The Lady's candidacy is not yours to question."

"I must," Garend responded. "For the sake of Pendaire. Though no Sorcerer, even I am aware a gifted healer can simulate virginity well enough to pass your examination. If this missy were an ordinary candidate, Ielond surely would have presented her case before today. I say the Prince is incapable, and that fact is what prompted his Guardian's great delay."

A muttering swept around the table, killed by Taroith's forceful exclamation. "Nonsense! Ielond was the most respected Master in Pendaire; that was the reason he was appointed Guardian to begin with. You do him and Elienne both a disservice by mistrusting her candidacy. I personally believe she is someone special, that Ielond took pains to select her above other more available women. Whether true virgin or not, she cannot be pregnant without her examiner's knowledge. And I remind you all it is Darion's *ability to father offspring* which must satisfy the Law, not the past history of his Consort."

"But suppose Ielond was capable of creating pregnancy and shielding it by sorcery," Garend persisted. "The possibility must be considered."

Surprisingly, Faisix himself ended the controversy. His lips slid easily into the thin, brittle smile Elienne recalled from the icefield. "My Lords," he admonished. "Are we so easily made victims of hysteria? Pregnancy cannot be fabricated without employing the Black arts. If such is the case, it will be quite obvious even to the green eye of an apprentice."

The Regent paused, allowing his words to take effect. His gaze touched each man present for a brief second before he resumed. "I will allow a conspiracy might be present to falsely establish Darion's rights of succession. Therefore, as a deterrent to injustice, I move another Sorcerer be present during our candidate's examination. The task would normally be Taroith's alone, as Master of the Sorcerers' League. But

Ielond addressed his writ solely into Taroith's hands, which is not common custom. Most likely, the gesture was innocent. But it might be wise if I attended Elienne's examination for candidacy, and also at her confirmation of pregnancy should she be blessed with the good fortune to conceive."

"I second," said Garend at once.

Elienne's blood ran cold. She hardly felt Taroith's squeeze of reassurance beneath the edge of the table. Faisix was a master of manipulation. One smooth move had shed doubt on Taroith's integrity and assured the Regent access to her through two critical examinations. The Select molded to his touch like soft wax. Round the table, the votes in favor of his motion were entered with swift and deadly ignorance of its possible consequence.

Elienne battled rising uneasiness. She had only just begun to appreciate the practiced sophistication of the Sorcerer who opposed her. If she wasn't careful, he would shift her out of his path without even the unpleasantness of a confrontation.

Discussion resumed over a host of lesser details. Time and date were set for Elienne's examination, followed by arrangements for a ceremonial banquet celebrating the royal betrothal. Normally, an endorsed Consort was permitted to pass her time of leisure as she wished, but Garend questioned Elienne's right to freedom on the grounds that another man might bed her in the Prince's stead. This idea was bandied about at wearying length. Some deemed it demeaning to confine one who might become Pendaire's Queen; others felt an assigned escort to be an appropriate and tactful precaution. Elienne herself listened without visible sign of rancor until she saw the beginnings of another smile take shape on Faisix's features.

The back of her neck prickled with apprehension. Faisix, like a man manipulating chess pieces, was eliminating her options through a series of carefully planned moves. Small, petty arguments would soon be welded together into another, wider purpose; and rather than allow Faisix to arbitrate to his advantage a second time, Elienne gave her seething temper free rein. Even Taroith started in surprise as her small hand crashed down on the tabletop in exasperation.

"Must you peck the issue to death like crows?" she said in sharp annoyance. "The Prince has but days to establish his rights to succession. You do him no favor by wasting his time over trifles."

"Missy—" Garend snapped over stunned silence.

"*Lady*. I'm not your relative."

"Missy, his Grace is, at this moment, disgustingly inebriated. His condition is so deplorable that he is incapable of bedding anything but himself. For a good many hours to come, he is unlikely to wish anyone's company, far less that of a well-born maiden."

Acidly suspicious, Elienne was not so easily put off. "Does his Royal Grace usually drink himself senseless? That doesn't sound to me like the behavior of a man who might face execution in seven days' time. I think the Prince had help, outside help, with his indulgence."

Immediate protest arose from the Select, but the most dramatic response came from Faisix. He pushed himself forward in his chair. White anger tautened the lines of his face, and his voice cut like a whip through the general outcry. "Silence!"

The Regent settled back. More calmly he said, "My Lady, your words are both treasonous and ridiculously ill-founded. You have neither voice nor vote in this Council. Disrupt these proceedings again, and I'll have you sent from the room."

"You're afraid I might smell the fish beneath all this finery." Elienne started at the sudden grip of a hand on her arm. She shrugged the clasp off, then turned and met the bland, round face of the door steward.

"Escort her out," said Faisix with incisive finality. "And keep her with you until this Council adjourns. She must be available afterward for physical examination."

Elienne slid her chair back. She bent over with a muffled exclamation and fussed with the fit of her shoe—the position placing her head within inches of Taroith's knee, well inside his sphere of influence should he wish mental contact. Her tactic was rewarded. Taroith's response came as a light touch upon her mind. *I'll forestall the Regent. Wait patiently. Don't stir up any more trouble.*

Elienne finished with her shoe, rose, and walked out of the room without a backward glance. Left standing by himself, the steward stumbled awkwardly over her chair in his haste to follow, and with varying degrees of disgruntlement the Select of Pendaire's Grand Council resumed debate.

Chapter 4

Prince's Consort

Elienne wanted time to herself, which meant shedding the presence of the steward who had been assigned escort duty. She watched the man emerge from the council room; he shut the door firmly behind himself and leaned on it, puffing. After appraising the paunch that strained the seams of his white and gold livery, Elienne judged he was not a man who loved exertion. She tailored her methods to suit.

The mammoth oval expanse of the Grand Council Chamber was quite empty, yet the ornate decor held splendor enough to rouse a stranger's curiosity. Elienne feigned a country girl's ignorant enthusiasm and, with apparent innocence, began to rove the room and admire.

The steward grunted like an unhappy sow, but the effect was irresistible. He pushed his bulk away from the door and followed while Elienne wandered the length and breadth of the room. No detail was too slight for her interest, though nothing commanded her attention quite long enough for her to linger. When the lower level and every detail of its mosaic floor had been exhausted, Elienne investigated the dais. Up and down twenty-five marble steps went the steward at her heels, his breath by now a stertorous wheeze.

Elienne failed to notice his distress. She plied him steadily with questions, then abandoned the dais and went on light feet straight to the staircase that led to the upper galleries. The steward balked and parked his bulk against the banister.

"Missy," he gasped. "No more steps."

Elienne turned in mid-flight and gave him a round-eyed look. "Oh, I'm sorry. I'm quite carried away. I've never in my whole life seen the equal of the craftsmanship in this room."

She paused to gaze wistfully upward. "Mightn't I just take a look? You can always call if the Select wish me back. I'll come straight down."

"Very well." The steward grumbled to himself and took a seat on the bottom step. Elienne could not leave without tripping over him. She would be secure enough, and his responsibilities did not include guard duty.

Elienne ran briskly up the remainder of the flight. She toured the upper gallery in a methodical fashion that had little to do with her earlier display of false curiosity. She covered all three levels from end to end, thoroughly, until she was satisfied that no other entry was possible except by way of the stair. Then she leaned with artful recklessness over the topmost railing and shouted down to the steward.

"There are soft chairs up here. Would you mind if I did my waiting sitting down?"

The steward nodded immediate assent, as much to get her away from the overhang as any other reason. He settled more comfortably on his step, relieved Elienne had at last decided to stay quietly in one place. No meeting of Pendaire's Select had ever been brief; this one was unlikely to differ.

Elienne chose a railing seat that offered an unobstructed view of the lower floor. Until her opposition elected to reveal its plot there was no way to gauge the extent of her personal peril. She dared not let the first move surprise her. Nor could she depend on Kennaird and Taroith for shelter against harm. Trathmere's fall had shown how easily the best defenses could crumble. If she lost the Prince, her fate might be worse than any she would have suffered in Khadrach hands.

Elienne pulled forth the thick gold chain that hung beneath the neck of her gown. The mirrowstone dropped, warm and weighty, into her palm. For a long, still interval, she held it without seeking the image contained by the jewel's depths. After fourteen hours in Pendaire, this would be her first, unhurried glimpse of the man she had promised to marry.

Carefully, Elienne tilted the gem. The clear, reflective surface became immediately congested and dark. Set like yellowed ivory against a field of black, she saw a man's face, lit by the dribbled stalk of a half-spent candle. A tangle of brown hair arched over one ear. The long, spidery lines of shadow cast across cheek and brow lent an impression more sinister than neglect. Garend had said the Prince was drunk. Puzzled, Elienne wondered why no servants attended his Grace's comfort until the effect of the spirits wore off.

Elienne bent closer. The planes of Darion's nose, forehead, and chin had the spare grace of a draftsman's sketch, but there all semblance of harmony ended. The mouth drooped open, slack as the empty pouch of a forester's pack. A small scar bisected the jawline, stark as an ink line against the pale, dry skin drawn taut against a lean framework of bone. The Prince was obviously ill.

Elienne frowned. Often she had sat with Cinndel's younger brother when the aftermath of his carousing had laid him low. The face she remembered had always been flushed and sweating. Whatever held Darion under certainly was not drink. And in a palace as richly adorned as Pendaire's, she doubted whether the dim, drab place where Darion lay was anywhere near the royal suite.

Elienne bit her lip and found herself shaking. The Prince's enemies were confident indeed if they could remove him on the pretense of drunken stupor and hold him without being questioned. Were Ielond alive, they would never have dared. Without him, Darion had no other to act in his defense with the possible exception of Kennaird. And Kennaird had been kept busy through the night with her.

Elienne cursed. The jewel in her hand was the only weapon Ielond had left her. Darion's oppressors did not expect him to be seen by other eyes, and according to the Sorcerer's instructions, communication was possible as well. Perhaps the Prince could be awakened.

Placing her fingertip against the cold surface of the mirrowstone, Elienne leaned close and whispered. "Darion! Your Grace, can you hear me? Darion!"

She released contact. The image flooded back, clouding the stone like dark smoke. The Prince roused enough to stir. This time the magic exposed him full face; his lashes quivered, spiking his cheek with trembling lines of shadow.

Elienne cupped the jewel closer and whispered again, urgently. "Darion, wake up."

Faint as the distant roll of surf in a shell, she heard a coughing sigh. The Prince closed his mouth. His eyes flickered open, irises wide and black in the candlelight. Hazel, Elienne recalled from her brief impression on the icefield, but they remained unfocused and confused.

"Darion, you've been drugged," said Elienne through the mirrowstone.

She held her breath as the Prince threw one veined wrist across his face. If anyone were present, such movement would surely attract attention.

As though answering Elienne's fear, a large hand appeared, momentarily obscuring her view. The Prince moaned thickly. Elienne looked on in horror as a second hand moved into sight. Fingers marred by an old, puckered scar pressed a twist of soaked linen firmly over Darion's nose and mouth until his weak struggles subsided.

"Oh, poor man," Elienne whispered. Hot tears blistered the inside of her eyelids. When the hands removed the drugged cloth and passed from sight, the mirrowstone's dark depths returned Darion's image with faithful clarity, even to the angry red imprint where the rag had roughened his skin.

Elienne shoved the jewel back inside the neck of her dress. The heavy gold setting had gouged purple grooves in her palm where she had gripped too tightly. Angrily she closed her fist over them. Something would have to be done. She no longer found it tolerable to sit like a lady while the Council's Select dallied over trivia. She could start an inquiry after a man with knowledge of drugs who also had a scarred hand.

Elienne rose and ran between the rows of chairs. She took the stairs two at a time while formulating a plan to forestall the steward. Just below the first landing, she all but bowled over someone who ascended the flight in the same state of haste.

"My Lady!" Kennaird divested himself of an armload of yellow silk skirts.

Elienne paused only to draw breath. "Darion's been

drugged," she said tersely, and described what she had seen in the mirrowstone. Kennaird was already familiar with the jewel. He had seen it around her neck the night before; it was the only item on her he had been unable to remove.

"I'll see what I can do," Kennaird promised. He grabbed Elienne with both hands as she tried to slip past him. "I said *I* would look after it."

"But—" Elienne began in protest.

"No." Kennaird shook her with curt annoyance. "No. You'll stay here as you were told. Darion is not the only one in danger. I came to warn you to guard your own life."

Elienne stopped resisting Kennaird's hand, and only then realized his homely face was drawn with anxiety.

"Tell me," she said.

Kennaird released his hold with a tired sigh. "The ward over the study door was broken when I returned." He shut his eyes and leaned back against the paneled wall of the stairwell. "All of Ielond's papers were stolen from the desk. Someone now knows more of you, Lady Elienne, than is meet."

Kennaird staved off Elienne's response with a raised hand. "Wait, Missy, until I finish. Ielond was not careless enough to leave written all the facts about you. There was nothing in his notes that would prevent your—"

"Shh!" Elienne pointed down the stair and whispered. "The steward."

Kennaird obligingly lowered his voice. "They can't stop your Consortship with the contents of those papers. But every facet of the culture you came from was outlined in detail, and among the documents taken was the written summary of the birth chart Ielond cast for you. He left out everything that pertained to your former marriage. But well outlined for my own purposes was a list of the dates and times your natal stars warn you will be vulnerable."

Elienne felt the constriction fall away from her chest. Astrology she understood. The Guild had placed great stock in the movements of planets and events, but Elienne had never paid much attention. No Guild seer had been required to foretell disaster in the path of Khadrach's armies. She spoke at last, concerned mainly for Kennaird's loss. He seemed greatly upset.

"Can't you recast the chart?"

Kennaird shook his head. "Ielond spliced *Time* to find you, Missy. Ma'Diere only knows when and where you were born."

"Well then, look after Darion." Elienne shrugged lightly. "There's no use fretting."

Kennaird regarded her anxiously. "Lady, you had better hear me. Ielond knew his craft. Trathmere's Loremasters were as blind men feeling their way among the stars in comparison. That list in the wrong hands could spell your bane in this world. Guard yourself well."

"I will." Elienne needed no warnings to emphasize her current danger. Aggravation made her response more curt than she intended. "But since I am in no direct danger at the moment, see to Darion, I beg you."

Kennaird made no move to depart. "Beware of Minksa, Lady. She means you ill. I suspect she may have been involved with the theft of Ielond's papers. Restrain your sympathies where she is concerned."

"All right." Elienne bit back impatience. She failed entirely to see how a little girl could have broken a Sorcerer's ward, but that small point was not worth delaying Kennaird with argument. Darion needed help, and in another moment she would disobey completely and search for him herself. But Kennaird was through lecturing.

"Ma'Diere keep you, Lady." The apprentice walked with her to the foot of the steps. Leaving her in care of the steward there, he hurried across the council chamber and disappeared through its wide double door.

The meeting of the Select did not adjourn until well into the afternoon. Escorted by the door steward, Elienne returned to the white and gilt paneled chamber in compliance with a summons from the Regent. She entered with reluctance. A surreptitious peek at the mirrowstone only minutes before had shown Darion's condition unchanged. Kennaird had not yet managed to aid the Prince, and Elienne fumed inwardly at the barriers of formality that hampered her from taking action herself.

As expected, Taroith and Faisix awaited her in the recently vacated council room. Elienne held her eyes downcast, but not through any maidenly deference. Though she wished to alert Taroith to the Prince's present danger, she dared not risk eye contact with the Regent. On the ice plain, the man had displayed a mindbender's skills without visible sign of effort. Better Taroith should remain ignorant than risk having awareness of Darion's drugged state plucked from her thoughts.

"Come here, Lady Elienne," said Taroith. In response to her evident apprehension he added, "This examination will neither hurt you nor disturb your dignity."

Elienne obediently sat in the chair the Sorcerer offered. With the same rigid indifference she had shown when Ielond transformed her dress, she held still as Taroith brought his focus to rest on her abdomen. The touch roused a chilly prickle of awareness. The Sorcerer cupped his hand, bent fingers eclipsing the white blaze, and exerted gentle but firm pressure.

Elienne felt cold slip like water through the fabric of her dress. The light penetrated the skin beneath, then muscle, and sank deeper. An alien presence invaded her innards like frost.

"Relax." Taroith smiled and quietly slipped his other hand around her waist and placed it flat against her back.

Elienne took a slow breath. The icy, tingling sensation of the soulfocus within her body totally absorbed her attention.

"The Lady is innocent," said Taroith presently. "Test for truth if you wish, Excellency."

Faisix rounded the chair and knelt beside the Sorcerer. He reached out and placed his narrow hand over Taroith's. Despite all effort at control, Elienne's stomach muscles knotted.

"There is nothing to fear, Elienne," said the Sorcerer gently. "The Regent will only attune his awareness to mine. There will be no pain, I assure you."

Elienne closed her eyes, forced herself to remain calm. The sensation of cold in her middle sharpened and grew heavy. Since she had no way of knowing whether Faisix could exert any control over Taroith's probe, Elienne tried to limit herself to trivial thoughts as a precaution, until the trial should end.

A small bubble of surprise rose in her mind. Startled by a swift flare of annoyance, Elienne repressed a shiver, certain the emotion was not her own. The feeling vanished as Faisix removed his hand. He had passed briefly through her awareness, and some of his own reaction had leaked through the contact. The Regent had expected to find evidence of Ielond's meddling, Elienne realized. Faisix *knew* that she carried some means of establishing pregnancy. But the Prince's Guardian had predicted accurately; no trace of her child by Cinndel could be detected yet through conventional sorcery.

Elienne found little comfort in the fact she had passed safely through the examination. Faisix would now be forced to seek her ruin beneath the Law, and in a strange court with unfamiliar customs she had little defense against treachery.

Taroith lifted his hands. Like a spark fanned by an air current, his focus withdrew from Elienne's body. Numbness lifted and her own warmth flooded back like circulation returning to a cramped limb.

"The Lady is indeed innocent." Faisix mastered his disappointment with finesse, and his yellow eyes seemed empty of malice. "I owe you an apology, Master Taroith, for expressing doubt against you earlier. The Law has been satisfied. The Council will place its seal of approval on the required documents this afternoon. I will personally send word to the kitchens to prepare a banquet in celebration." The Regent bestowed a smile cold as a snowdrift on Elienne. "Congratulations, my Lady Consort. May the Prince's favor become you."

Elienne rose warily and curtsied. Her mistrust of the Regent proved justified; she had barely completed her gesture when the door opened and admitted two strapping women in armor. Their hair was cropped short as a child's, and wide mesh belts clinked with weaponry. Broad, calloused hands and sinewy wrists offered mute evidence that scabbarded steel and heavy ash spears were not at all ornamental.

"Aisa and Denji," Faisix introduced. "They will stand guard at your door, Lady, until the royal grace period is past. They have orders to kill any man who enters your chambers—

other than the Prince, of course. Questions will be asked
afterward, should such a situation arise. Pendaire's succession
is no light matter, and with Ielond dead, the Select chose
caution."

Elienne said nothing. Plainly, she would have no chance
to speak alone with Taroith. Rather than place her escort on
their guard, she smiled sweetly and allowed herself to be
marched from the room. The muscled height of the guardswomen made her small build seem fragile by contrast. Elienne
hoped with all her heart the impression would cause Faisix to
underestimate her. She needed every advantage she could
foster, however slight.

Elienne was given a suite of rooms in the top of a keep
overlooking the sea. Aisa and Denji guarded the only door,
which gave onto the stair. The room was built on the defense
wall, and arrowslits pierced the stone in place of casements.

Left to herself, Elienne looked out. Hundreds of feet
down, green, foam-laced breakers crashed against the black,
splintered rock of the headland, and sunlight struck rainbows
through the spindrift thrown up by the surf. Chilled by more
than damp air, Elienne turned away. Though savagely beautiful, the view foreclosed any hope of escape. Even the spartan
ugliness of the arrowslits became a blessing to her eyes.
Windows, in that place, would have left her susceptible, not
to attack from the outside, but to a push from within. And all
too likely, the guardswomen were hostile. Until they proved
otherwise, Elienne chose to regard her surroundings with an
eye for her own defense.

The chambers themselves were lavish. In keeping with
what she had observed of Pendaire's palace, the furnishings
were handsomely adorned with stone and inlay of silver
filigree. Thick, patterned carpets brightened the parquet floor,
and a fire burned in the grate to drive off the damp. Through
the doorway, a maid labored over a carved double bed,
patting smooth silken sheets and embroidered coverlets in
deferential silence.

Yet the beautiful decor did nothing to allay Elienne's
sense of vulnerability. With stiff self-reliance, she began at

once to rearrange the furniture. The maid emerged from the bedchamber, startled to find the new Consort pushing a heavy chest across the floor.

She curtsied deeply. "My Lady, did you not find the room to your liking?"

Elienne shook her head and leaned like a draft horse. The chest rumbled another foot across the parquet. She abandoned it in the middle of the chamber and gathered the ornaments from a small side table.

Puzzled more than politeness would permit, the maid tactfully curtsied again. "The Lady mustn't spoil her dress before this evening's banquet."

Elienne responded with a preoccupied smile, both hands full of glassware. When she deposited the items on a cushioned chair and hefted the table toward the other side of the room, the maid salvaged the awkward situation as best she could by offering her help.

"Thank you." Elienne nodded toward a stuffed stool. "That can go there."

She and the maid labored for a time in silence. After a particularly trying struggle with an armchair, Elienne said, "Why won't Aisa and Denji speak to me? Have I offended them?"

"The shieldmaids?" The woman's eyebrows rose in her round, sweating face. "My Lady, they are deaf-mutes."

"Forgive me; I'm foreign," said Elienne quickly. "I didn't know. Is it common practice to put out ears and tongues in Pendaire?"

"Ma'Diere, no, my Lady." The maid wiped sweaty palms on her sleeves. "That pair belonged to the royal family of Kedgard."

Elienne's face remained carefully blank.

"It is an island kingdom," explained the maid. "The Regent took pity on them during a diplomatic visit and bought their freedom. They have served out of gratitude since."

"That was a kind act." Glad she had not trusted the guardswomen, Elienne bent and began to wrestle with an immense potted plant. "Is his Excellency often moved to charity?"

"I wouldn't know." The maid sighed. "Lady, must you move that?"

Elienne gave the plant a determined shove. Branches swayed, bobbing small pink fruits precariously against stem moorings. The tree was top-heavy, and would likely upset if she disturbed it further.

"I suppose the thing will do well enough where it is." Elienne critically surveyed the room and finally nodded in satisfaction. "That will do. And thank you."

The maid's reddened face reflected little appreciation for Elienne's taste. "I'll send a girl up to help tidy your hair and dress, with permission, Lady."

Elienne hesitated. She disliked personal fuss. As Duchess of Trathmere, she had often declined the services of a maid, and since her arrival in Pendaire she wanted nothing better than to be left alone. "I'd rather manage myself."

The maid pursed her lips with evident disapproval. Elienne's labors with the furniture had badly mussed her dress, and her dark, copper-brown hair sported loosened wisps like a peasant woman's. Should she appear in that state before Pendaire's best blood, she would disgrace her royal partner.

Elienne sighed and tilted her head toward the reddened slice of sky visible through the nearest arrowslit. "It's only sunset." She smiled with girlish innocence. "I have until the ninth hour of the evening before the banquet, and nothing at all to do between. If I have to sit idle, I think the excitement will ruin me."

"Very well, my Lady." Dubious still, the maid curtsied and departed, weaving her way through a tortuous maze of tables, chairs, and hassocks toward the door.

Elienne sank into the nearest chair the moment the heavy, inlaid panel closed and left her solitary. She was hot and tired, and the excuse she had just uttered had been an outright lie. The necessity of acting and reacting with strangers who had no awareness of her recent loss strained her. Not even in Trathmere, as prisoner of the Khadrach, had she felt so bereft, and until now Darion's difficulties had denied her the rest and quiet she needed to reach acceptance of foreign surroundings and the role she had agreed to play through.

Unbidden, Cinndel's face arose in her mind as he had appeared the night his son was conceived. Elienne thrust the memory forcibly away. Darion's uncertain succession endangered her own safety, and only the Prince's enemies would gain advantage if she indulged grief to the exclusion of caution.

Reluctantly Elienne rose, pulled a stick of kindling from the bin by the fireside, and wedged it beneath the fruit tree. She gave the ornate pot an experimental shove. It tottered unsteadily. Satisfied that an easy push would topple the ungainly plant, Elienne crossed the chamber and sat down before the lady's dresser. Brushes, combs, hairpins, and a manicure kit gleamed in neat array beneath a gilt-framed mirror.

Elienne sorted the items until she located a cuticle knife. Though the wrought gold hat was delicately set with pearls, the blade was tempered steel. Elienne experimentally pared a broken thumbnail. The knife parted it like butter. Nothing but the best would serve for one who might become Queen of Pendaire. Thoughtfully Elienne returned the instrument to a tooled leather sheath. Faisix would hardly have troubled to see her legally locked in a remote palace keep without devising a threat to match that advantage. She tucked the knife beneath the cuff of her dress and smoothed yellow silk over the lump; Darion's enemies would not catch her entirely defenseless.

The light through the arrowslits slowly failed. Oppressed by the deepening shadows, Elienne located a flint striker and lit the candle on the dresser, then busied herself with the pins that held her hair. Freed, the locks tumbled down her back, rich as dark mahogany. Fanned in wide, curling waves over her shoulders, the hair provided a perfect screen for her hands should the guardswomen look unexpectedly through the door.

Elienne drew the mirrowstone from her collar. Silver highlights gleamed coldly over its polished face, eerie against the warm yellows of the candle flame, yet Elienne noticed little beyond the image beneath.

Darion lay still, exactly as she had last observed him. But

now the dribbled stalk of the candle had burned out. Elienne observed a scene carved into clarity by the frosty glow of a Sorcerer's soulfocus. Even as she watched, Taroith's veined fingers entered into view and gently unfastened the Prince's shirt. The Sorcerer bared a tautly muscled chest adorned by a pendant wrought with the golden stag device of Pendaire's royal house. Elienne held still. The mirrowstone transmitted sound along with its image, but only faintly.

"Can you rouse him?" said a voice to one side—Kennaird's, surely, by the impatient inflection.

"Not here." Taroith leaned forward and placed his ear against Darion's ribs. The soulfocus drifted lower, hovered closely over the Prince's forehead. A long moment passed. Then Taroith sighed. As he moved to rise, his hair snagged in the Prince's pendant. He freed the lock with an abrupt gesture that roused a flickering sparkle of reflection from the mirrowstone's depths. "Not here," he repeated. "I fear Nairgen overdid himself. The Prince suffers severe overdose. To heal him now would require deeper trance than I wish to risk in this place."

"He must appear at the banquet in three hours." Kennaird sounded frantic.

"Then we must move," Taroith said.

The image in the mirrowstone dipped and spun as hands lifted the unconscious Prince from the pallet. Elienne caught a blurred glimpse of shelves stacked with glass jars, a shuttered window, and the supine figure of a woman on the floor. Then a sound beyond her own door recalled all her attention.

She thrust the mirrowstone back under her collar. Someone climbed the stair without, and by the weight of the tread, sharply punctuated by the ring of booted heels, her visitor was male. Without protest from the guards, the latch tripped sharply. Elienne whirled as the door swung open.

Over the threshold stepped a man of medium build, resplendently dressed in a white tabard blazoned in gold with the royal stag device. Through the blurred shadow of twilight, Elienne saw a polite smile of welcome spread across Darion's features.

"Good evening, my Lady Consort," said the man in a

light, pleasant voice. "I have waited long for this day. Permit me to express admiration for Ielond's choice. He has sent a true beauty, far finer than my most fanciful dream. I hope you shall find happiness with me."

Elienne barely noticed the compliment. Faisix had aptly demonstrated the powers of Pendaire's masters to alter faces with illusion; the man was surely an impostor, shape-changed by sorcery to the Prince's image. If she trusted that the mirrowstone from Ielond had reflected the real Darion, this one was surely a stranger and a threat.

"Come here, Elienne." The man politely offered his hand. "Let me have a closer look at you."

Elienne's heart pounded with leaden strokes against her breast. The guardswomen were deaf. She could expect no help from them.

"My Lady?"

Elienne curtsied and forced a smile. Her lips responded woodenly. "There is better light here, your Grace."

Her only choice was to play along, delay the man with coyness until she could catch him off guard. There was risk no such chance would present itself, but Elienne shied from the conclusion of that possibility. As the man wound his way between the furnishings, she rose warily, left her stool placed in his path, and rested one slippered foot on its embroidered cushion.

"I thought I was not to see you until this evening's banquet." Her voice, maddeningly, reflected false bravado rather than surprised nonchalance.

The man stopped before her. His smile brightened. Animated with life and spirit, the Prince's face was handsome—not so gentle as Cinndel's, but certainly not unpleasant. "I was impatient." He studied her with frank admiration. "Can you blame me? And having stolen this glimpse of you, I become all the more so, Lady."

He reached out as if touch her fallen hair. Elienne kicked the stool at his shin and stepped back, but the man dodged lightly to one side.

"Minx." With easy good humor, he moved again in pursuit. "You'll not escape me. You are my Consort, by the seals of the Grand Council, and by Ielond's writ. Do you play games with me for sport?"

"You're a stranger." Elienne paused, taut with alarm, behind a table. Her hands left sweaty prints on the rare wood, vividly betraying her fear. Yet subbornly she resumed her charade. "I would like to know you better. I cannot please a man I've only just met."

"But you have." The impostor stopped and leaned expectantly toward Elienne across a spread of ornaments on the tabletop. "You have pleased my eyes past bearing. I have but seven days to establish my right of succession. We'll have time enough later for talk. Years' worth."

His hand shot out and seized Elienne's arm. The grip was light, almost bantering, but Elienne saw threat in the contact. She shoved the table rim hard into the man's groin. Glassware pitched over the brink and struck, decking the parquet with a sparkling spray of costly fragments.

The man gasped. But instead of losing his hold, his fingers tightened cruelly and he yanked Elienne to him.

"Lady." The word came half-strangled from his throat. For a long moment he wrestled for breath. "That was an affront. A man in Pendaire can face execution for striking a Prince."

Elienne went lax in the impostor's arms, and smiled, clothing the murder she felt inside with tenderness. "But I am no man," she said softly.

He chuckled. "Bless Ma'Diere, you certainly aren't." Entirely without courtesy, he brushed the hair away from her face, leaned down, and kissed her mouth.

Elienne permitted him. She could do nothing effective with her arm pinned, and resistance would not entice the man to drop his guard. Though the touch of the man's lips revolted her, she feigned response, grateful she was not the inexperienced virgin she had been made to appear. Fatigue and excessive responsibility had made Cinndel difficult to please in the last months before his death; this man's wants were simpler, Elienne sensed, and when he raised his head at last, his face was flushed, and a light sweat shone on his brow.

"Ah, Missy, that was more polite." But his grip on

Elienne did not loosen, and his intention was evident. He wished to bed her ahead of the Prince. If he succeeded, her Consortship would be suspended until it could be proved she had sustained no pregnancy. There would be no way to avoid having Cinndel's child ascribed to this stranger's paternity. Should that happen, Elienne realized Darion's chance, and her own, would be irrevocably lost.

Chapter 5

The Hand of the Healer

The man easily lifted Elienne off her feet. "You're a small thing," he said, and stepped over the fallen glass toward the bedroom door.

Elienne leaned against his shoulder and teased his ear with her tongue. The taste was bitter, but she maintained her ruse. "Be easy with me, my Lord," she whispered. "I beg you."

The man squeezed her, studying her face in the firelight. "A moment ago you were willing enough to play rough."

Elienne lowered her eyes. "Your pardon, Lord. My sister once said men prefer women who show a little spirit."

"And did your sister teach you that kiss?" he mocked lightly.

Elienne flushed. Hoping her squirm would be mistaken for embarrassment, she buried her face in the loose satin that clothed the man's arm, and strained to loosen her wrist from his hold. Once her hand was free to reach the knife in her sleeve, there would be no need to endure further.

The impostor's smile returned. Reddened by firelight, his expression this time displayed wolfish eagerness.

Chilled even through the warmth of the man's embrace, Elienne said, "Please, you're hurting me."

"All right, Missy." The man became serious. "My Council members tell me that you were gently born. We'll make that gently bred as well." He laughed quietly to himself, as though wanting to taunt Elienne into further rebellion. Although the jest made Elienne's pulse leap in her veins, she controlled her instinct to resist.

The man laid her on the wide bed in the darkness. The

fingers that circled her wrist tightened cruelly as he brushed her forehead with his lips. But passivity could not conceal the heavy, racing pound of her own heart, loud in her ears over the distant rush of surf. The man seemed not to notice. "Shall we have light for our first time?" he said in her ear.

Elienne masked raging annoyance with complaisance. "If my Lord wishes." The maneuver with the table had evidently warned the man off. He wanted light so he could keep an eye on her. Her only chance was to bait him until desire made him careless.

Elienne kissed the fingers that rose to caress her face. They tickled across her jawline and came to rest, heavy with implied threat, across the bared column of her throat. After a suggestive squeeze, the man released her wrist and fumbled after a striker for the unlit candlestick on the bedside table. The spark flared, gleamed whitely against a puckered scar crossing swarthy knuckles.

Fear numbed Elienne's resolve. *That same hand had drugged Darion.* She reached to draw the knife then, despite the hold on her neck, but the man leaned suddenly over her, compelling her to wait. Her tenseness this time did not escape notice.

"Frightened, Missy?" he said softly.

Elienne swallowed and tried for a smile of seductive invitation. "Of what would I be frightened, my Lord?" The meek tone she intended came out sounding cowed, yet she had no other alternative. If she fought him openly, his size and weight would quickly overpower her.

Elienne threaded her arm beneath the impostor's elbow and drew him into an embrace. His skin smelled sourly of ash soap and herbs. The odor repulsed her. But without use of her other hand she could not draw the knife, which waited cold and heavy in her sleeve. The man pressed against her and covered her lips with his mouth.

Elienne endured, and while he was occupied, explored the fine cloth of his tabard with spread fingers. What lay beneath roused a stab of warning. The man was muscled like a bull. He stretched out alongside and wound one arm under her shoulders. Elienne felt her wrist pinned helplessly beneath his weight. She tried in vain to shift position. The man kissed her again, demandingly. His free hand roved from her throat, across her breast, and downward. Overwhelmingly conscious her move must be made quickly, Elienne leaned into his embrace with a show of sudden passion. The man sought the fastening of her bodice. She rolled and managed to block him.

Undetered, he pulled clear and ran his palm, hard, down her leg. Though she had not planned to kick, he must have thought she might try. His booted foot ground her ankle into the coverlet. Elienne started in pain. Her show of acquiescence had not convinced him. She felt the limp silk of her chemise slide inexorably upward. Cold air raised gooseflesh on her exposed thighs.

With lips and tongue, she strove to delay him. But panic caused her to shape her response too thoroughly. The man broke into hot sweat, and a deep quiver shook his frame. Elienne immediately realized her mistake. The man was now inflamed enough to finish what he had started without need of further motive. His shaking fingers tore away her last, thin undergarment with a sharp jerk.

Terror exploded across Elienne's mind. She twisted her face away from his kiss and clasped his broad back, desperate to free her pinned hand. The man rolled, half crushing her. He fumbled at the points that fastened his hose. A hard, sweaty fist yanked at knotted laces and jabbed Elienne in the stomach. She gasped. The man swore. His breath blew ragged and hot against her face. His belt buckle mashed her hip as he shifted against her.

But in his haste, he miscalculated. Elienne seized her chance and tugged her numbed arm from beneath him. She shoved her freed hand between his shoulder and the moist flesh of his neck, the knife in her other sleeve almost within reach.

The man strained against her, intent upon conquest. He arched his back to hold her while he wrestled free of his tangled points. His shoulder quivered, dropped, and Elienne's fingers closed at last over the knife's pearl handle. Half-smothered by the animal heave of the man on top of her, she clawed the blade free of its sheath. Though the awkward angle of her arm prohibited a sure stroke, hesitation would place her beyond all remedy. As the man lifted himself to take her, she twisted the knife and struck.

The man felt her tense with the thrust. He jerked instinctively back. The blade's sharpened edge glanced across bone and opened a gash in his scalp.

Blood coursed down Elienne's wrist. Hot as tears, it splashed her face as the man flinched. His bellow of surprise stung her eardrum, and his hand closed reflexively, pinching the exposed flesh of her groin. She cried out. One fleeting, startled moment, his grip relaxed. She tore free. He cursed and pitched himself across the bed after her. Heavy fingers caught the trailing end of her hair.

Elienne lashed out. The man fell back with bloodied knuckles and a fist full of trimmed curls. His quarry withdrew, beyond reach.

"Animal," said Elienne hoarsely as he dragged himself off the mussed coverlet and stood. The fine gold of his tabard was splashed red, and beneath, loosened points hung snarled like the frustrated remnants of a child's thread game.

The man hitched at his hose. "I'll have you executed." He tossed away the severed hair.

"You're not Prince Darion." Elienne's voice shook. She stood her ground behind a large wingchair, sticky fingers clenched around the little knife. "More likely you'll face execution for laying hand on what isn't yours."

"Bitch." The man reached up, felt the slice on the back of his head. "You'll regret this."

He lunged and caught the wingchair full in the chest. Though Elienne was small, long days spent in the saddle in Trathmere ensured she was not weak as her size suggested. As the man recovered his balance, she ran through the door into the sitting room. He followed, gasping for breath.

Elienne said boldly, "I know you for an impostor, and I can even guess your name. It is Nairgen, is it not?" She positioned herself behind an ungainly potted fruit tree.

The man swerved in pursuit, smashed his shin on a footstool. *"Demons!"* The room was arranged like a maze.

"You drugged the true Prince," Elienne accused as he approached.

A spiky cross-weave of branches effectively prevented him from reaching around to catch her.

Elienne spoke again, galling him intentionally. "Taroith and Kennaird have surely found him. They will rouse him from the drug."

"None of that will matter in a few minutes," the man responded, and he thrust his arm through the bush to grab.

Elienne dropped down and threw her weight against the pot above the wedge of kindling left positioned beneath. The plant overbalanced, bearing the man with it. He back-stepped, tried desperately to save his footing. But a diabolically placed chest tripped him up. He fell heavily. His head struck a marble statue of a fish. The tree crashed awkwardly over, jabbing him with twigs and a shower of loose fruit.

Elienne approached him carefully. Her knees shook. Knife held ready, she snapped off a bough and prodded the prone body on the carpet. But the man remained limp.

Elienne uttered a rude epithet and discarded the stick. She would have to bind the man, and the room was dark. She fetched the candle from the dresser. As an afterthought, she also included the nail scissors.

Her attacker lay as she had left him, but light revealed a changed face. Elienne started, despite her certainty that the man had been shape-changed. In place of Darion's image, she saw sallow cheeks, peaked brows, and a narrow, hooked nose. Iron-gray hair trailed in a growing scarlet puddle. But hawking after small game in Trathmere had accustomed Elienne to blood. Pragmatic out of necessity, she knelt and dipped the nail scissors in the gore and threw them on the carpet. Then she wiped the knife clean and sheathed the blade beneath her sleeve. She might have further need of a weapon.

Elienne rolled the tree aside and tied the man at wrist and ankle with drapery cord. The fall had only stunned him. She worked quickly lest he rouse before she finished. Though the wound on his head was shallow, it bled fiercely. Elienne stanched the mess with a pillow cover. Then she flung open the main door and beckoned Aisa and Denji inside.

If the sight of a middle-aged man prone on her floor and dressed in the Prince's device startled them, their faces showed

nothing. Unsettled by their cold expressions, Elienne panto-
mimed explanation as best she could. A rapid exchange of
sign language passed between the guardswomen. Then the
taller, Denji, motioned Elienne back with her spear. Aisa left
the room, weapons ringing in time to her step. She vanished
down the stair as Denji positioned herself like a sentinel over
the man's still form.

Badly shaken and in need of quiet, Elienne returned to
the bedroom. She straightened her clothing and hair; a maid's
assistance would be required to even out the gap in her curls
were she had cut herself loose, but there was no time to fuss
with appearances now. Elienne combed out the tangles. She
had just finished tying her hair into a knot when Aisa
returned, accompanied by Garend and Faisix.

Still puffing from his ascent of the keep stair, the elderly
councilman sank into the nearest chair. Garend's red-rimmed
eyes passed distastefully over the prostrate impostor and fixed
upon Elienne as she came through the adjoining door. "A
pity," he said, between wheezes. Whether he referred to the
man's misfortune, or her own, was unclear.

Faisix accepted the incident without immediate comment.
After the briefest glance at the unconscious man, he dug a
flint striker from a nearby drawer and set about lighting the
wall sconces. Elienne watched him progress from sitting room
to bedchamber, aware that his eyes missed little. The distant
crash of the surf masked his graceful step, lending an eerie
quality of pantomime to the scene. The glare of multiple
candles made Elienne feel helplessly exposed to his dispassionate gaze.

Faisix set his boot against the chest lid by Nairgen's foot
and leaned forward on crossed wrists. "Lady, what passed
here?" The gold trim on his doublet glittered as he drew
breath. "Aisa informs me you claim to have been assaulted."

Elienne received his inquiry with alarmed apprehension.
Whatever she said, certainly Faisix already knew why a man
had sought entrance to her chambers. She related in bald
terms what had occurred, but the knife was exchanged for the
nail scissors in her account, and she omitted mention of
Nairgen's actions against Darion.

Faisix regarded her narrowly when she finished. After brief hesitation, he said, "How did you know this man to be other than the Prince, whom you have yet to meet?"

Elienne chose not to reveal the mirrowstone. "Excellency, my Lord Garend insisted his Grace was incapable. Drunken and senseless, I believe he said. This man didn't smell of spirits, nor did he act in the least unfit. Truthread, if you doubt me."

"That won't be necessary." Faisix straightened decisively. "I'd rather see what the man who molested you has on his mind. That might be more informative."

Wary of soiling the impeccable black and gold silk that clothed his lean height, the Regent knelt on a clean patch of carpet. Tapered white hands fastidiously clasped the unconscious man's head at either temple. Under his touch, the eyes soon flickered open. But Elienne barely noticed Nairgen's unfocused stare. She chose instead to observe the Regent.

"What is your name?" Faisix tempered his words with sorcery. The command touched Elienne's own throat with the desire to answer. But since the truth call was not directed at her, she was able to keep her silence.

"I am called Nairgen, Dar's son," said her attacker in an inflectionless tone.

"Nairgen," Faisix repeated. He bent lower. "*What* are you?"

The reply followed mechanically. "I am a healer by profession."

"A healer. I understand." Faisix glanced quickly at Garend. "Listen carefully, my Lord. I'll require your word as witness."

He addressed Nairgen once more. "And did you, in Darion's image, enter this room with the intention of forcing the Royal Consort?"

"I did," Nairgen intoned.

Light glanced off the trim on Faisix's cuffs as he shifted his grip. "Were you successful?"

Elienne stiffened, but managed to concel her outrage. If the Regent had not broached that question, Garend surely would have in his stead.

Nairgen dutifully admitted failure. Faisix swiftly delivered his next demand, words sharpened with a keen edge of threat. "Who sent you to undertake such an act?"

Elienne felt the words pierce her singly. She shrank in acute discomfort, as though live bees crawled across her skin. The command certainly held more than simple truth sorcery. Nairgen thrashed weakly in Faisix's hold. His eyes bulged like marbles, and spittle dripped from quivering lips. Without warning, he screamed. The sound made Elienne's hair prickle, and even Garend flinched in his chair.

Only the Regent remained calm. Implacably he repeated his question. "Who? *Tell me*."

Nairgen groaned and drew a rattling breath. His body arched against the grip that clamped his head. Faisix's knuckles whitened with stress, and the tendons bulged beneath his immaculate sleeves.

"Speak!" The corners of Faisix's eyes wrinkled with concentration. "Who sent you?"

A terrible spasm shook Nairgen, leaving his body limp as wet cloth. A breathy stream of unintelligible words poured from his lips. Garend bent intently forward in his chair. "Who sent you?" The Regent stooped lower, impatient, and the intensity of his expression touched Elienne with dread.

"Taroith," murmured Nairgen, softly but with unmistakable clarity. "Taroith sent ..." The words trailed off into stillness like death.

Elienne felt as though she had swallowed ice. The testimony was false. She was certain.

The Regent sighed. Pale with weariness, he looked up at Garend. "Did you hear that?"

"A pity." The elder's forehead puckered into a frown as he sank back. "Who would have guessed? Master Taroith is not a Sorcerer one would associate with treason by conspiracy. Those are base charges, for a League Master."

"I greatly regret this." Faisix blotted sweat from his temple. "League Master or not, he'll have to be detained until the Grand Justice can be convened." Regretfully he regarded the bloody head in his hands. "This one will be needed as evidence. Best we get him healed at once."

The Regent closed his eyes. Sunny golden light appeared

above his fingers, and at the sight of what must be a soulfocus, Elienne knew fear. Nairgen must surely have condemned Taroith under a mindbender's influence. Faisix had that capability. If he had used it, Nairgen would never be permitted to recover, lest he contradict a forced confession. But Elienne dared not intervene. Her own peril was too great.

Nairgen quieted under the Regent's touch. His mouth gaped open, and his eyes glared, sightlessly spiked with spearheads of reflection as the focus slowly lowered and touched his forehead. Faisix knelt motionless as a velvet-clothed statue in his trance. Sweat shone fine as gilt on his brow, and his pale eyes fell closed. His breathing slowed and almost seemed to stop.

Suddenly his soulfocus guttered like a blown candle, and went out. The Regent started. He glanced up, but his handsome features remained woodenly still as he set Nairgen's head gently down and steadily faced Elienne.

"You appear to have broken the unfortunate man's neck." He blotted stained fingers on the rug. "What a shame. He is dead."

Murdered, Elienne thought. Hostility rose within her, heated and restless as fire. Nairgen had suffered cuts and a bruise at her hand, nothing more. But she held her protest. How easily Taroith had been framed with responsibility for an act against her. If she denounced Nairgen's testimony, she might force Faisix to silence her as well, and where better than in a keep surrounded by his own allies.

"I was frightened." Without difficulty, Elienne allowed tremulous uncertainty to color her voice. "I'm sorry. I didn't mean to kill him."

Faisix rose and stood over the corpse. "You spared him the unpleasant process of trial and execution. And you would be of little use to Darion if the fellow had had his way with you."

His appalling attempt at sympathy offended Elienne. She looked away as the Regent made a fluid sequence of signs with his fingers. Aisa stooped and shouldered the body. Faisix grimaced in distaste as she carried it out. Then he turned back and studied Elienne closely.

"You're untidy," he remarked at last. "I'll send you a maid for your hair and clothes. A drudge will be along to mop up and straighten your rooms again."

"Thank you, Excellency." As the Regent moved to depart, Elienne curtsied, alert to the fact he would never again underestimate her resourcefulness. His sharp gaze had not missed the altered array of furnishings, and she had seen him note the kindling she had used to wedge the pot. It had been a mistake not to remove that. Faisix certainly knew she had anticipated an assault, and prepared well for it.

The moment Garend's shuffling step carried him beyond the door, Elienne reached for the mirrowstone. Taroith would have to be warned of his impending arrest. She prayed he was still in the Prince's presence, within reach of the jewel's interface. She could then call the Prince, and hope the Sorcerer would overhear.

The stone's image showed Darion slung across Kennaird's shoulders like a barley sack. The apprentice walked down a flagstone path bordered by topiary and flowering trees, similar to those Elienne had seen in the palace gardens. Though full night had fallen, the scene was illuminated by cold, silver light, as though by a full moon.

Elienne knew relief. She had seen the moon set earlier, in crescent phase. Such light could be shed only by a soulfocus. Taroith surely followed just behind Kennaird. Elienne called his name through the mirrowstone. There came no response. Kennaird's feet rose and fell in regular strides; the click of his boot heels against the flags carried faintly over a background chorus of crickets. Elienne tried again, urgently.

Kennaird turned a corner. Darion's dangling arm brushed a stand of snapdragons, and dew fell, sparkling like cut gems in the soulfocus light. Either the apprentice heard nothing, or he ignored her call deliberately.

Elienne jammed her thumb over the stone's image and shouted an epithet pungent enough to make a fishwife blush. She ended with a demand that Kennaird stop still in his tracks. Nothing happened. Elienne cursed and blinked back tears of frustration.

Perhaps the mirrowstone's interface worked only on a

mental level, and Darion alone could have heard her. Whatever the reason, Elienne could get no message through. Taroith would face arrest unwarned.

Sudden sounds disturbed her from thought. Voices echoed in the stairwell. Apprehensively, Elienne slipped the mirrowstone beneath her collar. She faced the doorway just as the heavy, oaken panel opened, and servants invaded her suite.

Faisix had kept his word, in quantity. No fewer than ten maids arrived in answer to his summons. Only three were drudges. Elienne frowned. The remainder no doubt were intended to forestall activities that did not involve personal appearance; the wedge of firewood and the maneuvered array of furnishing had plainly shown the Regent she was warned against treachery. If he saw fit to distract her, there would be a cause.

Moved by an unpleasant prickle of intuition, Elienne turned her back on seven obsequious curtsies and chased the drudge with the broom and dustbin who marched through the bedroom door. The woman moved with the purposeful efficiency of one who sought something specific.

Elienne quickened step. By the time she crossed the threshold, the drudge's quick hands already brushed the blood-soiled scrap of hair Nairgen had cast aside. The woman bent to tip the dustbin into a sack that hung from her apron.

Fears confirmed, Elienne acted at once. She tipped and slammed with feigned clumsiness into the drudge's stout back. The woman staggered, grunting with surprise, and the contents of her bin tipped onto the floor.

Elienne recovered first. "Oh! I'm sorry! Here, let me make amends." She snatched the brush and dustbin with what she hoped would pass for contrite embarrassment and recovered the spilled hair.

The woman was not fooled. "The Lady needn't trouble herself." She tried to regain her implements, but Elienne had anticipated the move. She smiled brightly and flung the lock into the fire. The drudge glared as flames leaped, fizzling, to consume it. Dark smoke trailed upward, noisome with the reek of charred hair.

Elienne stepped back and felt the dustpan jerked angrily

from her grasp. Though chilled by the vehemence of the drudge's reaction, she removed the candle from the night-stand and thoroughly examined the bedspread, carpet, and floor, until she satisfied herself no strands remained. If hair bound Darion's image to the mirrowstone, she dared not leave herself vulnerable to the possibility an enemy Sorcerer might weave a similar enchantment for use against her. The drudge's annoyance confirmed her suspicion. Faisix had issued orders to retrieve that lock.

Elienne returned the broom to the glowering woman. Then she pitched herself to the task of dealing with seven maidservants, not one of whom could be trusted.

Washed, groomed, and poised despite the multiple concerns that preoccupied her, Elienne paused above the stair overlooking the vast banquet hall where the court of Pendaire gathered in her honor as Prince's Consort. The decor matched the grandeur of the council chamber, aglitter beneath chandeliers expensively tiered with thousands of wax candles. Clean, smokeless flames illuminated a scene colorful as a flower bed, dusty with the glimmer of gems and gold-thread embroidery. Pendaire's courtiers dressed with costly extravagance. Elienne wondered again how one kingdom could support such vast wealth.

A stern voice interrupted her thought. "My little Lady." A tall, lanky man with a harried face and balding, frizzled hair loomed over her. Peach brocade went poorly with his sallow complexion. "You *must not* make an appearance before you've been properly announced."

The comment identified him as Master of the Revels. Elienne gestured at the elegantly spread tables which seated the crowd at the foot of the stair. "Were you responsible for preparing all this in the space of a single afternoon?"

The Master of Revels sketched a self-conscious bow. "I did my best."

"Do you always conjure miracles?" Elienne smiled warmly. The man must have worked himself half to death. Never had she seen such an array, and at a glance, it seemed the entire Grand Council, along with every living relative, had attended.

The Master of Revels grinned with awkward pleasure, as though unaccustomed to praise. He took her hand and bellowed over the heads of his guests. "Our Lady Elienne, official Consort of Prince Darion, fourteenth heir of Halgarid's line."

Elienne descended the steps to the sound of polite applause. Aisa and Denji followed, the cold steel glint of mail and weaponry jarring in contrast with the finery of Pendaire's courtiers. The crowd stood. As she passed between the ranks of tables, Elienne endured row after row of faces marked by aristocratic appraisal. Pendaire's ranking ladies exhibited great curiosity over the foreigner Ielond had seen fit to import for their Prince. Elienne walked the gamut of their scrutiny, and felt clumsy. Under other circumstances, the escort clanking noisily at her heels might have amused her. But with one attempt of treachery against her already, anxiety clogged her sense of humor. She searched the packed room, unable to locate Kennaird.

The sharp pinpoint light of a soulfocus drew her eye. It belonged to a Sorcerer in green. He watched her approach, eyes pale and flat as a cat's. Elienne passed him uneasily. Taroith, also, was not present. She wondered what had happened to him.

A snowy length of carpet paved a path between the guests to the marble dais where the royal table stood. Seated there were the Select of the Grand Council, the Regent of the Realm, and several others whose faces were unknown to Elienne. A great stag rose from their midst as centerpiece; golden hooves lay banked in a drift of white starflowers, and a love wreath of myrtle circled the raised, gleaming neck. Black antlers shadowed two highbacked chairs embossed with carving and pearl inlay. Both appeared empty.

Elienne gathered her skirts and climbed the dais steps. Where was Kennaird, and more important, Prince Darion? If this banquet could go on without the Prince, the event would be the most costly sham she had ever witnessed, and her own Consortship no more than a courtly show of manners. Elienne repressed a frown. She swept across the dais, skirts fanning disturbed air through the starflowers.

Aware of little but her own angry thoughts, Elienne almost walked into the man who rose and pulled out a chair for her. She checked precipitously, blocked by a move that seemed calculated to make her look awkward. Small, flame-haired, and exquisitely dressed in blue silk with white fur trim, the courtier languidly observed her discomfort from narrow-lipped, arrogant features. But Elienne paid his rudeness scant notice. Her attention moved beyond man and chair to another who lay slumped, face downward, with both hands buried to the wrist in starflowers.

"Ma'Diere's mercy." Ellienne knew a moment of horrid recognition. "Your Grace?"

"Charming, isn't he?" said the red-headed man. "I'm almost ashamed to admit he's my cousin."

Elienne slipped past without answer. She stopped beside the prone figure, her cheeks blanched like wax. The Prince of Pendaire never moved. The fine white tabard, twin to the one worn by her attacker, lay twisted untidily across lax shoulders. A fillet of gold bound an uncombed snarl of hair, and his head was pillowed on the crested china of his dinner plate.

Darion's cousin blinked pale eyes and broke an awkward silence. "My Lady, you'll feel better if you sit down. There. Darion is indisposed. He'll recover after a while, I assure you. He took Ielond's death rather hard. That's understandable. He lost his mother at a very early age, you must be aware. His Guardian was all the family he had."

Elienne regarded the Prince. Taroith evidently had not had time to reverse the drug. Though another present held a Master's powers, no one had troubled to act in Darion's behalf. The opposite had been the case. The Prince's person reeked of spirits, a detail so crude it lit her temper.

"This man belongs in bed with a healer to attend him." Elienne turned a withering glare upon the courtier. "As his cousin, you should be ashamed to allow a public exhibition of him in such condition."

Light fingers settled on Elienne's shoulder. She started, and found Faisix behind her. "Come," he admonished with a smile. "Would the Lady argue before being introduced?" Elienne stiffened under his touch, suspicious he might try her mind with sorcery; but if the Regent had plotted the move, he exhibited only courtly courtesy. "Lady Elienne, meet Lord Jieles, brother of Darion's late father, Duke of Liend, and present heir of this realm."

Elienne found courtesy impossible. She stared in flat distaste at Jieles and said succinctly, "I'd rather not. I find him unworthy of his ancestry."

Faisix chuckled and removed his hand, settling himself into the seat on the Prince's immediate right. "I think the Lady won't be demanding much in the way of dinner conversation," he said to Jieles. "She likes her words sharp and quick. And she has shown an astonishing knack for tripping up men who are larger than she."

Jieles laid a patronizing arm across Darion's back. "We might have guessed wrong. Perhaps word of Ielond's choice drove his Grace to drink."

Elienne ignored the insult, her initial flare of temper controlled. If Darion was incapable, she would see him through the ordeal of the banquet with as much dignity as she could. With two unresponsive victims, Jieles soon saw further antagonism was wasted breath. He left the Prince and sat, just as the Regent rose to address the gathering.

Elienne heard little of his speech. She slid her heavy chair closer to Darion and worked to straighten the rumpled tabard. The slick silk of the stag blazon resisted her efforts. Elienne tugged the cloth over limp shoulders, conscious the flesh beneath was lean and well muscled; this Prince Darion was not a man who spent himself in decadence. Elienne recognized the same hard fitness Cinndel had acquired when the Khadrach had forced him from peacetime pursuits into daily training with arms.

The comparison shocked her. Cinndel was beyond need. And in Faisix's presence, even her husband's memory endangered her. Though grief roughened her throat, Elienne moved her hands briskly on.

Darion's hair lay matted across a fevered, dry forehead. The fine chestnut strands resisted Elienne's fingers. In the end she contented herself with smoothing the stubbornest tangles beneath the fillet.

At last she turned to Jieles. "Help me get him upright."

Jieles grinned. "I rather thought his ear would make a fine trencher for the roast."

"You're unpleasant." Elienne returned his smile with venomous annoyance. "I'm not above trying out that suggestion on your own anatomy."

Heads turned in their direction, decked with frowns of disapproval. Garend furiously gestured for silence.

"What a fool I was, to call you 'Lady,'" Jieles murmured, but he moved to lend a hand.

Together they raised the Prince like a puppet from the table and propped him against the chairback. Elienne sent the table page for cold water and, the moment the ewer arrived, began to blot Darion's face with her napkin.

Faisix completed his speech. Jieles filled the expectant hush that followed with a barbed excuse for his cousin's ineptness. Forced, uneasy laughter swept the tables below the dais. Elienne endured in tight-lipped silence. When Jieles tried to prolong the issue with pleasantries, she stepped hard on his instep beneath the table.

Jieles sat precipitously and turned a wide, furious gaze upon her. "You could face the headsman for striking a descendant of Halgarid," he whispered sharply.

"It would shame your manhood to put me to trial," Elienne replied without lowering her voice. "And you're the second man who's threatened that in a single evening. I find the repetition dull."

A page arrived with a covered dish. Jieles seized upon the diversion, red under the interested stares of his neighbors across the table. An uneasy meal commenced. Even the conversation below the dais seemed dampened by tension. Elienne studied the exquisitely prepared food and pitied the Master of the Revels. Though she had forgotten when she had last eaten, her plate went largely untouched. The others around her fared little better. The drug caused Darion to be violently ill at the table. Elienne struggled to support him in an upright position as his body was wracked time and again with spasms.

Servants descended like a swarm of insects. While they labored to clear the mess, the guests continued their toasts to the Prince's health as though nothing were amiss. But Darion's apparent drunken stupor cast doubt like blight over his integrity. That was inevitable, Elienne knew. Little dignity could be gained from the Prince's present condition, and even the table pages found difficulty showing his Grace the deference due an heir of Halgarid.

The evening dragged through endless ceremonies. Tongues loosened with the wine. By the time dessert was served, the toasts had turned ribald, and a few were maliciously barbed at the Prince's expense. Elienne never so much as blushed, but she did request leave to retire with the Prince. Jieles overheard, and laughed.

"You can't go, Missy, until after the Seeress of Ma'Diere's Order of the Seed and Scythe delivers the Trinity of Fortune."

"I'm foreign," said Elienne flatly. "Explain."

Jieles did, with a self-important display of mock courtesy. At a betrothal banquet, tradition required a Seeress to deliver three prophecies, one for the Consort, one for the Prince, and one for the realm. Not even the guests might depart until after the custom had been met.

"If the Seeress's words are unfortunate, the celebration will end early, but I don't see much cause for impatience." Jieles glanced deferentially at the Prince's still form. "Just now my cousin doesn't seem a particularly rousing bedfellow."

Elienne braced herself to endure. Servants cleared the plates away and returned with cordials and baskets containing comfits and sugared nuts. For the thousandth time, Elienne peered beneath the stag's glossy belly and searched the diners below. She failed to locate Kennaird.

A bard, a troupe of jugglers, and a knife dancer all performed and were applauded. The candles in the chandeliers overhead burned slowly lower. Elienne waited anxiously for the next of the revels, but sudden quiet settled over the long hall. A bent figure swathed in black and yellow waited, motionless, on the stair at the entry.

"Ma'Diere's Seeress," announced the Master of Revels. "Archmistress of the Holy Order of the Seed and Scythe."

The Seeress's lame step carried her down the stair and, slowly, the length of the white carpet that led past the table to the dais. As she approached, Elienne saw she was aged beyond estimate. The slice of face visible over her shroud of veils was as brown and creased as a dead leaf.

Elienne felt sweat dampen her palms.

The hour was well past midnight. Most of the candles had burned out. Those left alight guttered, couched in pools of wax, and long shadows flickered over a crowd of expectant, upturned faces. Silence reigned as the Seeress shuffled to a stop by Elienne's seat. The woman's eyes were milky, all but blind. The hands that caught the chairback for balance were crabbed claws of age, and the heavy robes reeked strongly of herbs and moth poison. The smell made Elienne dizzy.

"Lower your head, Missy," the Archmistress commanded.

Elienne obeyed. A dry, bony finger rested against the crown of her head. The silence deepened until it seemed to pound against her eardrums between heartbeats. After a pause the crone leaned forward. Her breath brushed hot as a desert wind against the skin of Elienne's neck as she delivered the required prophecy in a dry, quavering whisper.

"Foreign one, you will die truthful."

Sudden gooseflesh prickled Elienne's back. Numbed through with shock, she watched the Archmistress move on to Darion. Could she be destined to fail? For Cinndel's child to become Darion's heir was itself a falsehood, one upon which her life depended. Elienne fell faint.

"You know," Jieles said softly to her, "the prophecy always comes to pass."

Elienne buried her distress as the seeress delivered Darion's third of the Trinity of Fortune into an ear that surely heard nothing. Then she limped to the table and rested bent hands on the back of the golden stag. Eternity's stillness claimed the packed hall below. Servants and nobles alike froze, motionless. The crone spoke.

"The true blood of Halgarid will inherit the throne of Pendaire, and there shall be a son to stand fifteenth in succession from that seed."

Faisix rose and repeated the prophecy loud enough for all to hear. Cheers erupted across the breadth of the hall and speech became impossible. Hundreds of glasses raised in toast. Ignorant of Darion's curse, the court believed the Seeress had spoken of his own inheritance. Even the steward who poured the wine offered Elienne congratulations and a wide smile.

Elienne nodded in response, her features stiff as paint on a child's doll. Darion was the fourteenth heir of Halgarid. Cinndel's unborn son, key to his succession, was a stranger's get, an impostor. If the prophecies held true, logic demanded that Jieles claim the crown. He was the only other genuine blood descendant, and no curse would bar his conception of a natural son. Shaken, Elienne raised her goblet. The wine ran bitter on her tongue. She would make that succession difficult, she decided. And before fear could destroy her resolve, she drained her wine in toast to that end.

Chapter 6

Interface by Mirrowstone

The Seeress of Ma'Diere's Order of the Seed and Scythe was ushered out amid a wild pandemonium of celebration. There followed no more ribald comments on Darion's apparent lapse of morals; Pendaire's court rejoiced in the heat of restored faith. But at the royal table, the atmosphere remained subdued. Though Elienne felt emotionally bereft, she still managed to maintain a polite façade.

Jieles called for more wine and saw her goblet refilled. "Drink to Darion's fortune with me. It would seem I am to remain forever a Duke. Or did your own prophecy say differently?"

Elienne clenched her teeth. A graceful reply was going to be difficult. But Garend spared her the effort.

"You would think someone would notice, despite the felicity yonder, that the Seeress's words implied more than one alternative. You, my lord Duke, are equally descended from Halgarid. And you possess already two fine boys, one almost old enough to be declared for heirship."

Elienne had had enough, suddenly, of intrigue. Aware her temper might shortly triumph over manners, she searched the crowd beneath the dais with growing desperation, and at last spotted Kennaird shoving between the packed mass of guests. She rose at once, impatient, but careful not to show the uncertainty the prophecy had inspired. She smiled sweetly at Garend. "My Lord, it would be less offensive if you could withhold your list of alternative heirs until they are lawfully necessary. Don't obligate me to prove you a fool. Of the remaining prophecies, one left no space at all for discrepancy."

Rewarded by a flush of anger on the withered cheeks,

Elienne turned with perfect timing and greeted Kennaird. She spoke quickly. "I wish to retire at once with his Grace."

The apprentice needed no urging. After one brief appraisal, he hefted the unconscious Prince from the chair and made at once for the stair. Elienne followed, Aisa and Denji on her heels.

"Ma'Diere's mercy, my poor back," murmured Kennaird as he threaded a path between jumbled ranks of tables and guests grown raucous with drink. A wave of raised goblets toasted the Prince's departure, undignified though it was. Elienne felt as if the room would extend to Eternity, and the staircase before the door loomed like a mountain.

"Can I be of assistance?" said a kindly voice.

Elienne looked up. The Master of Revels stood before her with offered hands, but Kennaird responded before she could reply.

"Just help me get his Grace up onto my shoulders. Beyond that, I can manage."

Both men labored to lift the Prince. Shortly, Darion lay slung across Kennaird's back exactly as Elienne had seen him earlier in the mirrowstone. Chestnut hair curtained pale features, and strong, well-shaped hands dangled limply from shirt cuffs stiff with embroidery. From the apprentice's bowed stance, it was evident the Prince wasn't light. Elienne wondered, with a twist of uneasiness, how he had come to be overpowered.

Kennaird shifted his load, and something fell, glittering, from the Prince's person. The Master of Revels caught the object before it struck the floor. He had barely identified what he held before his face registered distress. "My Lady, this belongs with you."

Elienne reluctantly extended her hand. The possibiity of a gift from a man she had never known rankled, and Cinndel's memory rose, unbidden at the thought. But instead of placing the object in her palm, the Master of Revels slipped it onto her finger. Startled, Elienne pulled back from his touch and stared at a thin gold band set with a topaz. Slightly large, it circled her flesh like a snare, cold reminder of an alien destiny.

"That is the Consort's betrothal ring," said the Master of

Revels softly. Tears lined his wise hound's eyes. "His Grace was to have presented it to you this evening."

"Then I thank you in his stead." Elienne hoped the shake in her voice would pass unnoticed. "I won't forget your kindness." Whatever happens, she added to herself, and taking her leave, she followed Kennaird from the banquet hall.

The return to the suite in the keep was a long walk. Except for Aisa and Denji, and the occasional palace guard on sentry duty at the arched entrances of corridor and portal, Elienne was alone with Kennaird.

"What happened to Taroith?" Elienne spoke urgently, aware this might be her only opportunity to find out.

"He's been confined to a warded cell." Kennaird grunted as he stumped up a decorative staircase. Exertion made his next words raggedly breathless. "Accused of conspiracy against the Prince."

"The charge is false." Grateful her wardens were both deaf and mute, Elienne briefly related Nairgen's attack.

"That was bold, for the Regent." Kennaird sounded more thoughtful than upset. "He usually acts with more subtlety. Perhaps, for once, we've caught him on the defensive."

"But what does that matter? So far we've gained nothing but a muddle of prophecy that points toward failure."

As they reached the courtyard at the foot of the keep, Elienne stopped abruptly and faced Kennaird. Darkness hid his expression. "The Trinity of Fortune?" Kennaird walked stoically past her. "You'd better tell me."

Elienne softly repeated the Seeress's prophecy, eyes caught by the rumpled blazon on the Prince's tabard. The leaping stag shone dull gold by starlight, but an unlucky fold shadowed the animal's neck, rendering it headless as a sacrifice. Trapped by a sudden sense of foreboding, Elienne could not keep her voice steady.

Kennaird was strangely silent when she had finished. Elienne waited through an uncomfortable interval as, oblivious to the din of chain and bolt, Aisa unbarred the keep door. Kennaird followed her inside, the faint gleam of Darion's finery marking his progress up the stair. He spoke at last, words half-smothered in echoes.

"Incomplete, the Trinity of Fortune is invalid. The King's prophecy often provides the key to its meaning. Ask Darion, when he wakens. If his third also spells ruin, we must then disbar Jieles from inheritance by exposing Faisix; Ielond's instructions, Mistress. It will be easiest for all of us if you keep Darion alive. His execution would discredit us all."

Elienne felt despair. If Darion's prophecy held the key, the Trinity's meaning was irrevocably obscured; at the time of the Seeress's appearance, the Prince had been been senseless, beyond reach of any spoken word. And even if, by some miracle, Darion was able to achieve his heirship, Elienne saw no future for herself or her unborn child in the court of Pendaire. *"You may confide in my apprentice, Kennaird,"* Ielond had said. But the man had not inspired her trust. Unable to voice her fears, Elienne set feet like numbed weights on the stairs. A misstep earned an impatient shove from Denji. Absorbed in her own misery, Elienne let the indignity pass.

A sharp, metallic clink and a heated expletive from Kennaird disturbed a tangle of echoes. Startled, Elienne looked up. Kennaird stood at the head of the stair, sweating in the spill of light from the open door beyond. Bright as new flame, Aisa's shortsword rested against his breast. Each labored breath transmitted an orange flash of reflection.

"Godless bitch!" Slowly Kennaird bent. Darion slid, uncontrolled from his shoulders, and sprawled awkwardly on cold stone. One wrist tumbled over the lip of the top step and dangled. Aisa gestured curtly with her blade. "Father killers!" the apprentice shouted over his shoulder. A backhanded blow from Denji sent him stumbling down another stair. "Elienne, look after his Grace!"

Denji unslung her ax. With a rising sense of helplessness, Elienne watched as Kennaird was driven from the keep. Though the mute's unguarded back invited a swift push from behind, Darion was her first responsibility. Elienne turned back in time to see Aisa's booted foot roll the Prince, coarsely as a hunter's kill, over the threshold of his own chambers.

Anger left no breath for insult. Elienne launched herself at Aisa, hands grasping recklessly for the knife that swung from the studded belt. Warned by movement, the mute whirled. Elienne's knuckles brusied into an armored hip. Mailed hands caught her shoulder, sent her reeling sideways through the door. Her foot caught on Darion's inert bulk. She fell clumsily across his chest. Above her, Aisa smiled. Elienne caught the oaken door and hurled it shut with all her strength. The bar fell with a dissonant clank, shutting the guardswoman out.

Elienne discovered herself shouting Cinndel's name, and her rage suddenly broke before terrible, wrenching grief. Bruised, exhausted, and overwhelmed by all she had experienced since her arrival, the despair that had stalked her since the prophecy at last overcame her. Ielond had been a fool to believe she could be effective against Pendaire's entrenched palace intrigue. Stripped of allies, she was left no defense, and no guide. Tears slipped unnoticed down her face, glittering like jewels on the gilt embroidery of Darion's tabard. A faint sound echoed in the passage without; Denji bolting the outer door after Kennaird. His last shouts sounded distant, futile and thin as a child's protest.

Elienne wept for a long time.

The savage thunder of the surf that pounded the reefs below the wall gradually lulled Elienne's shattered composure. Her sobs quieted. Through swollen eyes, she took stock of her surroundings. The room had transformed since afternoon to a shifting sea of shadow. The candles guttered fretfully in the sea breeze, which slipped through the arrowslits. Ignited by flamelight, gemstones glittered, hot as sparks, from the ornamental gilt of furnishing and hanging, but the air was damp and clammy. Elienne shivered.

Darion's face lay buried in chestnut hair. The gold fillet, symbol of his royalty, had fallen off. With hesitant fingers, Elienne pushed heavy locks, so like Cinndel's, away from features inescapably different. The brow beneath was iced with sweat. Elienne froze, afraid. Her lapse into self-pity had been dangerously indulgent. Darion's life, and her own security, depended upon her clarity of mind. The Prince required immediate care.

The bedchamber door lay beyond a wide expanse of

carpet, cluttered still by the trap of obstacles she had contrived earlier. The servants had long since departed. Aching with stiffness, Elienne rose, hooked her arms beneath the Prince's shoulders, and attempted to raise his torso from the floor. Silken cloth rucked beneath her hands; the royal head lolled back and thumped into the rug. Elienne swore. Gracelessly straining, she hefted the Prince higher and tried to drag him, but the carpet's thick pile resisted her efforts, and after barely a yard she was forced to stop, panting. Why couldn't Aisa have left the Prince his dignity and allowed Kennaird to desposit him on the bed? Elienne lowered Darion back onto the rug. Bereft of intelligence, his hard, swordsman's body became an awkward parody, and she would see herself damned before she allowed those *mervine* who guarded the door the satisfaction of finding the Prince on the floor in the morning.

Elienne left Darion where he lay, and with ferocious energy began to move furniture. Careless of sweaty fingerprints or chipped inlay, she labored until the wall beneath the arrowlits was as untidily stacked as a junk merchant's stall. Elienne cleared a path up to the bedchamber door, then crumpled the rug and left it heaped by the hearth. Bared and gleaming in the candlelight, a well-oiled expanse of parquet stretched between Darion and the bedchamber door. With quick hands, Elienne plowed sheets, pillows, and coverlet away from the bed. The mattress was horsehair quilted with down, luxuriously costly. She hauled it onto the floor and by the fire fixed a makeshift bed. The delicacy of the silken coverlet was too flimsy for her intentions, and she searched the room for a substitute. A tapestry from the next room, torn from its hanging, better suited her purpose. Elienne bundled the Prince's senseless body onto an exquisitely stitched falconry scene, then seized one edge and pulled. Darion slid easily on his improvised sled. Callously deaf to the scraping rebuke of the gemstones scratching into wood, Elienne dragged her burden from sitting room to bedchamber. More effort saw Darion transferred onto the mattress.

Elienne removed his heavy jeweled belt and gold-stitched boots. The tabard gave her difficulty. The garment had no fastenings, and the stiff, decorative fabric had been snugly tailored to fit shoulders broader than Cinndel's. The comparison rose unbidden. Hot and tired, Elienne blinked back fresh tears. She wrestled the tabard over slackened limbs and with renewed gentleness began unlacing the lawn shirt beneath. The Prince lay like a corpse beneath her touch. His skin was gray with pallor, his breathing barely perceptible. Elienne's own breath caught in her throat; Darion's condition had worsened considerably since the banquet. The drug might easily kill him. With growing apprehension, she recalled Taroith's mention of overdose.

Elienne seized a limp wrist, horrified by the touch of flesh as moist and chill as autumn earth. The pulsebeat was weak and erratic. Pity wrung her heart, followed by fear. What could she do for his Grace except try to warm him? Kennaird had offered no advice, and Taroith was imprisoned, beyond reach.

Darion's chest heaved as Elienne removed the damp shirt. The stag medallion he wore glanced in the flamelight, red as a gate to Hell. Elienne smothered it with her hand, unwilling to face any more omens of death.

"Ielond gave his *life* to save you," she whispered, and paused, arrested by the sight of a silky tangle of white hair twisted in the links of the medallion's chain. A memory from the mirrowstone surfaced: Taroith, raising his head from examination of the Prince, hair snagged in the ornament; the impatient gesture that had jerked it free.

Elienne gripped the Prince's shoulder hard. Hair, Ielond had said, bound the interface that allowed her contact with Darion through the mirrowstone. If the stone were unset, and the Prince's hair exchanged for Taroith's, might she be able to reach the Sorcerer by means of the same enchantment? Kennaird had said the cell that confined Taroith was warded. Elienne wondered whether its defenses would exclude a force applied from without. She looked at the mirrowsone, hesitant. She had little knowledge of lore, even from her own time. Meddling might well destroy the spell that bound the stone's function. Elienne touched Darion's lifeless cheek, suddenly firm in her resolve. The Prince's condition would not wait; and if he died, the jewel's linking properties would be useless anyway. With trembling hands, Elienne untwisted the hair from the chain. Then she covered the Prince well with blankets and seated herself by the single candle left burning on the nightstand.

The thin gold of the mirrowstone's bezel yielded easily to the cuticle knife's edge. Elienne tasted sweat on her lips as she pried the gem clear of its setting. Half-braced for the dazzling flare of a broken spell, she sat rigid as the stone tumbled into her palm. But the crystal only flashed with reflected light, teardrop cool and inert in her hand.

Elienne released a pent-up breath. Coiled tightly against the gold backing lay a strand of chestnut hair. She tipped it carefully onto the table and laid the silvery thread she had robbed from Darion's chain in its place. When she returned the mirrowstone to the setting, the gem's glassy depths clouded instantly.

"My Lady?" *The voice was Taroith's!*

Elienne flinched, startled. Jerked by its tether of chain the mirrowstone's setting tore from her grasp. A winking arc of light marked the jewel's fall, extinguished at once by the table's shadow.

Elienne swore, bent, and groped across the carpet until her fingers touched ice. Prepared now for the unexpected, she retrieved the stone and set it back into place over Taroith's hair.

"Elienne?" The inquiry this time was gentler, less surprised. "In the name of Ma'Diere, who taught you the art of mindspeech?"

The jewel's interface worked, then, on a mental level. Elienne released her hold on the mirrowstone, rewarded by a view of a narrow, stone cell lined with closely spaced iron bars. Taroith sat on a wooden bench, white head disheveled and ascetic brows raised in astonishment.

Reluctantly, Elienne covered the gem with her finger. "Gifted? I've had no training. Only a jewel Ielond left to allow me contact with his Grace."

Elienne *felt* rather than saw Taroith's nod. "A mirrowstone? I understand. But how did you alter the interface?"

"Never mind that." The words sounded sharp, even to

Elienne's ear. "Forgive me. Darion is very ill, perhaps dying. The guardswomen would not allow Kennaird to treat him."

"He hadn't the skill, in any case." Taroith rose and paced the cell. "I have been consumed with worry.... Elienne, you must explain how you changed the mirrowstone's interface. The precise nature of the enchantment is crucial if I am to help the Prince. And you are right, without care he might well die. Nairgen was recklessly heavy-handed with the drug."

"I used hair," Elienne said, and added a concise account of her deductions.

Taroith shook his head, bemused. "I have to concede Ielond's judgment, my Lady. You have been admirably resourceful." The Sorcerer paused with clasped hands. Framed by the bleak, barred expanse of cell wall, his face looked lined and weary. "Tell me how his Grace fares."

"Not well, Gifted." Elienne described the Prince's condition ignoring her own self-doubt. Even with Taroith as consultant, there seemed little she could do to relieve the Prince's condition. Yet when she released the mirrowstone, the Sorcerer had summoned his soulfocus. The cell's close confines blazed with the blue-white brilliance of a lightning flash, and Taroith's features carried a hammered look of determination.

"Lady, there is only one course of action open to us."

His evident apprehension made Elienne's stomach tighten unpleasantly, but she held her questions. Taroith's gaze caught her through the mirrowstone. "I can—possibly—escape the prison's ward if I transmit myself, in spirit, across the jewel's interface."

Elienne fought dismay. The linking enchantment was surely too tenuous to act as a bridge for anything more complex than words.

Taroith understood her concern. "There is danger. But Ielond's work was exceptionally thorough. I trust his hand better than my own."

Though intended as reassurance, the carefully measured phrases implied a risk all the greater for being left unmentioned. "Gifted, no!" At once ashamed, Elienne wished the words unsaid.

Taroith was patient. "Have courage, my Lady."

"Courage!" Elienne shook her head. She swallowed, half-sickened by fear. "Then, I beg of you, be cautious."

The Sorcerer returned a quiet smile. "I shall be, for Darion's sake, as well as my own." His face sobered as he explained how the transfer would be effected. "Lady, are you ready?"

Elienne forced herself steady. A large measure of Taroith's safety rested in her hands, and his confidence wrenched at her heart. She laced the mirrowstone's loosened setting securely between her fists and nodded.

Taroith set his soulfocus, first to trace and define the construction of Ielond's spell. Physical sensation failed Elienne from the first instant of contact, and, despite all previous warning, the sudden plunge into black, weightless silence came as a shock. Blinded, deaf, and adrift in what seemed oblivion, she strove to regain the attitude of calm Taroith required, but her fear fed off that unnatural night, enfolding her like the wings of some monstrous creature. Just when she thought she would suffocate, a pinprick of light appeared.

Watch. Taroith's thought reached Elienne, strangely disembodied. *Every Master's work is unique. Ielond's sorceries were wrought with indescribable beauty.*

The light source waxed brighter, acquired a bluish tinge. Elienne recognized Taroith's soulfocus. Where it moved, she saw a thin needle of luminosity scribed against the gulf of negative space. Elienne seized the distraction hypnotically, following the focus's progress as it shuttled to and fro, tracing out—curve and countercurve—the path of Ielond's artistry. A structure gradually took shape. Awed, suddenly, by recognition of geometrically perfect symmetry, Elienne forgot herself. The spell's pattern extended delicate as interlaced threadwork, line for line a harmonic consummation of balance.

Taroith patiently mapped an interlocking mesh of circles. Elienne wondered at the delicacy of his touch, until a flat, angular flash of reflection caught her attention. Intricate as glass lattice, a crystalline array of planes appeared across the spell.

The mirrowstone's matrix, Taroith sent. *The enchantment*

passes through the stone near the origin. You may experience a sensation. Keep steady, whatever happens.

The master pattern narrowed, converged into a series of straight doubled lines. Elienne sharply recovered awareness of her body, as an alien touch hooked the vitals behind her heart. There followed an uneasy feeling of tension. Elienne fought revulsion. The sorcery tugged like fish line. Gooseflesh prickled her neck and arms.

I have crossed the prime command. Taroith's soulfocus drifted, separated at last from the softer luminescence of the spell. *As I thought, Ielond aligned the interface outward. Lady, you are the source. The mirrowstone will activate for communication to your touch alone.*

Which reduced the risks to Darion, Elienne knew. But the success of Taroith's transfer would rest all the more heavily upon her. If she lost contact with the stone while he crossed the interface, the dissolution that would result might well carry his spirit with it, since his entire awareness would be attuned to the link. Elienne battled fresh fear. When the interface assumed a psychic burden beyond its intended capacity, much of the stress would be transferred directly to her. And however soundly Ielond had wrought, the strength of his original handiwork was limited by her own frailty.

Taroith tried to encourage her. *Lady, Ielond had faith in you. My safety is in good hands.*

But Ielond surely had not known of the Seeress's prediction of failure. Elienne's grip on the mirrowstone was slippery with sweat.

Let me know if the discomfort becomes more than you can bear. Elienne nodded with false bravado.

Before her, the spell's linear pattern blazed to blinding brilliance as Taroith left his physical body and merged conscious awareness with his soulfocus. The result shone with the solitary splendor of an evening star, framed by the ingenious subtlety of Ielond's interface. Yet the display's raw beauty escaped Elienne entirely. As Taroith's spirit began the journey across the net, the physical pull within her increased to a searing pain.

Elienne cried aloud. Her hands clenched convulsively

over the mirrowstone. The ornamental setting bore deeply into her palms. For long, agonized minutes, unfamiliar forces closed over her with the cruel bite of trap jaws. Breath dragged in her throat. She tried to call Taroith's name, and found speech impossible. As a whirlpool of dizziness sucked at her consciousness, Elienne clung to her ebbing senses with an animal's blind instinct.

The crippling sensation suddenly ceased. Elienne slumped forward onto the table, drained and shaking. Something strangely insubstantial touched the fingers still fisted around the mirrowstone.

You may relax, Taroith assured her gently. *My release is accomplished.*

Elienne looked up, eyes assaulted by doubled images. The Sorcerer stood beside her in spirit, a luminous figure bound into existence by the pattern of the interface, which glittered like shot-glass thread through the bedchamber. Solid as a beacon, it seemed, while candlelit furnishings and stone walls wavered as though diffracted by water.

"But I won't hear you if I let go of the stone." Elienne transferred the jewel to one hand and pushed a damp lock of hair from her face. "And how else will you reunite yourself with your body in the cell?"

My return is no difficulty, Taroith explained. *The prison's ward is polarized only against sorcery applied from within. I will care for Darion. You should try to sleep.*

Elienne rose, swayed, and caught the table for balance, betrayed by unsteady legs. The weakness made her cross. "Gifted, save your concern for your Prince."

Insubstantial as a drawing in silverpoint, Taroith knelt on the pillows at the Prince's head. Darion lay still as death in the light of the Sorcerer's soulfocus. Elienne studied the waxy pallor of his features through the cross-weave of Ielond's enchantment. In Trathmere, a healer would have treated the Prince with an elixir containing an antidote or, if none existed, strong potions steeped with herbs. She wondered how Taroith would effect a cure with nothing at hand but will.

Taroith glanced up as though she had asked aloud. *Every*

creatures possesses innate awareness of its physical self, by Ma'Diere's Law. It cannot be permanently altered, except by Black Sorcery.

Elienne watched as the soulfocus drifted lower and touched Darion's forehead. Taroith continued his explanation. *A trained Master can call forth that awareness, and reinforce the original pattern with inanimate, elemental forces. Drugs, diseases, even injuries have no natural place in the structure and so cannot maintain existence.*

As the Sorcerer finished, the soulfocus blurred, expanded, and enveloped the Prince's comatose body in a shroud of illumination.

Darion.

The strength of Taroith's call made the very air seem to quiver. Ielond's enchantment pulsed with power, echoing the rush of surf against the headland beyond the palace walls. Elienne could feel the seething hiss of current and the tumble of sand grains against the seabed as if she stood, drenched by breakers, upon the rocky spine of the reef.

Darion.

Taroith's second call all but summoned stars from the sky. Cold, fresh air settled around him, and the chamber expanded with silence. Elienne forgot her fatigue, fascinated as the faintest flush of rose touched the Prince's cheeks.

Darion.

Taroith's last call was but a whsiper. As if his control was pent, the light that clothed the Prince flickered, then dimmed. Elienne felt the heightened awareness fade beyond perception, until the bedchamber lay stripped of enchantment, shadowed and stale, and hemmed by stone walls filmed with fog. The candles guttered, burnt low in rimmed sockets. Darion remained unconscious, his features limp and lifeless between Taroith's hands. Elienne watched through burning eyes, unwilling to recognize defeat, unable to accept that all their efforts had resulted in failure.

Taroith stirred, the soft glow of his presence barely visible in the gloom. *I could not maintain the final sequence in spectral state. But all is not lost. I believe the drug has been reduced to safe limits. The Prince should sleep off the final stages on his own. Let him waken naturally. And, Lady?*

Elienne looked up.

Ask Darion to have Nairgen's woman questioned. She may provide evidence of his guilt, or possibly names of his accomplices.

Elienne nodded quickly, shamed by neglect; Taroith had entered no plea on his own behalf until now, and, swept away by concern for herself and the Prince, she had forgotten to offer any help. "I'll see he does, Gifted." Contritely Elienne touched Darion's hand. The fingers were warm. But before she could voice her thanks, Taroith and all evidence of Ielond's spell vanished, leaving her alone in near darkness.

Even worn out, Elienne decided to restore Darion's hair to the mirrowstone's setting at once. The aftermath of Nairgen's rape attempt had taught her never again to leave evidence of her activities for Faisix's eyes. Though her fingers responded clumsily and her eyes stung in the dying flicker of the candles, the ceaseless threat she had known since arrival in Pendaire drove her to complete the task. Not until the jewel was securely crimped in its setting did she return to the Prince and settle her aching body at his side.

The hollows around Darion's eyes had lost the taut, sunken look of fever. His skin was resilient to Elienne's touch, and his breathing was deep and regular. Confronted with tangible progress toward his recovery, she wondered, through a fog of exhaustion, what she would have to say to him when he woke. The thought tangled unpleasantly with a memory of Cinndel, bloody and still in the dusty bailey where he had fallen. Drowsily Elienne's reflections drifted into nightmare.

A faint scraping of leather against wood brought her back to awareness. Elienne whirled to face the sound and caught sight of a furtive movement beyond the tumbled pile of bedhangings. A small face, fringed with dark hair, withdrew hastily into shadow.

Recognition eased Elienne's initial stab of fright. "Minksa?"

The girl flinched at the mention of her name, widened eyes fixed on Elienne in distrust. Uneasily Elienne wondered whether the child had slipped in to hide during her absence; if Minksa was sent to spy, how much of Darion's recovery would be reported to Faisix? Quite obviously, the child was terrifed.

"I won't hurt you." Elienne hoped she sounded sincere enough to reassure. From the first encounter, she had been inclined toward compassion for Minksa, whose nervous, hunted expression seemed that of a child sorely deprived of affection. Ignoring Kennaird's warning, she decided her best defense lay in winning the child's trust.

Elienne gathered Darion's hand into her lap as an indication that she had no intention of moving in pursuit. "Come out, child. You must ache from staying still so long, and it's chilly under the bed."

Minksa hesitated. Her eyes darted significantly toward the door to the sitting room.

Elienne strove to recapture her attention. "My sister's daughter was about your age, I believe. Are you twelve?"

The girl stood, visibly torn. Nervously she plucked at the elflocks that spilled over her thin shoulders. Her shift was loosely cut, shamefully large and worn for the niece of a Prince.

Elienne patted the pillows at her side with heartfelt sympathy. "You look troubled. Do you want to talk?"

Minksa chewed her lip, then shook her head in violent refusal. A single candle revealed what might have been tears on her pallid cheeks.

Careful to move without threat, Elienne offered her hand. "Will you let me help, Minksa?"

But whoever had sent the child to spy had traumatized her beyond coaxing. Minksa bolted madly for the door. The wake of her rush smothered the candle, and in darkness, Elienne heard the slap of sandaled feet crossing the floor at a run. The sour clank of the outer bar and a sudden draft of cold air marked Minksa's departure. The guards made no move to stop her. A moment later, Elienne heard the muffled sound of the door closing. The soft note of the latch carried clearly over the low roar of the surf.

Chapter 7

The Heir of Halgarid

She woke with her head pillowed against the Prince's thigh. His hand lay in her lap where she had last placed it, now cold-lit by dawn light from the arrowslits. But the wrist was no longer limp, and the fingers curved protectively against her waist. Abruptly aware of his conscious presence, Elienne caught her breath, glanced up, and met dark hazel eyes regarding her with close attention.

Nothing had prepared her for this moment.

The Prince's hand stirred. Elienne tensed for the inevitable caress, yet Darion withdrew his touch. His expression of polite restraint remained unchanged as he folded his arm across his chest.

"My Lady?"

Elienne searched his face, relieved to find no trace of passion. She inclined her head. "Good morrow, your Grace."

"Taroith left me with the awareness of how deeply I stand in your debt." Darion's voice was courteous, but distant. Probably he wished to win his right of succession and be done with her.

That suited Elienne. Thought of the physical involvement she had promised Ielond revolted her suddenly, and she wished the obligation finished, quickly, without kindness or commitment, so that she could forget. "Your Grace, you owe me nothing." With self-control tight as any she had shown before Faisix, Elienne began to unclasp her bodice.

Darion reacted instantly. "Lady."

Deaf to his urgency, Elienne continued to disrobe with mechanical efficiency. The loosened silk of her blouse slithered back, baring one shoulder to the chill air. Her fingers trembled as she reached to shed the garment entirely. But Darion caught her hands with his own and firmly resisted her intent. "Mistress."

Elienne's heart turned with sudden fear. "Mistress" was formal title for a married woman, not an affianced bride. She studied the Prince's features anew, prepared for betrayal and cornered by need to defend herself and Cinndel's unborn son.

The eyes which met hers were calm. "Yes, *Mistress*. Ielond broke the barrier of time and gave his life to send you to me. He told me you would already carry the son who would become my heir." Darion pressed her hands down into her lap. He smoothed the fallen sleeve back over her shoulder with a touch that was gentle but remote. "You come to me straight from the arms of a lover who is dead. Ielond promised me that the lady he would send would not be missed elsewhere." The Prince's smile was bitter. "He was a Sorcerer who kept his word."

Elienne shivered. "Please," she began. Adversity had forced her emotional turmoil at bay behind a wall of restraint. She found sympathy threatening that barrier, and grief was nothing but a liability. "My Lord, please, simply do what you must."

"Do you think me a man without feeling?" Darion's voice was no longer quite selfless. "Lady, you've been through Hell itself to give me my right of succession. If you're going to be imagining another man's face over mine when we love, I'd prefer to know who he was. I would rather respect his habits and his memory, that our time together might tax you as little as possible."

"Stop!" Elienne tried to curb the tears that brimmed at the edges of her eyelids. "I beg you, be done with this."

"No." Darion was final. "Lady, allow for me, if not for yourself. I would rather give Pendaire to Jieles than use you like a street wench. You cherished someone enough to grant him a child. Why don't you start by telling me his name?"

The sincerity of the Prince's compassion struck Elienne like a blow, crumbling her defenses. Unwanted sobs wrenched her throat, rendering speech impossible. Darion's features softened, then blurred through a rush of tears. Elienne buried her face behind her fingers, only vaguely aware of the arms that circled her and gathered her close. Grief allowed her neither pride not will to resist. Cradled against the warmth of Darion's chest, she wept for the husband and the home torn from her by the Khadrach.

The Prince held her, stroking the hair that spilled down her back long after crying had left her exhausted. Quiescent, she lay against him, accepting his comfort, and resigned to its inevitable conclusion.

Yet Darion's touch remained passionless, and a lengthy interval passed before he so much as spoke. "Lady, your man must have been exceptional to inspire such love. Please, tell me about him."

Crowded by vivid memories, bewildered by the enormity of her loneliness, Elienne found herself tempted to accept the consolation of communication. But Darion was a stranger, inescapably removed from all she had known and loved. "Cinndel was beyond words," she said at last. How could she speak of the rapport, the humor, and the joy she had shared with a man now dead? "Why ask me of him? You cannot take his place."

"I never expected to." Darion's tone was complaisant. His hands never broke their rhythm over her hair. "I wish only to understand you, Lady. If Cinndel was important to you, he is important to me. If you feel I seek to manipulate or use you, I will leave you now. I'll not establish my Kingship through another's pain."

Elienne pulled away from Darion's embrace. She sat up and stared through tear-swollen eyes, and on his features read honesty like flint. "Ma'Diere." Her voice shook. "That scruple could cost your life, and Ielond's sacrifice in your behalf will be wasted."

A fine web of wrinkles tightened the skin around Darion's eyes. Yet his voice showed no strain. "Even so, Lady."

Reminded of the mirrowstone's image of the Prince confronted by the headsman's ax, Elienne drew back, suddenly white. Assured and unselfish, the man who would bestow her freedom was not one to waste himself for a fool's sense of gallantry. About his stillness she caught a shadow of the quality that had so haunted her on the ice plain. Behind the Prince's concern lay a need greater than her own, a need she now knew herself incapable of denying.

"My Lord, love for my husband never made me cold." Hesitantly, Elienne laid her hands in the Prince's. "I want you to live, and claim your kingdom, though it costs me pain. Forgive the fact I haven't yet strength enough to lay my past aside. That is my burden, not yours."

Darion drew her close, the stress coiled tight within him now openly apparent. "Lady Consort, I make that burden mine as well."

The perception and grace behind the statement demanded no less than the warmth of an understanding response. "I refuse you that, Prince of Pendaire." Elienne lifted her head and kissed the man who would soon be her husband, not with passion, but with honest appreciation of his individuality. "I came to grant you release, not to add to your troubles."

Darion responded with tenderness. The kiss he returned was a compliment rather than a demand, and the hands that slipped the clothing from her body were gentle and unhurried. Elienne felt herself stirred to intimacy. She might not love this man, but out of sympathy she could return the gift of his compassion. She pressed close to him, awakened to desire, and recognized the familiar tension of shared physical passion. She fought to keep her words light. "My Lord, won't you rid me of Kennaird's handiwork? I find it a nuisance."

Darion laughed softly. "My Lady, that would be a pleasure." Yet the smile abruptly left his face, and the bantering tone turned serious. "But I am in no way deceived."

He soothed her with his touch until the barriers of her loss gave way before a torrent of physical passion.

Sparked into flame like kindling, Elienne accepted him fully; until, caught utterly by surprise, she felt her desire peak with him. The moment caught like pain.

Peace shattered before a cruel need for Cinndel, who alone had shared this intimacy.

Darion cradled her like a child. "Have I hurt you?"

Elienne turned her face away in distress.

Darion gently withdrew, and began to rub her back. "You miss Cinndel. There is no shame in the fact."

Elienne barely heard him. But beneath his ministrations, knotted muscles slowly eased, and exhaustion began at last to claim her.

The Prince settled the coverlet over her and continued to stroke her shoulders through its warm folds. "Lady, I respect your courage. From this moment, you may, if you choose, have nothing but formal relations with me. You have more than accomplished your promise to Ielond, and between us I demand no falseness."

Elienne stirred and drew a long, shaky breath. "Your Grace, I cannot pretend to love you. But you have won my admiration as Cinndel's equal, and your friendship is a gift greater than any I could have wished."

Through eyes grown heavy with weariness, Elienne saw Darion smile as she sank into dreamless sleep.

Movement roused her. Darion had risen, and as Elienne rolled over, she saw him stretch once, striped with golden morning sunlight, before he reached for the hose and tabard she had discarded on the floor the past evening. He caught her staring as he dressed. To her delight, he colored slightly, embarrassed.

"I don't mean to abandon you, Lady." He knelt by her side, concerned but impersonal. "The Grand Justice will meet shortly concerning the charges of treason against Taroith, and I must be present."

"I understand." Elienne wanted to inquire how much information Taroith had left the Prince concerning Nairgen's plot against the succession, but his mood was not one that invited interference. "Master Taroith asked me to request that you question the healer's wife."

Darion frowned. "I should have in any case. Are you comfortable? If you have needs, I will see they are attended."

Elienne tried to soothe his sharpened edges with a smile. "Acquit Taroith, your Grace. I want for nothing more than time to myself."

Darion rose and buckled on his swordbelt. Even as he

stood barefoot, with childishly disordered hair, daylight unveiled with stark clarity the intelligence and the grace the drug's debilitating effects had robbed from him. Elienne perceived with fresh understanding Ielond's dedication to such a Prince, and renewed outrage stirred in her against the faction of Pendaire's court that valued power over the realm's well-being. Even victimized by injustice, Darion proved himself formidably suited for the kingship that should have been his without hindrance or doubt. Had Cinndel fallen heir to the same lot, in honesty Elienne wondered whether even he could have handled himself with the same finesse.

"Ma'Diere give you peace, my Lady Consort." Darion bestowed a courtly bow and departed. As his step faded on the stair, Elienne realized, by his absence, how deeply he had touched her. Beyond her own fight for survival, he had won her willing support. While turning that thought over in her mind, she drifted into drowsy reflection, and thence to sleep.

When Elienne awoke at noon, the room was empty. The sea's restless surface threw needles of reflected light across the beamed ceiling. Annoyed at her laziness, Elienne rose at once and found fresh clothing laid out for her, alongside a basin, towels, and a basket of fruits and cheeses. No servants appeared to attend her. Elienne washed, grateful that Darion seemed to have taken her request for solitude seriously. The dress was wheat-gold, trimmed with black, mercifully plainer than the one Ielond had fashioned for her, yet richly woven despite its simple cut. Elienne dressed quickly, anxious to know how Taroith fared, and afire to see how Darion's enemies would react to his restored health. Yet she dared not consult the mirrowstone without advance precautions.

The sitting room stood deserted. Elienne surveyed the jumble of furnishings, then the rucked hump of carpet before the dead ash of the fireplace. The peach in her hand stayed untasted. The fact that no one had been sent to straighten the chamber struck her as oddly excessive, despite her desire to be left alone, and a fresh stab of anxiety caught her. Though famished, she abandoned the peach on a side table; left by an unknown hand, it might contain drugs, or worse.

Elienne sighed and dragged a stuffed chair from the pile. Rose and orange against oiled wood, the fruit she had abandoned seemed to taunt her insecurity. It was probably harmless. Impulsively driven to anger, Elienne grabbed the peach and hurled it through the nearest arrowslit into the sea. War had first taught her distrust. In Pendaire, she found its harsh lesson of caution a hateful companion. Unsettled, Elienne seated herself, surrounded by the unfamiliar tang of cedar wood and salt air. The mirrowstone would provide her with a window through the uneasiness that imprisoned her.

The stone held an image of tiered walls of books and scrolls, racked neatly behind finely glassed lattice cases. Darion sat, candle-lit, at an oaken table, his stag tabard replaced by a gold-trimmed doublet of black. A document lay spread beneath his fingers, and a stooped, elderly gentleman hovered anxiously at his shoulder.

"Elienne," the Prince mused softly. "She is called Elienne." The parchment's seals glanced in the light as he laid it aside. Elienne recognized Ielond's writ.

The gentleman crowed with delighted laughter, retrieved the document, and tucked it reverently into a jeweled slip case. "Ma'Diere bless the woman! Your Grace, she must have been exceptional to have busied you to the point where you have to consult archives to find her name."

Apparently bemused, Darion stared at his hands. But Elienne glimpsed the concern that lingered like a shadow before he schooled his features and looked up. The morning they had shared troubled the Prince still, though he masked himself with an actor's smooth skill.

"My Lord Librarian, on that score, I find even memory has failed me." The response sounded genuinely amused. Elienne found the light humor cutting because she knew it was forced.

The Librarian chuckled. "I have lived to see you smitten, your Grace, surely as the stars turn."

Darion rose. The mirrowstone's image followed him as he started toward the door. "Keep my secret, will you please?"

He stepped into the corridor, and brass-bound panels shut firmly on the Librarian's conspiratorial glee.

"Demons!" The Prince's expletive echoed down the marble hallway, and he suddenly looked tired. *Ielond, I was selfish. I never allowed for the potential of simple misunderstanding to cause your Lady discomfort. Ma'Diere grant me forgiveness.*

Elienne dropped the mirrowstone as though burned, surprised to find its linking properties extended even to the thoughts the Prince directed toward her. She had not intended to eavesdrop on his private thoughts.

Preferring to make her presence known at once, Elienne placed her finger on the mirrowstone. "My Prince, you need ask no forgiveness. My place here is little more than a lie, deserving of lies. I won't suffer."

In the darkness of the hall, Darion saluted her with a smile of irony. "On that we shall see, Lady Consort. Beneath Pendaire's glitter lies ugliness greater than you yet imagine. And our Grand Justice, you will discover, is nothing but a rude display of puppetry."

The pungency of the Prince's warning reassured Elienne concerning her decision not to eat the peach. Her finger must have strayed across the mirrowstone, because Darion's expression turned grim.

Lady, the fruit basket is safe. I fetched it myself. His mouth thinned with annoyance as he stepped away from the library door. *But you were wise not to trust until you were certain. Ma'Diere! Had I been as cautious, Nairgen's little snare would never have placed Taroith's integrity in question.*

Piqued by curiosity, Elienne said, "How? I've wondered."

Darion answered with open disgust. *Wine, sent by Garend as condolence of Ielond's death. He brought the gift personally, and I wasn't quite bloody-minded enough to refuse to open it in his presence. Scruples, Ielond once said, would shape my bane.*

There was more. Elienne saw the flash of suppressed thought behind his glance. After a moment the Prince decided to share it. *You may as well know. Ielond's death also signified your arrival. I was nervous as Hell's kittens you'd take a dislike to me. My Guardian promised me the Consort he chose would have*

*prickles enough to shake Jieles's arrogance to the soles of his boots.
Do you?*

Elienne burst into honest laughter, remembering the banquet. "Ask his Lordship about last night."

Darion grinned. *Demons! I wish I hadn't missed it.*

The chamber of the Grand Justice was deserted at the time of Darion's entry. Half-lit by a high row of lancet windows, the mirrowstone followed Darion's progress across an echoing expanse of mosaic floor. Though this room was considerably smaller than the Grand Council Hall she had visited the day before, Elienne saw the decor was equally opulent. Dark, paneled balconies overhung a lower level, centered by a dais. The Prince steered a course through the maze of spooled railings and stuffed brocade chairs that crowded the chamber at floor level. The image flickered and dimmed as he passed under the shadow of the far balconies, then stepped through a narrow door into darkness.

The mirrowstone's image pooled like ink. Elienne heard the faint creak of wood as Darion seated himself to wait. He intended to observe the proceedings for a time before he made his presence known, so that his own strategy could be timed to best advantage. Elienne spent the interval sampling the fruit basket's contents. When she next consulted the mirrowstone, Darion was newly visible, silhouetted against a narrow square of illumination. Beyond the door of the cubicle where he sat, servants could be seen lighting the wall sconces in preparation for Taroith's trial.

Elienne returned to her chair by the arrowslit and looked out. The hazy band of a fog bank had erased the sea's horizon. Though blue sky and sunlight shone fair over the castle's towers, Pendaire's coastal location made it a land victimized by changeable weather. Elienne studied the brooding, gray curtain of what surely ordained a squall, ears filled with the seethe of current over the rocks below. She wished a fire still burned in the hearth. It had been a mistake not to ask Darion for a maid.

In the chamber of Pendaire's Grand Justice, notables had begun to gather. Elienne leaned over the mirrowstone and tried to pick out faces amid the mottled patches of color that moved on the dais, but the image was far too small for details. She used the link to communicate her frustration to Darion.

Faisix is there, the one in the Regent's robes of gold, white, and black. The red sleeves denote his own house of Torkal. He will preside, today, over the Grand Judge, since the case is treason against the crown. The Grand Judge wears the white and silver, signifying impartiality. The third member of the tribunal which heads the Grand Justice is a Master. Emrith, the Sorcerer in green at Faisix's left hand, will verify the truth of testimony, as necessary. Unfortunately for us, he was Ielond's most outspoken critic.

Elienne put her finger on the mirrowstone and mentally assumed the memory of the Sorcerer who had directed the flat, impersonal stare upon her at the betrothal banquet.

He's the one, Darion sent. *The row immediately opposite the dais holds those who will testify. Garend and Kennaird are there. Listen closely, they're starting.*

Faintly Elienne heard the tap of the Regent's scepter. The distant hum of background conversation subsided as Faisix rose and began the opening ceremony. Yet he did not retire after the closing line. The mirrowstone reflected Darion's sudden uneasiness, and Elienne understood the Regent's additional speech was a departure from strict custom.

"Your Lordships, honored members of the Collective, Excellencies, I ask your attention this moment for an appeal." The raw conviction of the words carried clearly, even across the mirrowstone's tenuous link. "We are gathered today to pass judgment upon a member of the Select of Pendaire's Grand Council, at a moment of grave and imminent uncertainty. Until the royal succession is assured, we are a kingdom in peril, vulnerable through our lack of definitive sovereignty. I beg all of you to examine the accused's case with extreme care, that the verdict not be influenced by the concern we all share for our Prince. If treason has been committed against His Grace, let us face it untempered by emotion. I personally hope Taroith proves innocent. Through his years of Mastership, I believe he has served the crown faithfully and well. By Ma'Diere's Grace, I would be pleased to grant an acquittal, and commend him to more of the same."

A low murmur swept the chamber as Faisix returned to his chair. Elienne swore savagely, the mirrowstone heated as a coal in her hand by the resonance of the Prince's anger. A court herald began to cite the charges of treason and conspiracy, but the list was obliterated by the thought Darion directed through the link.

Cleverness has always hallmarked our Regent's style. The accumulated evidence will condemn all the more swiftly by contrast after that brazen show of idealism. How I long to break that façade.

The chamber quieted as the Grand Judge called for the accused to be brought before the Tribunal. Bent intently over the mirrowstone, Elienne saw Taroith's entry as a blur of gray flanked by the black and gold surcoats of guardsmen. His soulfocus was either absent or dimmed to the point where it could not be seen through the mirrowstone.

The herald's recitation was overlaid immediately by a strong surge of outrage from Darion. *They've fettered him. Damn them to Eternity, they'll soon regret that piece of foolishness.*

A Master's word, Elienne understood, was a bond after which the steel was an insult. The Prince's fury bored through the interface with tangible force, but the visual image of his person showed only flawlessly calm restraint. Darion made a formidable opponent, Elienne observed, suddenly glad her quick temper had not had the chance to alienate him.

The court will now hear testimony in defense of Taroith's innocence, Darion sent, in answer to Elienne's ignorance of procedure. *Then the opposing case will be set forth, after which the accused may speak in his own behalf. The Tribunal then calls for a vote from the Collective gathering, the result of which counts as one, followed by a vote of equal weight cast by each member of the Tribunal. Three to one, guilty, and Taroith is condemned. A tie demands a second hearing.*

Elienne listened with impatience through the two elders who spoke in Taroith's behalf. They lectured in broadly general terms on the Sorcerer's good character, and briefly listed charitable causes he had championed. The Collective fretted in their chairs. Kennaird's statement was badly weakened by his nervous delivery, and his description of Taroith's visit to Nairgen's cottage was heard through an atmosphere of restless disbelief.

"Taroith acted in his Grace's best interests," the apprentice said, over a rising barrier of background conversation. Lamely he took his seat.

The Regent formally closed the defense proceedings. Garend stood to contest Taroith's innocence, and by contrast, his presentation proceeded with devastating directness. Kennaird's claim that Darion had been drugged was dismissed as fabrication. Tales of his Grace's drunken stupor had widely taken hold, and fact corroborated that Darion had spent the hours following Ielond's death alone in his chambers. The men-at-arms who had stood guard duty outside the royal apartments attested, under oath, that the only visitor had been Garend. The Prince himself had seen the Sorcerer to the door upon his departure. Emrith verified the truth of their account.

"So you see," Garend concluded softly, "this mention of drugs is the product of an unsettled mind."

The attempted rape of the Prince's Consort and its aftermath unfolded with damning simplicity. The story was received with horrified surprise. Elienne felt her stomach knot. Faisix played the questions with deadly precision, tuning the Collective to a clamor of outraged animosity against Taroith.

The Grand Judge finally had to call for order. "Your Lordships! The subject is distressing, but I implore you, maintain your objectivity."

The crowd subsided reluctantly. The chamber stilled as the Grand Judge at last called for the accused to speak before the court. A hush of anticipation fell as Taroith rose to his feet. The rattle of the chain savaged the silence.

"Your Lordships, Excellencies of the Tribunal," Taroith began, so quiet, Elienne had to strain to hear, "I deny all charges of conspiracy against the crown."

The Collective shouted in protest. Faisix stood and forcefully demanded order. Elienne shivered, sweat chilling on her body as, beyond the arrowslit, fog extinguished the sun with the stealth of a strangler.

"*Gentlemen!*" Faisix's rebuke cut across the chaos and

restored a semblance of calm. "I remind you of the Law, which grants the accused the right to be heard before this court." Flax-colored hair glinted as he nodded for Taroith to continue.

"I thank you, Excellency." Arid with irony, Taroith pitched his next words solely for Faisix's ears. "I have only now come to appreciate the virtues of our late Guardian." Elienne, bent over the mirrowstone, was impressed by Taroith's quiet dignity. "Had I known the extent of your influence, as Ielond did these past years, I could not have held myself as silent. You will perhaps succeed in having me executed to preserve your intentions from public exposure. The risk to you is minimal, ultimately. What is another score against your soul, when already you stand thrice damned before Ma'Diere?"

"A conspirator's words carry little weight," Faisix said. "You waste time."

Taroith bowed. "I am not yet sentenced, Excellency. But I have no need to expose you. Ielond has worked your demise already."

Faisix's expression could not be read through the mirrowstone's tiny image. Yet his composure seemed unruffled as the Sorcerer once more faced the Collective and lifted his voice before the Grand Justice.

"Written Law allows for one accused of treason to have another speak in his behalf. I ask the Prince I have allegedly betrayed to come forward and plead my case."

The request was answered by laughter from Garend. "Master Taroith, I fear your cause will remain uncontested," the Elder said smugly. "His grace retired to his apartments early this morning, and specified that he was not to be disturbed."

The Prince rose quietly. Elienne applauded his choice of timing as he stepped to the door. The lighted chamber visible through the mirrowstone widened as he passed through.

Oblivious to the royal presence, Garend continued, "I spoke with Darion's chamber page. His illness, and his night with his Consort, left him badly indisposed."

"I beg your pardon, Lord Garend."

Heads turned. The Prince of Pendaire stepped from the

shadow of the galleries behind the dais, the understated sobriety of his dress accenting his restored health. The Tribunal twisted in their chairs for a better look.

"Has this court lowered itself to the point where it will weigh even the gossip of servants?" A rustle of whispers followed Darion's progress up the dais stairs.

In the tower, Elienne's knuckles whitened on the mirrowstone, and rain pattered, unnoticed, through the open shutters onto the parquet at her feet.

The Prince stopped at the accused's side. "Contrary to opinion, I did not waste the morning in illness. Instead, I saw fit to question Helein, the wife of our deceased healer." He paused and regarded a chamber taut with expectancy. "She told me, Lordships, Excellencies, the one fact her husband beat her to keep silent. She will attest, under truth examination if you like, that Nairgen was shape-changed to my image *immediately following announcement of Ielond's death*. The man the guardsmen saw with Garend at the door was an impostor. At that time I was unconscious from drugged wine."

A loud murmur swelled the room, cut by Garend's protest. "Unconsciousness may be caused by wine alone, your Grace."

Darion's clean laughter dispelled an ominous silence. "Whether I was overcome with spirits or not bears little on this case, Lordship. Don't grasp at straws. You had Nairgen shape-changed to provide you with an alibi so that I could be left senseless without suspicion."

"You have no proof."

Above, on the dais, the Grand Judge leaned forward, suddenly rapt. Faisix sat motionless at his side.

Darion's reply held the sheered edge of self-righteous anger. "You are wrong, Garend. Ielond left my Consort a mirrowstone interfaced to provide communication with my person. Lady Elienne *witnessed* a scarred hand placing a cloth with a sleep potion to my face during an attempt to rouse me through contact. Examination of Nairgen's corpse will reveal the selfsame scar."

Garend sank back, deflated, but Elienne was more interested in the Regent's expression of startled calculation. The mirrowstone had been a surprise to him, she realized, and to the court as well, by the tumult of talk that burst forth.

The Grand Judge pounded for order. Yet it was Darion's call for silence that finally calmed the uproar.

"I will reconstruct what actually occurred," said the Prince, "but not before Taroith's fetters are struck."

"He has not been acquitted yet, your Grace." Faisix spoke with the patience of a parent admonishing a child.

"Since when do we bind a Master of the League?"

The Regent inclined his head to the Grand Judge. "Kindly inform his Grace."

The Grand Judge fingered his silver-trimmed collar uncomfortably and cleared his throat. "Master Taroith refused to give his oath of self-restraint."

The Collective loosed a gasp of astonishment. Elienne saw Taroith nod in response to the Prince's inquiry. Clamor arose, stilled by Darion's raised hand. "Master Taroith, will you deliver the oath in my presence?"

"I swear to it gladly, your Grace." Light flashed through the mirrowstone as the Sorcerer's soulfocus sprang into existence. Darion motioned to the guardsmen.

Awakened, suddenly, to the downpour that drenched her feet, Elienne stood and banged the shutters closed with shaking hands. The closer Taroith came to acquittal, the greater her anxiety Faisix would engage a counterstroke. If her observations through the mirrowstone were viable as evidence, Taroith's innocence could be established beyond question, revealing Nairgen's confession to the Regent as false. Alone behind doors guarded by mutes loyal to Faisix, Elienne sat and cupped the mirrowstone in damp palms. It took all of her will not to burden Darion with her own fears as he delivered his final speech. Over the pounding of rain against shutters, Elienne heard the clink of steel as Taroith's wrists were freed.

"It is my conviction that there was a treasonous conspiracy against my succession, but Taroith was not involved." Darion directed himself toward the Collective, but his attention never strayed from the Tribunal. "I am prepared to produce evidence, that this case may be lawfully and justly concluded. Garend, together with a Sorcerer capable of completing a shape-change, sought to hasten a declaration of my unfitness to rule by creating the semblance of a weakness for alcohol. Nairgen the healer was given my form so that Garend could deliver drugged wine to my chambers and be observed to leave with my health apparently intact. Neither his Lordship, nor the Sorcerer involved, was aware Ielond had arranged selection of my Consort prior to his death.

"When this fact became known, Garend saw an opportunity to discredit the validity of Elienne's Consortship. Nairgen, in my likeness, provided a tool too convenient to be wasted. When his attack failed, I recall your attention to the names of those present when his confession named Taroith as instigator." Darion paused.

The Grand Judge shook his head. "I concede the possibility of Garend's participation. But I see no cause for inferring the Regent's complicity, or Taroith's innocence."

Darion looked up, and Elienne saw hardness in his eyes. "The facts seem to mesh neatly, I admit. Except the Lady Elienne, at considerable risk, used Ielond's interface to summon Taroith's assistance when the drug's effects threatened my life. I stand before you today, alive and well, *because the Master you accuse of treason restored me to health.*"

Uproar ensued, but Faisix's unemotional calm prevailed over the noise and recaptured the Collective's strayed attention. "Your Grace, I presume you accuse me of tampering with Nairgen's confession solely upon the testimony of a girl unknown to this court until yesterday? I remind you that Taroith was instrumental in establishing her Consortship through highly irregular circumstances. Exercise care. She could be privy to his plot." His voice was smooth and convincingly sincere, as always. The Prince seemed young and rash next to Faisix's understated strength. Elienne felt panic twist her gut. Already she saw heads nod among the Collective, conceding the possibility the Prince had been deluded.

And abruptly there followed the realization that she could reverse the tide of opinion. She seized the mirrowstone. "My Prince, Jieles's daughter, Minksa, witnessed all that occurred in your chamber last night. A truth reading will establish my innocence, and Taroith's as well."

Minksa? What was she doing there? Yet Darion quickly mastered surprise. "I ask this court to truth question Jieles's child, Minksa. She will corroborate, though it is well known she bears me no affection."

Faisix stood, white-lipped, but not yet unnerved. "I will fetch her, your Grace." Elegant in his rich robes of office, he started for the dais steps.

"Halberdiers!" Darion snapped. "Do not allow the Regent to leave this chamber."

Taroith's guardsmen leaped to obey. Steel flashed in an arc as they lowered weapons and barred the Regent's path.

Faisix stopped. An expression of annoyance stiffened his features, and a blaze of yellow light heralded the awakening of his soulfocus. It peaked to blinding intensity immediately before the crossed shafts of the halberds. The Regent stepped smoothly forward and vanished by sorcery.

Darion's shout cut through blossoming confusion. "He will have gone for my Consort! Taroith, get to the West Keep!"

But his arrival would be too late; Elienne already heard steps on the stair, followed by the harsh rattle of the latch. She turned in time to see the door swing open.

Chapter 8

Sphere of Influence

Faisix stepped over the threshold, his robes untouched by the rain. "Good morrow, my Lady." Aisa and Denji entered with him.

Though the greeting was formally polite, Elienne could not hide her fear.

The Regent stopped short. All semblance of courtesy left him, and Elienne saw once again the expression of ruthless purpose she recalled from the ice plains.

"She's aware of what has happened." Faisix motioned to the mutes. "Take her quickly."

Aisa nodded and advanced, but Elienne had recovered her wits. Affecting a startled expression of dismay, she said, "You aren't deaf at all." Delay, she thought frantically. If she could stall her enemies, even for a few minutes, Taroith might reach her in time for rescue. "I should have guessed. You probably talk also."

Aisa laughed, showing the grisly stump that remained of her tongue. Denji grinned as the Consort recoiled with a gasp and retreated against the ledge beneath the arrowslit.

Elienne noted the mute's reaction with satisfaction. Let them believe she was afraid. Her step back placed her on the far side of the rain puddle, by now sheened with oil from the parquet. Elienne waited, the drum roll of the storm loud in her ears, watching the mail-cowled faces of her attackers. She did not draw the knife until Aisa had lunged to seize her.

Denji howled wordlessly in warning. The sound lifted the hair on Elienne's neck, but her aim was steady as she struck at the unarmored gap between Aisa's gauntlet and forearm. The knife nicked steel and caught flesh. Aisa checked on the slick parquet and crashed heavily to one knee. She caught herself left-handed against the shutters just as Elienne ducked beneath her guard.

But Denji swung her spear across the gap. The oak shaft struck Elienne in the ribs. She gasped and fell sprawling, dimly aware that Aisa had regained her footing behind. *Delay,* she thought desperately, and rolled beneath the stuffed chair.

Faisix shouted in agitation, "Hurry!"

Denji raised the chair, cast it tumbling away. Elienne whipped the little knife at the hands that reached to snare her. Running steps and voices sounded on the stair. Beyond Denji's armored bulk, Elienne saw Faisix whirl and slam the door. Light bloomed under his fingers as he touched the lock. "Just catch hold of her!"

Aisa kicked Elienne's wrist. Pain numbed her fingers. The knife flipped out of her grasp and skittered across the floor. Elienne dove after. A gauntleted fist closed on her leg. She kicked with her free foot. As the hold loosened, she strained to reach the knife. But Denji plucked the weapon neatly away from her groping hand and grabbed Elienne's arm. Mailed fingers dug into her flesh.

Taroith's voice carried clearly through the closed door. "I cannot, your Grace. Faisix has set a blocking ward."

"Darion!" Elienne thrashed frantically. Aisa caught her ankle, then circled her knees in a bear hug. Elienne twisted desperately. Her hair tumbled from loosened pins, obstructing her vision, and her cheek banged into a table leg.

"Hold her!" Black and white cloth brushed Elienne's forehead. Faisix stood over her.

"No!" Elienne flung against her captor's hold.

Light flared, sulfurously yellow. Blinded by glare, Elienne cried out. The floor seemed to upend beneath her. All sense of solidity exploded violently out of existence, and darkness enfolded Elienne's consciousness, cold and silent as Eternity.

The ward on the lock split asunder with a coarse scream of sound. Taroith seized the latch with sweat-drenched hands and flung wide the door. At his shoulder, Darion squinted through the flurry of red sparks showered by the fading spell. The chamber beyond lay deserted.

"He's transferred by sorcery," Taroith's voice was deadened by the lash of rain against the oak slats of the shutters. "Inevitably, his destination will be Torkal. How much does Elienne know of enchantment, and the laws of self-infringement?"

"I don't know." Darion stepped past the Sorcerer and swept the room with haunted eyes.

"You must not despair, your Grace," Taroith said gently. "Lady Elienne is resourceful and spirited. And she has the mirrowstone."

Darion failed to answer. Across the room, by the arrowslit, the parquet was marked with blood. *"Taroith."*

The Sorcerer left the doorway and crossed the floor with measured steps. Shadows leaped as his soulfocus sprang alight overhead. He knelt and touched one scarlet drop with a forefinger.

"Aisa's," Taroith pronounced at last. "Your Lady is a fighter. Ielond chose well, Darion. Trust his wisdom."

But Darion seemed not to hear. "She was *alone*. Taroith, what happened to the maidservants I sent to attend her chambers? Were they waylaid? Did Faisix hold sway even over the ones I trusted? Just how much of a stranglehold does our Regent *have* over this court?"

Taroith rose slowly. "We have no way of knowing."

"Ielond knew." Darion suddenly bent and pulled something shiny from beneath the splintered strut of an oaken side table. The Consort's betrothal ring gleamed in his fingers, rimmed with blood. "A fine example of negligence I've made of that legacy!" Darion's fist closed fiercely over the ring. "I want a full-scale attack on Torkal."

"The Council won't deny you, your Grace," said a new voice from the doorway.

Darion whirled, saw the Sorcerer Emrith cross the threshold. Green robes dripped bright beads of rainwater onto the floor. "There is no longer any question of the Regent's corrupt ambitions. Taroith has received acquittal, along with apology from the Grand Justice."

The Prince twisted the ring in his hand. "I doubt the

Grand Council knows the smallest fraction of the Regent's treasonous activities." His tone turned bleak as winter. "If my Consort is harmed, they will learn quickly."

Darion pushed open the shutters and gazed through the arrowslit. Below, through ragged streamers of mist, breakers crashed over rocks, jetting lacy geysers of spray. "There's one who didn't waste time abandoning a sinking ship." Wind gusted, sheeting rain across the stone sill. The view dissolved behind a blurred curtain of water. Darion stirred irritably. "Faisix's allies might grant me lip service, but who can I trust to help me against him?"

Taroith touched the royal shoulder in gruff sympathy. "You love her well, I think. Ielond knew what he was about."

"Ma'Diere!" Darion pulled away. "How can you stay so calm? We both know what her life is worth to Faisix."

"Faisix feared your Guardian," said Taroith emphatically. "Remember that. And Elienne is Ielond's last bequest. She will therefore be his finest weapon against the adversary he spent his life to defeat."

"I beg you, help me win her back," said Darion.

Taroith returned a look of bemused patience. "Was there ever any question, my Prince? I would not do otherwise, though it called for the ruin of Torkal."

Startled by such a passionate threat from a Master of the League sworn to peace, Darion stared at the Sorcerer. "She has won your heart also," he accused.

Taroith nodded and started across the room. "And why ever not, your Grace? The Lady Elienne was the choice of a kindly and perceptive mind. Where in Ma'Diere's creation do you suppose Ielond found her?"

But the Sorcerer received only silence in reply. He wondered, as the shadow of the stairwell obscured the expression, what prompted Darion's silence.

Elienne recovered awareness slowly. Cold, wet rocks grated against her knees. One of the guardswomen held her wrists in a grip of steel behind her back. Mist and rain blurred her vision and ran in chilly runnels down her collar. Foam-webbed waves thundered against rock scant yards away. She licked lips bitter with the taste of blown salt. Not even her most fearful expectations had included drowning.

Faisix and Aisa stood a short distance off, deep in conference. Elienne could not hear over the seethe of the breakers, and Aisa's sign language was unintelligible. For the second time in her life, she faced the despair of total helplessness. The worst had happened, beyond hope of change. Faisix surely intended to kill her. Elienne found no comfort in fatalism. Again, as with the Khadrach, she responded with the reckless insolence of one who has nothing left to lose.

When Faisix left his conversation with Aisa, Elienne faced him with rugged anger. "I swim quite well, Excellency. You had better make sure of me with a rock, first."

Faisix's brows rose, and he gave way to startled laughter. "Mistress, I am never that crude. My purpose in stopping here was a practical one. Your Prince's urgency allowed me no time to route us a transfer to Torkal Manor with safety. Here we will not be pressured with interruptions."

"My knees hurt." Elienne tossed wet hair out of her eyes. "And the handling of your guardswomen is certainly crude."

"Do you call Aisa's slashed wrist civil?" Faisix folded his arms, amused, as though his ruined name meant nothing and the spoiled velvet that clung soddenly about his shoulders were entirely commonplace. "Denji, bind the Lady's hands and allow her to stand."

Elienne awarded the sarcasm the same disregard as the leather thongs that bit into her reddened skin.

"I regret the barbarity," he said civilly, watching her first stumbling step as she regained her feet. "But really, I don't want a visit from Taroith or the Prince just now, and Ielond seems to have forgotten to put a catch on the trinket he gave you."

"He knew your ways," she said, though the cold made her teeth chatter. "I find you pretentious."

Faisix smiled with delight. "Spare me your opinions. Since your death would only arouse public sentiment in Darion's favor, you will accept the hospitality of Torkal Manor for a time. Unless you have had the extreme misfortune to conceive, you have nothing to fear at my hands."

With a terrible, undermining sense of dread, Elienne acknowledged sound judgment. So long as Darion's difficulties did not make him a public martyr, the established laws of succession would condemn him soon enough. Jieles would inherit. And Cinndel's child would die. Elienne felt her brash courage dissolve. She would rather have taken her chances with the sea than become a guest in Torkal Manor. But already Faisix had lost interest in verbal debate. A dazzling flare of yellow heralded the second stage of the transfer. Denji caught Elienne's waist from behind as rocks, ocean, and misted skies were torn out of existence by a fiery explosion of sorcery.

She returned to her senses with agonizing slowness. Disorientation blanked her mind, persistent as fog. For long minutes she shivered, aware only of wet clothing and the staccato spatter of wind-driven rain against glass. Her limbs felt oddly weighted. She attempted to stretch and found her hands were bound. She was lashed to a chair with arms carved in the shape of demon's claws. The room's only casement showed the drenched limbs of a wind-tossed cedar, and the scrape of needles across glass set Elienne's teeth on edge.

"You'll be given your liberty shortly, Lady," said Faisix.

Elienne turned her head and saw a hearth flanked by bookshelves. The Sorcerer stood by the mantel, dry and comfortable in a gray doublet and soft calf boots. His fair hair hung lank with dampness.

Elienne battled to stabilize unfocused vision and a maddening recurrence of vertigo. Nausea toyed with her stomach. "What have you done to me?" The words sounded slurred, even through the roaring in her ears.

"Nothing permanently harmful." Faisix stepped forward, footfalls silenced by richly patterned carpet. Firelight made his shadow flicker. "Only a tiny dose of the elixir Nairgen gave to Darion. Not enough to put you out."

Elienne swallowed, a bitter taste on her tongue. "Why?" The question seemed silly, even as she uttered it, and the carpet appeared to melt into the form of the man in the flamelight.

"I don't wish Darion to be privy to the nuances of my hospitality." Faisix's reply seemed distant as a faded nightmare. "Aisa has gone to fetch a file."

With great difficulty, Elienne shepherded straying thoughts. Shortly she heard footsteps, and the steely jingle of mail. Then cold hands caught the mirrowstone, and chain snapped taut against her neck. Elienne tried to pull away.

"Hold still." Faisix moved closer, but seemed oddly reluctant to touch her.

Why? wondered Elienne, but the drug fuddled her reasoning. Aisa hefted the file, and her sinewed wrist flexed as she brought the tool to bear against the slender gold links. Sparks flew. Static crackled over the file's edge. Aisa bellowed in surprise and flinched back; the chain jerked in her hand, cutting Elienne's flesh painfully. The file tumbled to the carpet. With a snarl of anger, Aisa retrieved the tool and raised it for a second attempt.

"Stop!" Faisix's outcry was uncharacteristically curt. "Ielond has evidently warded the chain." He paused, and the glance he directed toward Elienne chilled her blood. "I regret the barbarity, Lady, but I fear I must restrict your powers of speech and set a blocking ward about your thoughts—at least until I find means to break the defenses set about your necklace."

The Regent cupped his hands. A glow pale as marshlight haloed his fingertips. Alert enough to recognize the threat of sorcery, Elienne shied back against the chair.

"Aisa, restrain her," said Faisix sharply.

Elienne failed to duck the icy fingers that clamped her head. She thrashed, but the mute's grip held.

The light of Faisix's summoning wheeled hazily directly before her. Had Elienne been able to free her hands, she would have covered her face. The spell's ghostly outline filled her with dread. Horribly, Elienne found herself unable to blink or look away.

"I have her now." The Regent's satisfaction overlaid Elienne's alarm. The spell that bound her swelled, brightened, and acquired hard edges like a glass bubble. Elienne's eyes ached, the reflexes of her pupils slowed by the drug. Faisix's sorcery seeped into her mind like spilled water and suddenly crystallized, imprisoning her will. In panic, she tried to call out, but the sound emerged as a whimper of despair.

The light in Faisix's hands flicked out abruptly. "My dear, I suggest you improve your relations with the mutes. They might consent, out of kindness, to teach you sign language."

With ungentle haste, Aisa untied her hands and guided her unsteady steps through the door. Faisix called after them. "Aisa, after you have seen Elienne to her chambers, locate Heggen and send him to my study. I have a summoning to perform."

Elienne lay back on the silken coverlet of an elaborately carved bed and waited for nausea to subside. Denji stood guard beyond the door. Vainly Elienne strove to remember the route from the study to bedchamber. The corridors had been dimly lit, and Aisa mercilessly impatient. When Elienne had exchanged her dress for a dry one found in the wardrobe, her arm had been imprinted with marks left by the mute's harsh fingers. Despite Faisix's pretense of mannered gentility, he had treated her with less regard than an animal; manipulative as a chess master, he seemed unconcerned that the game pieces in his bid for power were human flesh and blood. Elienne wondered, through the lingering discomfort of the drug, what motivated him. Greed alone did not seem an adequate explanation for the Regent's obsessive desire to disrupt the lawful succession of Pendaire.

The drowsiness caused by the elixir wore off gradually. Restless, Elienne studied the quarters that confined her. The small, richly decorated chamber was consistent with the air of established wealth she had observed throughout Pendaire's royal court. Fabulously patterned carpets covered the floor, and gilt-trimmed walls were paneled with rare wood, somber and darkly shadowed, yet tastefully adorned with paintings. Above the polished onyx slab of the mantel, candles burned in exquisitely crafted gryphon stands. Elienne admired the prismatic flash of the flamelight in etched crystal wings, and gold talons and eyes of jet crafted with lifelike cunning; no treasure in Trathmere had been so fine.

Though walking made her head swim, and her steps were still unsteady, Elienne studied the contents of every cabinet, table, and dresser. Yet she found nothing, not even a manicure kit, that could be utilized as a weapon. Discouraged, she settled herself at last in the cushioned alcove by the casements.

The rain had stopped. Through honeycombed panes of amber glass, Elienne saw a vast expanse of pine forest, bounded beneath the manor walls by the pewter shine of a moat. Well-groomed rows of hedge, lawns, and flower gardens graced the land within. At third-floor level, the window of Elienne's chamber overlooked the curved towers of two keeps, but Torkal was more palace than fortress, and Elienne saw neither craft village nor the farmlands that would have surrounded a normal holding in Trathmere. Faisix's manor was bordered, at least on one side, by trackless wilds.

As she knew nothing of local geography, Elienne had little hope of escape. Even if she managed to get free of the walls, she would face the immediate difficulties of provisions and shelter. The assumption did not follow that a road existed beyond Torkal's gate; for all she knew of Pendaire's Regent, he might arrange his travels to and from court entirely by sorcery.

Discouraged, Elienne sought the mirrowstone. Though denied its powers of communication, Faisix had not yet interfered with her visual link with the Prince.

The gemstone revealed a rain-sleek courtyard choked with men-at-arms and the hard, pinpoint blaze of more than one Sorcerer's soulfocus. Wrapped in a cloak of oiled wool, Darion frowned intently over what appeared to be a supply list. Chestnut hair clung to his neck, curled with moisture, and on the hand that held the parchment Elienne saw the soft gleam of the ring torn from her own finger during the transfer from the keep.

Taroith appeared at the Prince's shoulder, dressed for the saddle. "Your Grace?"

As Darion glanced up at the Sorcerer, Elienne was shocked by the change in the Prince's face since morning; he looked haggard.

"I have confirmation for you," said Taroith. "Lady Elienne

was taken to Torkal by way of the shoals of East Inlet. The reef was laid bare by tide at the time, and fog hid the sorcery from the sentries."

Darion's mouth tightened with grim anger. "You traced her through Ielond's interface?"

Taroith nodded. "The jewel was in Elienne's possession, and still operable before Faisix raised protective wards and closed our access to Torkal."

"She hasn't contacted me." The anguish in the Prince's voice made Elienne wince. "By Ma'Diere, if she's been harmed, Faisix will come to rue it."

Taroith said nothing, but his lined features reflected sympathy.

Darion bunched the sodden parchment in his fist with bitter anger and stepped back. "To horse!" His shout brought order to the jammed bailey. "We ride for Torkal!"

Elienne let the mirrowstone fall from shaking hands. However brief their acquaintance, Pendaire's royal heir plainly had come to value her with more than political significance. Given time, Elienne realized, her feelings for this Prince might grow beyond friendship. She quenched the thought at once. Already the cruel promise of the seeress's prophecy made her destiny an intolerable burden. If Darion fell to the headsman's ax, she wanted none of her emotions involved. And if by miracle he was granted life, her own falsehood exposed, his anguish at her loss would be lessened if she had never fostered his love. Firmly Elienne hardened her heart. A man comely as Darion would never lack for mistresses. And surely, if she kept herself aloof, he would direct his affection elsewhere.

Twilight fell early, hastened by a cloak of tattered clouds. Through the mirrowstone, Elienne watched the steaming torches carried by the Prince's outriders, while in her own chamber the candles burned low and guttered above the glass crests of the gryphons. She had no means to estimate the distance that separated Torkal from the royal palace. The men-at-arms traveled a muddy highway between fenced pastures and well-kept fields. Post stations were numerous, and efficiently staffed, which was fortunate, for the fast pace set by the royal company demanded frequent change of mounts.

The crofters Elienne glimpsed through the mirrowstone's narrow field of view were neat and adequately dressed. The Prince's retinue was received, invariably, with courteous deference, and even the horse boys seemed well fed. Confronted by mile upon mile of peaceful farmland, Elienne saw Pendaire's great wealth was probably the accumulated reflection of prosperity under fourteen generations of sound rule.

Faisix would end that. Elienne had seen how quickly honest, hardworking people could sour under the corrupt demands of the Khadrach. Why, she wondered again, would any man wish to disrupt the succession of a Prince as worthy as Darion?

Her thought was disrupted by the scrape of the door latch. Elienne dropped the mirrowstone, looked up, and saw Minksa enter with a tray of food and fresh candles.

Surprised, at first, by the child's presence at Torkal, Elienne swiftly realized why Faisix might wish the girl removed from the royal palace. If she had been sent into Darion's chamber to spy, the Regent would not care to have her closely questioned. Surely the summoning he had mentioned as Elienne was led off had referred to the child.

Minksa scuttled to the hearth and dumped her burden on a low table with a dissonant clatter of fine porcelain. She bestowed a wide, startled glance upon Elienne and cringed as though expecting reprimand. The child was desperately frightened. Elienne longed to express understanding; the tray was far too large for a child to handle gracefully. Enraged by the sorcery that prevented her from making even the simplest expression of sympathy, Elienne gestured for the girl to continue her chores.

Minksa gathered the candles from the tray with small, grimy fingers and paused, balanced on crossed feet, before the mantel. The shelf lay beyond her reach. The girl looked nervously to either side, in search of a footstool or chair.

Elienne rose to help her. Minksa started and whirled, poised for flight, her face a small, white oval in the flicker of flamelight.

I won't hurt you, Elienne thought. Slowly, carefully, she extended her hand.

Minksa shook her head. Tangled hair tumbled around her thin shoulders as she stepped back. But when Elienne walked to the far end of the mantel, the child held her ground. After an anguished interval, she hesitantly offered the candles.

Elienne stooped to the child's level and smiled reassurance. She had barely caught hold of the candles when Minksa let go and retreated, well beyond reach of a kindly touch. Elienne buried disappointment and rose. The girl waited, tense as a cornered hare, while she pinched the tired wicks of the old candles and located the flint striker to ignite the replacements. New flames wavered and lengthened, spreading soft light over crystal and gemstone. Elienne returned the striker to its hook and began a smile of encouragement for Minksa. But the fresh illumination revealed a detail she had missed earlier: the livid, congested weals of a recent beating marked Minksa's wrists and neck.

Elienne gasped, her heart wrung with pity. But before she could extend any comfort, the girl whirled and fled like a blown leaf through the door, oversized brown skirts billowing around her thin, bare feet.

Who had punished her? Elienne wondered. Could Minksa have suffered because she had been seen leaving Darion's chambers? Forgetful of caution in her concern for the child, she ate the bread, chicken, and wine on the tray without thought about the possibility of drugs.

Her mistake overtook her as she pushed her chair back after the meal. A violent wave of dizziness overturned her sense of balance. Startled and furious over her carelessness, Elienne rose at once to force herself to vomit. But she fell in the attempt. The hand she flung out to save herself landed on the tray; porcelain skidded across the tabletop with a crash. Plates and saucers flew like game pins and shattered against the hearth tiles. Elienne tumbled after, accompanied by the clamor of silverware as the tray upended and crashed to the floor.

Prone on the heated stone before the hearth, Elienne felt the room lift and heave about her, precarious as a ship's deck.

Booted feet wavered before her face. Elienne tried to recall whose they were, but her memory dissolved in the jaws of a poisonous black vortex. Sounds bounced like echoes across her thoughts.

"She's under." The cold voice was a stranger's. "Faisix wishes her taken to his study at once."

Hard hands gripped, then lifted her. Elienne lost track of reality. Jumbled impressions burst against her mind: a man's shaven skull, framed by a cowl of night; a staircase of marble the color of old blood; and the spinning sensation of descent. Keys rattled and a heavy bar clanged, echoing against stone walls. Elienne blinked, dazzled by sudden light. Amid a gleaming forest of flasks and braziers, she at last saw a face she recognized. A smile curved hated lips.

"Denji, kindly set the lady here." Faisix's image whirled in the kaleidoscope of her delirium. Elienne fought rising panic.

"Hold her."

Black-gloved hands circled her wrists. The cowled man towered above, black-eyed and still except for a rhythmic twitch in his cheek. Elienne felt a frantic burst of fear. Her own scream shattered the quiet.

"Silence," said a voice, and a baleful yellow flame arose in the air. Light brightened painfully, and smashed into Elienne's consciousness. Everything spun. Sucked downward into darkness deeper than mortal awareness could encompass, set adrift from all physical sensation, Elienne tumbled over and over in a bleak, limitless spiral toward the ultimate of Ma'Diere's secrets, the Eye of Eternity.

Pursued by her own raw terror, Elienne tried to break free. Cold tendrils curled around her. Elienne cast in desperation for some landmark upon which to ground her reason. Yet nothing met her search but the silent depths of the infinite. The threat engendered by Faisix acquired new meaning; for in the cold stillness surrounding her, Elienne recognized the steely presence of Ma'Diere's Scythe. Bereft of the means to protect her unborn child, she cried out, from the depths of coma, for mercy, and movement answered.

Blurred by fog, Elienne caught the fleeting glimpse of a

cloak hem bordered in silver and black. The impression of cloth swirled at the limits of perception and vanished in the mist, but not before Elienne had recognized the pattern.

"Gifted!" Elienne whirled and pursued the elusive clue. "Ielond!"

Mist resisted like water, dragged at her running feet. Elienne forced herself forward. Before her, the fog thinned reluctantly and yielded a dim outline of a cloaked figure walking with measured steps ahead.

Elienne shouted frantically, "Ielond, I beg you!"

For an edged, despair-ridden moment, the appeal had no effect. Then, slowly, the figure paused and turned to wait. A silvery spill of hair trailed from the velvet hood, bracketing shadowed features. Elienne drew uncomfortably close before she could discern the face, familiar though it was in memory.

Ielond was frowning. "Why have you followed, Lady?" Though gravely stated, the question was not without compassion. "This is no place for the living, and your time is not yet come."

"Gifted, I am sent against my will." Elienne stopped before the Sorcerer, and the yellow silk of Pendaire's Royal Consort billowed and drifted about her on the currents of her dream. "Faisix and his henchman would do me harm. I ask your help, for your Prince, and for my unborn son."

Slowly Ielond shook his head. Eyes light and clear as summer sky regarded her with deep sorrow. "Mistress, no action I take here can affect the living. By Ma'Diere's Law, my work is finished. You must rely on your own resources."

Despair struck, like madness. Elienne stepped back, unable to express the enormity of her pain. "Have mercy!" The words tore. Not even the Khadrach had made her beg.

"Mistress," said Ielond softly, and his gentleness soothed shattered composure. "Hear me. You are the culmination of a five-thousand-year search. Do you believe I would sacrifice myself and risk Darion's life as casually as a man would wager gold on a horse race? Did you think I manipulated Time itself, and yet had neither wisdom nor thought to search the future for the consequence of my action? You are anything but defenseless. Even now Faisix is reminded of the fact."

Elienne shook her head, and tangled hair clung to her tear-streaked cheeks. "Gifted, I don't understand."

Ielond searched her face. Beyond his shoulder, the mist rolled and tossed, formless as tidal surf. "Faisix wishes to remove the mirrowstone I left you; even as I speak, he seeks to break the ward I set. But shortly he will discover the chain's continuity is linked inextricably with his own existence. Should he cut the chain, or kill you, his own spirit would be drawn after mine across the Eye of Eternity. He cannot change this without forfeiting all that binds him to life."

"That won't stop him." Elienne thought of the mutes and shuddered. "He would as readily take my child's life, or see me crippled. It is Darion he wishes to strike down. I am nothing but a pawn in his hands."

"Not a pawn. You underestimate yourself." The cloak swirled, midnight and silver against the murk, as Ielond turned and started forward.

Elienne hurried to match his long stride, fear supplanted by sudden anger. *"How can I fight his sorceries, Gifted?"*

Ielond stopped, and amusement claimed him, wholly. "Mistress, are you daft, or merely forgetful? You all but achieved my ruin on the icefields, once."

Elienne checked, white with shock. "Sphere of influence," she said softly, and recalled the explanation the Sorcerer had once given for Faisix's arcane manifestation. *"When you resist me, even in thought, you match your polarity to that of my enemies, augmenting their strength. You provide them opening, since you are within my defenses, and through your dissent I am made vulnerable."*

"You see." Ielond nodded and moved off. "Faisix takes a very great risk in meddling with you, *especially* when he shapes his snares with enchantment."

"Wait!" Elienne moved quickly and stepped in front, blocking Ielond's advance.

He sidestepped, impatient. "You delay me, Lady. *My part is finished.*"

But Elienne would not allow him to pass until she had

voiced her deepest fear. "The Seeress's prophecy, Gifted. Ma'Diere's Archmistress forecast I would fail your Prince."

Ielond's features hardened to opacity. Even his eyes took on the remote, impervious glitter of gemstone. "Did she, in truth?"

Elienne swallowed. "She said I would die truthful. And that Halgarid's bloodline would inherit."

"Let me pass, Mistress. I once spared your life, but my task is now complete." Ielond gestured for her to move aside, and the hood tumbled, loosing his white hair to the breeze.

"Gifted." Elienne stood fast, held the Sorcerer's cold gaze though it took all of her will.

At last Ielond looked away. He pulled the hood back over his head, and for a moment silver-banded sleeves eclipsed his face. He spoke, finally, with extreme reluctance. "My Lady, no trial you have yet known will test you so severely as one to come. Through your darkest hour, maintain your courage. Remember I have looked beyond and seen a beginning."

"The prophecy is true, then?" Elienne regarded the Sorcerer with hope dying in her heart, and the appeal on her features caught him like a knife's edge.

"Forgive me, Lady. Tragedy linked each of the choices I placed before you in Trathmere." The Sorcerer turned his back.

"No!" Elienne's cry echoed, lost, into emptiness. "No, I beg you, spare me Cinndel's son!"

But this time Ielond did not slacken his step, and mist swiftly obliterated detail until he was reduced to a shadowy silhouette. "Lady," he cautioned over his shoulder, "attend your own defense, at once, or all is indeed lost."

Elienne longed to follow, to demand outright an explanation for the threat that marred her future. But a dull ache began to pressure her forehead. Warned beyond the barriers of unconsciousness by the sensation, Elienne knew she must obey Ielond's directive.

Mist swirled, thickened, and acquired the sickly consistency of cobwebs. Elienne's step dragged. A sultry flash of light blinded her inner vision. When sight returned, she found her perception of her flesh, and even the brilliant yellow silk of her dress, dimmed to the bleached white of old bones. A shadow crossed her heart. Faisix sought access to her mind through sorcery. Suddenly the pain behind her eyes mounted to the focused agony of a knife thrust. Elienne screamed.

Anguished and outraged, she turned against the source, roused awareness aligned like a weapon against the enemy who invaded her thoughts. Mist eddied, shredded, and Elienne whirled haplessly with it, sucked through a vast tornado of force. Then the shrill soprano of breaking glass splintered against her ears, and her eyes opened upon intense light.

Chapter 9

Duel of Masters

Glare shuttered against dream-roused senses. Elienne squinted. She lay on a tabletop, ringed by a net of forces that shone with the blue-violet corona of a lightning flash. The sorcery was not hostile. Though still numb from the elixir, Elienne realized that her own resistance had admitted this influx of energy. The harmonics that tingled against her ears were familiar; Taroith's trained awareness had detected the gap in Faisix's defenses. The lash of his response as he exploited the break had fallen with immediate and visible result upon those who threatened her.

Thrown from his feet, the cowled man sprawled amid smashed furnishings and the icy, frost-point glitter of broken glassware. Above him, Faisix clung to the edge of a cabinet, knuckles whitened as though his body were savaged by galewind. Though awed by the intensity of power permitted access through her dissent, Elienne retained wits enough to roll onto her elbow and reach for the mirrowstone.

"Heggen!" Faisix shouted. "Stop her!" His yellow eyes narrowed, intent upon murder. "I will break Taroith's defenses."

The black-clothed man stirred. His thick fingers closed, gashed by gritty slivers of glass, yet he seemed oblivious to pain. Through the brilliance of the light, Elienne watched him rise and stumble toward her, cowl fallen back to reveal a hairless, hideous face.

Faisix shouted in a foreign tongue. The light flickered. Elienne swore, dazed beyond immediate recognition of threat. Vivid as nightmare, yet strangely remote to her drug-stunned senses, Heggen stretched blood-streaked hands through the barrier to seize her.

Elienne recoiled. The man was recklessly confident; he thought to take her easily as a boy would pin a moth against a lantern. Elienne exploded into sudden fury. Denied speech to voice her contempt, she spat on Heggen's raised palms. Instantly, the vehemence of her denial admitted a tortured crackle of sound. Blinded by the flaring brilliance, Elienne heard Heggen scream.

Faisix shouted curses, his cool façade abandoned.

Elienne clutched the mirrowstone in feverish fingers. Rage mounted, tangible as fire within her, and the polarity generated by her resistance widened, unleashing the powers of those who defended her. Destruction resulted. A flask erupted into a fountainhead of shards. Heggen yelled warning. A shelf careened off the far wall, spilling a thunderous avalanche of books over Faisix's head. He dove clear. Spilled liquid met hot oil and flame. Yellow fumes roiled upward; sparks flew, acridly laced with smoke.

"Master!" Heggen's appeal was hoarse. "Drop the wards over Torkal." A candelabrum whirled and toppled, streaming tongues of fire. "Would you destroy us? Release the binding before we are stewed like fishes in a pot!"

Elienne heard Faisix curse again. Then a coarse sound like the tear of canvas ripped the air, and a starburst of light slammed her eyes. Wind clawed her hair. Faintly Elienne heard voices.

"She's done it!" The triumphant words were Taroith's. "The wards over Torkal are down!"

A reply from the Prince reached Elienne's ears, distant and ragged with hope. "Ma'Diere guide you. Bring my Lady back unharmed."

Elienne drew breath and found her speech freed. *"Darion!"* The cry raised a gust of wind. Glassware tumbled. Then the air before her split, cloven by sorcery. Within the rent appeared a tall figure clad in wet riding leather and gray wool cloak. Soulfocus light blazed down on sodden white hair and the familiar face of Taroith. Relief flooded Elienne's eyes with tears.

The wind died as though strangled.

"My Lady!" Taroith's summons cut urgently through the soft sigh of the flames. "Come to me, quickly."

Elienne pushed herself into motion. Her limbs responded with reluctance. Drug-blurred senses misjudged the height of the tabletop, and she stumbled, betrayed yet again by shaky legs. She clung to the oaken furnishings, consciousness riddled by yawning gaps. Blackness worried at her balance.

"Hurry!" Urgently, Taroith flung out a hand to assist.

But a thin red bar of light shot between, barring Elienne from the Sorcerer. Surly in his spoiled black doublet, Faisix lifted his voice in challenge. "Greetings, Master Taroith. If you wish the Lady's company, you must win it from me."

The red line blazed malevolently through the spectrum of oranges to a peak of dazzling yellow. Faisix smiled, then whipped his spell fluidly about Taroith's thin shoulders.

Taroith said, "You are foolish to contest me." He broke the enchantment's continuity with a gesture. Light danced and died.

"Spoken like a true and loyal Master of the League," Faisix mocked. "How you detest violence." With the grace of a panther, he stepped across the tangled wreckage of his study. Glass crunched like gravel under his boots. When he stopped, the braced stance he assumed stirred Elienne with uneasiness. His confidence seemed unshakable as Eternity.

"If you want the woman, *fight for her*." Faisix's deference offered cruel invitation, as though Taroith's resistance would shape some subtle victory. Elienne felt the skin on her arms prickle. Unseen forces aligned about her, a predator bunched to spring.

"Strike first, then," Taroith said softly. "And remember whose choice initiated this conflict."

Faisix performed a formal courtier's bow and, with an arrogant lift of his chin, flung sweat-tangled hair from his face. A sunburst blossomed overhead with the movement. Elienne narrowed aching eyes. Never, in her presence, had Faisix's soulfocus shone so brightly. The small room blazed, ruddy with reflections.

Even Taroith flung up an arm and shielded his face.

"Faisix!" The shout was whetted with rebuke. *"Are you possessed? We've set no precautionary wards!"*

"What care I if natural continuity is disrupted? *I* took no oath of Mastery, nor am I subject to the restraints of the League."

The focus brightened. Radiant heat raised a sinuous twist of steam from Taroith's damp shoulders. The Sorcerer licked sweat from his lips. "Faisix, desist, at least until we have erected proper restrictions. Two others in this room might suffer unjust consequences."

The Regent shrugged elegantly. "Heggen can look after himself. If the Lady's safety concerns you, weaken your own defense and shield her."

With staccato snaps, the leaded panes of the casement spawned marks like starbursts.

Faisix lowered his head, pale hair beaded with light. "Stand your guard, Taroith," he said sweetly, and struck.

The focus arced through the air. Shadows pinwheeled across floor, walls, and ceiling, and a flare of incandescence dazzled Elienne's eyes. Power tore into her; she staggered back and smashed with bruising force into the table.

"Ma'Diere, have you no scruples?" Taroith cried, shocked. Fuzzily she realized Faisix had directed the brunt of his assault against her, taking Taroith entirely by surprise.

Savage with disgust, the League Sorcerer roused his soulfocus. Light sheeted, mirror-bright, and deflected the Regent's attack. A lesser flash sparked across the room as Heggen shielded himself from the backlash.

Elienne clung to the table, helpless and disoriented. Sweat drenched her hair, face, and neck, and her body shook beyond voluntary control. Vaguely she noticed Taroith had provided some protection. Light still lanced her vision, but damped now to the sullen flare of marsh gas by the thin film of a ward.

Ozone whetted the air with a prickling scent. Elienne straightened, desperate to assess the action. The conflict beyond the barrier flickered, distorted as though viewed through a swift current. She saw Faisix hurl a raging mass of force. Elienne gasped, fearful Taroith would not escape.

But the elderly figure in gray raised up a glimmering net. The shield appeared delicate as opalescent glass. Yet the terrible, raw blaze of Faisix's offense recoiled harmlessly aside. The ward surrounding Elienne opaqued, mercurial silver, and shed the backwash of energy. Transparency returned with a soft flicker of blue light as Taroith's formidable control unbound the energy set against him.

The Sorcerers battled on more levels than mortal awareness could encompass, but Elienne understood enough to know Faisix held strategic advantage through his initial assault upon her. Burdened by her defenselessness, Taroith could not let his protection lapse until the Regent was totally subdued, lest the tactic against her be repeated. Diverted attention prevented the Master from assuming the offensive. Time after time, Elienne watched him deflect the fury of Faisix's attack.

The contest continued, lacerating her eyes and ears with unnatural forces. Her skin wept clammy sweat, and tension clenched her stomach. Heggen apparently shared none of her discomfort. He stood at Faisix's shoulder casually, an icon's secretive smile on his lips. Distastefully, Elienne wondered where Faisix had acquired such a companion. The man barely seemed human.

"Faisix." Taroith's sharp tone made Elienne start. "One last time, I ask that you abjure violence and heed the voice of reason."

The Regent's expression turned expansive with delight. "I'm touched by your concern, Master Sorcerer, but the sentiment is wasted." Slim, sure hands raised another inferno, voracious as the fires of the damned.

"I am left no alternative." Taroith frowned. "You compel me to turn the effects of your own summoning back against you."

Faisix gestured contemptuously. "I will easily regain mastery of what originated at my command."

The light swelled. Heat waves shimmered the air. Elienne saw this attack would surpass those which had gone before. Her grip tightened apprehensively on the table edge. The towering wall of fire made Taroith's stance seem marked by exhaustion and poignantly human frailty.

"Faisix, you misjudge me," said the Sorcerer quietly.

Yet the spell only blazed the brighter. Drafts stirred the drapes, and tapestries swayed like ghosts against the wall. Faisix's laughter arose harsh as metal against a grindstone above the crackle of fire. The Regent folded his arms with studied nonchalance, licked by shifting orange reflections. "I am not moved at all. Your threats, I think, are designed to frighten children."

Suddenly, startlingly, Heggen stirred, dark skin blanched the color of old bone. "Have a care, Master!" He raised an incautious hand to restrain the Regent. "The Sorcerer's words are well founded. You are overmatched."

"Fool!" Scornfully Faisix ducked Heggen's hold. "Would you ruin us both? I know what I am about." And a swift, blurred motion loosed his attack.

The ward this time failed to opaque. An explosion of light ripped Elienne's eyes. Through flash-dimmed vision, she saw Taroith respond with a neat, graceful gesture. The surrounding space gained transcendent clarity, as though he stood isolated in a sphere of focused perfection.

Faisix's blaze struck with a cobra's speed. Taroith intercepted with his soulfocus. Impact ignited a starred pulse of blue-white light. The energy deflected, as though from a mirror, yet even Elienne's limited perceptions detected alterations in the reverse flow. Somehow Taroith had translated the motivation of Faisix's intentions into tangible existence. The result was Evil, Hatred, and Greed, ruinously personified. Elienne shuddered in horror. She beheld what seemed the very death of hope. She tore her gaze away quickly, grateful not to be the victim of the Sorcerer's riposte.

Faisix's shout split into a scream.

"Yield," commanded Taroith, relentlessly impersonal.

The Regent reeled backward. His breath caught in tortured gasps, and trembling fingers clawed at the brass latch of a cupboard. *"Heggen."*

Though the appeal was no more than a ragged whisper, Heggen moved in answer.

"Yield," said Taroith again.

His soulfocus pulsed at the extreme edge of violet.

Energy backlashed, distilled into nightmare. Faisix flinched, pinned grotesquely against the cabinet doors. His hands scrabbled at the latch. "Heggen!"

Sweat gleamed on the cowled man's knuckles as he caught the latch and wrenched the cupboard open. Knives gleamed within, eerily ablaze with reflections from Taroith's sorcery. Faisix seized the handle of the nearest.

Taroith moved sharply forward, and his steps spun glass fragments across the floor. "Put up your blade. Physical violence will gain you nothing."

A ghastly smile curved Faisix's lips. He whirled with deadly grace and drove the dagger to the hilt in the heart of his assistant. Heggen gasped in mortal surprise, and crumpled. Blood splashed across the tiles. Too late, Elienne covered her eyes. The image of the murder was already clenched forever in her memory, along with the rustle of Heggen's contortions as the life left his frame. A stench thickened in her nostrils. Sickened by the taste of bile, Elienne choked and, looking up, saw Faisix trace symbols upon the air with crimson hands. Smoke boiled forth, backlit by the yellow glow of runes. Impressed by a sense of wrongness, Elienne knew at once she witnessed Black Sorcery.

A hard glimmer of blue-white drew her eye. With an expression seamed and grim, Taroith erected a protective lattice of light. Concentration made him seem inhuman. Colored highlights flickered over shoulders stiff as flint, as though he channeled the sum of his being into the spells carved into existence by his mastery.

Yet Faisix moved first. Elienne watched him stoop over Heggen's corpse; the runes fanned a crown of broiling smoke above his hair as he traced an arrow in wet blood upon the floor, then uttered a guttural phrase. His cipher pulsed and came to life. Fumes roiled ceilingward, and the blood leaped forth and ran in a sizzling stream toward Taroith's corner of the room. Its evil advance struck the clean luminosity of the Master Sorcerer's defenses with a hideous shriek of steam. Wind fanned the chamber in a hot breath, extinguishing Taroith's sorceries like blown candleflame; even the ward surrounding Elienne flicked out with a brittle snap.

Gray-black streamers of smoke caught acridly in her throat and left her choking. Through tear-stung eyes, she saw the blood settle, a scarlet puddle at Taroith's feet, with edges geometrically frayed by runoff into cracks between the tiles.

Faisix stood, unsteady and breathing hard. "Which of us is helpless now, *Master?* I can unbind your most powerful ward."

Taroith offered no reply.

The Regent smiled with courtly diplomacy. "I am not unsporting." He gestured with streaked hands at the pool beside his opponent's boots. "I have evened the odds between us; quite generously granted you means to triumph over me. Once, before the Grand Justice, you denounced me for Black Sorcery and named me condemned by Ma'Diere's Law." The smile became honeyed with sarcasm. "Join me in Damnation, and you might save your Prince's Consort."

Expressionless with exhaustion, Taroith lowered his head. Eyes dark as old ebony fixed, stricken, on the stained floor, and sudden apprehension locked the breath in Elienne's chest. Surely Taroith was wise enough to resist such an end.

Yet Faisix resumed his taunts, confidently anticipating a victory. "You hold the advantage, with all your League training. If you dared apply the Black arts, you would defeat me."

Taroith said nothing. The knuckles of his locked hands whitened with stress. Heggen's blood inches from his boot, the sorcerer seemed tormented by indecision. Elienne recalled a statement of Ielond's, uttered in anguish on the ice plains: *"I'd suffer Damnation gladly, Mistress, if I could spare Darion! But my Prince forbade me permission to work the darklore."*

The royal Guardian's love for his ward had instead driven him beyond the known limits of sorcery: he had broken the barrier of Time to ensure his Prince's succession. Elienne bit her lip. The temptation to battle Faisix with Black Sorcery was great; Ielond's prodigious sacrifices in Darion's behalf might easily make Damnation seem inconsequential if the royal succession might be secured as a result.

"Why the great delay?" the Regent goaded. "Don't you know? You have no choice."

He thinks to save himself, Elienne thought and, with a

horrid flash of perception, realized Taroith's use of Black
Sorcery might jeopardize the integrity so recently and
precariously restored him by the Grand Council's acquittal.
Should he fail now, all past actions could become tainted by
doubt; a lifetime of honorable service undermined at a stroke.
Faced by such betrayal, Pendaire's fickle court might well
turn back to the familiar leadership of Faisix.

And still Taroith seemed torn by doubt. Spent as he was,
Elienne wondered whether he realized his present danger.
Necessity forced her to control the fear that shackled her
against action. Like a hunted animal, she searched for some
measure she could engage in her own behalf, should Taroith's
wisdom falter. Her attention caught on the bright, deadly
glitter of a glass shard. Cautiously Elienne extended her foot
and scuffed the fragment within reach. That moment, Taroith
looked up.

White hair lay limp over the damp folds of his hood,
bracketing an expression of raw sorrow. "Faisix, there is
always choice," he said softly.

The Regent kicked Heggen's hand out of his path and
stepped forward, triumphant. "Ah, you're ignorant. Didn't
you know? The Lady Elienne is the sole key to Darion's
succession. Without her, he will certainly face the headsman's
ax."

Dread chilled Elienne to the marrow. *Faisix intended to
expose the fact that Darion's seed was sterile*. And if her son by
Cinndel was revealed to be other than the royal blood of
Halgarid, the vindictive rage of the court would surely destroy them both. Elienne stooped and caught the glass from
the floor, her only recourse to end the conflict before Faisix
could speak and ruin her.

"Ielond knew." Faisix prepared to drive home his crown-
ing blow, sure as a cat toying with prey. "The Prince cannot
possibly—"

"No!" Elienne's shrill exclamation sliced through the
exchange like a sword blade. Trembling, she extended her
arm, the cruel edge of the glass laid against the delicate skin of
her wrist. She drew a ragged breath and said, "Taroith. Listen

to me. If you use the darklore to save either me or Darion, I will take my life. *I'll not see you damned for my sake.*"

"Bleeding can be stanched," said Faisix conversationally.

"But you would welcome my death, Excellency. Do you think Taroith could subdue you in time enough to save me?" Elienne glanced quickly back to the Sorcerer. "Gifted, don't."

Taroith turned his face fully upon her, and with a wrench, Elienne noticed the tears that traced his lined cheeks. "Lady, your wisdom is the blessing of Ma'Diere. You already understand why I must abandon you here, though by so doing, I leave you in great danger. Do not despair, I shall not transgress natural law. I only hesitated because I could think of no gentle means to explain my withdrawal to you."

Elienne spoke quickly, barely able to maintain her resolve. "Leave with my blessing, Gifted." She laid the glass fragment aside with hands suddenly too unsteady to grip it with safety.

"Keep your courage up," said Taroith. "Neither Darion nor I shall rest until your freedom is won."

Unable to bear the sight of the Sorcerer's departure, Elienne squeezed her eyes shut. By force of will, she held herself from begging the Sorcerer to reconsider.

As though sensing her weakness, Faisix smiled. "You abandon her to a singularly unpleasant fate."

Taroith responded sharply, "Beware, Defiler. The Sorcerer's League will act in the Consort's defense. You'll be shown no mercy unless you release the Lady to my care now."

"She is significant only as long as Darion remains alive," said Faisix.

Through the words, Elienne heard a rustle like velvet rubbed across wool, and a soft breeze chilled her wet cheeks. She opened her eyes to find Taroith gone. Faisix approached her, madness upon his smoke-grimed features. "Above anything else, you will come to regret your part in Darion's life, Lady Consort."

Though the wide casements were not barred, and no lock secured her door, the bedchamber on the third floor of Torkal Manor became Elienne's prison during the days that followed.

The hallway without never went unguarded, and the only soul she saw, beside the mutes, was the girl Minksa, who brought her meals, water, and fresh candles. Elienne tried to win the child's confidence, with little success. Sometimes Minksa lingered over her tasks to listen to her companionable chatter, but the offer of friendship seemed to increase the girl's apprehension. Discouraged yet again one evening as the child bolted from her chambers, Elienne sighed. She rose and pushed the door closed, shutting out the view of the guardswoman in the hallway beyond.

Alone for the night, she settled herself on the chilly cushions of the window seat and gazed out at the gardens beneath a half-moon. The forest spread dark beneath sooty streamers of cloud. For the thousandth time, Elienne wondered what form of trauma had disturbed Minksa. Such reserve was unnatural for a girl of her years. As always when she was troubled, Elienne reached for the mirrowstone that hung from the chain at her neck. Even Faisix's barrier of Black Sorcery could not prevent sight of the Prince through Ielond's interface, though communication was still impossible.

Within the stone, moonlight struck through a canopy of foliage. Horses moved in thick shadow. Cloaked against the cold, Darion hunched in his saddle, his face a pale blur in the darkness. Daylight would have revealed angular hollows at cheek and temple, and eyes set deep in circled sockets. The Prince paced when weariness forced his men to make camp. Restlessness robbed him of all but the lightest of sleep, and Elienne had observed him in the throes of nightmare more than once. Had Taroith been present, he might perhaps have reassured the Prince. But the Sorcerer had not returned to Darion's side since the conclusion of the duel with Faisix. Elienne tried to recall how long ago that had been; hours ran together into days, and since nothing other then weather differentiated one from another she lost track. Had it been seven nights, or eight, since the duel with Faisix?

Elienne leaned her shoulder against the windowframe, and closed her eyes. She could not guess how far the Prince's retinue was from Torkal. And though Faisix had left her entirely alone, she doubted he had forgotten her. Often Elienne smelled the acrid fumes of Black Sorcery.

Permitted no diversion, Elienne exhausted herself battling the despair that threatened hourly to overwhelm her. Accustomed lifelong to activity, she fretted in confinement. Sleep tormented her with visions of freedom, and her waking thoughts strayed too often into nightmare.

Curled in the window seat over the mirrowstone, Elienne finally drowsed. Snared by an uneasy dream, she beheld a meadow whitened like snowdrifts with the blossoms of starflowers, but the rare and peaceful beauty of the place was marred by the pathetic sounds of an infant's cries. Elienne searched, but found no child.

"*Forgive me,*" Ielond said from behind. She stopped and turned, but saw no trace of him. The voice resumed, implacably. "*Tragedy linked each of the choices I placed before you in Trathmere....*"

And close by, the infant continued to wail.

"Mistress!" Someone shook her.

Elienne woke with a start. Minksa gripped her elbow urgently.

"Mistress, I'm frightened." The girl's small hands were damp with sweat, and even by wan moonlight, Elienne saw her eyes were widened in terror.

Though empty of confidence herself, Elienne gathered the child's trembling body close. "I'm your friend. Can you tell me what has upset you?"

For a long time, Minksa clung, speechless. Then a sob wrenched the thin shoulders in Elienne's arms, and she felt the child's fingers grope and lock among her skirts.

Minksa drew an unsteady breath. "Mistress, it's Faisix," she began, and twisted her face toward the door.

Moonlight burnished her pale forehead like bone, and the shadowed eyesockets beneath seemed momentarily vacant as a skeleton's. Elienne shivered. Then her ears caught the ring of footsteps in the hallway beyond.

Minksa gasped. "He comes here, Mistress."

Firmly Elienne gathered her ragged composure. "Who comes? Faisix?"

Minksa nodded, tears silvering her cheeks.

"My friends don't call me 'Mistress,'" Elienne said quickly, glad the wait had ended at last. "Why don't you hide behind the bedhangings? The Regent need not know you came."

Minksa swallowed and tilted her small sprite's face up at Elienne. "Mistress, Lady, he is not angry with me. You are the one who has displeased him, though he will beat me if he finds I have warned you."

"I won't tell him." Elienne squeezed the girl's hand reassuringly. "Hide yourself quickly."

But Minksa failed to move. The steps drew closer, paired by the dissonant jingle of mail and weaponry.

Elienne gave Minksa a small push. "Go, child."

Yet, surprisingly, the girl resisted. "Lady, he already knows I am here."

Elienne tried to hide her uncertainty. "Then we'll face him together." She blotted a tear from Minksa's cheek, just as the door crashed back.

Light sliced the chamber, darkened almost at once by Faisix's slim height. He wore mail and a black surcoat trimmed elegantly in gold, which Elienne found oddly, disquietingly familiar. At his back, a hand-held torch flung heated reflections off Aisa's armored and weaponed shoulders. Minksa shrank against Elienne's knees as the Regent and the mute stepped into the room. Denji entered behind them both, fingering the haft of her battle-ax. The Regent checked by the bed, startled to find the gold-sewn coverlet smooth and unmussed.

"I'm over here," said Elienne coldly. "Your hospitality doesn't encourage sleep."

Faisix spun and faced the window seat, abandoned utterly to fury. "Woman, count on it. I'll make your existence a living Damnation. You'll wish for death."

Pushed past her fear by a blaze of sudden anger, Elienne tried to provoke him. "How sporting of you! I see Darion has not yet fallen prey to your schemes. Tell me, does frustration *always* make you strike unarmed men and women?"

Faisix's jaw tightened. He took a sharp, thoughtless step forward.

"And children," Elienne said scornfully. "Ma'Diere knows you've used this girl. Your methods, certainly, are gutlessly crass." If he could be angered enough to strike her, she might once again disrupt his sphere of influence and summon Taroith.

But her hope misfired. Faisix jerked his head at the mutes. "Bind her," he said, "and the girl too."

He accepted the torch from Aisa, and watched coldly while the guardswomen dragged Minksa and Elienne roughly from the window seat. "I am lately returned from a most irregular paradox. You might recall a time when you were not such a staunch ally of the Prince. Once you resisted Ielond's will and summoned me to the ice plains of Ceroth. I think you recall the unpleasantness that occurred there quite well." He paused.

Elienne's breath stuck in her throat. The paradox of Ielond's Timesplice had only now caught up with her. The meeting on the ice plain must have just occurred, for the Regent.

"I see you remember." A fierce gleam lit Faisix's eyes, and his voice thickened. "I spoke with Ielond, yet Ielond is dead. And you are with child, surely, by a man other than Darion. Whatever tricks your Prince's Guardian has played with the natural laws of progression, I assure you, his efforts will come to nothing."

"You bluster like the wind," said Elienne hotly. Her heart labored against her breast, and her mouth went dry, but she continued. "Ielond has already defeated you."

Faisix's brows rose thoughtfully. "Has he indeed? I shall unravel his mysteries, Mistress, and discover the origins of a certain chestnut-haired man who was once dear to you. Then we shall see who suffers defeat. But such a search will cost me time, and I intend to ruin Darion first. Without him, your fate won't matter. And since you've shown such touching concern for Minksa, I've decided the child shall help."

Horror snapped the threads of Elienne's composure. "No!" But Faisix simply smiled at her protest as the mutes bundled her and Minksa toward the open door.

Chapter 10

The Path of Damnation

The study had been cleared for the worst wreckage from Faisix's duel with Taroith, but broken glassware glittered still in the recesses beneath furnishings, and the floor bore the crisscrossed scars of scorch marks and ugly rust-colored stains. Pushed by calloused hands into a wooden chair, Elienne heard Faisix move to the cupboards against the left wall. Beyond the mute's bulk, she glimpsed the jars that held the reduced remains of Heggen's corpse. Elienne was grateful Minksa's back was turned. The girl was young for such a grisly sight.

Faisix selected a flask from the shelf and spoke without leaving his work. "Aisa, please restrain the Lady in a manner which leaves her left hand at liberty. I wish her free to watch her Prince's demise in the mirrowstone."

Elienne barely felt the bite of the cords, concerned as she was for Minksa; the girl offered no resistance as Denji turned her over to Faisix. Like a hare trapped in the jaws of a wolf, she seemed suspended in paralysis. When the Regent caught her hand, she followed willingly, and cued by her attitude of submissiveness, Elienne realized the girl was no stranger to the practices of sorcery.

Faisix spoke to the mutes without looking up. "You are both excused. Set the bolt from the outside as you leave."

The raw clank of weaponry belled in Elienne's ears as Aisa and Denji departed. Why should the Regent require the door locked from *without*? Elienne licked parched lips, avoiding thoughts of Darion, alone with his men-at-arms, and bereft of Taroith's guidance. Gripped instead by recall of the scorched and wretched corpses bloating beneath Trathmere's walls, she experienced an echo of Minksa's submissive despair. Defeat became a haven of familiarity beside the horror of confronting yet another incomprehensible barrage of sorcery. Her life, surely, had ended with Cinndel's at the hands of the Khadrach; every action since seemed pallid and futile as that of a ghost.

"Stand here, child." Faisix indicated a clear space in the center of the room.

Mutely obedient, Minksa followed with dull, uninterested eyes as he delved into a nearby chest and returned, both hands laden with candlestands. As he arrayed them on the floor by the girl's feet, Elienne noticed the bases were carved of black stone, each one a squat, leering demon. The girl seemed indifferent to the ugliness around her.

Faisix lifted the flask from the table and anointed his left hand. Bloody, dripping fingers traced a line from candlestand to candlestand, enclosing Minksa within a red triangle. The torches cast grotesque, hunched shadows about him as he bent and scribed a wide pentagram, then framed the configuration with runes.

The child stood motionless while Faisix set bluish-white candles into the demon stands and lit them, each with a separate incantation. When he had finished, he stood within the pentagram and spoke a word guttural with consonants. The gory tracings upon the floor sizzled, then burst into flame.

That moment, Minksa cried out, like a sleeper wakened from a nightmare. The sound twisted Elienne's heart. Pendaire's Regent was a monster, to shape his snares with a child. Better she lose Cinndel's son than suffer the rule of such a man.

"Minksa!" Elienne shouted. "Recite Ma'Diere's Laws! Do you know them?"

The child seemed stunned, as though the rhythmic rise and fall of Faisix's chant robbed her of hearing.

Elienne drew breath to repeat the Laws herself, but poisonous fumes from the candles choked her throat. A spasm of coughing mangled the words beyond recognition. Half-smothered by the smoke, Elienne blinked watering eyes and, in the sulfurous glare of flamelight, saw Faisix raise his arm.

The darkness of oblivion appeared before him, framing a doorway in the air.

"Come here, Minksa." His voice was barely above a whisper, yet the child heard. She raised her head and took a slow, tranced step forward. For a moment, Elienne saw her outline blur. Then Minksa crossed the threshold into night.

The blackness flickered, suddenly suffused with streaks of dull red. The girl screamed once, high and thin like a wounded rabbit. She swayed, and her legs buckled as her senses left her. Faisix caught her body as it fell through the gate he had fashioned. Her limbs dangled from his arms as he laid her like a corpse at his feet.

Flayed by emotion, Elienne found her free hand clenched fiercely around the mirrowstone. The jewel was drenched with sweat, and her palm ached where the gold setting had gouged her skin.

"The girl is not dead," said Faisix conversationally. "See for yourself." The Regent inclined his head toward the triangle, and following his nod, Elienne saw a pale, spectral shape move within. Faisix's sorcery had separated spirit from flesh. Imprisoned by the red barriers of the warding spell, Minksa's soul desperately sought escape, to no avail. Elienne shivered, stirred to anger. As Faisix initiated his next invocation, Elienne sought the knotted cords that bound her right wrist behind her back.

The torches streamed and flicked out. Only the ensorceled candles remained alight, flames casting sickly, greenish halos in the dark. Sweat slicked Elienne's back, and the tendons ached around stressed joints. Strain as she might, the knots stayed just beyond reach. Beyond the perimeter of his pentagram, Faisix had scribed a second triangle, and above it, still another dark gateway. The name he called into the obsidian void was that of Darion's sister, Avelaine, who had died of a fall from a horse at age fifteen.

With a leap of horrified intuition, Elienne perceived the Regent's intent. If Faisix merged Minksa's hapless flesh with the spirit of the Prince's dead sister, he would create for himself a formidable weapon. Half-crazed with concern for

Darion, Elienne wrenched desperately against her bonds. But the knots held.

Sparks flared through shifting billows of smoke. Elienne bit her lip to keep from crying out in frustration.

The Regent bent over Minksa's possessed body and applied the arts of shape-change. As though aware of his meddling, the girl's spirit beat like a moth against the sorcery that confined her. Elienne watched in growing apprehension as the girl's fleshly contours altered under Faisix's touch. The apparition that finally rose to its feet before him bore little resemblance to the plain child fathered by Jieles. Luridly underlit by guttering candle flames, Elienne beheld a tall young woman with rich, dark hair and a determined jawline. A jeweled pin glittered at her throat, and her slim figure was expensively clad in riding leather of masculine cut.

"Brother, why have you called me back?" she demanded in a clear, imperious voice.

Hearing the words, Elienne realized that Faisix had himself assumed the Prince's image. When the two were seen together, the likeness to the royal features in the woman's profile was unmistakable.

"I have summoned you because I am in grave danger, sister."

The Princess glanced aside, as though to examine the hellish glow of the ciphers that ringed her round. But Faisix recalled her straying attention. "Avelaine! Will you listen? My life is threatened."

Avelaine faced him with an imperious toss of her coroneted head. Dark hair glanced like raven feathers in the dim, smoky room. "Darion, you have changed much since I saw you last."

"I haven't time for idle talk. I am pursued by a man shape-changed to my likeness. Not even Taroith can tell us apart." Faisix added a gesture of theatrical vehemence. "Bring him down for me, sister. I offer the chance to avenge the death of one dear to us both."

Avelaine frowned. "*Who.* I think you lie, *your Grace*. The brother I knew would never disturb the dead. Not even for his own life's sake."

"Ielond lost his life for the sake of the succession. Must I be murdered as you were, or will you help?"

Avelaine's eyes narrowed. "Faisix!" She said suddenly, "Ma'Diere have mercy, was my death not enough?" and took a sharp step back. The heel of her riding boot knocked inadvertently into a candlestand, and, as though wakened, the carved base came alive.

Elienne gasped. Though fumes scoured her throat, she shouted frantically, "Avelaine, it's a trap!"

But the woman in the triangle seemed deaf to her warning. The demon shape bloated like a soap bubble. White and foul as a slug, it burst, releasing a writhing coil of vapor that rose and twined malevolently around the Princess's head. Avelaine gasped.

"You are mine now," Faisix said softly. "This geas I lay upon you, Avelaine of Pendaire. You shall never rest until your brother lies dead at your hand."

The Princess stood, reasonless as a beast. Her hands accepted the sword Faisix offered with a dreamer's incomprehension. No longer wearing Darion's face, the Regent drew a thin, ceremonial dagger from his belt.

Faisix took the knife and nicked his palm with a swift motion. Blood welled, black against pale skin. He muttered an incantation, then raised his slashed hand and let the wound drip like a libation over the ring. A thunderous blast reft the air. Wind tossed the hair back from Elienne's face, and the candles streamed like specters gone mad. The pentagram flared, red to violet, and crackled sparks, seeming for a prolonged moment to enclose the blackest pit of Hell.

Within, Elienne saw movement: a glint of scales like smoky quartz edging the arch of a serpentine tail. Then the darkness parted and dispersed like smoke, and she beheld the equine demon Faisix had once ridden over the ice plains of Ceroth. Sparks shot from restless hooves, and, yellow as lamps, its eyes gleamed with a man's intelligence. Dazed by fumes, and battered beyond mortal reason by the proximity of unnatural forces, Elienne was slow to recognize she viewed the Regent himself, hideously transformed.

She wrenched at her bonds until pain made her dizzy.

Through blurred eyes, she saw Avelaine mount. The sword flashed once in the flamelight, severing the five candles at the apexes of the pentagram. Thin wax shafts toppled, trailing ragged flags of smoke, and extinguished with a sheared-off hiss against the floor. The connecting lines flickered out. Elienne swallowed, tasted sweat. A triad of candles burned at the angles of the ward that confined Minksa's soul. All else lay shrouded in darkness.

Elienne seized the mirrowstone, braced for disaster. The stone's depths shone warmly, lit by an open-air campfire. Darion sat on a gilt-trimmed saddlecloth, with knees drawn up, and his head resting on crossed wrists. Lumped like dark hillocks about him, the men-at-arms slept under damp wool blankets, armored still, she saw, by the light that pricked helms, weapons, and mailed limbs.

Faisix's apparition had not yet arrived.

The mirrowstone slipped from nervous fingers. If she was to help the Prince, she had little time to act; her only chance lay in the glowing triangle across the room, where Minksa's imprisoned spirit huddled in abject despair. If, somehow, the child could be freed, Ma'Diere's Laws might lend advantage enough for her to regain command of her possessed flesh from Avelaine, and so disrupt Faisix's geas of murder. The chance was slim, and dangerous; Elienne knew her own ignorance of sorcery might precipitate disaster. Yet Ielond had not chosen her for timidity.

The cords could not be loosened; the chair, then, would have to be included in her plans. Elienne grimly bit her lip and shoved against the floor with her feet. With a screech, the legs skated a foot across the tiles. Elienne battled a queasy rush of vertigo. She lowered her head quickly, to prevent herself from fainting outright.

She would have to change tactics. Even if she managed to retain her senses, the noise alone would surely attract the mutes. Urgently, Elienne searched the shadowed room for inspiration.

Her eye fell on the rucked outline of a throw rug piled beneath a book stand. Grasping the chair seat firmly, she yanked upward as she kicked, her intent to lift the chair clear of the floor. But the motion jarred her arms to the shoulders, and pain channeled like molten metal down her nerves. Against all effort of will, she cried out. Sweat dripped like tears down her temples and cheeks.

Elienne drew a shallow, ragged breath. The rug was beyond her means, but any cloth would do as well. She tugged at her skirts and with shaking fingers tore the soft chemise from beneath. Then she tilted the chair and eased the fabric under its legs with her foot. This time the chair slid more smoothly, noise reduced to a muffled rumble, and with clumsy persistence, Elienne propelled herself toward Minksa's confined spirit. The chair caught once, on an uneven square of tile, but Elienne pressed doggedly forward.

The chair rocked to a halt before the heated line of the triangle. She picked out the thin glimmer of the figure within. The girl bent, tightly crouched, her face buried in the crossed shield of her arms.

"Minksa!" Elienne's voice seemed slurred, even to her own ears. The spectral shape did not stir. Perhaps the child could hear no spoken word, removed as she was from her flesh. But Elienne refused to abandon hope.

"Minksa, are you listening?"

The child stayed motionless.

"Minksa, you must..." Elienne's voice cracked, and new tears sprang hotly in her eyes, silvering the faint, phosphorescent image of the imprisoned soul before her. "Minksa, his Grace's life depends upon us now. I think we can save him, if you will help."

Within the triangle, the child stirred. Elienne knew a wild surge of hope. The small, translucent hands unclasped, and Minksa raised a face imprinted with misery. "Lady, I cannot."

Cut to the quick by the need for haste, Elienne's response was brisk to the point of brutality. *"You can try."*

Anguished, Minksa shook her head.

"Does our friendship mean nothing?" Elienne reached fiercely for the candle at the nearest corner of the triangle, as though to pinch off the greenish flame at the wick.

"No! Lady, I beg you!" Minska flung herself at the barrier. "You'll come to great harm if you touch that."

The enclosure flared red as Minksa struck its perimeter. She fell back with a cry of pain, and knelt, weeping, though no tears fell.

Elienne tried to balance urgency with gentleness. "Minksa, Darion could be killed if we don't act quickly. Then all of Pendaire would suffer. Will you help?"

Minksa sat back on her heels, an expression beyond her years molding her thin face.

"Child, what in the Name of Ma'Diere troubles you?"

"Lady, I daren't help your Prince, for my life's sake." Minksa turned her face away. "Darion of Pendaire would condemn me to the headsman should I leave my Lord Regent's protection."

Elienne felt sick. Was there no end to the intricacy of Pendaire's court intrigue, that even children were involved?

"I am older than I seem," said Minksa, startling Elienne with realization she had voiced her thought. Bound by the triangle, Minksa sprang suddenly to her feet, quietude shattered. "Lady, I was there when Faisix bound the Prince to his bane. *My own sister died, as sacrifice,* and I as witness committed high treason against the crown."

Elienne forcibly restored herself to a semblance of calm. Minksa was close to panic. Logic alone would win the girl's complicity in the struggle to aid Darion. Braced with patience she never knew she possessed, Elienne gently urged the child to elaborate her tale. "Darion is a just man, not a vindictive one," she added. "I can't believe you acted entirely of your own free will. Do you trust Faisix, who abuses you, more than me?"

Minksa sat, uncertainty evident even in her gesture of denial. In the oppressed, shadowed room, stale with ash and spent smoke, Elienne waited for the girl to sort her allegiance. The candles flickered and spat by her feet, winnowing sparks like the fireflies released each year at the summer festival in Trathmere.

Elienne sighed, and decided impulsively to gamble. "Minksa, listen well. There shall be an heir. I am with child."

"But Darion is cursed. *I saw.* He can father no children."

Elienne drew a steady breath. With the caution of a wolf stalking deer, she knotted lies with half-truths and tried not to examine the enormity of her risk. "That is exactly what Faisix wants you to believe. What if you're wrong? You must have been very young. The Grand Justice cannot hold you, as a child, accountable for what you saw. You say your sister was murdered, at Faisix's hand, and that fear of reprisal bound you to secrecy. You are innocent of treason, child, but if you fail to act now, you will not be innocent long. The blood of your Prince and his unborn heir will be upon your hands."

Minksa shook her head, agonized. "Please. Would you have me act against my own father?"

Patience abandoned, Elienne struck with sharp and remorseless honesty. "Would a loving father ever exchange his own daughter's life for a crown? Minksa, *if* the child I bear is not the Prince's, *think why.* His Grace might choose not to claim his birthright through murder, though his own life were forfeit. *Don't you realize that such a curse could be reversed in the same manner in which it was cast?*"

Distressed by indecision, Minksa buried her face in her hands. Her bowed shoulders quivered, reminding Elienne how cruelly young the girl was for the burden of loyalty and betrayal thrust upon her. Yet lives depended upon her choice. Though pierced to the core with pity, Elienne dragged words past the wretched knot in her chest and weighted the conviction of her cause with all she had left to offer.

"Minksa, I am going to put out the candle."

"Lady, no." Hysteria threaded Minksa's tone. "The wards will defend against interference."

"I know." Elienne tried to control the fear inspired by the warning, with poor success. Her resolve to disrupt the ward seemed the action of a fool too dim to comprehend defeat. The carved demon on the candlestand mocked her with an expression of poisonous despite. Should the Prince be condemned to the ax, the plight of a foreigner would rouse little comment at court.

"I beg you, Lady," said Minksa. "You are my friend. I don't want you injured."

Yet Faisix's mad intent to inflict vengeance was no more tolerable. Elienne clenched her fingers into a fist. "Minska, if you value that friendship, you will help me by setting your will against what confines you here."

She raised her arm, and caught Minksa's eyes with her own. "Fight back, and Darion's supporters will act to defend us."

Minksa shrank back in terror. "Lady, please!"

"No." Elienne cursed the quaver in her voice. "If you choose, Taroith can reach through your desire and free you. I doubt very much whether Avelaine can continue to rule your body without your consent. *Act against Faisix, if only for your dead sister's sake.*"

"Lady, no!"

But the protest had no effect. Driven by loss, by betrayal, and by her own reckless anger, Elienne smashed the candle from its stand. An aureole of scarlet sparks rinsed the room of shadows. Her skin flamed agony. Someone screamed. The sound seemed to rend the very fabric of sanity, and darkness rushed through the gap. Elienne felt as though her fingers handled magma. The screams, she discovered, were her own. Time hesitated, seconds stretched to span the Eye of Eternity. Then a starburst of blue light shattered her vision.

A log settled, and an upsurge of flame tossed a flurry of sparks adrift in the dark. Darion shifted position, weary of the wait, and worn by the forest silence, which pressed his ears until they ached. At sundown, Taroith had sent word that the Regent's counterstroke was imminent, and the trap to take him prisoner set in readiness. Yet the night was better than half-spent, and nothing had marred the stillness but wind. Darion avoided thoughts of Elienne. He was never a patient man, and a fortnight of concern had frayed his nerves until even the stamp of a restless horse made him start. The flames snapped and hissed at his back as he scanned the black, shadowed forms on their tethers.

A high, whistling snort cut the night, and maned necks lifted, tautly arched. Something had alarmed the horses. Darion caught the dew-soaked leather of his scabbard with sweaty fingers and rose quickly. His booted foot disturbed a bridle, and something struck a buckle with a clink. One of the men stirred and sighed in his sleep. But above the nearby sounds of the camp, Darion heard what the animals' keener senses had detected ahead of him. A horse approached, driven through the wood at a hard gallop.

Certain the animal would have a rider, Darion called softly to his captain, "Waken your men." And steel glanced blood red by the flamelight as he lifted his sword.

Around him, the men rose and armed themselves. A less experienced company might have protested that such measures were excessive against what obviously was nothing more than a single horseman—but where Black Sorcery was involved, one foe could easily be the match of twenty. Darion rode to the center of the shield wall that ringed the camp. He would not meet Faisix in the open, alone and vulnerable.

The captain paused at the Prince's side. "I should think he has reached the League's ward circle by now." He folded his arms across his huge chest and scraped an itch on his jaw with a gloved knuckle.

Darion frowned. "Not yet."

That moment, a horse screamed. The captain started violently. Darion's hand froze on his sword hilt, as every animal on the picket line erupted into frenzied panic. A tree branch splintered, and dirt clods thrown up by shod hooves rattled among the bracken.

"Cut them loose!" shouted the Prince. "Quickly. They'll injure themselves."

A man put aside his pike and ran, dagger drawn. He slashed the halter ropes. One after another, the freed horses wheeled and plunged at a crazed gallop into the brush. The snap and crash of sticks soon obscured all sound of the approaching rider. Cold sweat threaded Darion's temples. Faisix surely was aware of the net of sorcery that the League had set about the camp. He would come prepared, and probably in a form no right-thinking man would sanction.

Suddenly light flared. Shadows leaped, stark as spearshafts from the tree trunks, as with a gusty rush of sound a

Sorcerer's ward girdled the shield wall and camp it defended within a sheet of blue-white illumination.

"He's crossed the League's boundary!" shouted the captain, exultant. "We have him prisoner."

"Only if we can subdue him." Grimly Darion squinted, tried to see between silhouetted trees, convoluted and black as blown ink against the dazzle of the ward. His knuckles tightened on the swordgrip. The extraordinary brilliance of the League's defense was itself a warning that Faisix's sending was no trifle. By Taroith's estimate, the man's ambitious cunning had developed beyond reason into madness. *"The Regent has forgotten restraint,"* he had said, following his attempt to rescue Elienne. *"He is a killer whose actions hold no thought of morality. Any who intervene do so at great peril."*

Yet whatever he had told his colleagues had moved the entire League of Sorcerers to uncharacteristic aggression. Consumed with concern for Elienne, the Prince resisted the impulse to rub his aching eyes.

The approaching hoofbeats stopped. The forest was eerily still. Expectancy gripped the entire company. A pikeman shifted his weight, outlined in light, and the man next to him swore aloud.

"Maintain your guard, soldier!" snapped the captain. But a scream of rending foliage made his reprimand unnecessary. The attack was upon them, from behind.

Darion spun around, saw two men hurled bodily into the air. The watery gleam of a scaled beast reared beyond, equine, deadly, and straight out of legend. Hooves raked the shield wall like hammers. A man screamed, horribly, drowning the thump as his comrades struck earth, limp as rags.

"Close ranks!"

In dreamlike disbelief, Darion stepped forward, sword held lifted in frozen hands, and eyes fixed upon the apparition that reared above the heads of the men. "Ma'Diere, he's raised the Demon of Hellsgap."

A pike struck a scaled shoulder and glanced, rattling, aside. Its owner fell, but Darion had eyes only for the rider. The familiar, light hand on the rein caught in his memory like a barb.

The captain caught his arm roughly and jerked him back. "Let the men handle it, your Grace!"

Something struck a shield with a belling clamor, overlaid by the brighter chime of swordplay. Darion whirled, half-lit features stamped with denial. "By Eternity's Law, they cannot!" He tried to fling off the restraining hand. "The rider of that fiend from Hell is my dead sister, Avelaine!"

Steadfast and experienced, the captain tightened his grip. He spoke calmly over the clang of arms. "Then leave her to the men. What can you do, except throw your life away, as Faisix intends?"

Iron struck steel with a screech, countered by a choked-off human cry. Darion flinched and tore free. "I can stop her killing." And he saw the captain's face slacken with fear as he turned to meet his nemesis.

A ragged shout arose as another man went down. The shield wall crumpled like a burst dam. The demon horse surged through the gap, its rider's hair a spray of ebony against the glare of the ward. Shod hooves chewed gouts of soil from the earth, and slitted eyes glimmered, hooded by horny sockets.

The Prince braced himself, sword upraised. The stag blazon on his surcoat leaped in the ward's light as his chest heaved with each labored breath. Close up, he saw memory had not tricked him. The face beneath that wind-tossed net of hair was his royal sibling's, but the gaze she fixed on him was inhuman as a cat's.

"Avelaine!"

Darion's voice came hoarse from his throat. The demon steed reared over him, fetlocks spurred like a fighting cock's. He parried, jarred to the shoulder as steel cracked against a taloned hoof. Air buffeted his ear, plowed up by the other hoof, and the spur caught his sleeve like a razor. Cloth fluttered, opened to expose the fine mesh of mail beneath.

Darion stepped back, recovered, and saw the thin, hard edge of Avelaine's sword thrust at his throat. He twisted, ducked, vision filled by the bullion tassels of the beast's saddlecloth, and an armored boot driving at his face.

"Sister!" The word was a gasp as he dodged. He slashed

at the horse's hamstring, but it sidled, serpent tail smashing downward. He took the blow with his sword edge. Steel quivered, and stung his palms, but the blade opened a line of scarlet between closely lapped scales.

Darion recoiled, his sword poised. The horse snorted, breath like streaked smoke on the night air. Muscles bunched under scaled hide, and both forelegs lifted to deliver a second barrage. Darion back-stepped. He thrust upward, hoping to catch the softer heel of the hoof, or the exposed ridges of tendon above the spurred fetlock. But Avelaine yanked the reins hard left, driving her steed off balance, and into safety. She parried Darion's lunge and riposted, her slim body utterly at home in the saddle as the beast recovered equilibrium, sidestepping.

Steel struck steel. Darion feinted and retreated to recover himself. His heel mired in the folds of an abandoned blanket. He blocked a thrust at his neck and sprang clear before his footing could be spoiled. Sweat burned his eyes, transforming the reflections off scales, weapons, and caparisons into starred points of light. Dazzled, he blinked, and almost missed his parry.

"Avelaine!"

The plea caught between breaths. Dimly, he heard shouting. The horse reared. One or the other forehoof would smash him before he could impale it. The sword dragged at his wrists. Yet he lifted the blade, and noticed that he had somehow bloodied his knuckles. The demon loomed over him, black as the shadow of Eternity. Its evil head seemed to rake the sky, neck muscles rippling against tasseled reins. Darion angled the sword's point for the belly just behind the dark line of the girth, oblivious to the flash of Avelaine's steel, which swung at him from the side.

A snap like a whipcrack sounded almost at his elbow. The night split with a cruel flare of light. The horse screamed and staggered back, its rider thrown into the black tangle of its mane. Her sword scraped Darion's mailed shoulder, scattering sparks.

He stumbled, blinded. His own blade struck earth, plowed up leaf mold. He freed it instinctively and looked around, saw the blue-white blaze of a warding spell circling the spot where he stood. And the shouting, finally, resolved into words in his ears.

"Your Grace, stand guard!" The voice was Taroith's. "The circle will stay the demon. But the woman is flesh. Her weapon will wound."

Sweat trickled coldly down Darion's temples. *"She is flesh?"* He shaped the words with disbelief, eyes pinned on the girlish form that reined her horse around to renew the attack. "Ma'Diere's mercy, *you expect me to kill her?"*

Her sword flashed in a feint at his chest. He parried and stepped back. "Taroith!"

The Sorcerer spoke again, somewhere to the side. "Her body has been borrowed from another soul and shape-changed to your sister's likeness."

"Whose?" Darion deflected a vicious riposte, but did not press his advantage in the opening that followed. The hesitation cost him. Avelaine scored a light touch on his shoulder. The stag on his chest showed bloodstains as he loosed a pent-up breath. "Damn you, who is she?"

Taroith answered with weary patience. "We don't yet know."

And Emrith qualified with what might have been a deliberate effort to throw him off stride. "The body might be Elienne's."

Darion flinched, and gained another slash in his surcoat. The cloth gaped, stag blazon neatly beheaded. "No. It can't be." His voice lacked conviction. Such a combination would match Faisix's style.

"Defend yourself, your Grace!"

Yet more than Taroith's reprimand, something in the knowing stare of the demon horse's eyes stung Darion to muster his self-command. His fingers tightened on the sword's blood-slicked grip, and his body moved, blocking the blade that sought his death until his arm ached to the elbow from the endless, jarring blows. He was tiring. His feet dragged and slipped over torn earth. Mounted, Avelaine's advantage of height easily countered his greater reach. Her weapon licked down from above. Darion deflected the stroke, knuckles lined blue with reflections from the ward circle. He wondered whether Faisix had augmented Avelaine's natural endurance with sorcery; the skilled swordplay he parried certainly had never been hers in life.

Lights flickered suddenly at the corner of his vision, bright and brief as fireworks. Taroith had engaged in sorcery, but pressed by Avelaine's steel, Darion dared not glance aside.

"Your Grace!" the Sorcerer shouted.

Darion barely noticed, intent upon the weapon that flashed toward an opening in his guard.

"It is Jieles's daughter, Minksa, possessed by your sister's spirit." Taroith ran forward. Something faint and luminous trailed him.

Darion twisted, caught the blade in a bind on his crossguard. For a suspended moment he swayed, tried to force his spent muscles to hold Avelaine's weapon locked and harmless. Yet she jerked free with a ferocity that wrenched every tendon in his wrist. Unbalanced, Darion stumbled back. Avelaine's sword rose.

"My Prince!"

Taroith's words held no meaning in his ears as he parried, beat, and lunged offensively to drive her back, allowing himself a brief space to recover. That moment, Avelaine's outline shimmered and blurred. Her blade hesitated, mid-swing.

Darion realized, horrorstruck, that his stroke would go home, unimpeded.

"...Jieles's daughter!" Taroith cried, desperate.

He dropped the sword, there being time for nothing else. The grip fell, tumbling the weapon in the air. Steel rattled across Avelaine's mailed calf and chimed against her stirrup. Darion glanced up, seeking the return strike that would take him disarmed, and saw Avelaine's features run like wax. The weapon flew, spinning from her hand, straight for his throat.

The Prince threw himself flat, felt dirt carved up by the blade spray his neck and shoulders. When next he looked up, the girl on the demon mount had transformed. Gone was Avelaine's effortless grace in the saddle. A child clung in her place, white-faced with terror, her slippered feet too short for the stirrup, and her hands inexperienced on the rein.

The black horse screamed, and tried to throw her. The stamp of iron-shod hooves shook the ground where Darion lay. The child cried out, piteously. The Prince rolled and pushed himself to his feet.

"Don't leave the warded circle, your Grace." Taroith flung himself between, blocking Darion's rush. His voice gentled. "The League will protect her."

And the woodland night exploded with the brilliant, pinpoint blaze of a dozen soulfocuses. The demon form plunged, bellowing, black mane softened to smoke against the light. Scales winked, dimmed by misty fumes, and the Sorcerers of the League converged inward, their circle narrowing. Wind arose, and the fumes cleared. A man stood with wrists shackled in bands of light. His head was bent, as though with sorrow, and a small girl cowered at his feet, trembling still with fear.

One of the Sorcerers held out his hand. "Minska?"

The girl rose, went to him, and buried her tearful face in his embrace. At Darion's side, Taroith released a pent-up breath, and the sharp blaze of the wards snapped out like a pinched candle, leaving only the ruddy glow of the campfire.

"Torches!" The captain's order roused a flurry of activity, and voices. Somewhere in darkness, a wounded man moaned. A healer arrived at the Prince's elbow, inquiring after his hurts.

Darion shook him off. Though his muscles quivered with exhaustion, he reclaimed his fallen sword and followed Taroith to the place where Faisix stood captive. The circle of Sorcerers parted to admit him.

"What have you done with the Lady Elienne?" he demanded sharply.

The fair-haired man at its center stirred reluctantly and looked up, tears startlingly bright on a face that seemed rinsed clean of madness. "She is at Torkal," said Faisix softly, "held under guard by the mutes."

Chapter 11

Foreshadow

Through a haze of delirium, Elienne heard running footsteps, half-blurred by echoes. There followed a sudden crash of splintering wood, and a draft buffeted her. Nearby, someone blundered into something metallic.

Elienne flinched. Though her vision blurred and spun with dizziness, she focused enough to receive an impression of dribbled candles, laced still with the opalescent glimmer of unspent spells. Beyond, an armored figure plowed through a tangle of furnishings, the needle-gleam of polished steel in one hand.

"You've come for me," said Elienne indistinctly, certain she addressed the Khadrachi Inquisitor. "Is it sundown?"

She bit her lip, abruptly aware that her cheeks were wet. The tears annoyed her. Cinndel disliked women who cried.

A thick shadow loomed above her, and fingers gripped her shoulder. Elienne looked up, saw a woman with closely cropped hair bending over her with a knife; not the Inquisitor. Terror caught the breath in her throat.

"Aisa!"

The dagger moved and sawed at the cords that bound her to the chair. A blinding rush of pain tore at her senses. Elienne heard a male voice call her name. Then Aisa jerked her upright, and the world upended, tumbling her sickeningly back into oblivion.

"...trying to delay us," said Taroith in a tone spiked with urgency. "Faisix left the mutes with instructions concerning your Consort, should he fail to return to Torkal."

Elienne struggled weakly, unable to move. Aisa's hands

gripped her roughly from behind. Her eyes burned, gritty with ash. She blinked and attempted once more to sort her surroundings. Suddenly a door banged open. Light slashed across the murky haze of smoke-laden air.

"Here!" shouted Darion. "I've found her."

A clash of steel punctuated his discovery. Echoes shimmered against Elienne's ears. Dimly she realized Denji had engaged the Prince, and that he fought, hampered in the narrow hallway, to win control of the doorway.

"Your Grace, put up your blade," commanded Taroith. He came into view beyond Darion, his lined face anxious with worry. "Your Lady will not be won back through violence, I think."

And only then did Elienne identify the thin edge of cold against her neck: Aisa pressed an unsheathed dagger against her throat.

The fighting ceased at once.

Elienne swallowed, and felt an unpleasant sting. Blood traced a hot line across her collarbone.

Darion swore. "Eternity witness, you'll pay for that." The Prince stood just beyond the doorway, sword rested point downward against the floor. His face dripped sweat, and his surcoat hung, slashed and stained, from shoulders that trembled with fatigue. Suddenly he stiffened. "Taroith, Elienne is injured!" He stepped forward.

Denji raised a mailed fist in warning. Aisa's grip tightened harshly. Elienne gasped. A flash of pain pricked her neck. The room turned under an onslaught of vertigo, and her vision dissolved into slivers of light.

"She's going to pass out," Darion said.

The hands around her shifted.

Then Taroith said something low and urgent. An object struck metal with a high-pitched clink, against which Darion's reply fell like a peal of anguish. "Ma'Diere's mercy, Taroith, they're going to kill her right in front of me!"

"Wait," said Taroith. "Aisa, listen to me."

Through ebbing consciousness, Elienne felt the mute gesture denial.

The Sorcerer addressed the guardswoman again, but

more gently. "Did Faisix never tell you your tongue, and your powers of speech, might be restored?"

Elienne sensed stillness, and realized Aisa had stopped breathing. Taroith had her attention. Yet the arm that held the knife pressed like a rock against her chest.

"The Sorcerer speaks truly," said Darion. "By Ma'Diere's Law, any injury not natural at birth can be reversed." With desperate sincerity, he turned his sword and offered it, point reversed, to Denji. "Here is my oath, as Halgarid's heir."

"I will bargain with you," Taroith said. "I offer healing and freedom in exchange for the Prince's Consort, unharmed. That's a fair trade, I think."

Aisa moved. Elienne knew a horrible, numbing sensation of falling, and darkness obliterated her mind.

Elienne drifted, lost in a fog of oblivion, until a gentle voice spoke her name repeatedly and shepherded her back to awareness. The mists that held her captive began gradually to lift. Her wrist no longer ached. She lay cradled in someone's arms, wrapped warmly in a cloak that held the clean scent of leaves and woodsmoke. A hand lightly smoothed the hair back from her face.

"Your Grace," Taroith said softly from a place very close by. Satisfaction shaded the note of exhaustion in his tone. "Your Consort has suffered no lasting harm. And I can tell you, beyond question, that she is with child."

Elienne opened her eyes, saw Darion's face bent over her. His features relaxed into a smile, and his arms tightened protectively, drawing her close against his chest. The gesture dissolved the last of her confusion, and full recognition burst through. She was free of Torkal; Cinndel's son was safe. Tears started, sudden and bright, down Elienne's cheeks.

In a voice that shook she said, "My Lord?"

The Prince leaned down and kissed her. His lips tasted of salt. Elienne clung to him, and for that moment Trathmere and Cinndel were obscured by an almost forgotten sense of peace. For the space of a second, her heart lay open to the man who held her.

Darion raised a face transformed by joy. "Did you hear?" he shouted. "My Lady shall bless the Kingdom with an heir!"

A raucous cheer arose. Elienne realized they stood ringed by the entire company of men-at-arms. Yet the Prince allowed no chance for embarrassment. He shielded her from public view with his own body and spoke quietly into her ear. "Let us go home, Lady of my heart."

His words twisted Elienne's thoughts and killed the spontaneity of the moment. She had no home. Recognition of reality chilled the warmth within her. She could not afford to allow the Prince's love for her to grow, trapped as she was by her fate. Although Faisix was imprisoned, the mutes had overheard her relate the Seeress's prophecy of failure to Kennaird the night of the betrothal banquet. Now, presumably, they had won their speech and their freedom from Taroith, making that knowledge a threat to her safety. The Prince would have to be told. But Elienne could not bear to murder his moment of triumph after so many had labored to win her back. No harm would result if she mentioned the fact another time, and when Taroith urged her to rest, she made no effort to resist.

Elienne wakened, disoriented, in a strange bed surrounded by luxury. Puzzled, she raised herself sleepily on one elbow and stared in horrified disbelief at gold-sewn bed hangings, paneled walls, and a white silk coverlet emblazoned with the royal stag of Pendaire.

"No," she said softly. Anger blazed within her. "Eternity take it, what have they done to me?" She remembered nothing beyond blankets and an open-air camp among the men-at-arms.

"Your Grace?" A beautifully groomed Lady-in-waiting stepped into the room and accorded her the courtesy of a Princess of the realm.

"Where in Ma'Diere's Name am I?"

The Lady smiled. "You are in the suite reserved for Pendaire's royal family, at the Prince's request. Neither he nor Taroith thought it fitting for you to return to the castle in the company of the men-at-arms. The Sorcerer sent you back while you slept."

Elienne rolled over and glared mutinously through the casement to a breathtaking view of the seawall, silvered still with morning dew. She said to the scenery, "Is Taroith back yet?"

"No, my Lady. He returned to Torkal to escort Faisix to captivity." The woman's features pinched into a frown. "Is anything amiss?"

Reminded of her manners, Elienne fingered the coverlet and strove to contain her agitation. "A small matter has me concerned. I'm sorry. Would it be possible for me to see Kennaird after I have dressed?"

The Lady-in-waiting's expression thawed slightly. "That could be arranged, your Grace. But wouldn't you rather eat first? Your maid has breakfast waiting."

Elienne sighed, resigned. Whether she liked it or not, she was going to be fussed over. "All right, I agree to breakfast beforehand." A rueful smile escaped her. "But must I be saddled so soon with titles? 'Elienne' is a lot less clumsy."

"You are unaccustomed to court life?" said the Lady, surprised. She cocked her pert head and suddenly her poise broke into unrestrained warmth. "I am Mirette. Shall I call the maid for your wardrobe?"

Elienne made a face and tossed off the covers. "Yes, but I don't think I'll ever get used to the formality of having help with my dress." She paused, caught by impulse. "Mirette, is there any way I can speak to the Seeress of Ma'Diere's Order?"

"She talks to no one." Mirette bent and pulled a dressing robe hurriedly from a chest. "Not even the initiates of her own Order. Following initiation, the Seeress delivers nothing but prophecies, and those only if the realm is threatened, or changed in some way, as with the royal succession."

Elienne accepted the robe, her fingers damp with sweat. "I cannot see her?"

Mirette froze, china-blue eyes widened under perfectly arched brows. "Lady, the custom for breaking her vow of silence is ritual suicide. What troubles you?"

But Elienne was not willing to share her secrets with strangers. She shrugged lightly. "I was curious. Can you forgive a foreigner's ignorance?"

Mirette nodded, not entirely convinced. Her stare lingered overly long upon Elienne's face before she left to call the maid.

The breakfast that followed was tedious. Elienne could not warm to the companionable chatter of the Ladies assigned to attend her as royal Consort. Their interest was piqued by the foreigner chosen for their Prince; though they did not pry openly, Elienne found their friendly inquiries trying, preoccupied as she was with her uneasiness concerning the Trinity of Fortune. If the prophecy was correct, she was not out of danger. Yet with Faisix imprisoned, she had no visible enemy to defend against. The mutes' knowledge of the Seeress's words was the only threat she could perceive, and over that she fretted endlessly, while one after another, Pendaire's nobility arrived to bestow felicitations upon her for her coming child. Though not officially announced, word of her pregnancy had somehow been noised abroad. Aware inheritance of a throne rested upon the fragile life within her womb, Elienne felt vulnerable. She wished her privacy had been maintained until after Darion's return, and said as much to her women after a lengthy interval of staring out the window.

"Lady, you ask too much." Taxed by her charge's moody silences, Mirette rammed her embroidery needle irritably into the surcoat she was stitching, and almost broke the thread. "Eternity." She paused to untangle a snarl. "In case you've forgotten, Darion's twenty-fifth birthday passed a week ago. The Grand Justice, by law, should have condemned him to the headsman then, except that Taroith won an abeyance until you could be rescued, on the chance you had conceived. That in itself was a precedent. Count yourself fortunate."

Shaken, Elienne murmured apology. Yet her repentance proved short-lived when, a moment later, Mirette arose to announce still another visitor.

Elienne turned from the window with an oath in questionable taste for a Princess, and added, "Ma'Diere, will they never let me alone?"

Mirette's well-bred face looked strained as a small figure in dark skirts rushed in from the antechamber, thin brown hair combed back and unfamiliarly tied with ribbons.

Elienne's bad temper dissolved into welcome. "Minksa!" she exclaimed, delighted, just as the girl flung herself into her arms.

"Lady, the mutes didn't take your baby from you. I'm so glad." She tilted her face upward, radiant. "And Taroith promised I could ask a place in your service. Will you have me?"

"Are you certain you wouldn't rather keep the company of girls your own age?"

Minksa shook her head, and seeing again the shadows of abuse in eyes which had known too much for a child, Elienne knew the girl's decision was not lightly made. The realization filled her with sudden warmth. "Of course I'll have you, Minksa."

That moment the antechamber door crashed open. Minksa started, hands closed convulsively in Elienne's skirts. Mirette jumped to her feet, exclaiming, just as Elienne looked up and saw Kennaird enter, his face flushed above black robes of mourning.

"Well, it's about time you got here." Gently Elienne disengaged Minksa's clinging fingers. "Relax, child. Kennaird won't bite. You belong here now, remember?"

The apprentice planted himself before her and said quickly, "My Lady, send your women away."

Though Elienne disliked the stiff formality of court etiquette, his abrupt lack of courtesy rankled. At her side, Minksa shifted with uneasiness. Elienne placed a sisterly arm around the girl's shoulders. "Whatever you have come to say, I have confidence my ladies can support it."

Kennaird fidgeted and said crisply, "I think not." His heavy blue eyes rested upon her, faintly annoyed. The authoritative air he tried to assume only made him seem foolish. "The Seeress of Ma'Diere's Order is dead."

"How?" Elienne felt Mirette's sudden stare, and a familiar, hollow quiver invaded her gut. *No,* she thought desperately. *Not so soon.*

"Apparently someone caused her to break her vow of silence." Flatly Kennaird elaborated. "She took her life with a ceremonial dagger reserved for that purpose alone. The initiates of her Order found her shortly after noon. Now will you send your women from the room?"

Elienne nodded, uncomfortably aware of Mirette's speculative interest. She knew there would be gossip concerning her request to see the Seeress only that morning, but that was unavoidable. Minksa's offer of service had seen a rude beginning, as well.

Nettled by Kennaird's tactlessness, Elienne tried her best to ease the girl's uneasiness. "Go along with Mirette, child. She will look after your needs in my place until I am free."

The instant the door closed, Elienne rounded upon the apprentice. *"Who could have caused such a thing?"*

Kennaird shrugged, disturbed. "No one knows. Not even the initiates." He sounded strangely irresolute, like a guilty child.

Elienne struggled to master her own fear. "The mutes? Do you suppose there's *another* Sorcerer in league with them?"

"No. Definitely not." Kennaird stepped back awkwardly and sat down on Mirette's embroidery. Fortunately the needle had been left poked through the stuffed arm of the chair. Oblivious, the apprentice continued. "Emrith checked. Aisa and Denji have not left Torkal."

Elienne felt the blood beat in her veins like the wings of pigeons startled into flight. "Then who? I told no one of the prophecy other than you."

Kennaird sighed and pushed a fallen lock of hair ineffectively over his bald spot. "Not even the League knows how it happened. Faisix has been in their custody the entire time. . . . The incident may not be connected with the succession at all, but I thought you should be warned."

But it was connected, Elienne was certain, and Kennaird's attempt to dismiss the matter only augmented her concern. Though Ielond had recommended she trust him, he seemed a poor ally. But until the return of the Prince, a fortnight distant, Kennaird, Minksa, and Mirette were the only allies she had.

*   *   *

Yet despite her foreboding, the interval before the royal arrival passed without mishap, except that Minksa grew careless the morning of Darion's return and cut her finger on a breadknife. Elienne herself attended to salve and bandages, that the child could watch for the royal cortege from the battlements. Unsettled by the cheerful company of her women, Elienne finally made excuses to Mirette and donned a cloak to join the child's outdoor vigil. As she buttoned the garment, she overheard whispers that the Prince's absence appeared to have tried her sorely: how thoughtless she was to expose herself needlessly to chill during pregnancy.

"Never mind the rain," said Mirette, nettled still by her mistress's rebellious insistence. "Pray the air will improve her temper."

Elienne sighed. The women believed her impetuosity to be the inevitable result of new love. Actually, she needed a chance to compose herself, that Darion's homecoming not take her unprepared. She waited on the battlements to allow space to contain her emotions before she greeted Darion in the courtyard. At all costs, she must not allow his love for her to continue. With the exposure of Cinndel's child unavoidably to come, disaster would result if sentiment prompted him to defend her against the wrath of a betrayed court.

Elienne left the keep stair and stepped out onto stone sleek with puddles. A sharp wind dragged at her skirts. Through a misty curtain of rain, she saw Minksa curled expectantly against the wall that overlooked the main gates. Her hood had fallen back, and loosened hair had blown into tangles, threaded with sodden red ribbons.

Elienne crossed the open space between. "You don't look much like a Consort's Lady, Missy." She straightened the girl's damp locks and tucked them back into her hood.

Minksa lifted a face pink with excitement. "That's too fine a cloth for bad weather, your Grace." She capped her accusation with a mischievous grin.

"I know." Elienne glanced ruefully down, saw the delicately embroidered fabric now wilted miserably against her shoulders. "This was the plainest cloak I could find in the wardrobe."

Which was one thing she would change at once, she decided, if Darion would allow her a seamstress. She had always been accustomed to activity in Trathmere, and riding and hawking might become her only release from the pressures of the intrigue that ringed her round. Pregnant or not, she had no intention of sitting indoors day after weary day.

Lulled into reverie by the steady splash of the storm, Elienne nearly missed the first sight of the Prince's escort. Minksa's exclamation roused her. Small, cold fingers plucked insistently at her elbow, and following the girl's gesture, Elienne caught a glimpse of banners muted by mist before the cavalcade vanished behind a stand of trees. The nervous rush that followed caught her totally by surprise.

Irritated, Elienne bit her lip. What possessed her, that she felt suddenly overwhelmed? *I don't love this Prince,* she insisted to herself. But she could not deny she cared, and that she was honestly glad to see him.

The horsemen reappeared closer and swept at a canter around the final bend in the sea road before the castle gates. "There's his Grace," said Minksa, startling her once again from thought. The townsfolk who had turned out in greeting raised a rough cheer.

Elienne leaned over the battlements to see better, and a sudden gust streamed her cloak like a banner. Attracted by bright, yellow-gold cloth against gray sky, Darion looked up and immediately recognized who awaited him in the rain. The weary line of his shoulders straightened as he lifted a hand from the rein and swept off his helmet in salute to his Consort.

Elienne felt her stomach tighten with unwanted emotion. She stepped back stiffly from the battlements. Bitterly Elienne remembered the uncontrolled moment of warmth she had shown the Prince upon her rescue from Torkal, and regretted that loss of restraint. As Elienne made her way down the keep steps, Minksa's joyous shouts of greeting were like a knife in her back.

The courtyard was cold and exposed to the bite of the sea

wind. Elienne stood amid an expanse of rain-pocked cobbles as the ranks of horsemen clattered through the gates. Darion was soaked, but resplendent, in enameled armor chased with gold. He dismounted, smiling, and threw his reins to the groom who ran at his stirrup.

"My Lady!" His shout lifted easily over the crack of hooves and the rattle of winches from the gatehouse.

He crossed the yard at a half run, and Elienne saw he was stiff with fatigue from the saddle. He deserved nothing less than warm welcome, hot spirits, and back rub. A thick lump knotted her throat; desperately, she forced her emotion back.

"My Lady?" Darion reached her, arms outflung to embrace her.

Threatened by unwanted empathy, Elienne avoided his eyes. She curtsied formally, and felt Darion's hands touch her shoulders in a belated attempt to recover his equilibrium.

"My Lady, I am glad to see you are recovered from your captivity." His words sounded forced.

Elienne raised herself, glad of the rain that hid the wetness on her cheeks. "Welcome back, your Grace. Your presence has been greatly missed at court." She sensed the longing in his voice and knew she was not callous enough to risk a prolonged encounter. "Your Grace, I have a request."

"You need only to ask." Warmth crept back into his voice.

Elienne steeled herself against compassion. "Could you arrange a horse and a hawk for me? I am weary of the indoors."

For a moment, Darion stood utterly still. Then he raised a hand to rake wet locks back from his collar. "Of course," he said at last, disappointment completely controlled. "I shall speak to the Stable Master at once, and the Master Falconer." He paused. "You'll want proper attire. I'll have the steward appoint you a tailor."

Elienne murmured polite thanks, and repeated her curtsy. Darion took her hand, lightly kissed it, then moved off without comment. She dared a look at his back then, and at once saw the cost of her resolve to spare him from entanglement. His anguish stopped the breath in her throat. Her façade shattered, Elienne fled back into the castle.

Elienne returned to her chambers soaked and shaken. Mirette and her women accosted her immediately with scolding and hot towels. And that, suddenly, became more than she could bear.

"Leave me," she said, driven beyond politeness. "I want to be alone."

The women were slow to respond.

Elienne whirled sharply on Mirette. "Did you hear? Get them out."

The door closed with accusing control. But Elienne was far beyond noticing nuances. She flung herself headlong across the stag medallion on the bed and wept for the man who had ridden himself to exhaustion for five weary weeks in her behalf. Memory of his stony-faced kiss returned to cut her. Had he shown anger or resentment at her rejection, her cold response would have been easier to justify. Instead, he had mastered his disappointment, determined despite his own desires to grant her release and leave her free to find happiness unencumbered by guilt. "I cannot promise I will love your Prince," she had said to Ielond on the icefield. "Husband he may be, but only in name. My heart is not available for bargain."

Caught by a wave of misery, Elienne failed to hear the click of the door latch. Her women were not present to warn the pageboy who entered of her presence. His chatter died, mid-sentence. Startled, Elienne raised flooded eyes and with a horrid shock recognized the black enameled armor he carried.

"Mikon, is something wrong?" called a familiar voice from the corridor, and unaware of her, Darion appeared, framed by the lighted square of the doorway. Elienne confronted him knowing she had no hope of concealing the evidence of her tears.

His features momentarily registered shock. Then he looked suddenly away, all brisk efficiency, and lifted a towel from the hands of the page who stood, stunned and staring still with curiosity.

"Leave us," he said gently. "I will attend to my own needs this once, and I think if you ask the cooks nicely, there are pastries waiting."

The boy deposited his burden with a noisy clatter and departed in high spirits for the kitchens. Darion ruffled his wet head with the towel, then rescued his swordbelt from a precarious position against the wall and hung it carefully on a chairback. He stood with hands rested on the gold boss of his buckler and glanced across the bed where she sat.

"Lady, do you still grieve for the one you have lost?"

Though allowed space to compose herself, Elienne groped for a plausible response. Should Darion discover the feelings she kept hidden, her posture of assumed indifference could never be salvaged. Having no better excuse than the one he already offered, Elienne made herself speak. "I miss him, your Grace."

Stitched leather buckled under Darion's fingers, and his features assumed the rigid mask she recalled from the mirrowstone's view of his confrontation with the headsman. Elienne looked away. She raged at her own thoughtlessness, for forgetting her place of refuge had been the Prince's own apartments. His discomfort tore her the worse for being her own fault.

Darion answered, presently, in a voice that was too steady. "I should never have moved you in here. I'm sorry."

"No. I'm sorry." Elienne stared helplessly at the stag medallion on the counterpane as Darion stepped back through the doorway. She heard, through the open door, a quietly phrased request that the old Queen Mother's apartments be opened and aired. Mirette's voice queried him once, sharply.

"Never ask that again, madam," said Darion softly, but with unforgettable force. "Concern yourself with your mistress's well-being. She has need of a friend."

Elienne heard his step on the stair. He did not return. Presently Mirette entered. She had been weeping. After a hostile glare at Elienne, she began to empty the wardrobe.

"You are to be moved to other apartments, my Lady," she said tartly, and Elienne perceived that the woman's bitterness was rooted in sympathy for the Prince. In time, she knew her strained relations with Darion would create irreparable enmity in a person who had closer contact with her than any other, a situation she could ill afford.

Elienne made an attempt to avert the worst. "Mirette, can we talk about it?"

Mirette banged down a chest lid and reached to fasten the latch. Her hand shook. "His Grace said you were not to be faulted. I have no desire to know more."

Wounded more deeply than she cared to admit by the rebuff, Elienne wondered briefly whether the bed of the Khadrachi Inquisitor might have been the easier fate to manage.

She saw little of Darion in the following weeks. Those meetings which were unavoidable were always public, and handled invariably with deferent reserve. Elienne found even the briefest encounters abrasive. Time did not smooth her tangled emotions, and Mirette's stiff silences became a constant reminder that her adherence to solitude was gracelessly cruel to a man who deserved better. Elienne escaped to the stables as often as she could.

The Horse Master had chosen her a pert chestnut mare, spirited, but obedient to the rein. Though Elienne had preferred more challenging mounts in Trathmere, she was content during pregnancy with a quieter animal; and the mare had good stamina and comfortable gaits. Accompanied by a groom and two men-at-arms in royal livery, Elienne spent long hours riding the hills above the harbor. Her escort quickly learned that she desired silence. Out of respect, they often hung back and allowed her to ride ahead in solitude, for which Elienne was grateful.

The Horse Master glowed with pride over the mare's glossy new growth of muscle. "The Lady'll make a fine Queen," he boasted to her groom, unaware that she had lingered in the stall to give the mare a carrot. "Pushes the best out o' that animal, yet never a mark of abuse. And she's tough. Rides even with the morning sickness, did ye know?"

The groom knew. Elienne colored and laid her cheek against the mare's silky neck. She had twice had to dismount, only that day. But not even nausea was enough to keep her indoors, under Mirette's accusing eyes. And though Minksa remained a staunch friend, Elienne's reticence toward the

Prince distressed her. Where initially the girl's confidence had begun to blossom under the first love and understanding she had known in fourteen years of life, now she lapsed often into odd periods of silence. It was a pity, Elienne reflected. She let herself out of the stall and set the bolt securely. The child at present was the only measurable good she had done anyone since her arrival in Pendaire.

The stable was strangely deserted for mid-morning. Elienne paused in the aisle, alerted to the reason by the clang of the gate and a rattle of hooves and harness in the courtyard. A large cortege had just arrived. Though the commotion probably heralded nothing more than the arrival of a border patrol, she shook the straw impatiently from the hem of her habit and hurried outside.

The courtyard was jammed with riders. Cloaked against the early autumn chill, they dismounted from animals slick and steaming with sweat. Elienne identified the gold and black surcoats of the royal guard, but, backlighted by a cloud-streaked sky, the standard at the head of the column bore the argent and blue blazon of the Sorcerers' League. Taroith must have returned at last, from the keep where Faisix was held in custody. In the midst of the jumble, his tall, white-haired figure caught her eye.

"Gifted!" Elienne started forward, pleased.

Though her hail could not possibly have been heard above the din, the Sorcerer glanced around. His smile of welcome gave her a twinge of discomfort; inevitably he would ask after the Prince.

Taroith left his horse with a groom and made his way through the press to where she stood. "You look thin," he observed as he tugged the riding gloves from his fingers. "Is the pregnancy giving you difficulty?"

Elienne saw advantage in the excuse. "A bit. Yet not enough to keep me indoors." She attempted to divert the Sorcerer's scrutiny with a change of subject. "Gifted, I'm glad you're back."

Taroith's gaze stayed on her face, and he made no effort to answer. Uneasily, Elienne stared at the bustle of men-at-arms and horses being led away. Whether or not the Sorcerer guessed that she had estranged herself from Darion, he would soon find out. She regretted her impulsive greeting and wished instead she had returned to her chambers without calling attention to herself. The sun burst through a break in the clouds, drenching the scene in light. Bright amid the gray steel helms of the guardsmen, a fair-haired head caught her attention.

Elienne felt gooseflesh ripple the skin on her neck and arms. "Faisix is with you?"

Darion's antagonist stood, unrestrained, amid a group of halberdiers. An unfamiliar Sorcerer stood with them. Shocked that a traitor who had engaged Black Sorcery against the crown should be permitted the liberty of escort without bonds, Elienne glanced questioningly at Taroith. "They aren't going to free him, are they?"

The Sorcerer's eyes left her at last. "No." He gazed at his hands. "He will not be released. The League will plead for his life, but he may yet face the headsman. It is a pity."

"A pity?" Elienne scuffed savagely at a tuft of moss between the cobbles. "You said yourself he was mad. A killer. And the Seeress was murdered by someone who wished to know her secrets."

Taroith touched her gently on the arm. "There is no way known to League mystery, or Black Sorcery either, that Faisix could personally have been involved with breaking the Seeress's vows of silence. His death would achieve nothing. Alive, he has something left of dignity, and a chance to recover from his mistakes."

Though Elienne had seen enough of death to sympathize, the Sorcerer's logic did nothing to relieve her inner distress. Perhaps she was hopelessly prejudiced, but she was unable to imagine that the man who had tormented her could ever recover humanity enough to be trusted.

"You don't believe me." Taroith withdrew his hand and sighed with weary regret. "Lady, look at him. See for yourself. Perhaps then you'll gain a measure of understanding."

Elienne did not wish to comply. The raw forces that once had swept her from Ielond's arms during transfer were too potent a memory for simple forgiveness, whatever sentiment the sight of the man who had wielded them might arouse. Since she could not dismiss the issue without appearing hard-hearted, reluctantly she looked again.

The square had cleared partially, allowing a clear view of the prisoner. Though his tall frame and elegantly handsome features were recognizably the same, the man himself had changed profoundly since Elienne had seen him last. From bared head to the plain, unassuming set of his shoulders, the former Regent exhibited a poignant humility that alienated all previous impressions. Even from a distance, his expression of sorrow touched the marrow of Elienne's soul. She swallowed, suddenly subdued. As though purged by remorse and loss, Faisix seemed reawakened to compassion. His attitude of deferent gentleness made her heart cry out for reprieve, even against the recent scars of remembered terror.

"I don't understand," she said softly.

"That's not surprising." Taroith steered her across the cobbles toward the palace door. "You lack the background. Faisix's father, the old Earl of Torkal, was killed in a drunken quarrel with his steward. His son was ten at the time, and motherless. Ielond took him in, reared him as his own. The boy idolized him."

Taroith opened the heavy, studded panel door and waited for Elienne to pass. "As a child, Faisix had tremendous aptitude for sorcery. Everyone assumed, when he came of age, he would apply for League training."

The Sorcerer fell silent. His booted step echoed hollowly down the corridor. At his side, Elienne waited patiently for him to resume. Taroith halted abruptly. Tall lancet windows silhouetted his gaunt frame as he drew breath, and his words fell as an incantation upon stillness.

"The requirements for apprenticeship are unimaginably stringent. It takes a bold heart and a dedicated, disciplined mind to undertake the examination for candidacy. Only the strongest are permitted to try, for the slightest irregularity of character is enough to constitute failure. And failure, without exception, engenders emotional loss greater than anything else a human soul can endure. The effect can be crippling; some aspirants never recover."

"Then Faisix was found unsuitable?" said Elienne. A gust rattled loudly against the leaded glass casements. She had to lean close to hear Taroith's reply.

"Ielond himself conducted the test. He was a fair judge, though the adverse decision must have cost him great pain. At first Faisix seemed to handle it well. He went on to become a brilliant statesman and was granted the Regency when Darion's parents perished in the fire." Taroith gazed out over wind-tossed gardens. "No one knows what turned him, whether he became jealous of the Prince for sharing Ielond's affections, or whether, all along, resentment of his rejection from apprentice-ship festered in him. Whatever the cause, the League assumes full responsibility. I will save him from execution, if I can. The Prince supports me."

The statement came as a surprise, reminding Elienne of the distance that separated her from Darion. Weeks had passed since she had last reached for the mirrowstone, and for days at a stretch she had avoided his company. Caught suddenly by a chill of foreboding, she realized how easily that isolation might augment the threat to her child and Darion's succession. For though Faisix's repentant attitude roused her to pity, she did not trust him.

Despite Taroith's insistence, she was not convinced that the Seeress's death was coincidence. The only justification she had to balance her distrust lay in the third of the Trinity of Fortune that was hers alone. Elienne laced her fingers tightly together to keep from shaking openly. Above anything else, she did not want to confide that information. In the wrong hands, the knowledge could ruin her.

"Gifted," she said at last. "I think you are making a grave mistake."

Chapter 12

Ielond's Paradox

Taroith abandoned the window, his expression sharply surprised. His dark eyes met hers with a directness that turned Elienne's chills to sweat.

"Tell me why, Lady."

Elienne fought an onset of discomfort. Ielond had urged her to seek Taroith's guidance, yet intuition made her suddenly doubt the advice. Repentant or not, Faisix sought her destruction. Uncertain how to express her mistrust, and pinned by the intensity of the Sorcerer's attention, Elienne groped clumsily for a reply.

A shout in the corridor spared her. With characteristically poor timing, Kennaird burst around a bend into view, the hem of his mourning robe splattered heavily with mud. "Master Taroith!" He paused to catch his breath and rubbed a nose pink with chill. "Have they told you? The Grand Council has appointed you Regent until Darion's coronation."

"I was aware." Taroith stepped back from the window and resumed his interrupted course.

Kennaird tagged along as though waiting for the Sorcerer to comment. When none was forthcoming, he said, "Aren't you pleased? It's quite an honor."

The Sorcerer answered reluctantly. "I have accepted as a formality of Law." He reached the doorway to his own chambers and paused with his hand on the latch. "I informed the Council members that Darion will make the decisions. I have enough to occupy me without adding troublesome matters of state to the list."

Elienne observed the apprentice's crestfallen expression with distaste. Kennaird seemed to relish gossip like an old crone, an odd and embarrassing trait for one who had reputably passed Ielond's examination for apprenticeship. Briefly Elienne wondered what the dead Sorcerer had seen in the man, unaware Taroith echoed her thought.

But as Master of the Sorcerers' League, his concern went deeper; surely as the stars turned, when mourning for Ielond was past, Kennaird would appeal for continuation of his training. Yet that responsibility was seven months distant. Taroith put it from his mind.

"Good day, my Lady, Kennaird. The journey has tired me." The Sorcerer bowed respectfully to Elienne and retired to his chambers.

Kennaird sighed and walked on. Headed in the same direction, Elienne went with him, absorbed and silent.

Kennaird interrupted rudely with a question. "What has happened between you and the Prince?"

Elienne stopped cold and regarded him through narrowed eyes. "Ask his Grace."

"I did." Kennaird glared back, fingers knotted belligerently in his belt. "He refused to say."

Angered, Elienne produced a honeyed smile Jieles would have recognized. "Then I have nothing to add. I'm on my way to the privy. Are you going to follow?"

Kennaird's round face turned an unbecoming shade of puce. "You're the cause of a lot of talk."

"You're adding to it. I'm not interested." While the apprentice was still flustered, Elienne stepped past and left him standing stupidly at the foot of a flight of stairs. However highly Ielond had regarded his apprentice, she was unable to respect the man. Kennaird had irritated her ever since that first day he had scolded Minksa. With sudden longing, Elienne realized how greatly she missed the Prince's staunch logic. He alone had breached her loneliness. Yet even his friendship might endanger his succession, and the people of Pendaire needed his rule.

Fall wrapped the countryside in flame-colored splendor, and a fortnight of brisk, golden days blessed Pendaire. Darion gave Minksa a pony, and for a short while the girl accompanied Elienne riding. But the mild weather broke early that year. Thick frosts withered the late-blooming roses in the gardens beyond her window. Bent brown stalks rattled in the wind like ranks of aged spearmen, until autumn rains beat them flat. Elienne began to feel less ill in the mornings, and Mirette commented that her riding habits were becoming snug about the waist.

"You'll have to put the mare to pasture soon, I think," she said.

Elienne twisted her hair into a knot and pinned it with more force than necessary. "I'll have the seamstress let them out." She jammed her cap on her head and rose from the mirror.

Mirette gathered skirts of rose silk trimmed with fur and stepped out of her path. She had learned respect for her mistress's temper. "You shall not be able to ride much longer, Lady, without risk to your child." Her soft complexion and rich clothes made her look more like the Princess than Darion's Consort, who was dressed for bad weather, and whose skin was roughened from exposure to wind and sun.

Elienne tossed her cloak over her shoulders and left the room without answer. Once outdoors, she allowed her oath of aggravation to mingle with the rain. Would Mirette never understand her mare was the only thing left which gave her pleasure? She dreaded the day she could no longer ride; her mornings out were all that made her isolation from Darion tolerable.

She returned, chilled, and wet to the skin, having ridden farther than usual. Even her escort had complained. Elienne entered her apartment and flung off her dripping cloak, braced to endure Mirette's annoyance. Yet no scolding arose to disturb her.

Elienne paused with her hand half-raised. Her women were absent. Darion sat in one of the brocade armchairs beside the fire, alone. Elienne tensed, wary lest she reveal her vulnerability. His gaze fixed upon her, chilly as the breakers on the north beach, and the velvet of his surcoat rose and fell evenly, unmarred by quickened breath.

He looked down at his hands. "You asked to see me?"

The wet bodice seemed suddenly tight around Elienne's chest. Words became difficult. "I was worried."

"About Faisix?" Darion rose and smoothly turned the adjacent armchair toward the fire. "You're cold. Won't you sit?"

Elienne stepped back. "I'll spoil the brocade."

Darion smiled with sudden, unexpected warmth. "I believe you're worth it. But if you get much thinner, I'll have to reconsider. I thought the sickness had stopped?"

"It has." Trapped by a shiver of chill, she grinned back. "You explain to Mirette." She dragged her muddy skirts across the carpet and settled herself before the hearth.

Darion remained standing. "You were worried?" Cautiously he folded his arms and rested his weight against the chairback.

"Yes." The fact that he was behind her, out of view, set her somewhat at ease. "Jieles told me the Grand Justice meets tomorrow to determine Faisix's sentence. He thought they would spare his life."

"I would support such a decision," said Darion. "Do you wish him dead?"

A log fell, and sparks fluttered, brief and bright as fireflies in the updraft. Though Elienne wished to sound objective, a tremor invaded her voice. "Lord, I fear for the safety of my child."

He had leaned close to her. Elienne felt the current of his sigh tickle her neck. "Above all others, I expected you to understand the futility of executions."

Elienne closed her eyes, tried frantically to stem the emotion that locked her throat. She wanted to tell him of the Seeress's prophecy; that she would fail him, and perhaps lose the son she had left Trathmere to save. Yet the most she could do was shake her head.

Darion left the chair. He crossed in front of her and sat on the settle by her knee. The fire traced copper highlights in his hair. "My Lady, you have nothing to fear."

His sincerity made her afraid that the barrier of distance she had raised between them would shatter under the stress. But he only gathered her cold hands into his own calloused, warm ones in brotherly concern. "Elienne, trust me. Faisix will never leave the custody of the League. He regrets his actions, greatly, and spends his time in meditation. I have seen him, twice. He bears no malice toward you, or the child you bear. You are secure here, I promise. My word as Halgarid's heir."

Elienne shivered, unable to speak of the uneasiness she had felt since the day of the Seeress's murder. "Ielond discovered the secrets of Time through meditation."

"Ielond had League training, and the accumulated wisdom of a very long life." Darion chafed her wrists. "You're chilled. And you spend too much time alone, which does you no good. If my company causes you discomfort, try to confide in Mirette. She has a gentle heart and is trustworthy. I chose her for discretion, and Ielond never intended you to be without friends."

He released her hands and rose. "This is your home now. I want you to be happy. Will you try?"

Shamed, Elienne summoned a smile. "I've been rotten." She would plainly have to shoulder her doubts by herself, and the Prince needed no added burden of concern. "Can you forget?"

"About what?" Darion made a droll face and left her, still grinning, in the seat by the fire.

A few minutes later, Mirette appeared with dry clothing. She made no comment on the waterstained brocade. "My Lady, there's hot tea waiting."

Elienne stirred, and noticed an unfamiliar glitter on her finger. With a small gasp of surprise, she lifted her hand and saw the topaz and gold of the Consort's betrothal ring she had lost during transfer to Torkal. The band this time fit perfectly; Darion must have left it on her finger, and through her confusion, she had not noticed. She felt, suddenly, as though she had been knifed. "Ma'Diere, how can I support this?" She raised a face stamped with feelings she could not curb, and saw sympathy on Mirette's pretty features.

"I'm glad to see you don't hate him." The statement was one of observation rather than malice.

"No." Elienne thrust her hand into the soggy sleeve of

her riding habit. "No. I never hated him." And she permitted Mirette to fuss over her without stiffening in distaste.

The following afternoon, the Grand Justice sentenced Faisix, Earl of Torkal, to life imprisonment under wardenship of the Sorcerers' League. In response, Elienne lengthened her rides into the hills above the castle. She slept poorly at night. Within a fortnight, her exhaustion had advanced to the point where Mirette sought Darion's counsel. She met him seated at breakfast.

His reply was immediate, and mercilessly direct. "Have Kennaird escort Elienne down to the cell for a visit."

Mirette flinched in anticipation of Elienne's response. "She won't like it."

The Prince set his knife carefully aside. Morning sunlight fell through the diamond panes of the casement, spotlighting his hands as he laced them together and leaned forward. "Be easy on her. Elienne has good reason to be nervous. The man tried to kill her, twice."

Mirette's elegant features paled. "Your Grace, she never told me."

Darion stared at his plate. "I didn't expect she had." He said nothing more. Mirette curtsied, though he never looked up, and silently left him.

"I won't go!" said Elienne explosively, when told why Kennaird awaited her in the anteroom. Her knuckles tightened against the comb with which she had been straightening Minksa's hair. "What possessed him, that he thought I would wish to see Faisix?"

"He acts under his Grace's orders." Mirette braced herself, expecting sharp language in reply. Even now she did not regret her interference. The Lady Elienne was lately consumed from within by restlessness that nothing seemed to assuage. The Prince had been the only one who could reason with her at all.

Yet instead of her usual oaths, Elienne became suddenly still. Too still, Mirette thought.

"I suppose you informed the Prince I haven't slept," she

said softly. "I wish you had spared him. If I go quietly, will you promise the next time to keep your mouth shut?"

Startled speechless by a reaction she could not possibly have anticipated, Mirette nodded.

Elienne handed her comb to Minksa. "I'll finish your hair later, Missy."

Minksa dumped a fistful of ribbons on the dresser. "I want to come."

"No." Elienne was adamant. "Absolutely not. One of us is too many."

Though the corridor which led to Faisix's cell was nothing like the dank stone passages of Trathmere's dungeon, Elienne felt as though she had just been immersed in ice water. No good would come of this visit. A chill of foreboding preoccupied her as she followed Kennaird down a carpeted stair into a chamber unnaturally lit by harsh, blue-white light.

Before her, etched out by the glare of an enchanter's wards, was a steel-barred enclosure similar to the one that had imprisoned Taroith. The structure had no visible door. A Sorcerer stood watch to one side.

Elienne's eyes adjusted to the dazzling brilliance slowly. After an interval, she made out the image of a figure beyond.

"I have brought the royal Consort to see Faisix, at his Grace's request," said Kennaird.

The attendant Sorcerer dimmed the wards, allowing a clear view of the prisoner. The former Regent sat comfortably in a stuffed chair, profile toward them. He was thinner, Elienne noted. With his eyes closed in meditation, she saw beyond distractions of character and finely proportioned bone structure to an abiding harmony with life, which momentarily defied thought. The effect terrified her, as nothing had before. Elienne stepped clumsily backward into Kennaird.

He caught her in startled embarrassment, just as Faisix stirred and raised opened eyes to his warden.

"I see I have distinguished visitors." His honey-colored hair glanced in the light as he rose and bowed respectfully to Elienne. "My Lady, I'm glad to see you are well."

Elienne shook off Kennaird's hands. "It wasn't my idea to come here."

"That's understandable." The expression of peace on Faisix's features remained imperturbed. He seated himself smoothly. "They tell me you will give birth to a healthy son five months from now." His gaze touched the green velvet that girdled her thickened waistline. "I see this is so, and wish you joy upon the occasion."

Unsettled by his reference to the child, Elienne wanted to leave at once. Her reply came out edged with mistrust. "I won't forget."

"Neither will I." Faisix returned the hostility with frank acceptance. "I felt an apology would be worse than useless, even insulting. I want no more injury between us. And I think the Prince would understand if you go without belaboring the point. I'm not proud of reminders, either."

Elienne could not bring herself to answer. Inexplicably uneasy, she addressed the League Master who safeguarded the cell. "Gifted, I've seen enough."

The Sorcerer stepped forward to restore the potency of the wards. Though he worked with unerring efficiency, Elienne had a sudden, overwhelming premonition that all was not well. She looked up, just before the sorcery flared active, and saw that Faisix watched her still. His yellow eyes scarred her like a brand. Sudden dizziness spun her vision out of focus. In the blue-white deluge of light that followed, she thought she saw Ielond against the desolate emptiness of Ceroth. Memory of his words surfaced to haunt her. "*We're going to change history, my Lady, and send Faisix to his Damnation.*"

She wanted to cry out, to warn that the man in the cell was evil and still capable of inflicting great harm. But no words came. She swayed on her feet, caught by a firm pair of hands.

The face of the Master Sorcerer wavered above her. "...strength of the wards," he was saying. "The effects of close proximity have disoriented her. She'll recover quickly enough. Just take her out."

Elienne felt herself transferred to Kennaird, who guided her stumbling steps back the way they had come. Once she was clear of the cell, the vertigo passed almost at once. Elienne caught the railing of the stair, sweat cold on her skin. "I hope his Grace is satisfied," she said tartly to Kennaird. "I won't repeat that experience."

The apprentice regarded her with sympathy. "I doubt he would ask again. Are you all right?"

Elienne nodded, though her heart raced still. She climbed the stair unassisted, preoccupied by the remembered statement of Ielond's. Her fear was justified. But not even the wisest masters in Pendaire perceived Faisix as a threat, secure as they were in the powers of their sorcery.

"Lady, the hook won't fasten." The maid leaned to one side, hands clutching the waistband of Elienne's dress. "Do you want me to call the seamstress, or shall I fetch the blue skirt you wore yesterday?"

Elienne touched her swollen middle with a resigned sigh. "The blue will be fine. I don't expect the Prince's healers will let me ride much longer, anyway."

"I would think the weather would stop you," said Mirette from the window seat. "The sentries on the north gate came in complaining of frostbite."

Elienne shrugged out of the dress that no longer fit. "It rained only yesterday."

"*After* it snowed." Mirette set her sewing aside and flung back the curtain. A cold draft spilled across the room from the uncovered casement. "It's turned bitter."

Yet not even the sight of fields leaden-gray under a mantle of new ice prevented Elienne from making her usual trip to the stable. The Horse Master greeted her with a lighted pipe, a sure sign that he had not been overseeing the saddling of her horse.

"What's wrong?" Elienne knew a moment of apprehension. "Is Abette lame?"

The Horse Master puffed his reddened cheeks until his whiskers bristled. "She's at her hay, and well sound. But she won't stay so if ye go out. Ice'll cut her legs. Best to wait. There'll be a thaw."

Elienne returned to her chambers, disconsolate. The healer had granted her no more than one more week of liberty, and with a freeze as deep as the one currently gripping Pendaire, a quick thaw was unlikely. She had watched Mirette amuse herself with an endless succession of sewing projects, aware such activities would do little to maintain her spirits through the weary months to come.

"You could always start on things for the baby," Mirette suggested, and wondered afterward why Elienne requested books, her gaze fixed morosely on the ice-glazed gardens beyond the casement.

An oppressive silence lasted until Minksa burst in from the anteroom in boisterous high spirits. "Elienne!" Her skirt knocked Mirette's thread basket, and spools bounced helter-skelter across the carpet.

"Child, will your manners never improve?" Mirette rose, watching her feet. "And that was no proper address for a Lady who might become Queen of the Realm."

"I'm sorry." Minksa curtsied precariously among the spools and in the same motion bent to pick them up. "Lady," she said from her hands and knees on the rug. "The Prince has come to see you."

Caught unprepared, Elienne left the window. She directed a suspicious glare at Mirette. "Was this your doing?" But the Lady-in-waiting's startled expression was genuine. *Why,* Elienne wondered, and sat hastily in the chair farthest from the door.

A moment later, Darion entered, arms loaded with books and a small wooden chest inlaid with mother-of-pearl. He spotted Elienne by the fire and smiled. "I thought I'd find you sulking." With the controlled grace of perfect fitness he crossed the room and deposited his burden on the side table next to her. He sat down.

Elienne shut her eyes, unwilling to respond for fear loneliness would betray her.

"Please," she said softly. "I don't want company."

Darion opened the box, which contained chess pieces. "You play, don't you?"

"I'm insufferably out of practice." Elienne felt her palms break into sweat. He had known what loss of her daily ride had meant; his kindness besieged the integrity of her decision to remain separate, and left no avenue for graceful retreat. Tormented by desire to reach out and use what he offered, Elienne watched his hands as he laid out the board. Yet even that proved a mistake.

The beautiful, long fingers were roughened from weather, and calloused like a mercenary's. Elienne caught her breath. Even Cinndel's knuckles had not chapped that severely on campaign against the Khadrach.

Distressed, Elienne looked further, and saw wrists grown sinewy from long hours in the tiltyard. She understood, suddenly, what brought Darion to her chambers with chessmen. Exercise had been his outlet, also. Weather had deprived them both, and he had resolved to confront the source of his pain, perhaps to overcome it if he could.

His determination cut her. And Ielond's diabolical thoroughness had ensured she was a fanatical devotee of chess. Conscious of failing strength, and resolved not to let the Prince guess, she fought back. "You must have better things to occupy you."

Darion set the last piece in place with barely a pause. "I'll take black, for having nothing better. The council chamber offers little other than glorified scrapping among old men. Your move."

Elienne bit her lip, momentarily defeated by his charm. Intending to discourage him with dull strategy, she reached for a pawn.

Yet he caught her drift early in the game and managed to maneuver his own king into peril first. He sat back in his chair and watched her search in smothered dismay for a move that would not place him in check without sacrifice. There was none. The situation became suddenly comic. Elienne tried to choke back a grin.

"You must like stomachaches," said Darion, red-faced himself. A moment later, he doubled helplessly over the board, scattering chess pieces like smallshot. His laughter mingled with hers.

The irresistible rapport of shared amusement sobered Elienne first. Events seemed to conspire against her, displaying always the charm, the wit, and the high spirit of the man whose destiny Ielond had joined with hers; the Sorcerer had intended the attraction. Yet poisoned by the uncertainty of her future, Elienne still held back. This discomfort was surely kinder than the grief she had known upon Cinndel's death.

Conscious of her silence, Darion caught his breath. "We'll play again." He ducked beneath the table to rescue the fallen game pieces. His voice emerged, muffled. "This time, to the bitter death, with no bowing out."

With far more at stake than a chess game, Elienne chose not to put his challenge to the test. She rose quickly, while he was occupied and disadvantaged, and retreated to the bay of casements which overlooked the sea. Leaden combers battered the shoreline, carved into spray by black rocks and the wracked debris of winter storms. A dirtied wall of snow bounded the sand above the tidemark, seaweed piled like war dead beneath.

She heard the chair creak as he straightened. Wooden counters clattered in a cascade onto maple inlay. A few rolled onto the carpet.

His booted step approached her. She stared rigidly at the horizon's gray line, sensitized to the desolation she inflicted on the man at her back. He had stopped with his hands poised, but not touching her shoulders. His arms lowered after a moment, with a soft rustle of velvet and lawn. His ring clicked against his poniard as he hooked his thumb in his belt.

"Lady, will you forgive me?"

"What is there to forgive?" said Elienne, knowing the painful barb of her own self-reproach would strike like a whip of antagonism. The wintery landscape before her shattered, viewed through a prism of tears.

With her features open to anguish, she faced him. "There is nothing between us to forgive, your Grace. *But I find no peace in your presence*. How long, before you learn mercy and leave me alone?"

The scope of his response caught her like tide, left her dizzied with pain. Unable to speak or see, she caught the paneled wall for support. Nothing reached her except the clink of the door latch that signaled Darion's departure. Caught by an ugly, wrenching sob, Elienne laid her cheek against the cold panes of the window and watched the beach blur and fade beyond a white cloud of condensation. She felt, inwardly, as though someone had put the candles out.

"*I hate you*," said Mirette suddenly, out of the dark.

Elienne stirred and slowly leaned her back against the wall. "I'm sorry." The apology seemed to flounder on the stillness.

"Sorry!" Mirette rose, furious, and confronted her with loathing evident in every line of her pose. "Ma'Diere's infinite mercy, you abuse him! He gives you the best of himself, and you fling it back in his face."

Cornered and raw with exposed nerves, Elienne frantically sought escape. "Stop. Mirette, you don't know. I have a reason."

"No reason known to man would be enough to justify what you just did." The artfully painted lines around Mirette's eyes blurred, and tears spilled over her lashes.

Elienne watched the streaks glide down perfectly tinted cheeks. Understanding imprisoned her like a trap: Mirette's suffering was caused by frustrated love of the Prince. The assault of yet another person's pain was more than she could bear, with her own feelings vulnerable to exposure. Out of need for survival, she deadened her own response. "The Prince will find another woman. I won't be jealous."

Mirette seemed not to hear. "You're cold as Eternity. If I were Consort to such a Prince, I'd count myself blessed." And that suddenly pushed the situation beyond constraint.

Elienne knew white-hot anger. "Go to him, then, if that's where your sympathies lie!"

Mirette gasped, pale beneath her rouge. She answered with vicious honesty. "I've tried. Once we were lovers. But since Ielond sent you, his Grace has eyes for no other. I curse that day. And I curse you for your cruelty."

Punished into a frame where only the absurd became tolerable, Elienne laughed. Mirette's mouth opened in shocked protest. She whirled and fled the room, leaving Elienne alone, weeping, by the window.

The morning Kennaird chose to apply for continuation of his training, sunlight through mullioned windows patterned elongated yellow diamonds across the floor of Taroith's study. The Sorcerer sat at his desk, chin rested on laced fingers. A yellow tabby cleaned her paws by his elbow, untroubled by the concern that furrowed her master's brow. Though the spring equinox was nearly come, the weather had not broken. Icicles still runged the eaves. Yet from the yard below his window, Taroith heard the crack of quarterstaffs interspersed with an occasional thump or shout as a blow landed. Darion was at practice, again, though the ground was still frozen iron-hard.

Taroith sighed. The cat looked up, then resumed her washing. Through the long winter he had seen the relationship between Prince and Consort progress from stiff to strained. Darion was left preoccupied and temperamental; and Elienne had withdrawn inside herself until even rice powder could not hide the imprint of the unhappiness that left circles beneath her eyes. Though the court gossiped openly, Taroith had not interfered. Now, with the Consort's pregnancy near term, he questioned the soundness of his judgment.

Outside, a quarterstaff smacked padded leather. Someone applauded, and the Prince's voice called challenge to another opponent. Listening, Taroith reflected grimly that Darion would be the first heir to carry bruises at a peacetime coronation. The thought spurred his concern. In bringing Elienne to Pendaire, Ielond had initiated a master plan to preserve Darion's succession. Everywhere, Taroith had encountered evidence of the Guardian's handiwork, not least in the instant and undeniable rapport between Consort and Prince, which, broken, was starving them both. Though he had implicit faith in Ielond's judgment, he wondered increasingly what had gone amiss.

The wall clock chimed the hour, and Taroith frowned. Kennaird was late. The man's haphazard habits had always been irritating. As Master of the League, he had granted the apprentice an appointment strictly out of a sense of duty.

The flat crack of quarterstaffs resumed beyond the window. Between the interplay of blows, Taroith heard a running step in the hall, followed by a sharp knock. The door opened.

Kennaird stepped in, red-faced and breathless. "I'm late. Master, will you accept my apology?" He pulled nervously at the sleeve of his rust-colored jerkin.

"I would hear your reason, first." Taroith gestured to the chair across from his desk. "Sit. You're going to be here for a while."

Kennaird's eyes widened until full rings of white showed around the blue. "You're going to—" Taroith's expression stopped him. He blinked and dumped himself into the chair, startling the tabby from the desk top. "I forgot the time, Master."

Taroith leaned on his elbows and tried to be sympathetic. "I can take nothing for granted, Kennaird. As Ielond's apprentice, you were Ielond's responsibility. If you would become mine, I must gauge for myself precisely how far your training has progressed. There is no better way than to repeat the examination for candidacy. Do you object?"

"No." Kennaird pushed knuckled hands beneath his cuffs as though chilled. "No, not at all. I just hadn't expected another soul-search, even as a formality."

"This is no formality." Taroith rose and gently nudged the tabby away from his calf. "The only difference, I hope, will be the fact we require no drug to align your consciousness. You'll be able to resolve your focus?"

"Of course," said Kennaird, affronted. "I studied nine years under Ielond."

Taroith withheld comment. After nearly a decade under one of Pendaire's finest Masters, Kennaird showed remarkably poor progress. Unsettled, the Sorcerer left the desk and positioned himself behind Kennaird, his back to the sunlit window. Had the apprentice simply been slow, or had Ielond deliberately held him back? Either way, Taroith knew he would shortly find out. He placed his hands on Kennaird's shoulders. "Resolve your focus."

Obediently, Kennaird concentrated. A faint, greenish glimmer presently illuminated the air above his head. Taroith waited briefly for the force to brighten. When it did not, he silently summoned his own focus and directed its harsh white light through Kennaird's pallid glow. The apprentice flinched under his touch.

"Steady." Taroith adjusted the balance of power. The beam from his focus passed through Kennaird's like lamplight filtered by lenses and caused a pattern projected upon the floor. Though it was a geometric abstract, the Master Sorcerer's trained perception could read from the configuration the motives and the events that comprised Kennaird's life since birth.

The effect upon the apprentice was comparable to having the mind's most secret recesses exposed and minutely searched. Taroith felt Kennaird warm under his hands. He knew his subject would shortly suffer as aftereffects a headache, and perhaps nausea, and worked swiftly to forestall as much discomfort as possible.

". . . second time you've scored," said Darion, voice dimmed by concentration. "I must be tiring. Can you make one more bout?"

Taroith did not hear the opponent's reply. Sensation and sound left him. The design encompassed his entire awareness, surrounded him as a sculptured prism of light. Almost at once, he spotted imbalances in the symmetry. Alarmed, he probed, and discovered more. *Ielond, what have you done?* he thought, embarrassed to look further. Kennaird was not, and never had been, qualified for League apprenticeship. Taroith faced the fact that Ielond would not have overlooked so gross an error. He had chosen to train Kennaird himself; there would be a reason.

Grimly the Sorcerer conjoined with the pattern; by tracing Kennaird's instabilities through past events, he hoped he would find his colleague's purpose. The scenes he traversed impressed him with trivia: a petty squabble over a toy that ended with a young brother's bloody nose; a misdealt card; plates filched from the palace kitchens; and later, a maid maneuvered into a tryst she had not wanted. She had escaped with nothing worse than embarrassment, but gossip inferred otherwise. Distastefully, Taroith searched for reason amid a tortuous maze of small-minded actions. Over the course of an entire life, he found none.

He surfaced at last, preoccupied by dilemma, and allowed his soulfocus to dissipate. Kennaird stirred. Taroith lifted his hands, silenced by the scope of his discovery.

Ashen-faced and groggy, the apprentice pressed damp palms to his temples. "That was more unpleasant than I recalled."

Taroith settled on the window seat. The courtyard below lay empty, dull gray with frozen puddles under the noon sun. As Master of the League, he could never sanction Kennaird. Yet he was reluctant to refute the man's apprenticeship publicly before he had spent more thought on the subject. He had far too much regard for Ielond's vision to discard anomaly as a mistake.

"Well?" said Kennaird. Unsettled nerves and a savage headache made him cross.

The tabby leaped lightly to the windowsill. Taroith stroked her absently and tried to smooth the gravity of the situation without arousing suspicion. "I've seen enough to know how far you progressed under Ielond. After Elienne's child is born, we'll discuss the matter further in depth."

Kennaird's mouth gaped. He stared, resentment tightening his hands on the chair until tendons quivered beneath his cuffs. "That's *all*? You perform soul-search for half a morning, and have nothing more to say?"

Taroith rose and unlatched the door with dispatch. "We'll begin, I think, with the subject of courtesy."

Kennaird swallowed. "I'm sorry. I had no right to question."

"Ask the kitchen for broth," said Taroith with an effort at kindness. The apprentice would probably be wretchedly ill most of the day. He offered his arm to steady Kennaird's first few steps.

"Thank you." The apprentice pushed sweat-drenched hair from his brow. "I'll be fine." Yet his course as he departed down the corridor was anything but straight.

Taroith saw him out of sight and left at once for the Library. There he requested to see Ielond's writ. "The original," he insisted, "not a copy."

The Archivist vanished into the stacks, grumbling, and reappeared presently with a jeweled slip case. "Were you aware his Grace had to consult this very document for the name of his intended?"

"No." Taroith accepted the parchment, the seals rough against dry fingers. "Should I be?"

He carried the document to a carrel and blew out the wax candle in its glass stand. Taroith had not come to consult the official words of state inked in Ielond's bold hand. Enveloped in thick shadow, he focused his inner awareness and flicked one thumb down the left margin, much as he had that day Elienne had arrived in the Grand Council Chamber. At his touch, a row of glyphs flashed like starlight on the page. Thin as thread, and fainter than their original appearance, the message was still cipherable. In the dim silence of the Library, Taroith reread the lines Ielond had left for his eye alone.

> *Though you discover discrepancy, allow my choice to stand. I have seen the course of my decisions. Have faith. Darion will legally inherit.*

Slowly the message faded. Taroith ran cramped fingers through his hair and sighed. He had encountered discrepancies enough to undermine the stability of the entire Kingdom. Elienne's ancestry was straight out of legend. His Grace could father no children, as the Sorcerer had seen the night he performed the healing for drug overdose. And now Kennaird proved hopelessly incompetent for a post he had held for nine years. Where, thought Taroith, did faith end, and duty begin?

That moment, the stuffy silence of the Library was shattered by the resounding peal of bells from the tower of the East Keep. Taroith started upright.

"Damn it to Eternity!" The bells could signal only one event: Elienne had gone into labor. Taroith rose and banged his knee in the dark. She was early, by a full week, according to the League astrologer's conception chart.

"Discrepancy!" Taroith muttered. He abandoned the writ where it lay. "I call it mayhem!"

Chapter 13

Backsplice

Late in the afternoon, the endless tolling of the bells in the east tower of the keep was joined by sweeter tones from the belfry of Ma'Diere's Sanctuary. Although Kennaird knew the added peals signified the arrival of a new heir to the Crown, he took no joy in the occasion. From the lofty height of the window in Ielond's study, he gazed sourly downward at the guard captain who strode across the arch above the gate, arms clutched around a massive bundle of pennants. The fellow paused beside a leaning row of halberds, the owners of which industriously cleared flag halyards stiffened with ice.

Kennaird shivered. No fire had burned in the grate since Ielond's death, yet he made no move to lay kindling. Below, the first of a multitude of banners flapped slowly skyward, gold and black, and sewn with the royal stag. Cheers arose from the crowd in the bailey. Surrounded by mounted lancers, a tabarded official waited with a coffer; tradition granted largesse to the city's poor, that all might celebrate the birth of Elienne's son.

Kennaird retreated from the window before the coins were distributed. Noise only added to his headache. But the sound of the rejoicing populace disturbed him even among the still, dust-layered rows of Ielond's books. The crease between his sandy brows deepened into a frown of displeasure. Once the library of his former Master had provided a refuge from the dissatisfaction which had galled him since childhood. But now the place aroused nothing but emptiness and the torment of remembered happiness.

Kennaird touched a familiar calf spine in sudden longing.

Something had gone wrong during his appointment with Taroith that morning. He knew the Sorcerer's oblique dismissal masked refusal. Ielond had misled him. He would not be granted training to complete his Mastership.

Spurred by a bitter pang of loss, Kennaird swore and hammered the shelf with his fist. The blow raised a dense plume of dust in the air. He stumbled back, choking. The carpet absorbed his enraged step.

"Why did you lie to me?" he shouted, as though Ielond could hear.

Immutable stillness answered. The gold-leafed titles of ten thousand books taunted him with awareness of fulfillment he would never own. The void left an ache. Kennaird clenched shaking hands and whispered, "You promised."

Yet, in truth, Ielond had not, memory reminded. "*I offer you the chance to study*," the Sorcerer had said to the boy who knelt at his feet. He had never mentioned Mastership, though for years Kennaird had served apprenticeship under the assumption League investiture would be his. The Master had never seen fit to correct him, even when he voiced his ambition openly.

"That's as good as a lie." Silence swallowed the statement. Agonized by his misery, Kennaird sank onto the battered wooden stool by the desk, as he often had when Ielond was alive. The brown quill pen still stood in the ebony stand, though mice had gnawed the feather end. The Sorcerer had used that same nib to inscribe the writ which granted Darion his Consort. Ielond had spent his life to ensure his ward's inheritance. Kennaird cradled his chin on folded arms, resentful. "Did you leave no legacy for me, Master?" he said to the tenantless chair.

That moment, he discovered the box. It lay as though waiting for him, the shine of black lacquered enamel out of place amid dust-filmed surroundings. The top bore, in white, the same glyph Ielond had used to verify the writ.

Infused by a thrill of excitement, Kennaird straightened. Often as he had visited, he knew the layout of the desk by heart. The box had never been there before. Driven by curiosity and a giddy rush of hope, he reached out. As his hand touched the edge of the box, he felt the familiar, cold prickle of sorcery.

I am your legacy, the box informed through mindspeech. Unsurprised and trembling with renewed expectation, Kennaird tilted back the lid. Nestled within scarlet velvet lay a ring of gold, cunningly wrought in the shape of a scaled creature out of myth.

I am knowledge, whispered the ring to his innermost soul.

Kennaird hesitated. The glitter of the metal absorbed his conscious awareness like the magnetic pull of a compass. The beast shape seemed almost alive, so perfectly was it crafted. Carefully he lifted the box. Tiny, slitted eyes glared from beneath a spiked crest, and the interlocked loop of tail and taloned limbs was extraordinarily accurate. A current of uneasiness welled beneath his excitement. Never in memory had Ielond wrought any spell with a demon's form.

I am the completion of your training, the ring replied, as though in answer.

The words bounced like echoes in Kennaird's mind. Headache forgotten, he laid the box flat on the desktop, but did not withdraw his hand. "Explain," he said softly.

I am the key to Mastership, yours by right. I was left in this place by Timesplice for you to accept or reject, as your will dictates.

"But the demon," Kennaird whispered.

The ring cut him short. *Power can be used for good, or ill. The user chooses. A body of knowledge that contains the secret of Time would be poorly guarded were it left in a form an enemy might identify.*

Kennaird licked his lips and tasted sweat. Although Faisix was imprisoned, dissidents remained who would rather Jieles inherited in Darion's stead, a Master Sorcerer among them. And in the hand of one such as Emrith, the key to the arts of Timesplice could even now disrupt the succession Ielond had died to preserve. Kennaird studied the ring's sinuous contours, as though his eyes could somehow unravel logic and reveal a hidden flaw beneath the ring's smooth answer. Its reason had not entirely eased his distrust. He shifted position, conscious he wanted to close the box and ponder the matter further, yet reluctant to release his hold upon hope. The encounter with Taroith had introduced the joyless, bitter vista his life would become were his training suspended. Uncertainty opened like a wound in his mind.

Kennaird lifted his hand. The box's shiny finish lay marred by a film of fingerprints as he paced nervously to the window once again. The bailey was crammed with townsfolk. Above, thin, high clouds smeared the sky's edge, harbinger of thaw and spring rains, yet a band of street children burrowed like rabbits through the mob, towing baskets of paper lanterns to light the square by night. Carpenters labored over construction of a platform for musicians. There would be dancing, Kennaird remembered, but the celebration of the populace seemed transient and shallow beside the realities which hedged him. Without training, he was nobody and nothing. The ignominy galled.

Kennaird's fist tightened against the graveyard cold of the sill. He knew, then, with the simple pleasures of ordinary men spread like a tableau before him, that he lacked the humility to endure such a life. Having tasted the wide, solitary spaces of a Sorcerer's power, he could never again be content with common toil and marriage as his lot. The ring won him, in guilt, like a street whore's promise: desire assuaged without threat of rejection. But the price no longer mattered.

Kennaird returned to the desk, determined despite the hollowness in the pit of his stomach. He grasped the box with roughness born of self-loathing. Weakness, not strength, founded his decision. He knew, and accepted the fact. Yet having chosen his course, it angered him to discover he was not master enough to silence the whimper of his conscience.

I am your legacy, the gold soothed as he reopened the lid. With a trembling hand he scooped the ring from the blood-dark velvet. The demon curled like ice in his palm, bright with the sparkle of highlights. He thrust it on his finger.

The ring slid into place smoothly as water. Kennaird experienced a sharp, thornlike sting as sorcery entered his mind. An arctic tingle coursed through his body. The sensation did not surprise him; he had anticipated the ring would establish linkage of one form or another.

He lifted a hand now remarkably steady, and noticed blood welling from a cut knuckle. Yellow gold glinted, heated as flame against scarlet. Odd, Kennaird thought; the metal must have had a sharp edge. He would file it later. Deep in his mind, he felt the wound should have disturbed him. But the idea was discarded as the ring's influence unfolded him, filling the empty, insecure places with newborn strength and confidence.

An instruction surfaced. Obediently Kennaird leaned down and opened the lowermost drawer of Ielond's desk. Within lay notes penned in the Master's own hand. Kennaird lifted them out, excited and startled by recognition. These were the same documents that had vanished from Ielond's desk the afternoon Elienne had been presented before the Grand Council.

"But I searched that drawer," he murmured to himself.

The ring offered no explanation. Kennaird laid the notes flat on the desktop. Uppermost lay the page that listed the times and dates of greatest vulnerability Ielond had gleaned from Elienne's birth chart. One was circled in red. Kennaird bent closer and saw the marked entry was for that very night, eight hours past sundown.

"Of course," he said softly. With Elienne weakened by the ardor of childbirth, and the new heir only hours old, Ielond would certainly want someone to guard against harm. Exhilarated by a renewed sense of purpose, Kennaird touched the ring on his hand. Why, he wondered, had the form disturbed him, earlier? The Demon of Hellsgap seemed a right and natural choice of image for an object of power. Legend named it warden of mysteries Ma'Diere had decreed forbidden to Man, and the Secret of Time had certainly never been sanctioned by the League.

Warm under the dry weight of fresh blankets, Elienne lay with her newborn son cradled against her breast. She wished ardently for quiet. But Law decreed the birth an affair of state, since the event was linked with the succession of a Crown Prince. Beside the usual healer and midwife, numerous officials and no less than two League Sorcerers crowded her chambers. Elienne closed her eyes. Though Taroith had been present to ease the worst of the pain, the hours of labor had taxed her strength. She felt emptied, exhausted beyond thought. Only concern kept her awake.

The tiny bundle of life in her arms was perilously vulnerable. On his own, outside the protection of her womb, the infant became a helpless target for any faction anxious to disrupt Darion's inheritance. Elienne saw threat in the child's separateness. Fearful as never before that the Seeress's prophecy would wrench this precious new life from her, she resented the presence of every stranger Pendaire's unmerciful tradition forced upon her.

Taroith patted her shoulder in fatherly sympathy. "Patience, my Lady. They'll leave shortly. The documents, I believe, have just been signed."

Elienne looked up, saw Darion return to her bedside. His white and gold tabard glittered by candlelight, and his hands held a flat square of parchment weighted with colorful wafers of wax. "Lady Consort, I'm proud." His smile was only slightly shadowed. "This is official acknowledgment of my right to the crown of Pendaire." He knelt at her bedside and lightly kissed her hand. In a tone pitched for her ears alone, he added, "You have spared me execution and murder. What will you do for encore?"

Elienne smiled wanly amid a fortress of pillows. "Nothing, I hope. May you rule long and well." She meant it, earnestly.

Darion raised his hand, palm upward. An unfamiliar seal ring weighted his finger. Elienne glimpsed the stag blazon of Pendaire as he cupped the infant's miniature feet.

"I see he has the proper number of toes." Hilarity threatened the gravity of the royal expression. "That's a good start, for a Prince. Have you thought about a name?"

"The mother needs rest," Taroith interrupted. Beyond him, the room began slowly to empty. "The healer has sent for a wet nurse so she can sleep undisturbed."

Elienne half rose in protest, the child clutched protectively in her arms. "I require no wet nurse." Even that small move left her head spinning. She settled back, unnerved by her helplessness.

The midwife leaned over the bed and fluffed the pillows, her beefy features kindly with understanding. "Rest, your Grace. The arrangement need not be permanent. Your son will be astir before you, being fine an' healthy. All the better you weren't wakened, at least through the first night."

"No." Elienne returned the solicitous concern on the features of everyone present with acid mistrust. "The baby stays with me."

A knock sounded softly, and the door opened. "The nurse has arrived," Mirette informed from the hall.

"Send her away!" The words came out uglier than Elienne intended, but weariness and insecurity stripped her of tact. She dared not permit the child to leave her presence.

"My Lady," Taroith began.

"I won't hear it!" She met the Sorcerer's startled glance with the wariness of a cornered vixen. "I prefer to be awakened. Let the crib be brought here."

Although she had directed her statement to Taroith, Darion was first to notice the buried distress in her voice. Disturbed, suddenly, by what seemed stubborn, irrational hysteria in the woman Ielond had chosen for sensitivity and courage, he listened more carefully. If Elienne was over-wrought, there would be cause.

"Come now," said the midwife. She laid aside her towels and extended her arms toward the infant. " 'Tis a natural thing to feel a little set back after a birth. Time and sleep will restore your spirits."

Elienne regarded the pink, scrubbed hands like vipers. "Get away. *Don't touch him.* I told you, he stays here." Her voice turned brittle with anger. "If you want to help, fetch the crib from the nursery."

"Enough!" Darion stepped between midwife and Consort with the caution of a man ending a fight between mastiffs. "Leave us, please. I wish to speak with my Lady in private."

Taroith's brows rose questioningly. "In private," Darion repeated quietly.

The chamber cleared slowly of maids and attendants. As though reluctant to give ground, the midwife was last to leave. Taroith held the paneled door open for her wide girth. Then he winked at Darion and closed the latch with firm finality.

Alone with her child, Elienne regarded the Prince who stood before her, hands clasped neutrally at his belt. She said, "You won't change my mind."

"I won't try, Mistress, if you tell me what troubles you." The medallion on his chest flashed as he drew breath. "I don't believe your behavior was founded on whim."

"No." Elienne felt familiar tension return. Phrased with direct compassion, Darion's sensitivity invariably left her defenseless against emotion. Too spent to battle, she stared down at the coverlet, trapped yet again by the intertwined monogram of Darion's initial and her own embroidered onto the sheet. She spoke quickly, before control left her entirely. "But I would rather not speak of it." With the succession all but completed, the Seeress's prophecy was her own affair.

"Are you still worried about Faisix?" The Prince waited, motionless, for her answer. After lengthy silence, he said, without rancour, "Lady, Faisix has been in trance, meditating, for the past four days. I doubt he knows your child exists, yet."

Elienne shivered. She met the Prince's hazel eyes with open alarm. "He knows. Will you listen? *I have a reason.* Please, my Lord, don't allow them to take my child from me, even for a night."

Darion hooked a stool with his foot and sat down by the bed. "All right." He lifted a lock of her hair from the bedstead and smoothed its mahogany length upon the pillow. "You honestly feel the baby may be endangered?"

Elienne swallowed. "Yes, Lord. Ielond would not guarantee his life." Her body ached. She desperately wanted to sleep. But before rest, she needed to stay clear-headed enough to establish her son's protection from harm. His tiny, warm weight against her body was her last most precious link with Trathmere and her lost husband.

"I think we should name him Cinndel," said Darion without warning.

Elienne started, and caught him watching the child with an expression of awed tenderness. "What?"

He laid his forearm on the mattress and leaned on it. "I said, I thought he should be named Cinndel."

"No." Emotion rendered the word nearly inaudible. Elienne tried, and failed to curb her amazement. "No," she repeated more clearly. She shifted the baby closer to the Prince, but he was too young yet to be interested in the bright glitter of the seal ring. Mellowed by the generosity of Darion's offer, Elienne qualified through a haze of drowsiness, "This child would have died, except through the intercession of your Guardian. I wish to call him Ielond, if you'll permit."

"Permit?" Darion withdrew his hand and for a long moment pressed spread fingers across his face. Chestnut hair fringed his knuckles, and the soft glow of candlelight touched his bronze profile. He spoke without moving. "I'd be honored to call my heir by that name." His tone became fractionally unsteady. "Are you certain?"

Moved by his reaction, Elienne touched the velvet-clothed wrist draped still over his knee. "I decided months ago. I'm glad you're pleased."

"Overcome is more accurate." He lowered his arm, unveiling a wounding smile. Elienne's breath caught. She had no will left to trample the response that welled up within her. Her grip tightened against the warmth of his sleeve.

Darion covered her fingers with his own. He lifted her hand from his arm and folded it neatly over the child's blanketed body. "Lady, you shall have your crib. The maid of your choice will attend you. I'll have a pallet brought."

"Minksa," said Elienne promptly. The room seemed to roll like a ship beleaguered by storm swells. Only stubborn will held her eyes open.

Darion rose to his feet, a tall glittering presence seen through vision fuzzed by exhaustion. His voice resumed like a litany, above her. "Further, I will post my two most trustworthy guardsmen at the door of your chambers. They shall have orders to admit no one without your consent."

Elienne roused herself with an effort. "Kennaird," she murmured.

Darion bent close. "What?"

"Send Kennaird. I need to speak with him." Much as Elienne disliked the apprentice, he alone shared knowledge of the Seeress's prophecy. And Darion was unlikely to humor her very long without demanding the reason for her insecurity. The child's safety could only be left to one Ielond himself had trusted.

"Very well, Lady." The Prince saluted, as though to a commander of armies. He struggled with a solemn expression. "Kennaird will be summoned for audience with the Queen-to-be. I will personally oversee all arrangements, and not leave you, or Ielond, until the guardsmen have arrived. *Now, will you rest?*"

"Like the dead," Elienne promised. Weakened past restraint, she summoned a wan smile. "My Lord, about the chess game . . . someday I'll explain."

Darion watched his Lady's eyes fall closed. He stood for a long while over her still, slight form, while the child of a dead stranger blinked and slept at last in the bright drift of her hair. The sacrifices the two of them had made for his future left him indebted beyond human coin. He yearned for Elienne's happiness until its absence made him ache. Yet even when he coaxed a smile from her, grief and mistrust seemed always to rob the moment of pleasure. Perhaps the baby would restore her trust in life, he thought. The sharp trip of the latch started his reverie.

Taroith entered. "She's asleep, I see." He paused and raked a gnarled hand through his beard. "Are you going to reveal the terms of the truce?"

Darion laughed quietly. "A crib at her bedside, Minksa's presence, and two guardsmen."

The Sorcerer grunted. "You humor her. Your Grace, never spoil the one you marry. You'll rue it, sorely." He was smiling.

Darion shrugged, impossibly high-spirited. "She has achieved my succession. Let her have her way, for tonight." And he called for servants, his pageboy, and a scribe, that he could fulfill his bond to the lady who had at least granted him reprieve from the headsman.

*   *   *

Elienne woke in the night to the wind-driven batter of rain against the casements. Ielond lay quiet in his crib. Drowsily, she recalled that Minksa had wakened her earlier, and she had fed her child. There had been lights, then, and stillness. A solitary candle still burned on the table by the bed. Elienne dozed, her thoughts of Darion's forthcoming coronation. Ma'Diere's Order would bless Ielond as Prince and heir of the realm at the same time.... Lulled by the fury of the storm, for once she permitted herself the luxury of contemplating a future removed from dread.

Voices beyond the door drew her back. Half-roused, Elienne saw Kennaird enter her chambers. Water glistened in his thin hair, scattering droplets onto the carpet as he bent and carefully fastened the latch.

Elienne stirred and spoke in a voice thickened with sleep. "Kennaird? You came very late."

The apprentice crossed the floor without a reply. After a brief survey of the room, he unhooked his wet cloak and slung it over a chair by the hearth. "You're alone?" He sounded brisk rather than surprised.

Elienne raised herself on one elbow. Minksa slept on a pallet behind the decorative screen of the wardrobe. But the girl was no threat to her privacy. Elienne chose not to waken her. "I wished no women about until I had seen you concerning protection for Ielond."

The name caused Kennaird to check sharply.

"I surprised you." Softened by fatigue, Elienne smiled. "I'm sorry. The boy is named after the Sorcerer. I hope you don't mind."

"No." Kennaird's lips curled. Half-lit by the candle, his expression seemed strangely amused, as he resumed his interrupted course and paused at her bedside.

Elienne settled back against the pillows, more tired than she cared to admit. She looked up at Kennaird with relief. Shortly she could enlist help from a nurse without danger to Ielond. "Kennaird, I'm worried about the Seeress's prophecy. No one else knows the child may still be threatened. You are the only one I dared trust to ensure his safety."

The apprentice gripped the bedstead above her. Shadows bent his familiar features into a mask's hard angles, and eyes pale as winter searched her face, as though something about her annoyed him.

Chilled awake by the intensity of his silence, Elienne knew faint alarm. "You will help, won't you?" She pushed back the coverlet as though to rise.

Kennaird laid a hand on her shoulder. "I'll look after the child." He pressed her firmly back against the pillows.

His autocratic touch sparked annoyance. Elienne resisted, and felt his fingers tighten, gouging her nightrobe unpleasantly into her skin. "Kennaird!" Fully roused, she twisted angrily, and caught sight of a bright glitter of gold; the Demon of Hellsgap lay coiled like a garrote beneath his knuckle.

Terror flooded her, sharp and immediate as a knife. She drew breath to scream, found bedclothes rammed tight against her mouth. The cry emerged muffled. Kennaird shook her. She lashed out, felt her wrist caught and imprisoned in a cruel grip. Elienne wrenched in panic. Her assailant braced against her. His leg bumped the side table. The candle tottered, tossing pinwheels of shadow.

Driven by fear, Elienne flung against his hold again. Kennaird raised his knee and pinned her long hair against the mattress. The bedclothes shifted in his hands, ruthlessly suffocating her. Elienne struggled. Harsh fingers twisted the cloth to gag her. She tried to kick free of the blankets, without success. The sheet tightened like a rope across her mouth, salty with the taste of her own sweat. She heaved, desperate. Kennaird's hold slipped. Knuckles banged painfully against her ear.

Air sobbed in Elienne's throat. *"Guards!"*

A hard palm silenced her. Elienne thrashed. Kennaird forcefully thrust the gag back over her face. Her elbow cracked the headboard. But the pain of impact went unnoticed as the apprentice yanked the sheets into a knot. His face loomed over her, stippled with sweat, and unhumanly intent. Distantly, Elienne heard the rattle of the door latch.

"Eternity, it's locked!" someone shouted.

A heavy object crashed against the door from without,

but the stout oaken panels held. Kennaird finished with the gag. He released her with an expression of contempt and started around the bed. Beyond stood the crib where Ielond lay sleeping.

Elienne flung herself after Kennaird. *He would kill her child.* Linen snapped taut under the force of her rush. Cloth abraded her chin and ripped away. Elienne caught Kennaird's elbow and clung. Too weak to stop him, she could only slow him down. A fist battered her shoulder. The doors shuddered under a second blow.

"No!" Elienne kicked at his kneecap, missed, but saw a white figure move in the shadows across the room. "Minksa! Unbar the doors!"

The girl ran like a deer. Kennaird saw her and swore. He raised his arm and smashed Elienne brutally aside. She staggered. He struck her again, and she fell.

The door burst open. Guardsmen entered, running, just as Kennaird reached for the child.

"No!" Elienne made a frantic effort to rise. "Stop him!"

Gauntleted hands seized Kennaird, jerked him back. He tore free, whirled, and attacked the guards, though he was unarmed. Through a wave of weakness, Elienne heard the slick ring of a sword drawn from a scabbard. Steel flashed, yellowed by candlelight. But crazed as a beast, Kennaird rushed the guardsmen with suicidal fury.

The blade took him in the chest. Startled by the impact, the guardsman cried out in stark surprise and dropped his weapon. Kennaird toppled with a gasp. The steel crossguard thudded into the carpet. Driven home by the weight of his own body, the blade emerged, bloodied, through the back of his jerkin. But Elienne saw nothing beyond the flash of gold that tumbled from his outflung hand. The object spun, flickering in the darkness, and came to rest a scant yard from her face.

Elienne stirred. Blood rang in her ears, as though she might faint. She clung to consciousness. Like a living presence of evil, the ring lay just beyond reach, unnoticed by the guardsmen. Fear caught like ice in her throat.

"Ma'Diere, he was mad!" said a shocked voice, threaded

by a wail as the baby began to cry. "*He killed himself,* I'll swear by Eternity."

"Send for Taroith, at once." A booted step approached the crib. "The child is untouched. Girl, see to your mistress. Is she hurt?"

Elienne felt a trembling touch on her shoulder. Minksa bent over her, dark hair tangled against the white lace collar of her shift. "Lady?" She sounded as though she was weeping. "Lady, are you all right?"

Elienne's senses blurred and dimmed. Shadows pressed her vision, dense as water, and Ielond's lusty cries thinned with distance. "My baby," she whispered.

Minksa moved in response. Elienne shivered in the grip of pain. Sound tumbled against her ears, blended voices uttering words she could not understand. Pushed to the extreme edge of awareness, she forced her eyes open, determined to remain conscious at least until Minksa returned with the child.

But the girl had paused with her task incomplete. Elienne saw her bend and reach for a gleam of gold in the shadows.

"No." Too quiet to be heard, her warning went unregarded. Minksa's small fingers closed over Kennaird's ring.

As though the touch opened contact, Elienne felt the cold sting of sorcery lance her mind. She gasped. Vertigo claimed her and the room violently upended, tumbling her downward into night. The alien chill followed.

Her last, desperate protest was barely audible, undermined by ebbing strength. *No!*

Sorcery straddled the thought. *You will remember nothing of my presence,* said Faisix's voice within her.

Willfully, Elienne struggled. She punished fading thoughts back, forced recollection. She saw Minksa's hand reach down and pick up...what? She searched, frantically, aware the missing object jeopardized her existence. Yet her efforts yielded nothing but a void that rose up and enfolded her in darkness....

Only half-clothed, Darion entered his Consort's chambers at a full run. His steward trailed him with a harried expression, arms clutched about a shirt and a pair of boots.

The Prince skirted the bloody cloak-draped bundle on the carpet, eyes drawn unerringly to where Taroith bent over the supine body of his lady.

"Elienne," he said, and knelt. Nearby, Ielond wailed loudly in the gingerly grasp of a guardsman.

Taroith lifted his hands from her brow and looked up. "She's suffered no more than a bruise on the head. But she'll not waken until morning."

Darion touched the pale curve of her cheek. "You made her sleep, then. Is that wise?"

"Do you wish her to see the aftermath of this?" Taroith gestured pointedly at the naked sword that lay, dulled and sticky, beside the covered form on the rug. "She is exhausted beyond her strength, and terrified." The Sorcerer noticed the Prince's face and gentled his voice at once. "Ma'Diere, I know, your Grace. Your Guardian chose her for strength, but an attack on a child is a horror she will never forget. Let her rest, at least until she has recovered resource enough to master her emotions."

"Then let me get her to bed." Darion lifted Elienne's slight body into his arms. Long, dark hair tumbled warmly over his skin as he cradled her against his chest. Relaxed in sleep, her head rolled against his shoulder. The brief peace Taroith's healing had granted lay imprinted on the soft curves of her features.

The sight wrenched Darion from within. He wanted that contentment for her, always, but Pendaire had rewarded her generosity of spirit with nothing but violence, distrust, and cruelty.

Taroith stood by as Darion laid Elienne on the bed. The sheets were a twisted ruin. Annoyed, Darion snapped at the steward who hovered, still, at his elbow. "Can you do anything about this mess?"

The man bowed and dropped a boot. "Your Grace, your garment—"

Darion swore and, cued by the steward's gaze, glanced downward. He tightened the laces of his hose with unabashed dispatch and accepted the shirt without complaint. "Sheets," he said, voice muffled by cloth. "And fetch Mirette." His head emerged, disheveled, from the white lawn collar. Impatiently he jabbed an arm into a sleeve, while the servant stared. "Well? Don't stand there while I dress, man. *Go at once!*"

The steward departed, still clutching footwear. As he scuttled into the hall, Darion set Elienne's rumpled nightrobe straight and smoothed her hair across the pillows with gentle hands. Taroith relieved the guardsman of Ielond. The baby's crying trailed into silence.

"They told me the child was untouched." Darion sat with Elienne's head rested against his thigh. He settled a blanket over her shoulders to keep off the chill until Mirette arrived.

Taroith laid the infant by her side. "The boy was wakened by the noise. He frets now because he is hungry." As Darion made to rise, he touched the Prince's wrist. "I've already sent for the midwife. Leave Ielond's difficulties to her."

Darion lifted an anguished face from the still form of his Consort. "Ma'Diere! She trusted Kennaird. We all did. And Faisix is confined under ward. How in Eternity can this have happened?"

"I don't know." Taroith stood, gray robes clenched around bowed shoulders. He paced the floor. "I soul-searched the man only this morning. He showed no such motivation then. If he acted under influence of possession, I could find no trace, though I reached here only minutes after he died." The Sorcerer paused with his hand on the table by the bed. The candle illuminated troubled features. "Control could have originated from an object. If so, it is no longer on Kennaird's person. I shall search the room, of course. And the League will summon Faisix back from trance for truthsearch, though I know of no method he could have initiated to bring about this assault."

"We should have had him executed," said Darion abruptly. His dark brows bunched into a frown. Somehow Elienne had known this attack might happen. Repeatedly she had asked his protection. With a stab of guilt, the Prince remembered that he had granted her guardsmen as an indulgence of a whim. And her son had almost been murdered. The ugly fact sparked rage he could not curb. "Eternity! Is there no limit to the intrigue in my court? Who would kill a baby? Jieles?"

"Your Grace!" Taroith left the table, aged features set like granite. He gripped the royal shoulders forcefully with both hands. "Ielond taught you better than that!"

Darion flung off the Sorcerer's grasp and rose. "Ielond taught me compassion." He shoved the reddened swordgrip with his toe, his eyes intense with anger. "Show me the compassion in this, Master. If it was Jieles, I shall condemn him to the block."

Taroith bent his head and said nothing. Brittle silence stretched between Prince and Sorcerer, while the guardsman fidgeted uncomfortably to one side. After a time, Darion stirred and raked fingers through his disordered hair, ill temper gone from him.

"I'm sorry." He rubbed his hands across his sleeves as though chilled. "I think precautions are necessary, at least until we discover what caused Kennaird's defection. Let Elienne be moved to my own apartments. I want guardsmen in the chamber with her at all times."

"That's a wise decision, your Grace," said Taroith. "I'll grant you the services of a League Sorcerer as well, after Faisix has been interrogated."

A soft knock at the door heralded the arrival of Mirette. At the Prince's request, she sent for additional servants and a litter to remove Elienne and the royal heir to the family rooms. Darion rewarded her stoic patience with a tired smile. "I might be engaged through the morning with Taroith. If my Lady wakens, before I return, please tell her I shall do my utmost for her safety, and the child's."

Mirette's pretty features tightened, as though with disapproval. She said nothing.

"What's wrong?" Darion laid a hand protectively against Elienne's cheek. "Can't you tell her I care?"

"Lord, I'll tell her," said a girl's voice from the far side of the chamber.

Darion turned, startled, and saw Minksa seated in the shadows. "Have you been there the whole time, Missy?"

Minksa nodded and crossed the room, reddened eyes large in her white face. She had been crying.

The events of the night must have been gruesome for a

child her age; and Jieles, Darion remembered, was her father. At once he regretted his angered threats of execution. He tried to amend the damage. "Look after your mistress, child. Stay close to her. You're possibly the only friend she has."

Chapter 14

The Demon of Hellsgap

Rain hammered the slate roof of Pendaire's royal palace long after dawn soaked gray, chilly light through a thick mantle of fog. Though Mirette bundled the drapes back from the casement only at Elienne's insistence, she tried to be kind. "There's been a thaw. The weather will be good for riding by the time your strength returns."

Elienne blinked as her eyes adjusted. Sore abdominal muscles blunted her desire to ride, and the deep maternal bond she had experienced since Ielond's birth overruled the restless impatience with the indoors she had known during pregnancy. She glanced sleepily at the crib by the bedside. Ielond kicked contentedly among the sheets. The sight of his tiny red face reawakened memory of Kennaird, and violence. Elienne sat up, alarmed. She lay in a changed room. Two men-at-arms stood guard at her bedside, burly, weathered features out of place amid the ornate delicacy of the furnishings.

"Mirette." Elienne looked more carefully, and recognized the small chamber that normally housed Darion's squire. "Did the Prince...?"

The Lady-in-waiting left the window. "Beyond all else, his Grace wished you safe." She settled into a chair and arranged her skirts with stiff ceremony, as though she expected argument.

But Elienne's concern for her child overshadowed any emotional pressures imposed by Darion. Though relations with Mirette had been ruinously strained since the morning of Darion's chess game, she tried to reassure. "Mistress, I'm not displeased."

Mirette picked a wisp of lint from her sleeve and said

nothing. Elienne read exhaustion in the smudges beneath her eyes. "Were you up all night in my behalf?"

"Not quite." Mirette's tone was courteously neutral. "The midwife saw to the baby."

"And you saw to me," Elienne smiled. "Why don't you retire? Your staff can summon the midwife, if I need her, and Minksa will be back with breakfast shortly."

Mirette rose and curtsied with flawless formality. Peach-colored silk rustled as she straightened. "Ancinne is in the anteroom if you need her. The Prince wished you to know he will visit when his official affairs permit."

Elienne smiled. "I'll manage."

She watched Mirette's departure with relief. The Lady-in-waiting's strict adherence to duty rasped her nerves unbearably. The woman adopted ceremonial politeness like armor. "By Ma'Diere's everlasting backside, someone should teach her to swear," Elienne said aloud.

One of the guardsmen gasped in unprofessional surprise. He muffled a shout of laughter behind his sleeve, while the other, with more control, bit his lip and purpled slowly beneath his crested helm.

Elienne sank back against the pillows, conscious of tangled hair and puffy eyes. Inevitably, Ancinne would send after a maid to straighten her appearance, if the Prince was to visit. Elienne hoped the woman's innate laziness would delay the interruption. She wanted a chance to think, undisturbed by servants or Minksa's friendly chatter. Something unsettled her about the attempt upon Ielond's life the night before. But when she searched her memory, the feeling eluded her grasp like water.

Restlessly, Elienne rolled onto her side. Swollen breasts brought a twinge of discomfort. Annoyed that she had neglected to ask Mirette when the child had last been fed, she sighed. Ielond seemed quiet. His tiny hand thrashed the air with contented abandon.

Elienne closed her eyes. Reluctant to expose herself before the guardsmen without another woman present, she decided to wait at least until the baby became fretful. Uneasiness returned to nag her. Irritated, she sorted again through her recollection of the past evening's events.

A loud rattle of porcelain disturbed her thoughts. Minksa entered with a breakfast tray, Ancinne's stout bulk on her heels.

"Missy, have a care, you'll spill something."

"I didn't." The girl set the tray on the table by the bed with a precarious crash and thrust her hand in her apron pocket. She turned an excited face to Elienne. "Lady, the cooks are making tarts with icing for the banquet tomorrow."

Ancinne fussed with the pillows while Minksa removed the covers from a bewildering array of dishes.

Elienne sat up, dismayed. "I can't eat half that amount."

"You'll have more appetite than you think, Lady. You've a child to feed." Ancinne frowned at Minksa. "Missy, don't serve royalty with your hand in your pocket, ever."

Minksa set a pitcher down with a bump.

Elienne winked at her. "I'm not royalty until the wedding," she said to Ancinne, certain the girl's clumsiness was no more than high spirits. She started to ask the Lady-in-waiting to judge Minksa less harshly, but Ielond chose that moment to cry. Little as he was, his yell defeated conversation.

Elienne smiled. "He'll become a tyrant, I know it." And since Minksa was closest, she nodded in response to the girl's request to fetch the child.

Minksa turned with the slow step of a dreamer. She leaned over the crib, right hand eclipsed by her body as she removed it from her apron. Instead of reaching downward, she raised interlocked fists over the child's small form. Elienne saw gold flash on her finger.

Memory surfaced, deadly as poisoned steel, of the demon ring recovered from the floor. Her scream obliterated thought. She flung herself from the bed as Minksa's arms descended like a club.

The table rocked under Elienne's hand, scattering plates. *"No!"* Her shout mingled with a guardsman's curse. Too late, she reached her feet.

The bright clash of porcelain masked the impact of

Minksa's blow. Ielond's cries silenced. Blood flecked the blankets, then flooded in a sudden bright stain across the mattress.

"Oh, Eternity, no!"

Minksa lifted a tear-streaked face and laughed as the guardsmen's grip closed over her reddened wrists.

The wards over Faisix's cell flickered as Taroith stepped through the bars. He paused and rubbed a hand over his face, outlined in light, as the defenses brightened at his back. Of the Sorcerers who had originally accompanied him to question Faisix, six remained within.

Darion straightened stiffly. His back ached from long hours spent leaning against cold stone. "Did you find anything?"

"Nothing." Taroith lowered his arm and sighed. "You haven't been here the whole night, I hope. What time is it, your Grace? Mid-morning?"

"Almost." Darion worked a sore shoulder, still clad in the thin shirt forced upon him by the Steward. At some point he had acquired boots, but his hair was an uncombed tangle in the shadow of the stairway. "Tell me. Something isn't right, or you wouldn't have taken so long."

Taroith buried his fingers in his sleeves and fixed eyes distant with reflection upon the Prince. "We couldn't rouse him."

"What?" Darion's exclamation echoed against granite walls, and he suddenly noticed the chill.

"I said we couldn't summon Faisix back to consciousness." The Sorcerer started briskly for the stair. Gray robes rippled over the stone. "We entered his mind and searched. There was neither knowledge nor evidence of instigation in the attempt upon the baby's life. The only passion we could resolve at all was an intense desire to follow in Ielond's footsteps. That much we expected. Perhaps I gave it too little significance."

"But you couldn't recall him." Darion took the stairs effortlessly, two at a time, and caught up.

"No." Taroith rounded the landing. "They're still trying. His will seems beyond reach."

The Prince waited for the Sorcerer to qualify. When Taroith added nothing, he said, "That's not possible!"

"But it's happened." The Sorcerer stopped and caught the Prince's hazel eyes with a glance keen as a raptor's. "How did Ielond bring Elienne to Pendaire, your Grace?"

Darion stood with his back to the brass railing. The wall sconce flickered, tracing long, crawling shadows over his cheekbones. *"Reveal to no one what I've told you,"* Ielond had instructed the night of his death. *"I shall alter Time in Pendaire only once, to send you a bride. Let fate achieve the rest."*

"Answer, your Grace, or I shall ask Elienne." Taroith started slowly upward, his step suddenly tired. "For if Ielond left a riddle, I think Faisix has unraveled the key to it."

Above, a door crashed open. The wall sconce streamed in the draft, and someone descended the stair in reckless haste. "Your Grace!"

A disheveled servant skidded to a stop on the upper landing. "Your Grace, come at once. There's been violence."

Darion pushed away from the railing and raced up the steps, Taroith at his side. He caught the servant as he passed, compelling the man to follow at the same pace. "What's happened?"

"Minksa, my Lord." The man gasped, breathless from his run. "She's attacked your son."

"Possession," Taroith said with curt self-reproach. "There must have been an object, last night." And he swore with acid feeling.

Darion said nothing. He released his grip on the servant and placed all his attention into speed. *"Let fate achieve the rest,"* Ielond had told him. Bitterly, the Prince wondered whether Cinndel's child was an intentional sacrifice. He pounded the length of a hallway, haunted by Elienne's expression of gratitude spoken only hours before. *"This child would have died except through the intercession of your Guardian."*

Taroith's focus crackled to life overhead. Caught in a net of light, Darion wrenched open the latch. Sounds of furious struggle and a woman's screams battered his ears as he dashed into the suite. The door to Elienne's room lay ajar. The Prince slammed through without breaking stride.

Minksa thrashed in the grip of the guardsmen, pale arms streaked scarlet. Small as she was, two grown men had difficulty restraining her. Loosened hair whipped her face as she flung against their hold, screaming piteously for her father. Darion passed with barely a pause. The crib lay puddled with blood, empty. Elienne knelt on the floor nearby, a sodden bundle cradled against her breast. Ancinne clutched the bedstead above her, ghost-white.

The Prince brushed the woman aside and stooped beside his Consort, his worst fears confirmed by a glimpse of what she held. Firmly he caught her wrists, felt the slippery warmth of Ielond's blood. Horror checked his breath. "Elienne."

She did not look up.

"*Elienne!*" He shook her gently, and dark hair tumbled like ribbons down her back. "Elienne, *give the boy to Taroith*. If there's hope, Ielond must have care at once."

She raised a blank, stunned face. Eyes darkened with shock locked upon the Prince. Lacerated by her expression, he spoke again.

"*Give the boy to Taroith.*"

Elienne stirred like a dreamer. Taroith bent quickly and lifted the infant from her loosened arms. Darion caught her bloodstained shoulders and buried her head against his chest. Elienne quivered in his embrace. He covered the shell of her ear with his hand. "Taroith, make her sleep."

Shadows wheeled as the Sorcerer lowered his soulfocus. The light touched Elienne briefly; Darion felt her trembling slow and stop. She buckled against him, consciousness blanketed by the Sorcerer's contact. Darion lifted her, and discovered tears on his cheeks.

"The child is dead," said Taroith beside him.

"I guessed as much." Darion swallowed with difficulty. He lowered Elienne's body gently to the bed. "You!" he said to the maid. "Look after your mistress!"

The room seemed suddenly crowded. Darion left the bedside and saw three League Sorcerers, Emrith among them. The courtier he had passed in the corridor gaped in the doorway. The Prince leaped and slammed the oaken panel shut. When he returned, Taroith had laid the corpse of

Elienne's child in the crib. He covered it with a sheet and straightened, blotting bloodied fingers on his robe.

Emrith raised his voice over Minksa's cries. "I've sent for the Duke of Liend."

"I forbid him entrance," Darion said curtly.

"Would you deny the girl the comfort of her own father?" Emrith's brows rose over cool green eyes. "She's obviously lost her wits."

Taroith stepped briskly between. "I called for trained Masters, not relatives. His Grace's judgment is sound. Jieles has no business here." The Sorcerer shifted his attention to Darion. "An object definitely controls Minksa's possession. Allow no one else near enough to touch her. I want no risk of transfer." To Emrith he added, "You weren't summoned here. Since you seem to have volunteered your services, you will bring an ingot of iron to this chamber from the smithy by transfer."

For a League Master, the request was no difficulty, but the task would occupy Emrith wholly for a lengthy span of time. Sobered by Taroith's adroit diplomacy in the heat of crisis, Darion strove to bridle his own tangle of rage and grief. If trusted hands could be influenced to murder, no one in Pendaire was safe.

Taroith approached Minksa, who struggled still in the grip of her captors. "Hold her firmly," the Sorcerer instructed as his League colleagues positioned themselves at the guardsmen's shoulders. "She may turn suicidal."

Taroith poised his soulfocus over the girl's tangled head. The metal helms of her wardens mirrored the harsh light, and reflections burnished sweat-sheened features.

Minksa flung herself against their restraint. "Mercy! Let me go to my father!"

Her plea ripped Darion's heart. She was so very young. Taroith lowered his focus slowly toward the girl. Sparks jumped. With a crackle like breaking ice, a halo of scarlet ringed Minksa's body. She cried out and twisted against the mailed hands that prisoned her. One blood-slick wrist slipped and almost tore free.

Instantly Taroith withdrew his focus. "Hold her." The

sultry glow faded slowly to an after-image. He nodded to his colleagues. To the guardsmen his instructions were terse and verbal. "She is defended by Black Sorcery. We have no choice but to immobilize her through indirect contact. You'll experience some numbness. Keep steady. The sensation will cause you no harm."

Grimly silent, the two Sorcerers placed their hands upon the armored shoulders of the men-at-arms. The bunched mass of their shadows splintered into triplicate as they summoned their focuses beside Taroith's. Outlined in glare, one guard glanced uneasily upward.

"Mind the girl!" Taroith warned. "Any threat to you originates with the force she harbors."

Minksa wrenched desperately, thin cheeks awash with tears. Light flared above her, dazzling Darion's view. He squinted, through aching eyes saw the guardsmen stiffen into posed statues. The violence of Minksa's struggles gradually damped under the combined influence of the Sorcerers. The Prince had observed his Guardian enough to understand something of their method—by channeling their powers through the touch of the men-at-arms, they could breach Minksa's awareness without rousing the ward inherent in the will that possessed her. But progress was torturously slow.

Minksa's cries gradually subsided. Porcelain clinked, solitary harpnotes against the stillness, as Ancinne cleared the fragments of the breakfast dishes from the floor at Elienne's bedside. She worked with feverish concentration, as though she could somehow negate the finality of death by cleaning up the traces. Beyond her fat bulk, Emrith knelt in trance, arms wrapped in an aura of light. The translucent outline of an ingot drifted above his spread fingers, and sweat beaded his forehead.

Minksa hung motionless as a wax figure in the hold of the guards. Taroith walked forward and examined the streaked, bloody fist clenched like stone in the gauntlet of the elder man-at-arms. "I thought so," he murmured, beckoning Darion nearer.

The Prince entered the flood of brilliance cast by the focuses of three League Masters. He shielded his eyes. Rigid as glass, Minksa remained frozen in a pose of savagery. Her expression dismembered thought. Darion wrenched his gaze away.

"Look here," said Taroith at his side. "But take care not to touch."

The Prince bent close. The guardsmen seemed lifelessly immobile as their captive; even their breathing was suspended. Stunned by the scope of energy needed to subdue a mere girl, Darion took a moment to notice the glint of metal on Minksa's finger. Gummed with clotted blood, a gold ring nestled between her whitened knuckles.

The Prince recognized the form with an ugly shock. "The Demon of Hellsgap? *Faisix did this?*"

Taroith rubbed his neck with glazed knuckles. "Appearances may be deceptive, but yes, I believe so. Though I cannot begin to guess how he accomplished the feat from a warded cell."

"He'll pay with his life." Darion's words were clipped by rage.

Taroith made no attempt to dissuade him. Instead he drew the Prince aside. "I'm going to require help. When Emrith completes his transfer, ask him to summon all but two of the Masters from Faisix's cell. They're needed here."

The Sorcerer returned to Minksa. Darion waited fretfully for Emrith to rouse from trance. Rain snaked watery streaks across a view flat gray with fog. Caught in a dreamlike sense of isolation, the Prince crossed the carpet to Elienne's bedside. He sat, and tried not to think of the still form beneath the stained sheet in the crib. Beside him, his Lady lay peacefully asleep, long hair caught in her lashes. Darion smoothed the strands aside, dreading the moment she would wake and remember.

"We should never have interfered with you," he murmured.

Ancinne lifted a tray load of shards from the rug. "Your Grace?"

"Nothing." Darion stood restlessly.

Across the chamber, Emrith stirred and opened his eyes. He hefted a thick bar of iron, blinked once, and directed an interested glance at Minksa and the guardsmen. Darion rose and delivered Taroith's instructions promptly, anxious to see the Master gone from the room.

Emrith stood. He offered the ingot, black hair shadowless as night against the glare of his soulfocus. "My condolences upon the death of your heir, your Grace."

"Do you equate murder with death?" Darion's hand closed forcibly over metal still warm from transfer. "Save your pity for those tragedies without malice."

The Sorcerer bowed and moved silently to the door. He let himself out without looking back.

Though Darion knew he had spoken rashly, concern for Elienne left no space for regret. With her loved one's baby murdered by the only friend she possessed in Pendaire, mistrust might well drive her to solitary despair. He vowed he would prevent that, though he forfeit his own peace. Whether Elienne hated him permanently for interference, he would not abandon her to grief.

A crackle of sound and a blast of wind ripped the air at his back. Darion left the doorway and saw the League Sorcerers Emrith had summoned arrive by direct transfer from Faisix's cell. Three moved at once to Taroith's aid.

The fourth, a vigorous old man with a scarred cheek, strode over and lifted the iron from the Prince's numbed grasp. "Your Grace, you have my deepest sympathy. Should you or your Consort require anything, please don't hesitate to ask."

The Prince twisted the seal ring on his finger, eyes shadowed by a fallen wing of hair. "Spare the girl, Master Duaire. She was a tool ruthlessly used."

"Your Grace, we shall try." Duaire hesitated, as though he might add more. But after an uncomfortable interval, he quietly joined his colleagues, his face a mask of determination.

Darion settled wearily into a chair. Sounds of voices and footsteps filtered through the suite. A guard captain shouted for order. The Prince cringed inwardly. Already a crowd of courtiers had gathered beyond his door, curious and hungry for details. Let the steward handle them, he thought viciously, in no mood to confront the inquisitive pity of the household. Their loss was only symbolic.

Sorcery brightened the far side of the chamber. Darion glanced around, dazzled by a raw pulse of power. The League Sorcerers stood in a circle, stark as silhouettes against the glare. The Prince shielded his eyes, saw the crimson arc of the ring's ward snap back into existence. Minksa cried out, netted by a blaze of energy. The fist containing the ring was obscured by the stellar incandescence of League forces.

Presently the effect relented. Darion beheld the image of the Demon of Hellsgap outlined in fire above Minksa's head. The girl hung limp as death in the grasp of the guards.

Taroith suddenly stepped aside from the Sorcerers who ringed her still body. His robed form gleamed orange as metal under a smith's hammer in the sultry glare of the demon-form.

"Khavillein," he called boldly, naming the creature in the Loremaster's tongue. "Who has sanctioned your presence here?"

The demon-form writhed, sinuous amid smudged billows of smoke. It spoke like the scrape of stones. "Faisix, Torkal's master."

Darion felt perspiration chill between his shoulderblades.

"Khavillein," said Taroith again, his voice a peal of command. "By natural law, that is impossible."

Laughter filled the chamber and echoed cruel and impersonal against the walls. Darion felt his flesh prickle.

Taroith moved. Sudden light snapped from his hand. Wind fanned his robe. The demon-form dissolved onto a roil of scarlet. Its laughter changed pitch, and the inflections that answered were familiar.

"Ielond spliced Time to grant Prince Darion his succession," said Faisix in the same crisp tones that he had once used to address Pendaire's Grand Council. "I could do no less to achieve his ruin. But unlike my predecessor, I utilized means to accomplish simultaneous existence in the same locus. This extension of my will is the result." Torpid as grease, the smoke coiled in the air, dimly reassuming the serpentine outline of the demon. The voice resumed, triumphant. "Your Royal Grace, your heir is dead. Mourn him. Avenge him. You shall sire no other."

Darion tensed in his chair. Rage entered him like fire.

Taroith turned suddenly from the image of Faisix's summoning and shouted, "Your Grace, stand clear!"

Darion slammed his chair back and strode forward.

Taroith intercepted, caught the royal wrists in a grip like shackles. "Your Grace!" Sweat slicked his white hair. "Your Grace, if you loved your Guardian, stay clear! *What you see is a projection.*"

With more calm, Taroith elaborated. "This evil can be immobilized if iron is thrust through its center. But when that is done, all existing connections must end. Faisix's flesh will perish. The properties of the iron shall prison his spirit, since that metal conducts no resonance of Black Sorcery. Do you, as mortal sovereign, dare sentence a man's soul to eternal confinement?"

The Prince covered his face with his hands and stood motionless for an extended interval, shadow pooled like ink about his feet in the steady blaze of the wards. He answered at last in the gritty tones of exhaustion. "Yes." He unveiled an expression like etched stone. "Let it be done."

Abruptly Taroith released his hold. "Your Grace, let the responsibility be mine alone." And before Darion could reply, he caught the iron bar from Duaire.

Taroith's soulfocus flared into view, curtaining him in a white corona. The iron brightened, molten silver in his hands, and lengthened into a rod a slender yard in length. The Sorcerer raised the object like a weapon, whirled, and thrust it upward through the hazy coils of the monster that drifted above Minksa's bent head.

Light exploded upon contact. The bar heated to incandescence, bright and sudden as lightning. Taroith released it as though burnt. The metal tumbled, end over end, the chime of impact as it struck the floor overlaid by a scream from Minksa.

"Elienne!" The cry reflected restored intelligence.

Minksa called out again, her tone roughened by horror-ridden recognition. *"Elienne! Elienne!"*

The guardsmen released her. Anguished by memory, Minksa raised marked fingers to rake her face. Duaire stooped and caught her before she could inflict injury. His own focus flashed, flat as a mirror overhead. The girl fell limp in his arms.

She lay like a shot animal against his maroon robe. Duaire straightened, his features heavy with sorrow. "Ma'Diere's infinite mercy, what are we going to do with her?"

He glanced at the Prince. But Darion seemed mesmerized by the rod, which had come to rest at his feet, a cool blue-gray against the soft pastels of the carpet. The demon ring was imbedded deeply in the smooth sheen of the metal's surface.

Taroith answered, finally, blistered fingers poised against his forearms. "By law, she must be confined. But for her sanity's sake, not alone. Will you stay with her?"

Duaire strode at once for the door. But his departure was hampered by the arrival of yet another League Sorcerer.

The newcomer crossed the chamber and stopped before Taroith. "Master, Faisix has gone into a coma."

"I expected as much." Taroith bent and gingerly retrieved the iron rod. "He'll not recover."

With a short gasp of dismay, his colleague removed the object from his wounded grasp. Taroith murmured brief thanks and addressed the Prince. "Your Grace, the Grand Council must be called into session. As Regent, I can officiate, if you wish to be absent."

Darion stirred as though roused from deep sleep. "Your hands . . ."

". . . are no impediment, your Grace." Taroith's features softened. "I'd hardly be worthy of League status if I could not mend damage to my own person."

A guardsman's boot scraped uneasily against the floor. Darion fingered the creased cloth of his shirt and looked up, finally, hazel eyes darkly troubled. "I won't leave my Consort, at least until she wakens."

"That won't happen before nightfall," said Taroith. "But the Council has no need of your presence. Stay by her if you wish."

Darion crossed woodenly to the bed where Elienne lay. Oblivious to Ancinne's protests, he tossed off the blankets, lifted his Consort's slight body in his arms, and started for the door to his own chamber with the Lady-in-waiting at his heels. He lifted the latch. Ancinne tried to follow and found herself rudely excused. Darion crossed the threshold alone and kicked the oaken panel shut with untempered violence.

"Why, the nerve!" Ancinne braced plump fists upon her hips. "The very last thing Lady Elienne needs is a man's company."

Taroith's brow furrowed into a frown. "Madam, on that you're most assuredly wrong. Let them be, or I shall roast your silly tongue to a cinder."

By his uncharacteristic curtness, the League Sorcerers present realized just how greatly their Prince had been taxed by the morning's events. With unceremonial efficiency, they acted to relieve the responsibility from his shoulders.

Rain pattered steadily against the casements of the royal apartment when Elienne returned to awareness. Eyes closed, in utter stillness, she listened between the soft drip of water from the eaves for the thin cry of an infant. No sound answered. No sound ever would. Ielond was dead. His absence left a hollow of silence in which thought drowned, without echo. Someone's arms tightened gently around her, though she had made no move to indicate that she was awake.

She wished no words of consolation. But the other did not speak. Buoyed by the steady, undemanding haven of the embracing arms, Elienne recorded the firm warmth of the Prince's body sheltering her. His shirt smelled faintly of cloves; her head was pillowed in the hollow beneath his chin. His hands locked across her back, an anchor against the currents of grief. The shirt was unlaced at his neck; he still wore his hose.

For a very long while, he simply held her close, while the candle by his elbow burned slowly lower in its stand. Through dull, half-opened eyes, she recognized the bedchamber and remembered that the counterpane that covered her was emblazoned with the stag of Pendaire's royal house. The night surrounded her like Eternity, endlessly empty and cold.

When Elienne spoke, finally, her tone was dead against the sibilant splash of the rain. "She said I would die truthful."

Darion stirred, placed his wrist across the back of her neck, and cupped her face in his hand. A lengthy interval elapsed before he responded at all. "Who said?"

The candle guttered, all but spent. Elienne lay motionless without replying. He did not press her and for a long while the rain trickled unregarded down the blackened glass of the casements. Words came much later, with great reluctance. "The Seeress."

Darion's fingers moved. He caught her strongly and lifted her until her head rested against his shoulder. His face bent next to hers, eyes fathomless as pools in the dying wisp of flamelight. "The Trinity of Fortune? Are you telling me you knew of this in advance, even since the betrothal banquet?"

Numbed, Elienne nodded.

"Ma'Diere's infinite mercy," Darion said softly. The whisper of the wind claimed the silence his words left upon the air. Elienne caught the clean scent of thawed earth, and noticed that the casement had been left cracked open. Darion's fingers soothed her hair. She waited, between the stroke of his hands, for the kick of a child against her breast.

The Prince's touch stilled. "How did you keep your sanity?"

The candle flickered out, the wick a red pinprick against dark. Elienne felt a calloused palm brush her eyes, walling away the sight, along with any associations dredged back by a chance gleam of scarlet. She turned her face into his neck, felt the prickle of chestnut hair. After prolonged quiet, her voice emerged, muffled. "In Trathmere, the boy would have miscarried, consequence of my own misconduct."

There was more. Patiently, Darion held her, and waited.

Chapter 15

The Trinity of Fortune

Seconds passed, unregarded, into minutes or hours; suspended in grief, time had no meaning. When Elienne spoke at last, her voice emerged beaten and flat with exhaustion. "I left my land without hope. Had I stayed, I would have lived as a conqueror's concubine."

Darion stroked her back, his hands warm through the fabric of her nightrobe. Tortured by memory of Ielond's tiny face, Elienne continued, her old pain a shield against acceptance of the immediate past.

"My husband's son would have been raised an overlord, claimed as get of a Khadrach Inquisitor. He would have matured a cruel man, accursed by his own people, for the Khadrach know neither kindness nor mercy."

Elienne lifted her face to the Prince in raw appeal. *"Perhaps he is better dead."* A deep shiver ran through her, and her breath caught.

Darion shifted his embrace, clasped her tightly against him. She yielded, helpless before the agony of loss. Tears flooded, hot as blood, and splashed his dry collar. The Prince offered no word of consolation; only the steady comfort of his presence, as though he knew that every sensation, even the impersonal touch of the coverlet against her skin, created a reaction of pain. He held her in total silence.

The weeping that convulsed her eased and gradually calmed. Darion stroked dampened hair back from her temples, felt the slick tracks of tears that ran unabated down her cheeks. "Ielond was wrong to bring you," he said finally. "Your grief would be less, born in hatred."

Elienne stirred in protest and covered his mouth with

unsteady fingers. "No, Lord. In Trathmere, there would be none to comfort me in this hour of despair," and in forced, broken phrases, she described the Khadrach hordes that had invaded her land with armies and taken her husband's life. "Ielond spared me immeasurable suffering," she whispered when she had finished. "I would not have survived that first night with the Inquisitor."

Scraped raw with sympathy, Darion leaned close and kissed her. His lips caressed her with agonized tenderness. Trembling, Elienne responded, the salty taste of tears bitter on her tongue. After a space he lifted his head and cradled her face against his own. "I love you."

Elienne lay quiescent in his arms, the wind beyond the casement a lament in her ears. Cinndel seemed faded and distant as a childhood fancy. *"Through your darkest hour, maintain your courage,"* Ielond had said. *"Remember I have looked beyond and seen a beginning."* But the future stretched before her like a vista without hope—she could no longer deny that she loved Darion; and now, unavoidably, his life once again might be threatened. "My Lord, what of your succession?"

"Mistress, your sacrifice was not made in vain. The headsman cannot touch me now."

"But there can be no lawful coronation until you have offspring," Elienne interrupted. Her voice broke, torn short by a knot of pain for her lost child, and for the curse that prevented conception of another.

"I don't know," he admitted. Betrayed by her nearness, Darion's intended detachment came out transparently strained. "This is a precedent. The Grand Council will have to rule one way or another."

Elienne laced both hands in his hair and drew him into another kiss. He quivered under her fingers. "My Lord," she said in his ear. "By my life, I swear, I will see you get another heir."

His grip changed, and he drew her strongly against him. Elienne clung to him and buried the sliver of ice in her heart. Her promise to Darion was made in the knowledge that her life with him might be sacrificed. She lay quietly with him, and he who had not rested through two long nights at last slept with her twined in his arms. Slowly dawn silvered the black panes of the casement. The rain eased and stopped, and spring sunrise spilled rosy light beyond the darkened towers of the palace. In utter stillness, Elienne listened reflexively between the song of robins for the thin cry of an infant. No sound answered. No sound ever would. Ielond was dead.

The Grand Council of Pendaire seemed eternally in session. The murder of Darion's heir brought about intensive study of the ancient Laws of succession, and debate ensued concerning the legality of the impending royal marriage and coronation, since by tradition the ceremonies were held together. Though worn by exhaustion and grief, Elienne dealt with the irritability of an uncertain court with a sturdy self-reliance that bordered at times upon belligerence. She maintained quarters in the Prince's apartments and shared the wide bed with his Grace through two sleepless nights. He stayed available to her; painfully aware her women provided no comfort, he deferred the hour when court responsibilities would call him from her side.

The morning following the baby's funeral, Mirette brought the accustomed attire of mourning from the wardrobe and met with blistering rebuke.

"Put that back." Elienne sat stiffly upon the edge of the bed, hair coiled in elflocks around the delicate lines of her collarbone.

Mirette hesitated fractionally too long.

"I won't wear black, Mistress," said the Consort with such unrestrained vehemence that Darion left the attentions of his valet and set his hands lightly on her shoulders. Elienne started and glanced up at his face in sudden, anguished appeal. "I don't need to be reminded. Your Grace, the boy is beneath the soil. Let me put him behind me as swiftly as possible."

Darion gathered her close and spoke quietly to Mirette. "Please bring my Consort something else to wear."

The Lady-in-waiting curtsied with rigid courtesy and walked back to the wardrobe. Cued by the fixed set of her back, Darion resolved to seek an elderly woman who would not be discomforted by Elienne's difficult temperament.

Mirette returned with a white and gold dress gathered at the waist with a girdle of topaz and pearl. Elienne pulled free of Darion's embrace and accepted the gown without comment. He lingered while she donned it, impressed by her fierce determination to shed her loss and act for the future. In all his life, he had never known a woman with her resilience of character. "Elienne?"

She paused with one wrist halfway down a sleeve, dark eyes swollen and heavily circled.

Darion restrained an impulse to sweep her into his arms again. "I must leave you for the council chamber. Taroith reports further absence on my part might not be wise."

"I'm going with you." Elienne read protest on his features and forestalled him. "*Don't argue.* I know. They will toss Ielond's death about like drunks playing mumblety-peg. I'll weather it." She hesitated, the shadow of an uncertain smile upon her lips. "Do you suppose they can deny your right to marry before the wan and aggrieved presence of your betrothed?"

Darion caught his breath in wide surprise. After a moment he lifted his head and laughed aloud. "Eternity!" he said the moment he could manage speech. "Ielond knew what he was about." The Prince raked disordered hair back with his fingers. "Poor Jieles. He's going to be sorely disappointed."

Elienne stared. "I don't pity him."

"No?" Darion responded to the discreet touch of his valet and lowered his head to receive the ornate collar of state. "Then dress, you crafty shrew. We don't want to keep him waiting."

Yet despite the unprecedented and steadfast presence of the Consort at the Prince's side, the Grand Council managed to extend debate over a fortnight. The stress began to wear heavily upon the Prince. Attuned to his emotional state as she once was to Cinndel's, Elienne began cautiously to extend what release she could. Nights alone in the royal suite became a haven of shared solace for them both. Darion demanded nothing. Conscious her body required space for readjustment following childbirth, he settled, apparently content with the comfort of her presence. Yet lying awake in the darkness with his arms loosened in sleep across her breast, Elienne wondered whether he guessed her hesitation was rooted also in uncertainty.

The Seeress's prophecy troubled her still, though the Trinity of Fortune might have resolved completely with Ielond's death. Now no stranger's child by her could possibly claim the heirship. But the statement for the realm had yet to be determined. Either Jieles or one of his sons would have to be crowned for Halgarid's bloodline to inherit fifteenth in succession. Elienne's fingers tightened over the Prince's wrist. Though Darion was spared execution, the Grand Council might well deny him kingship until he had sired a new heir. How many years, she wondered, could he rule childless without dispute or conspiracy arising to supplant him?

The Prince sighed beside her, disturbed by restless dreams. Elienne traced the tense muscles of his shoulder, anxious to know whether she dared allow her love for him free rein. But bound to the Grand Council's decision, like him, she could do little but wait.

Outdoors, the days warmed under the first breath of spring. Elienne resumed riding in the early hours of morning, with the Prince mounted at her side. The exercise helped ease the tension generated from long hours in the council chamber, and through Darion's company, she saw the hills and forests of Pendaire in a new light. Landmarks inspired him to recite ballads from the early years of the realm, and gradually she absorbed knowledge of the local history. Set against the rich and varied past of an ancient kingdom, Faisix's curse of childlessness imposed upon the Prince awakened fresh depths of anger. For the first time, Elienne fully understood Ielond's motivation to break the barrier of Time in Darion's behalf. And though she would regret lifelong the loss of Cinndel's child, she accepted why the Sorcerer might have sanctioned the sacrifice in view of the greater good. The boy would not have survived in Trathmere. And in truth, the Sorcerer had not lied. *"I cannot promise such choice will be without peril, but the Prince is a just man, and your son would become heir to*

Pendaire's throne." Ielond had never guaranteed the child would inherit.

"You're very ,quiet," said Darion at her side. He ducked his head as his mount carried him under a low-slung branch.

Elienne watched him straighten in reserved silence, unwilling to voice her thoughts.

The Prince laced long fingers through his horse's mane. "You're brooding again. May I ask why?"

But Elienne neatly sidestepped the issue. "Do you suppose we could visit Minksa this afternoon?"

Darion checked, dark brows hooked sharply into a frown. "*Why?* Mistress, the girl is tormented with guilt. Duaire has all he can handle just preserving her sanity."

The mare tossed her head as Elienne pulled her up short. She met the Prince's displeasure with a raised chin. "I was her only friend. What happened was not her fault." Elienne felt her voice begin to shake, and cursed her loss of control. "*I want to forgive her.*" And maddeningly, emotion threatened her control.

Darion reached across and touched her cheek. "My tough Lady, I admire your courage. But the event is too recent for you both. If you break down and weep in Minksa's presence, you'll cause her no end of harm. Give yourself time. Everything doesn't heal in a day."

Elienne's expression turned mutinous.

"All right." Darion sighed and returned his hand to the rein. "I'll ask Duaire. But you'll abide by his judgment, won't you?"

"I'll beat you to the cedars," said Elienne with total incongruity. With an impish grin, she kicked her horse into a gallop. A mud clod thrown up by the mare's hooves struck the Prince and left a rich splatter on his impeccable white lawn sleeve.

"Bitch," he murmured fondly, and tossed his own animal its head.

Yet when Darion and his Consort returned from their ride, the subject of Minksa was never reopened. Taroith awaited them at the stables. Early sunlight burnished his hair to silver as he crossed the courtyard, his step urgent. Darion halted his horse, and Elienne saw the pleasure fade from his face.

"Your Grace, I bring news," said Taroith at once. "The Earl of Torkal's body has perished."

The Prince gave the Sorcerer a dark, unreadable glance and vaulted lightly from the saddle. A groom took his horse. He caught the mare's reins while his Consort dismounted, concern evident in his movements. "There's more, or you wouldn't have met me."

Taroith raised his voice over the crack of hooves as a second groom led Elienne's mare to the stable. "There is more. The Select met separately concerning Faisix's death. They also drafted a final decision on your succession."

Darion's response was clipped as he took his Consort's arm. "Has the Grand Council yet endorsed anything?"

Elienne looked from his tautly controlled features to Taroith, but the Sorcerer's expression was equally stiff. The birdsong and the bright, cloud-flecked sky seemed suddenly false as illusion around her, and happiness became a lost dream.

Abruptly, Darion started across the bailey.

Taroith matched his long stride and said cautiously, "Your Grace, the Council is presently in session, for the purpose of the vote."

The muscles of Darion's jaw tightened. He steered Elienne clear of a puddle and mounted the marble stair before the entrance without voicing the obvious: The Council might have waited for his return before presenting the Select's writ for approval. Instead, he said, "What are the terms?"

Taroith's sigh was buried by the boom of the door panel as it swung under Darion's hand. "That you marry your Consort at the week's end and head the Grand Council with a Regent's powers, coronation and kingship subject to the birth of a living heir. I think the writ will pass, this time."

Elienne clung to Darion's arm as he stopped just past the threshold. "Will Jieles retain the heirship in the interim?"

The door swung shut at Taroith's back, and his face fell

into shadow. "Lady, that much could not be argued. The Duke of Liend is of Halgarid's line."

Yet the pause that followed only fueled Elienne's apprehension.

"If the Grand Council is voting, I would prefer to be present," said Darion suddenly. He turned down the corridor, oblivious to his mud-stained shirt and the chestnut hair still disordered from the morning's gallop in the hills.

Elienne hurried to keep pace with him, heart pounding beneath the heavy wool of her riding habit. If Darion's life became the only obstacle between Jieles and the crown, the Prince's safety would never be secure. The Duke of Liend had once sanctioned his own daughter's murder for the sake of power. Elienne felt sweat spring coldly along her spine.

Darion approached the entrance to the Grand Council chamber and snapped a command, which the door steward leaped to obey. The servant performed his bow of obeisance to an empty hallway as the Prince and his Consort passed quickly within, Taroith behind them.

The moment she entered the wide oval chamber, Elienne knew the vote was already in progress. The galleries above were largely empty, observers having been denied entrance to the session. The vacant seats lent a sense of desolation, as though the people of Pendaire had no voice at all in the succession of their Prince. Elienne quelled rising alarm as Darion led her across the wide expanse of mosaic and up the stair to the central dais.

Taroith quickly assumed the seat appointed for the Regent. The Prince located a chair for his Consort, but Elienne refused it. Like Darion, she preferred to remain on her feet. Already the Chancellor of the Realm tallied the black and white chits deposited in the ballot box by the councilmen.

At length the Chancellor rose. He spoke softly to the Herald, who finally mounted the dais and stood before the stone rostrum. Sound died in the wide, tiered chamber as he drew breath to announce the result.

"Your Grace, Excellency, august Lords of the Grand Council, the vote is four hundred thirty-six to fifty-two in favor of the writ, now made official by Law." He repeated the terms Taroith had recited earlier: Darion and his Consort would be married upon the date appointed, the Prince's authority to be limited to Regency until the birth of a new heir.

Buffeted by courtiers who suddenly crowded the dais to congratulate the Prince, Elienne barely noticed as Darion's arms circled her.

"They expect me to embrace my bride," he said in her ear.

She returned Darion's kiss with unresponsive lips, feeling the tension that gripped his spare body. He released her to a thunderous roar of applause.

Elienne looked around and saw Jieles regarding her with exaggerated deference and hostile eyes. "My most sincere felicitations, Lady." He bent his fiery head and reached to kiss her hand.

He knows he will inherit, Elienne thought, disturbed by his blatantly aggressive overtones. She withdrew from the Duke's touch with an absent nod and spoke quickly to Darion. "Your Grace, please excuse me. I must see Taroith." And before the Prince could react, she slipped from his grasp and weaved through the press of bodies toward the Regent's seat. But Taroith had already gone.

Quickly Elienne searched the surrounding courtiers. The slightest delay would weaken her. The only possible way Darion could gain the throne of Pendaire was for her to renounce her place in his life.

A knot of officials drifted toward the dais steps. In their midst, Elienne glimpsed a gray robe banded in black silk. "Gifted!"

Taroith paused, cloak draped over his arm, and waited for her to make her way to his side.

Elienne ignored the frowning man whose conversation she had interrupted. "Gifted, may I see you at once, in private?"

The Sorcerer's brows rose. Sharp brown eyes studied her, and the courtier commented unpleasantly about the intransigence of women in matters of state.

Taroith responded shortly. "My Lord, I find your opinion

bereft of any grace, even intelligence. Will you excuse me?" And he escorted Elienne promptly from the dais.

"You would hardly approach me for something unimportant," he said as they passed beyond earshot. "Don't mind that ignorant fool."

Yet just such an ignorant fool had power to influence Darion's future; Elienne was not placated. She walked across the brightly tiled mosaic floor, reminded of a morning nearly ten months past when she had crossed the council chamber with the same Sorcerer, her purpose to warn him of Faisix's plot against the Prince. She wondered whether Taroith would prove sympathetic as he had during that first encounter.

The Sorcerer touched her arm gently, urging her forward. "We'll go to my personal study. You'll be comfortable. There's a fire, and no one will trouble us." His soul focus brightened overhead to light the way.

Elienne moved woodenly at his side. If Taroith proved unsympathetic to her plan, all she hoped to gain for Darion might be lost. She was grateful, suddenly, that she had not had time to change after her ride. The plain green wool of the habit became a symbol of unpretentious origins, before she had been ranked a Princess. Her resolve was strengthened by the belief she would be renouncing nothing that was honestly hers; Darion belonged to the people of Pendaire.

After uncounted turns and two flights of steps, Taroith guided her through a plain door. The room beyond was small, cozily furnished, and striped by wide bands of sunlight from a row of dormer windows. Elienne perched uneasily in the armchair opposite the desk while the Sorcerer laid aside his cloak and kindled the stacked logs in the grate with his focus. A small tabby cat slept curled on the scarlet cushions of the window seat. Elienne envied its peace. Taroith seated himself and waited expectantly. Chills chased her skin into gooseflesh; yet having gone this far, she would not flinch from completing what she had come to initiate.

"Gifted." She swallowed and started anew. "Gifted, in view of the Grand Council's decision, I've a confession to make." She met the Sorcerer's steady brown eyes with rugged determination. "I beg you to listen without judgment, and to stand with me in finishing the work Ielond began. If Darion is ever to claim his full birthright, I'll need your help."

Taroith leaned forward on crossed arms, hair coiled like sea foam around his black-banded collar. "Mistress, set your mind at ease. Much of what you've come here to relate may not surprise me. I am aware Ielond had a master plan; Darion's affliction is known to me."

Elienne gazed down at the scuffed leather toes of her riding boots, relieved to know the Sorcerer at least would not expose Darion's heirship as fraud. Bracelets clinked on her wrists as she forced her interlocked fingers to relax. In a steadier voice she said, "Then you knew my child was not legitimate, and that Darion's seed was cursed to sterility by Black Sorcery?"

Taroith straightened in his chair. "*Cursed!* Ma'Diere! That ritual requires the death of a virgin girl! How was such an evil thing accomplished?"

"Faisix murdered Minksa's sister. The Prince was seventeen at the time, yet he forbade his Guardian to work the counterspell. Ielond broke the barrier of Time in an effort to save him." She described her departure from Trathmere by Timesplice, and Ielond's certainty that her dead husband's child could not be detected by Pendaire's Sorcerers for a full three days following conception. Taroith did not interrupt. Her words came with difficulty as she related how the Seeress's prophecy obstructed any chance of conceiving another man's child to become Darion's heir. She finished flatly. "Our marriage will produce no children. But I know a way to ensure the Prince's succession, and satisfy the prophecy, so that Halgarid's line will inherit after him."

The tabby stretched in the window, pink tongue curled into a yawn. When she leaped lightly onto Taroith's lap, he stroked her fur with an absent hand, his expression thoughtful. "You have come to ask my help?"

Elienne mustered the last of her courage. "Gifted, I ask your cooperation. I cannot marry Darion, if he is ever to inherit lawfully. Discredit me as Consort. Betroth the Prince to Minksa, and get her pregnant by another man." Fiercely resolved, she raised hardened eyes to the Sorcerer's face. "Her child will be of Halgarid's blood, thereby satisfying the Trinity of Fortune."

Elienne leaned back in her chair, drained by stress, and poised on a knife edge of hope and loss. She had said everything necessary. The Sorcerer had only to approve, and Darion's future could be assured.

Taroith lifted the cat and released her on the rug. His cragged features showed little of his thoughts as he laced his hands together on the desk top. "What of yourself?"

Elienne answered briskly, "I am nothing in this world. Spare your Prince, Gifted. He is the future of Pendaire."

The Sorcerer bent his head and watched the tabby stalk across the carpet, tail held haughtily aloft. Beyond the windows, a quarterstaff cracked flatly as a hackbut against silence. Taroith swore. The Prince was at practice again.

"Mistress," he said at last, "your offer is the gift of an honest and unselfish heart. Yet I advise against such a course of action."

"What else can I do?" She felt cornered. "Gifted, for Darion's sake . . . I have no other choice."

"There is always choice, Lady." Taroith raised his voice over the din of weaponry from the courtyard. "Accept your Prince as husband. Unless my awareness of you errs badly, you love him as you once did the father of your deceased child."

"But the prophecy!" Elienne protested. To her annoyance, Taroith smiled. The thought that he might be patronizing her sparked anger. "Black Eternity, Gifted, does Darion's life mean nothing to you? Do you *want* Jieles to rule?"

The Sorcerer rose. Gray velvet rustled as he rounded the desk and caught her tense shoulders with firm fingers. "*Elienne, you base your assumption on flawed facts*. The Trinity of Fortune is incomplete without all of its parts. Did you think to ask Darion for his third?"

Elienne shook her head, stubbornly resistant to comfort. "Gifted, Darion was drugged unconscious at the time the Seeress delivered the prophecy to him."

"*It's not lost.*" Taroith's hold tightened. "A Seeress's words never pass unheard. Ask Darion for his portion of the Trinity.

Afterward, if you still wish to renounce your Consortship, come back, and we'll talk. But I caution you: Ielond chose you for the Prince's bride. Trust there was purpose behind his selection. Change might well disrupt the legacy he left his ward."

The Sorcerer urged Elienne to her feet. Beyond the window, the interplay of quarterstaffs reached a crescendo. "Score!" shouted Darion.

Taroith smiled. "You're dressed for the outdoors. Go to your Prince."

Doubts lingered in her thoughts as she reached the door. The tabby blocked her path, and Elienne bent to move the animal aside.

"Lady!" The Sorcerer shouted, razor-edged with urgency. "Summon Darion."

Elienne started and whirled around, surprised rather than frightened.

Taroith overtook her in two long strides. The cat streaked out of his path. "Use the mirrowstone, *at once*." He grasped her forearm and wrenched open the door.

Bundled unceremoniously into the corridor, Elienne gasped. "What's happened?"

"Call Darion to Minksa's chamber, *now*." Taroith turned a corner and plunged down the stairway, his fingers like iron upon her wrist. "Minksa's dying."

Elienne groped at her neck for the mirrowstone's chain. The echoes of her own footfalls beat at her ears as the jewel caught in her palm. She sent a mental call to the Prince; his surprise struck her in a wave of cold, and she sensed him fling aside his quarterstaff in dismay.

". . . stabbed herself." Breathlessly, Taroith ducked into a corridor. "Duaire tries to hold her to life, but her spirit is unwilling, for reasons—" He broke off suddenly, then said, "Oh, Ma'Diere. So this was the outcome Ielond foresaw." He stopped so suddenly she slammed into his side. The Sorcerer caught her close with his other hand. "Mistress, keep steady. We're going to transfer." And the narrow stair exploded into light.

Wind slapped into Elienne's skirts. A flash of energy

scalded her, and emptiness yawned under her feet. The sensations ceased with a snap. As her eyes adjusted, Elienne viewed a small, candlelit chamber, sparsely furnished. A tray of food steamed on a side table. Beyond, Duaire bent over a slight, familiar form, the hem of his robe darkened crimson. He spoke without looking up. "Mercy upon her. *She used a fork.* Taroith, I couldn't hold her. Something concerning a debt to the Prince and his betrothed, and far too strong to countermand."

"I know what it was," Taroith sighed. "Is she gone?"

Duaire's shoulders sagged as he straightened. "Yes."

Yet another loss, Elienne thought. Minksa had been a friend. Tormented as her short life had been, the girl had not deserved such an end. These were the fruits of the intrigues surrounding the succession of Pendaire's throne.

"Summon me a circle of seven Masters. But spare yourself, Duaire. You've spent enough of your strength." With careful hands, Taroith lifted Minksa's corpse from the floor.

Elienne watched dully as small, streaked fingers fell away from the smeared handle of the fork.

"Don't look," said Duaire unexpectedly out of the darkness at her side. He caught her close; the sounds of the other Sorcerers' arrival was muffled by the fine cloth of his sleeve.

Suddenly Darion's voice cut clearly through the noise. "Taroith! No! I forbid this!"

Elienne twisted clear of Duaire's hold and saw the Prince standing in the doorway, pale features set with denial. His shirt lay open at his throat, and sweat gleamed on his collarbones. Across from him, ringed by six League Sorcerers, Taroith leaned over Minksa's limp form, hands stained red from handling her, and head bent in apparent deference.

Yet when he looked up, determination etched new lines across his lean face. "Your Grace, the girl died believing she granted you deliverance."

"No." Darion made a trapped gesture with his hand, breathing hard. The stag medallion flashed on his chest. "You'll work no darklore for my sake. I refuse to see you damned."

But Taroith was not deterred. "Would you permit Faisix to reverse the curse against you?"

"He's dead." The prince spoke aggressively, clear warning his temper neared the breaking point.

"Not precisely." Taroith paused, as though waiting. His gaze stayed locked upon the Prince. A moment later, one of his colleagues entered carrying the iron bar that confined the demon ring which had once driven Minksa to murder. The Sorcerer handed the rod to Taroith, who raised it balanced across his palm. Stillness settled over the little room, and Elienne held her breath as he addressed the Prince. "Your Grace, if I release the ring and place it upon my own hand, Faisix's projection will supplant my will. With seven Masters present to direct his influence, I believe he may be pursuaded to reverse your affliction, in the same manner as it was originally cast. Our offense against Ma'Diere's Law will be but slight." His tone turned stony. "Faisix was not the only adept about with a touch for mindbend."

Darion stepped out of the doorway, stern profile bronzed by flamelight. "There's danger to you."

Taroith gripped the bar of iron on either side of the ring and stared at the bright gold glitter of the demon as though he and the Prince were alone. "Of course. Should my colleagues lose control, yes, there is danger. There is danger in all sorcery. But I assume that risk, as is my right." He looked up in sincere appeal. "Trust me, your Grace."

"I understand." The words seemed tortured from Darion's throat. Fallen hair veiled his expression as he blotted his brow with his sleeve. "Please take my Consort from the room. I will not risk her to Faisix again."

Duaire moved to Elienne's side and took her elbow.

"No, please. I wish to stay."

But Duaire paid no attention. He caught her with uncompromising firmness, just as Taroith set his hand on the ring, soulfocus stark as a beacon over his head. Heated air fanned her hair as Duaire steered her toward the door, and a harsh blaze of scarlet rinsed the walls. Duaire guided her firmly outside. The corridor went dark as the latch fell shut under his hand.

The subdued light of the Sorcerer's focus drove the blackness back. She sat down on the cold stone, weary, feeling decades older than the desperate woman who had first come to Pendaire with Ielond. "I wanted to forgive her," she said at last.

Duaire sighed, scarred features troubled by memories of his own. "Minksa could not forgive herself. All her life, she was used as a pawn in this mad play for power. She died believing your heirs would bring an end to the feuding. Mourn her loss, but do not dishonor her sacrifice, my Lady. The decision to take her life was hers alone."

Elienne waited in silence. From within the cell came a rumble of thunder and a sharp metallic clang; she heard a Sorcerer's voice say, "Your Grace, I suggest you burn that garment." After an interval, the door opened, throwing yellow light into the corridor. Darion emerged, shirtless, his face a mask. Taroith followed on his heels, haggard with weariness. He had rinsed his hands. Elienne watched the approach of the Sorcerer and the Prince and thought, It's over now. It's all over.

Gently Darion pulled her up from the stone. Elienne leaned against him and listened to the steady beat of his heart. Taroith shoved damp hair back from his brow and broke the silence with a curt command. "Your Grace, tell Elienne your third of the Trinity of Fortune."

Darion swore in mild surprise. "Wasn't she told?" And he leaned close, a trace of life restored to his expression. "The Seeress promised me my heart's desire."

"Your succession." Elienne traced his jawline with hesitant fingers. "I'm glad."

"Ma'Diere." Darion laughed and lifted her effortlessly into his arms. "No, love. My heart's desire was nothing less than a child of my own, by you."

"The curse has been reversed." Taroith raised an iron rod newly bent into a seamless ring. The demon glittered hotly, imbedded immovably in a surface that glowed white with wardspells. "Lady, I can promise with Eternity's finality Faisix will cause no more harm to your children."

Darion cradled her close. The Sorcerers fell behind as he moved off down the corridor. Elienne felt his grip shift as he started up the stairs.

"I can walk," she said. When he failed to respond, her protest turned heated. "Lord, put me down!"

But his arms only tightened. "Not here, my future Queen. I'm taking us both to the bedchamber. We've an obligation to the realm of Pendaire." He paused. Chestnut hair tickled her cheek as he kissed her long and gently. When he finally raised his head, a dawning glimmer of joy shone through his solemnity. "Our first male heir will be named Cinndel. This time, by right of sovereignty, I'm going to insist."

About the Author

Janny Wurts is the author of several highly praised novels. Among them are *Sorcerer's Legacy,* her first novel which was newly revised for this edition; *Daughter of the Empire,* coauthored with Raymond E. Feist; and **The Cycle of Fire:** *Stormwarden, Keeper of the Keys,* and *Shadowfane.*

She is also greatly appreciated as an artist. Her work can be seen gracing the covers of most of her novels, as well as those of other authors.

Wurts lives in Connecticut, where she is currently working on a new novel.

SPECTRA SPECIAL EDITIONS

Bantam Spectra Special Editions spotlight some of Spectra's finest authors in their top form. Authors found on this list all have received high critical praise and many have won some of science fiction and fantasy's highest honors. Don't miss them!